LOVE HER MADLY

A Novel

M. ELIZABETH LEE

ATRIA PAPERBACK
New York London Toronto Sydney New Delhi

ATRIA PAPERBACK
An Imprint of Simon & Schuster, Inc.
1230 Avenue of the Americas
New York, NY 10020

This book is a work of fiction. Any references to historical events, real people, or real places are used fictitiously. Other names, characters, places, and events are products of the author's imagination, and any resemblance to actual events or places or persons, living or dead, is entirely coincidental.

First Atria Paperback edition August 2016

ATRIA PAPERBACK and colophon are trademarks of Simon & Schuster, Inc.

For information about special discounts for bulk purchases, please contact Simon & Schuster Special Sales at 1-866-506-1949 or business@simonandschuster.com.

The Simon & Schuster Speakers Bureau can bring authors to your live event. For more information or to book an event contact the Simon & Schuster Speakers Bureau at 1-866-248-3049 or visit our website at www.simonspeakers.com.

Interior design by Kyoko Watanabe

Manufactured in the United States of America

10 9 8 7 6 5 4 3 2 1

Library of Congress Cataloging-in-Publication Data
Names: Lee, M. Elizabeth, author.
Title: Love her madly : a novel / M. Elizabeth Lee.
Description: New York : Atria Books, 2016.
Identifiers: LCCN 2016003646 (print) | LCCN 2016015406 (ebook) | ISBN 9781501112157 (paperback) | ISBN 9781501112164 (Ebook)
Subjects: LCSH: Female friendship—Fiction. | BISAC: FICTION / Psychological. | FICTION / Suspense. | FICTION / Contemporary Women. | GSAFD: Psychological fiction.
Classification: LCC PS3612.E2254 L68 2016 (print) | LCC PS3612.E2254 (ebook) | DDC 813/.6—dc23
LC record available at https://lccn.loc.gov/2016003646

ISBN 978-1-5011-1215-7
ISBN 978-1-5011-1216-4 (ebook)

For my parents

Love is blind; friendship closes its eyes.

—Friedrich Nietzsche

LOVE HER MADLY

PROLOGUE

Though seven years have passed since that night, my mind retains a perfect image of Cyn as she fell away from me into the churning black water. Only a moment before, we'd been together, her thin hand in mine as we raced into the dark ocean, fleeing the strange men who had charged out of the jungle and onto our beach. I didn't know them. I only knew that we were two young women alone in the night, messed up beyond reason on mushrooms and rum.

I pulled her to her feet, and we ran, her pink flip-flops tripping her up until she kicked them loose. We ran silently, breathing fast like foxes. If the full moon hadn't been there to illuminate our escape into the surf, we might have vanished unseen. But the men spotted us and began shouting. Geysers of water exploded up into our faces as we pounded through the shallows, but that was okay. We were together, and we were getting away. I looked back at Cyn. Her eyes were full of wild panic, one breast barely contained within her disheveled bikini top as I dragged her with me into deeper water.

"Glo, wait," she'd pleaded, and I had, pausing for what felt like an eternity as the waves crashed against our naked thighs, knocking us off balance. Over her shoulder, I saw the men on the beach stooping to unlace their boots, and I knew they were coming in after us.

I took Cyn's wrist and pulled, and for a few steps, she followed. As the water reached my ribs, I felt Cyn's hand jerk free from my grip. I spun around, my feet barely touching the sand as a strong wave passed through us. Cyn faced me, near motionless. The panic had evaporated from her perfect features, and she was serene, otherworldly, resigned. I shrieked at her to give me her hand, to come with me, but it was like reasoning with a sleepwalker. Her expression didn't change as she withdrew from my reaching fingers, slipping backward into dark water. I saw the splashes of white foam as two men entered the water, and I screamed her name again and again.

"Go. Get help," she said. And that was all. Her decision was made. I turned away, back out to sea, and kicked deep into the immense darkness, my mind reeling in shock at what my body was doing. I was leaving her alone, in that messed-up state, with those men. With each kick, I felt my heart rip itself to shreds, but I couldn't go back. It was too late now, and anyway, I had my orders.

I watched from the safety of deep water as they seized her and dragged her screaming off the beach and into the depths of the jungle. That was the last I saw of her.

Until now.

By the time Cyn Williams was officially declared dead, her name had become a sick joke. By remaining alive, I had the privilege of remaining obscure, the shadowy, red-haired best friend, hurried in and out of police stations by Jonathan Grant, my United States attorney, or as I thought of him, Mr. Nocomment, Esq. Yet it was perfectly true that I had no comment for the reporters that assailed us first in Costa Rica and then tenfold in Miami. I had done my best to explain to the baffled local police, then the *federales*, then the more important *federales* with nicer suits, that

Cyn was lost, that I didn't know what had happened to her. I didn't deny the obvious—that in the chaos, disoriented by narcotics and fear, I panicked and left her alone. I lost her on that island off the coast of Costa Rica, and unless someone found her soon, she wasn't coming back.

By the time the second night after my rescue had fallen, I knew she was dead. She was a lucky person, and so smart, and brave, too, but that wasn't enough to keep her from vanishing off the face of the planet. They were still out searching for her, but the instant I heard her whisper inside my head, I knew it was all pointless. She was gone.

The first time she spoke to me was in the municipal police station in San Jose. I was nursing my sixth cup of bitter coffee while I waited for another detective to arrive to take my statement. Grant was sitting across the table from me, exchanging peevish barbs with his ex-wife on the phone, while I examined the scores of deep red scrapes that crosshatched my legs. I was aching to scratch the insect bites that peppered my feet and ankles, but I didn't want to amplify my feral charm by openly bleeding in front of the next cop. In my efforts to resist, I must have sighed loudly, or groaned, because when I looked up, Grant was staring at my ravaged legs with a faraway look in his eye.

Another upstanding member for your fan club, Glo.

I began to laugh. Grant's eyes found my face, and he frowned. He had lost any real interest in me after the fifth or so interview, when it became clear that I was tapped out of salacious details re: crazy coed's last night in the jungle. No fresh leads meant fewer opportunities to address the cameras, which he'd already done a half-dozen times over the thirty-six hours or so we'd been acquainted, pausing to delicately blot the shine from his brow before stepping in front of the lights. His frown deepened, and I laughed harder.

She's cracked, he must have thought.

God, yes, let me crack, I wished.

Babe, you already have.

I gasped for breath, my laughter swinging toward the uncontrollable. My lawyer rose to his feet, his brow ropy with confusion. I could almost sense Cyn laughing with me, and it struck me like a huge wall of icy water that she who had been so real, so huge a presence in my life, was truly gone. The sobs swam up on me then, hijacking my laughter and transforming it into horrible convulsions that tore at my sides. I hadn't cried since they released me from the hospital the day before, and now there was no stopping it. My stomach lurched, and in between gasps, I vomited a shiny pool of coffee across the tabletop.

My lawyer narrowly rescued his briefcase from the table, disgust contorting his face. When it became clear that I would not be regaining my composure, he steered me through the police station hallways, pausing to stick his big, square finger in the face of an officer who objected to my abrupt departure.

"This is a United States *citizen*," he'd sneered, shaking my shoulder, as I was the citizen in question. "We will continue to cooperate with your investigation but—" I tuned out. Whatever was happening didn't really concern me. In embarrassingly little time, I'd grown accustomed to everything being completely beyond my control. I was merely the body that sat and waited, followed people down hallways, and answered the same series of questions by rote. In the vacuum that opened up where my free will used to be, my thoughts circled endlessly on one topic: Where was she?

"Come on," Grant said, and the next thing I knew, I was perp-walking through the reporters on the street and diving into a taxi that ferried us through the labyrinth of fading colonial streets to our hotel. In the elevator up to my room, he pressed a couple of pills into my palm and told me to take them. He left me at my door, reminding me to lock it from the inside. I swallowed the mystery pills and collapsed across the bed.

Before sleep took me, I heard her whisper: *Lights out, lovely.*

The next afternoon, three days after Cyn disappeared, the Costa Ricans released me without charge. Grant was very pleased. My questionable recall of the night of Cyn's disappearance hadn't made me seem particularly innocent, nor did the fact that I obviously, openly, blamed myself for everything. But there was no body. No clear motive. A dearth of hard evidence exonerated me but did nothing to clear up the mystery of where my best friend had gone.

On the flight back home, I experienced an entirely new level of emotional emptiness. Somewhere beneath my feet, Cyn's purple backpack was flying along with me, waiting to be "returned to her parents," while on the television, twenty inches from my nose, she was alive again. I took one look at her face, that magnetic smile frozen forever in time, and I had to turn it off. But there was worse ahead.

At the airport in Miami, I experienced firsthand the "Cynty mania" that had taken over the nation. I hurried through the terminal, hidden behind dark sunglasses and my formerly lucky green ball cap, praying not to be recognized. Images of Cyn and me together had plowed across the television airwaves like an unstoppable freight train. If I had at times resented how she outshone me in life, it was a mercy that she continued to do so in death. Walking quickly across the glossy airport tile, I attracted no curious glances.

Heading down the escalator, I spotted a teenager ascending the opposite direction wearing a T-shirt that nearly made my mind implode. FIND CYNTY! the tee shouted in four-inch bubble letters. My eyes swept below the text to behold Cyn, smiling up at me in cutoff jeans and a tight flannel shirt, her blond hair glowing. I had taken that picture of Cyn, posing cheekily in her thrift-store-sourced Daisy Dukes Halloween costume, and there it was, ripped from the Internet, silk-screened onto a novelty tee and purchased for $9.99 by some dipshit who knew nothing about Cyn. As he floated past, the kid sensed hostility radiating from behind my dark lenses and dashed a quick glance in my direction. Zero recognition. He looked away, untouched by my fury.

Don't be such a hater. It's a helluva photo.

I took a deep breath and reminded myself that it could have been worse. Many of the photos that had been released of Cyn were not nearly so innocent. What began as a shocking, college-girl-missing-abroad story became a tabloid gold mine as the press dug deeper into "Cynty's" background and discovered her sideline job as a lingerie model and dancer at a seedy adult store. As each passing hour unearthed some ripe scandal, Cyn's fame mushroomed. The news outlets breathlessly implied that her jobs were somehow connected to her disappearance, which they weren't, or that since she was so obviously a person of low moral character, she deserved what happened. That they never discovered the true scope of Cyn's secrets was a private joy to me.

Beside me, my lawyer cursed under his breath, and I glanced up to see a scrum of reporters and cameramen staking out the airport's exit. I felt my heart begin to pound. This was always the worst part.

"Hopefully this is the last run, champ," he murmured, shrugging his shoulders like a prizefighter trying to get loose. I doubt my parents had considered it when hiring him, but Grant was tall and had an impressive wingspan—useful qualities for clearing a path. I took a breath, pulled my hat lower, and followed him into the churning sea of flashbulbs and microphones. Immediately we stalled. A blinding flash exploded into my face, and I felt someone claw at my elbow. Grant stiff-armed one photographer away, but we were already surrounded three-deep. I felt my throat close up as bodies pressed tight around us, questions hammering down upon me. Time slowed to a terrible blur as I struggled to breathe. Grant bellowed something, and a pair of cops appeared to muscle me out of the crush. I glimpsed the revolving doors and the sunlight beyond, and I willed myself to hold it together for just two more minutes. No reactions for the photos. Sure as hell no tears. If I was a walking wound of a human being, that was my secret. I'd be damned if I betrayed one hint of emotion to the people who had so thoroughly savaged my dead friend.

It helped to know that on the other side of that mess, my parents were waiting for me. They'd take me home and try to make things better. They wouldn't ask me to talk about it, but I'd catch the worried glances exchanged over my head and sense the anxious vibration of their unasked questions. I'd tell them I was okay, that I didn't need to talk to anyone. Then night after night, safe and loved in a warm bed, I'd lie awake. Cyn's voice faded to silence, but our last moments in the water remained, cycling through my mind in a never-ending loop. I perpetually reached the same useless conclusion: things had happened too quickly for thinking. I simply reacted, and so did Cyn. We both made our choices, and that was why I was sleepless, guilt-ridden, and alive, and she was dead. I rechoreographed our last act, crafting ways in which we might have both made it back. *If only I had done X*, or *If she had done Y and not Z*. At the end of every reimagination session, at first light, I would absolve myself. *It wasn't my fault. It was our fault.*

Like hell it was.

Part I

What Happened Before

CHAPTER ONE

I hadn't pegged Cyn as a natural ally. When I first saw her, in the dismal cafeteria as we, the new freshman class, settled in for orientation, I thought, *Oh great, they've got those here*. She was blond, lithe, and seemingly absorbed in a paperback, as if unaware that her physical charms were rendering the rest of the females in our group of transfers and latecomers altogether invisible.

I should explain that this was not truly my first day at college. That had happened the previous fall, in what felt to me like another life. My aborted semester was staged at the State University, a massive campus-tropolis with ten thousand freshmen; a handful too many to goad into shy eye contact or stilted small talk through "sharing games." Tiny U, with a raging hippie ethos and an enrollment of nine hundred students, had the time to ensure that everyone got very well acquainted.

It was a damp January morning in Florida, and there weren't quite enough chairs. I took a seat on the all-weather carpet by a wall where I could scope everyone out on the literal down low. The aging air-conditioning unit above me rattled, straining to circulate the humid air, and from behind the closed swinging doors that led to the kitchen, a radio was blasting bachata.

Other than the Barbie-looking blonde, my fellow students were a motley bunch. The college attracted what could politely be called the misfit element: neo-hippies, homos, kids with fancy ideas and terrible posture, the narco-curious, the fantasy role-players, a handful of goths (their requisite black garb a sign of extreme dedication in the tropical heat) and me.

Why the hell was I there? Probably because the school seemed the polar opposite of what I'd experienced during my semester at Big U. I had felt so overlooked and invisible in my stadium-seating-only courses that, after the first couple of months, I simply stopped showing up. My grades tanked, naturally, but with some finagling involving the school psychologist, I managed to withdraw before my abysmal grades permanently screwed my chances of keeping my swimming scholarship. But Tiny U didn't care about sports. Their bag was molding eccentric, bookish high achievers into the next generation's nutty professors. My near-perfect grades and test scores were enough for them to grant me their own scholarship, and my crack-up at Big U seemed to further endear me to my admissions officer. She patted my knee and told me she thought I'd fit in nicely.

I sure hoped so. My social life at Big U had been pathetic. I'd been tossed into a tiny "suite" with three other girls. My roommates were nice enough, but proximity breeds contempt, and it quickly became apparent that I was the lone onion in a tight can of maraschino cherries. It was mostly my fault. Sheila, Mel, and Christina were polite to my face, but I knew that they hated me for stubbornly defying the open-door policy they'd enacted on our single bathroom. Maybe it was because I was an only child, but I couldn't tolerate someone evacuating their blackheads two feet from me while I showered. They found this impossibly rude, unaware that my watery respites were the only thing keeping me sane. I slowly earned their resentment and, eventually, their ostracism. The bright side was, they weren't my type anyway.

It certainly didn't help my mental state that as my world was collapsing, I decided to quit swimming. I'd been competitive in freestyle all throughout high school, passing countless hours watching the dark blue tile of the lane marker whiz by beneath me. Kick, flip, repeat. I was fast, scrappy, and I hated to lose. I'd never considered myself to be a capital "A" Athlete, but I felt right in the water. It felt natural, even the skintight suits with shoulder straps that left red grooves in my skin and the goggles that gifted me with dark rims around my eye sockets for hours after practice.

I lived for the euphoric high I got at moments when everything went right in the pool. I felt superhuman, as if I had some special ability to knife through the water and meld my limbs into the exact planes that would get me to the wall just a little faster than the next girl. Of course, I loved to win. Not because some other chick was losing, necessarily, but because I'd asked something of my body, and it usually found a way to deliver. Sad as it might sound, my relationship with my heart, lungs, and fast-twitch muscles was probably one of the most rewarding of my early life. I was good to them, and they rarely let me down.

Every afternoon and every other morning throughout high school, I would dutifully wrestle my mass of frizzy red curls into a ponytail, then snap the whole package under a swim cap, wincing through the inevitable tug of latex against delicate skin. I'd tiptoe across the chilly tile of the locker room, rinse in the shower, and emerge into the humid terrarium of the pool room. That the only Olympic-size lap pool in our Florida town was indoors was a dark irony to me. While my classmates were golden brown from their weekends at the beach, I, who spent hours in the water, was pallid. While most girls smelled of vanilla and orange blossom, I reeked of chlorine and Irish Spring soap.

By the time the summer between junior and senior years rolled around, I was beginning to think about quitting. I still loved competitions and was winning at meets, but I was bored out of my mind by the repetitive grind of practice. Then, like the mystical granting of a wish I hadn't made, Coach Mike appeared on the scene, and everything changed.

A collegiate-level women's coach from the frozen north, Coach Mike brought with him a wife and one-year-old daughter. He was a straight-up Adonis: sandy blond hair, fabulous muscles, eyes the color of the ocean, amazing yet hard-won smile. He quickly became my all-encompassing everything, and by trying to please him every goddamn day, I became a very, very fast swimmer. It could have stayed a crush, but his wife was struggling with postpartum depression, and there I was, adoring young person, ready and willing to be his secret keeper and confidant. I pursued him as stealthily as I could, finding countless reasons to steal a few chaste minutes alone with him. When I won the meet that guaranteed my scholarship, he took me out to celebrate. Back in his car, fueled by celebratory drinks, he touched me for the first time, and I could not fathom a greater happiness.

I graduated, and we continued to meet up and fool around for the remainder of the summer, spending languid, sweaty evenings pawing and licking in the semi-privacy of isolated parking lots. I never thought of myself as a home-wrecker, but rather as his misplaced intended, his star-crossed lover, his water babe. He seemed vastly more sophisticated than the high school boys I knew. He would listen to me when I talked, for one thing, and he repeatedly told me I was beautiful. He whispered rapturous compliments into my hair about the merits of my long legs, my heart-shaped lips, and even found good things to say about my nearly nonexistent breasts. I believed every word of it, hungry as I was for his approval. He'd move the car seat into the trunk to make space and give me this smile that melted away my thoughts of everything but the anticipation of his hands on my skin.

Despite our many lusty sessions, and even though I repeatedly told him I wanted to, we never had full-on sex. I wonder now if he feared I'd try to trap him with yet another baby. I was so obsessed with him at the time, it might have crossed my mind. He dropped hints that he'd leave his wife. He said she was crazy, and that he wished he could start all over with me. I was too blind to see that the little girl was the one who really had his heart. The end came when I went up to Big U. He stopped returning my calls, changed his number, disappeared. He was my first love, and he dumped me without a word of explanation. I tried not to let it get to me, and I reserved my crying time for the shower, which led to some long showers, which in turn, engendered the ire of my suite mates.

I could have told those girls what was up. I could have confessed my heartbreak and fallen into their arms, smearing snail trails of grief mucus all over their Big U sweatshirts. I don't doubt that they would have been kind to me and happy to listen. But I liked my misery complete and my depression abject, so I kept my mouth shut and my eyes glued to the calendar, counting the days until fall break would come and I could go see Mike in person.

When that day finally came, I drove directly to the pool to find him. Instead of finding Mike, I ran into Ms. Johnson, my old JV coach, who, while giving me a look that telegraphed exactly how little she thought of me and my trampy ways, breezily told me he was gone. He wasn't working at the school, and as a matter of fact, she'd heard he'd taken the wife and moved back north. So, heartbroken and misanthropic, I returned to my cramped, lonely suite, my pointless classes, and my nonexistent social life. Alarmingly, I had even lost all desire to step foot in the pool. I knew my scholarship depended on it, but I just couldn't force myself to care. I essentially shut down.

In truth, my epic failure as a student, and probably as a person, at Big U terrified me. It shocked me that I could surrender to apathy so easily, shaking off my dreams like slipping off a robe. It would have felt less alien to me if I'd picked up a heroin habit and became singularly devoted to my fix, because at least then there'd be something I wanted. Instead, I was bafflingly devoted to nothing. Under a bizarre haze of alien nihilism, I, the swimmer, was drowning.

I guess this is to say that the morning of orientation, the life preserver of my second-chance school was wedged so tightly around my chest that I wondered how I could breathe. I was feeling so hopeful that things would turn out better that it made me a little nauseated. Steeling my nervous gut against the discordant odors of ammonia and grilled cheese sandwiches drifting in from the kitchen, I told myself life was about to improve.

I was on the lookout for any evidence that my feeling was correct when an upperclassman girl switched on a microphone and began to rehash a bunch of stuff that I'd already read in the handbook. I spent the time surreptitiously searching for potential future friends. No one immediately jumped out at me, but considering my limited experience in that area, I didn't have much to go on.

I should clarify that it's not like I never had any friends. As a kid, I had playmates and did time in uniform on a few inglorious soccer squads. What I loved most, though, was dodging the asphalt-boiling summer days in the air-conditioned twilight of the local roller rink. In that glossy-floored paradise of Top 40 hits and snow cones, I felt at ease. I remember gleeful hours playing tag in my purple skates with the other girls. I went to all their birthday parties, invariably hosted at the rink and all serving the same rainbow-frosted ice cream cake. I even fostered an intense best-friend-forevership with another skating redhead before her family moved away to Georgia and we never saw each other again. I didn't see any signs of pariahdom ahead, but it was on its way.

Puberty struck with catastrophic vengeance. My bony frame erupted in fatty bulges, my skin went radioactive, and my hair morphed from soft strawberry blond waves to a hellish carroty bush. My mom put me in swimming classes to try to spare me the humiliation of being a pudgy, pimply ginger, and I realized that underwater, no one can hear you scream. My former friends morphed into shallow, vicious gorgons, consumed by their status in the junior high food chain. The skating rink parties of the past were now meaningless, as was every other pleasant or otherwise human encounter we'd ever shared. It wasn't just that our friendships were so quickly forgotten, it was that those girls seemed to suddenly *hate* me with such shocking purity that I spent countless hours wondering what I'd done wrong.

Obviously, my appearance made me a target. I did as my mother suggested, and pretended not to hear the mean jokes or nasty commentary. That worked great. Soon, I was feigning deafness seven hours a day (band class excluded), and I wised up to the fact that accepting the torment with a smile wasn't going to do shit for me in the merciless world of preteen girls. Instead, I aspired to master the special art of disappearing in plain sight. I cherished the days that no one spoke to me, and then I'd go to swim practice.

Girls from swimming helped fill the social vacuum that I'd earned with my celebrated awkwardness. Almost interchangeably quiet and sensitive, these girls and I would sleep over at each others' houses, bake brownies, and engage in speculative conversations about boys, but no friendships ever stuck. The faces would simply change by the season, without any of us feeling bad about it. By high school, my swim friends had become my competition, not only in swimming but also for boys, status, and presumably, the opportunity to mate and further our genetic codes.

By sixteen, my junior high pudge and acne had melted away

like a half-remembered nightmare. I'd grown tall and lean, and my features had arranged themselves in a way that still verged on the elfin, but attractive elfin. I knew this only because a girl on the team let it slip that her older brother referred to me as Tinkerbell. It was great to no longer be at the very bottom of the social totem pole, but as far as the cliques went, I was over it. I had stopped seeking out friends and demurred from most chummy overtures. I expected the worst, and besides, with high school more than halfway over, there seemed little point in forging new bonds. I had books, and TV, and enough acquaintances that I didn't feel like a total outcast, and while I was in the protective cushion of my home, that had been good enough. This time around, I knew I needed to find some people to call my own, or I'd be lost, lonely, or dead.

My future classmates began to stir, and I tuned in again to what the orientation leader was saying. She was copy-paper pale, with blueberry-colored dreadlocks, a nose piercing, and a wide smile that she wielded relentlessly. She began chirping that it was time to have fun and get acquainted through a really exciting exercise.

The essence was, she would play music, and we would all walk around, saying our names aloud to anyone we happened to make eye contact with. Then, when she stopped the music, we would partner up with the closest person to us, and we'd receive further instruction.

The music started, and it was perfectly awkward. I got to my feet and began circling with the others. We all felt stupid, so with a few exceptions, we were all smiling. I spoke my own name, dusty classic that it is, so often that it began to sound alien to me. When the music finally stopped, I was facing a wall. Someone tapped me on the shoulder, and I spun around. It was the perfect blond girl.

"Howdy, partner," she said, flashing me a smile.

The speakers screeched to life, and Dreadlocks' voice boomed across the sound system like a detonation. We all flinched and covered our ears. "Whoops," Dreadlocks said, her voice reduced to a tolerable volume. I glanced at the blonde, her face a portrait of sarcastic bemusement.

She was even prettier up close, unlike some blond girls who can sell the package at a distance but flatten and fade upon closer inspection. She had cool blue eyes spaced evenly under pale eyebrows that seemed arched in perpetual contemplation of a private joke. Her nose was small and slightly pert in the Nordic supermodel vein and buttressed on either side by high cheekbones. When she smiled, dimples and even white teeth appeared, completing the circuit of devastation. She was so naturally stunning that I didn't even feel jealous.

"Now everyone sit down across from your partner, join hands, and close your eyes."

The room filled with awkward murmurs. Blondie and I exchanged eye rolls.

"Now we do the traditional orientation séance, I guess," she murmured as we joined hands. Embarrassed by the intimacy of touching a stranger, I clamped my eyes closed.

"Now everyone share something about yourself with your partner."

Suddenly I had the distinct feeling that she was leaning in close to me, and I heard her whisper in my ear, "Oh, your hands, they're so . . . baby soft. Do you . . . exfoooliaaate?"

My eyes snapped open. She shot me a really lecherous leer and began circling the top of my hand with her thumb. She licked her lips and shifted her eyebrows almost imperceptibly. I realized she was putting me on. *Game on, weirdo*, I thought.

I dropped my head back and rolled my eyes around in mock ecstasy and moaned loud enough for a few surrounding parties to hear, following up with a strangled, "Oh yes!"

I opened one eye. Blondie looked startled, but her face quickly cracked into a smile, and she loosed a low, throaty chuckle.

"It's not funny. Why would you laugh at that? We're supposed to be sharing!" I stage-whispered, attempting outrage. Her face turned red, and she laughed harder. When she released my hands and shoved me, I broke. We tittered like hysterical preteens, rocking back and forth breathlessly, attracting stares.

Our mirth was just receding when Dreadlocks announced that we'd begin again and find new partners. As the music started to play, I got up, wiping my hands on my jeans with a show of disgust.

"Pervert," I spat.

She nodded appreciatively, brushing a smudge of dampened liner from beneath her eyelashes. "I'll be seeing you around, missy."

I proceeded to meet a few other unremarkable students, including an uncomfortable sit-down with my new roommate, Annie. We'd already met that morning as my dad was helping me move in. She'd appeared as a large, quiet shadow in the doorway, and as I was under my desk trying to jerry-rig an electrical hookup, I didn't notice her there until I heard my father say, "Oh, hello. You must be Ann."

We knew this crucial bit of information because I'd received a letter from the school with Annie's contact information, just in case we wanted to get to know each other before the semester started. It seemed that mutually, we did not. After my dad left and we were alone, I attempted to build a conversational bridge (progress!) while watching her thumbtack photo collages above her bed. She nailed, with particular wistfulness, a smaller, framed collage that featured only photos of Annie with a tiny fella (Thomas, I would soon learn) who looked like a miniature Clark Kent. In one image, taken at prom, he sits on her lap.

Anyway, it was soon established that we shared virtually no interests, be they political, academic, or arts and leisure. Our conversational fount slowed to a polite, if meager, drip and stayed there, permanently. I foresaw Annie as a quiet and sufficiently amiable cell mate, and one unlikely to invade my shower time to test-run eye shadow. I'll say it: I was satisfied with the match.

As for the blonde, I ran into her again that evening in the quad. She was sitting on a bench, surrounded by several students, smoking a cigarette.

"Hey, you! Ginger!" she called out when she saw me.

I pretended to look around like I didn't understand. When I pointed to myself in mock confusion, she laughed, which I suppose was my goal.

"Yeah, you. What's your name?"

"Gloria."

"Like an angel," came a voice from the grass. I looked down and saw a guy with a great shock of spiky hair and a delicate build smiling up at me.

"She's no angel," Blondie quipped. "My name's Cyn."

"How appropriate," I responded.

She grinned. "Short for Cynthia."

"Right."

Cyn laughed. "I've always wanted to befriend a redhead."

"Well, in truth, earlier today I was sure I wouldn't like you because you're so very blond."

"That's discrimination," she protested. This topic was rapidly debated by the assembled group, while Cyn sat smoking, already their queen. She studied me from her bench. "Do you always dislike people on sight?"

I laughed, because it was true.

"I'm trying to improve," I offered. "And you've already helped me so much because, although you are very blond, you seem utterly shameless, and I'm looking for a mentor."

CHAPTER TWO

The next few nights, I took to walking to the bay after dinner. The quay at the bay front was a thing of real beauty, and by far the college's crowning feature. An old mansion from the Roaring Twenties, now converted into classrooms, stood at the end of a long brick walkway. At its foot, a manicured lawn sprinkled with benches and palm trees offered an unimpeded view of sailboats. At sunset, the air filled with the scent of cheap tobacco and marijuana. By nightfall, the scene felt like *The Great Gatsby* transposed into the Summer of Love.

I found a quiet bench and sat alone for a very long time, trying not to think about the disaster I'd made of things in the fall, trying not to think about Mike. Laughter floated up from the students who splayed on the lawn not far from me. I suspected I could have approached any group and been received with friendship, but I just couldn't do it. The minutes lingered painfully as I remained trapped inside my head. When the agony of my stubborn shyness finally dug past paralysis to despair, I trudged back to my dorm alone. Annie was already asleep, oblivious to the party music floating up from the rooms below. I crawled under my comforter and felt with depressing certainty that I was destined to repeat all my mistakes and remain always alone, an outsider. I may have even squeezed out some silent tears of self-pity as the strains of "Space Oddity" echoed across the quad.

The next night, determined not to repeat my pathetic loner act from the night before, I walked to the bay again, a smile of pleasant curiosity plastered on my face. I would talk to someone, anyone, even if it killed me. As I rounded the mansion and the bay came into view, I heard someone call out, "Hey, Ginger! Over here!"

Under the glow of the lamplight, I spotted a halo of fair hair and a thin arm beckoning me over. My fake smile now authentic, I hurried over to join Cyn and her friends.

I sat on a low wall and was introduced all around. It was obvious to me that these, though mostly lowerclassmen, were the cool kids. They were more attractive, slightly more stylish (I say slightly because the hemp and Birkenstock ethos of the campus was worlds away from chic), but more than their exterior signifiers, they had an innate cockiness that advertised their utter confidence in themselves, in their intelligence, and in their right to assert themselves on the world.

Cyn lifted a bottle of amber-hued hooch and passed it to me. "Where you been, Ginger? I've been looking for you."

"Yeah?" I took a gulp from the bottle and grimaced at its fiery sting.

"Great stuff, huh?" She laughed. "Don't worry. Max here says that tomorrow, when the rest of the school comes back to campus from winter break, we won't have to settle for Brand X."

"Brand X?" I coughed. "More like Skull and Crossbones."

Cyn chuckled. Max, the delicate guy I'd met on the quad a few nights ago, snorted appreciatively, and the conversation moved along fluidly. My presence unchallenged, I began to relax, and soon everyone and everything seemed perfect and right.

A while later, after the bottle had been emptied and the group was discussing how to obtain further intoxicants, Cyn leaned over to me.

"Hey, you wanna be my bathroom buddy? I gotta go."

"Sure," I said, hiding my surprise that she'd asked me instead of Clara, the buxom German exchange student, or Lila, a wan, dark-haired pixie who seemed to be Cyn's obvious alpha female partner.

We left the others and headed across to the side of the mansion, flanked by a wooded area and floodlit for safety.

"Buddy system was the way to go on this one," I commented, wary of the inky darkness beyond the streetlamps.

"Right? They have those emergency call boxes, but no way those chubby campus cops could golf-cart over here in time to save us from dismemberment."

Safely inside the tiny ladies' room, I checked out my skin in the mirror while Cyn ducked into a stall.

"Your friends are nice," I offered, personally hating a too-silent bathroom.

"Yeah. Hard to believe I met most of them only yesterday. There seem to be a lot of cool people here."

"This is already so much better than my last school." Cyn remained quiet behind the door, so I kept talking. "I was at Big U upstate. Hated it there. Where were you?"

The toilet flushed, and Cyn reappeared at the sink. "I was nowhere."

I watched her wash her hands, which were loaded thumb to pinkie with ornate silver rings. "I got behind on the application. Missed the fall deadline." She turned off the water, and our eyes met in the mirror. "Actually, the truth is, I was working to make tuition. Out-of-state fees are absolutely ridiculous, but I fell in love with this place, so whatever. I'll worry about the money part as it comes." She opened her bag and fished out a pack of cigarettes. "You smoke?"

"No," I said, and she snapped the pack shut.

"I don't really either. It's more of a social thing." She tucked the cigarette behind her ear and untwisted a strand of hair that had become entangled in the star-shaped silver charm she wore around her throat. "You smoke weed?"

"I don't know."

"You don't know," she repeated. She studied me for a moment to see if I was putting her on. I shrugged, clownishly. "Glo, you are a character. I can already tell."

"Yeah? Well, so are you. You're like Cinderella with cigarettes. And probably drugs."

"That was my nickname in high school. Cynderella." She lit the cigarette with a salmon pink lighter and inhaled, lost in her own thoughts. Then she quickly ashed it into the sink and focused her spotlight-blue eyes on me. "Listen, I'm planning a trip to the big beach tomorrow. You wanna come?"

I opened my mouth to accept the invitation, but she was already exiting the bathroom.

"You'll ride with me. I think some of those miscreants out there are going, too. It'll be fun."

We walked back to the dorms together, chatting easily. She peppered me with questions about myself; the same investigative treatment I underwent with Annie a few days earlier, except a thousand times more fun. She interrogated me about my taste in music, books, movies, the countries I most wanted to visit, my ideal man. I found myself answering with surprising candor. I'd say something from the heart, and if she went quiet, I'd begin bracing for the inevitable rejection. But with Cyn, miraculously, it didn't happen. She wasn't judging me, and we were discovering loads of common ground.

Our dorms had been designed to be easily converted into apartments if our school failed, so each room had private entrances and its own en suite bathroom. It was a nice setup, even if our walls were a little moldy and the air conditioners leaked onto the carpets. Cyn's room was on the second floor, like mine.

As we ascended the open-air staircase, I saw a magazine cut-out of a wide-eyed toad taped to her door. Written above it in block letters were the words LICK ME!

"Nice frog," I said.

"It's a toad. *Bufo alvarius*. Its venom gets you high. My roommate hates Mr. Bufo already." She opened the door a crack, revealing a dark room. "She's the early-to-bed type."

"Mine's the always-in-bed type."

"What? She sleeps around?" Cyn whispered.

I had to laugh. "No. Just a lot. She sleeps a lot."

"Sounds fun. See ya tomorrow." She pulled me in for a casual, one-armed hug, just like I'd seen girls do in the wild, before slipping silently into her room.

When I returned to my dark room and saw myself in the bathroom mirror, I noticed that my face was flushed, and not from the booze. I felt giddy. I felt great. It was almost like falling in love.

The next day, I sacrificed my top sheet for use as a beach blanket, and Cyn, Max, Lila, and I squeezed together along its narrow expanse. No one had a beach umbrella, and even in late January, the sun was intense. Lila and I fetishistically applied sunscreen while Max looked on, manifestly disappointed to not have been asked for help with those hard-to-reach spots. Cyn slouched lazily under a cowboy hat and an oversize men's Oxford shirt, her bronzed legs stretched out into the sand.

Max fiddled with a boom box so ancient that it lacked a compact disc player. No one had any tapes, so he scrolled through the dial, switching stations as often as he redirected the focus of his flirtatious banter. At first, it was entertaining. He was like someone's cute little brother brought along for the ride, desperate to commandeer attention. Lila, having explained at length (truly, at length) that she had a boyfriend in Miami, batted back his weak come-ons like a churlish Siamese cat, while Cyn openly mocked him. Finding no success with either of them, his attentions turned to me.

He rolled in my direction, his eyebrows raised above the limits of his sunglasses, making them appear to be caterpillars in free fall. "So what's with the one-piece, Gloria?" he asked, reaching out to touch my racing suit. "Your synchronized swimming partner showing up later?"

"No. My fur bikini just happens to be at the cleaners."

Cyn snorted behind her magazine.

He blinked. "I see. So what are you, a swimmer or something?"

"Used to be. Want to race? I'll give you a big head start." I'd told Cyn a little about my swimming the night before. She whispered something into Lila's ear.

"Yes, Max. You should race," Lila blurted, failing to keep a straight face. "It's hardly manly to insult a girl's bathing suit and then turn down a challenge like that. Hardly manly at all."

"I'm being set up, aren't I?" he asked.

"Your chances of success are not for me to judge," I yawned, rolling onto my belly. A shadow fell across our blanket, and I looked up to behold Clara, the exchange student, with two hippie-looking guys and a stout goth chick with a barbed wire tattoo around her ankle.

"We *habe* beer," Clara announced to great approbation. They joined us, and the afternoon rolled along in fine fashion.

I sat by the edge of the water fingering the shells I had collected as the sky faded from fluorescent pink to violet. I thought of Mike, but only for a second. In contrast with my new life, he seemed so quaint. As I watched my new friends splashing around in the surf, I felt a tap on my shoulder. Looking up, I saw Tim, the very tall, skinny half of the pair of hippie dudes.

He raised a long, wet arm and pointed out the glimmering arc of a dolphin as it slipped between the waves.

Classes started and the first few weeks flew by in a beautiful blur. Cyn and I saw each other every day, without fail, and our makeshift family expanded to include Max, Lila, and Tall Tim, the second-year marine biology major from the beach whose lanky frame belied a startlingly deep voice. Cyn and I didn't cross paths much during class hours, since our studies were comically divergent. She was planning to major in chemistry and psychology, while I was hitting the humanities pretty hard. The only crossover we had was Spanish Conversation, led by a young and improbably handsome professor, Pablo Altasierra. Professor Pablo was Argentinian and spoke with an exaggerated lisp that we both adored and therefore mocked mercilessly.

Por ejemplo:

ME: *Thynthia, your mithuthe of the path't tenth is thimply thaddening.*

CYN: *Theriously, theñor?*

ME: *Theriously.*

CYN: *Thuck me, theñor.*

A month into classes, Cyn bounded into my room, her face lit up with excitement. She waved a hasty salute to Annie, who barely blinked, and leapt onto my bed like an oversize rabbit.

"Good news. I've made contact with the dealer." Her eyes were unnaturally aglimmer.

"The dealer," I repeated.

"Yes! Get this: his name is *Silence*. He's just what you'd expect. All hippied out, skinny as death, total space cadet, but he seems like a cool dude, and he's got access to all kinds of shit." She slapped my leg in excitement. I closed my book as a thousand doubts clouded my mind.

"Are you sure you can trust this guy?" I ventured, predictably. Drugs had been a frequent conversational topic throughout our intensive crash course in best friendship. Cyn's view on drugs was overwhelmingly pro-experimentation and pro-legalization. She'd read tons of books and scientific studies about the profound effects different chemicals had on consciousness, mood, and perception, and more to the point, she made getting high sound like a fucking blast. Having had no personal experience with drugs, I was intrigued by her tales of chemical adventures past, but because she was honest enough to include both the highs and the lows, I was wary enough for both of us.

"Of course we can! Everybody does. He's 'the guy' for the whole school. You know how many kids here do drugs, and so far, other than people stupidly mixing stuff, there've been no incidents with the product."

"Incidents with the product? You sound like a sixties-era mafioso."

"Maybe." She studied my face. "Okay, full disclosure, there have been two suicides, but no one blamed them on the drugs."

"Suicides? Are you kidding me? Cyn—"

She mockingly mirrored my horrified expression and fell backward on the bed, laughing. "Glo! No one commits suicide after a little smoke, okay?" She slowly pried a small plastic Baggie filled with something green out of her too-tight jean shorts pocket and tossed it at me. "Check it out."

I caught the bag and tossed it right back. She grinned, amused by my discomfort. My fears made me too spooked to even handle the Baggie, but inside, my curiosity was churning. I wanted to experience the strange visions and new perspectives that Cyn rhapsodized about. Also, pathetically, I was terrified to suddenly be left out. If my friends were doing it, prudence be damned. I wanted in.

"Fine. I'll try it. Then we can all jump off the bridge together."

Cyn smiled widely and crammed the Baggie back into her pocket. "So dramatic, Glo."

"And you have to look out for me. Make sure I don't do anything stupid."

She opened her mouth to respond with the wisecrack that I'd carelessly set myself up for, but I was faster. "I mean *too* stupid. You know what I mean." I shoved her, and she rolled off my bed and onto her feet.

"Sunset at the quad. Be there, and you'll no longer . . . be square."

"Get out," I said, tossing my pen after her as she darted out the door.

After Cyn left, my misgivings began thundering away like jackhammers. I tried to finish the essay I was reading, but the words just blended together, my consciousness only tightening into focus when I'd think about sunset. I shut my eyes, hoping that a quick nap might clear my mind. Across the room, Annie had nodded off, the rumble of the air conditioner muting her soft snores. I turned my face toward the wall and tried not to think of anything.

The dream that followed was as softly textured as a watercolor. I was by the bay, surrounded by people. Someone was repeating "Isn't It Great?" over and over again until it seemed that *Isn'tItGreat* was the voice of the surf itself. A blond, Cyn-like figure appeared; her smile, when she flashed it, startlingly jagged and overly toothy. "Isn'tItGreat," she hissed, before turning away and disappearing into the crowd. The faceless pastel throng that had surrounded me abruptly vanished, leaving just me and the flat silver sea. In a flash, the water surged forward, rushing around my ankles and quickly rising. It was astoundingly warm, and I felt pieces of slimy filament wrap around my bare legs as the tide rushed in. The water continued to rise, its surface churning with foam. I turned to look for Cyn but saw only tiny figures on a distant shore, miles of water between us. I wanted to yell out, but the roar of the surf drowned my voice. I wanted to move, but the water had stiffened around me like concrete. The sea rose to my neck, and then to my lips. A piece of driftwood appeared at eye level, rushing toward me on the tide. I watched in horror, unable to move as it spun wildly on a crash course for my forehead. I couldn't duck, couldn't even close my eyes. I stared in frozen terror, awaiting the devastating impact of coarse wood into flesh.

"Gloria! Hey. Gloria, wake up."

I opened my eyes and discovered Annie nudging my shoulder. I sat up quickly, the dream image of the log still careening dangerously in my mind's eye. Annie was already backing away to her side of the room.

"You were having a nightmare," she explained, redundantly.

"Yeah. I was. Thanks for the rescue. I think I was about to die." I closed my eyes, struggling to review the dream images before they faded completely. "I couldn't move, I couldn't scream, and I was about to drown. Did I scream?"

"You were moaning."

"Oh."

I stared at my desk, my sneakers on the rug, my dirty coffee cup, taking in all the real things around me, trying to sort myself out. My mind kept returning to the sensation of being sucked into the warm, quicksilver waters. But that wasn't what had filled me with terror, nor was it the spinning driftwood. What truly chilled me was the indifference of the people on the shore, toothy Cyn included, who couldn't be bothered to notice me die. I could discount the dream as a meaningless specter born of worry, but I wondered if there weren't some truth in it. Perhaps my subconscious was giving me a little heads-up that my treasured new social stature wasn't as secure as I believed. In truth, the sum total of my life experiences suggested that I was past due for a huge social takedown. I felt my dormant terrors shake to life and rise like hungry zombies.

It'll happen tonight, taunted a too-familiar voice. *Those people you think are your friends see your selfishness, your sad vanity, your fear and every other failing you think you've hidden. It's coming, it's coming . . .*

I shook my head violently, trying to clear the voice away, and locked eyes with Annie. She averted her gaze and sunk deeper below the rim of her textbook.

My gratis shrink from Big U would nail this emotional whirligig as a negative thought pattern. Back in treatment, she said the best way to handle it was to do something positive to counteract all the negative thoughts. *Actions are key*, she repeated over and over, *actions and self-compassion*. Since I couldn't toss out my paranoia like a busted pair of flip-flops, or generate much in the way of self-love, I decided the next best thing was to see Cyn. She was compassionate. She said she'd be there for me, and as much as I desperately wanted to trust her, I had to be sure. I told Annie's textbook that I was going out for some air, and I'm sure she was relieved to see me go.

Moments later, as I was climbing the stairs toward the psychedelic toad, Cyn's roommate, Joan, emerged, slamming the door behind her. Cute in a mousy sort of way when her forehead wasn't contorted with repressed rage, Joan was a poor roommate match for Cyn. As Cyn explained it, Joan had essentially disliked her on sight (as had I, it amused me to remember), her disdain escaping in passive-aggressive snorts at Cyn's conversation and the rearrangement of dorm furnishings in Cyn's absence. Joan was engaging in what Cyn described as a one-sided silent turf war. That Cyn tended not to notice Joan's timidly malevolent antics stung her all the more.

She didn't like me much either, as to her, I was an extension of Cyn. But because I was among the more orthodox of Cyn's visitors, she was passingly polite.

"She's in the shower," Joan said, throwing her abundant brown mane over her shoulder. It was long enough that she could sit on it, and though it was shampoo-commercial thick and shiny, it gave her a strangely rural air, as if she might have just escaped from a cult in Texas. "If you're lucky, she'll be out in an hour."

I entered Cyn's room, heard the water running, and crossed to the floor-to-ceiling windows that covered one wall, overlooking the palm-studded pavilion that was the social hub of campus life. It was an enviable room. My own sweeping windows faced a brick wall.

The shower turned off, and Cyn appeared a moment later, wrapped in a towel, with her hair in a tight emerald turban that made her look like a fifties movie star.

"Hey, what's up," she said, always unsurprised to find visitors on her bed. "Joan leave?"

"Yeah."

"Wonderful. I've been entertaining the idea of keeping a water pistol handy to shoot at her when she misbehaves. She's like a mean tabby. I think it might work." She smiled over her shoulder while she shimmied into her underwear. "Something wrong, babe?"

She walked over to me, and seeing her concerned expression, I suddenly felt stupid.

"Yeah, kind of." I felt my face flush.

"Oh no. What is it? Is it the weed? You know you don't have to do it if you don't want to."

This statement was so after-school-special obvious, I almost laughed. "I know. No. I want to. I want to try it with you. I guess I'm just nervous, because sometimes I have strange reactions to things and I guess I'd feel better if I knew I had someone looking out for me." It felt so raw to say the words, I could have died of shame.

"Aw, Glo," Cyn said with a soft laugh. "Of course I'm going to look out for you. What kind of friend do you think I am?"

"A great one, I think. But, I might as well just lay it all out now so you'll at least know what kind of a head case you're dealing with." My words came out sounding strangled and weird, but I pressed on, determined to get the humiliation over with in one go. "I haven't really had many good girlfriends, at all. I mean, ever. There were a few way back who said they were friends and turned on me, and I basically gave up after that. So I spook easily, and I get paranoid. But I don't want that to happen with us. So . . . that's my deal. Just so you know."

Cyn's eyes glittered with understanding. "Girls can be total nightmares for each other, can't they?"

I shrugged and nodded, unsure if I'd be able to speak normally. She hugged me tight, and I had to swallow hard and concentrate on the absurdity of Joan's vintage *Phantom of the Opera* poster to avoid tearing up. When Cyn released me, her face was thoughtful.

"I'm really glad and touched that you told me that. And you're right. We don't have to be that way. We just fucking won't."

"We'll be nice?" I ventured, managing a smile.

"Fuck no. We'll be real, and true, and kind. We'll love each other."

She straightened up to her full height, put a hand on her heart, and pronounced, with a full, Castilian lisp:

"I Thynthia Dawn Williamth do tholemnly thwear to alwayth be your friend and treat you with the utmoth't rethpect and thintherest affection. Do you, Gloria, whatever your middle name is—"

"Melissa," I said, hastily placing my hand across my own heart.

"Melissa? Really? Huh. Do you, Gloria Melitha Roebuck, vow thimilarly?"

"I thwear."

She gave me a hug. "Ugh. We do belong together. We're equally ridiculous." She went to her dresser and pulled out a tank top. "But I am glad you said something. It's like, we make these solemn pledges with guys to treat them a certain way when we date them, but with other women, it's all fast and loose, and loyalty is totally in question until it happens to be tested. But just so you know, I would have had your back anyway, pledge or no pledge. That's just how I roll."

"I believe you. I think I knew that or I wouldn't have said anything about my fucked-up psyche. I'm just scared of the world, I guess."

She blinked. "You don't seem to be. But I guess a lot of people are."

"You aren't?"

She examined her reflection in the mirror, adjusting the spaghetti straps on her tank top. "I'm missing that gene, I guess. Or maybe my curiosity is bigger than my fear. It's probably not a good thing."

I shrugged, wishing I were so lucky. Cyn tossed two pairs of cutoff shorts onto the bed and stared down at both, comparing. "I've been thinking about the infinite. Things that are limitless."

This was typical Cyn, her mind reeling toward the metaphysical while trying to decide between jean shorts.

"Okay," I gamely responded.

"There aren't many things that can be infinite, in my opinion. Time, maybe. Energy perhaps, but I'm not entirely sure of the math. Hope, certainly. Love."

"Mm-hmm." I offered. No telling where this was going.

Cyn decisively selected one of the near-identical shorts and stepped into them.

"I guess what I'm saying is love is one of the few things we've got that is absolutely, unquestionably infinite, yet our nature is to be pretty goddamn stingy with it. Why is that?"

"Takes energy to love? Energy might be infinite, but you aren't sure of the math."

"Glad that you're listening," Cyn snarked, tossing her damp hair towel at my face. "It's always puzzled me, why it's our nature to exclude and reject. What does it costs us? There may not be enough natural resources, but there is enough love. Something is just deeply wrong with our programming as a species."

"That's fucking deep, professor." I collapsed backward onto Cyn's pillow and examined the constellation of glow-in-the-dark stars scattered across the ceiling. "Probably competition screwed our chances for a love-based society. It's not productive to love someone if you might eventually have to kill them and eat their bones to ensure your own survival. Must have caused angst in caveman times, so we turned away from it, closed ourselves off, trained ourselves to assume enmity. That way, if we're wrong, it's a nice surprise."

"Darwinism. That's depressing."

"Consider your source. You just concocted a friendship pledge because I fear everyone."

Cyn smiled. "If I can save you, then maybe that's one small step forward for humanity."

"Now *that's* a depressing idea."

Cyn laughed.

"So anyway, back to your original concern: tonight's festivities. As far as smoking weed goes, you really don't have anything to worry about. You won't hallucinate or anything."

"Well, I know that much," I hedged. Secretly I suspected

that with me and chemicals, anything was possible, but I was determined to suck it up and be brave.

"Okay, good. Just trying to reassure you. Worst-case scenario, you get a little paranoid and we'll go for a walk and look at the phosphorescence in the bay. Either that or we'll go to the mini-mart and you'll get to reexperience ice cream as the most amazing thing ever."

"Either way, I'll be fine."

"Yes, my sister. That you will."

CHAPTER THREE

I don't remember much about that first time we all got high together, for obvious reasons. All I know is that it was not at all how I expected to feel, what with the tingly sensations in my feet and hands and my sudden, all-encompassing thirst, an outcome which we were prepared for, as someone had brought orange cola. I remember coughing so much and laughing so hard, and I remember that we all tried to make animal shapes with our shadows on the lawn from the glare of the floodlights around the mansion near the bay, and that the animals were all really deranged except for one giraffe shape that was pretty close. (Tall Tim was the neck.) The next morning, I had to contend with grass stains on my jeans and a really fuzzy head, but I was a new believer.

We started to go to a lot of parties. Some were on campus, in someone's heavily incensed dorm room, with the stereo blasting and video games flashing brightly across secondhand television sets. Others were more elaborate affairs held at off-campus homes. We would get dressed in our best party wear, which for Cyn meant ripped jeans that were just tight enough and a tank top, while I did my best with my wardrobe of cargo pants and T-shirts. We'd always walk, since no one lived very far away. Someone we didn't know would answer the door if they could hear us knock. If not, we'd let ourselves in, the party noise wrapping around us like a protective spell. We'd saunter through rooms thick with cigarette and weed smoke, hunting our familiars from the forms sprawled across sofas and pillows strewn on the floor. We'd find the kitchen, find the plastic cups, find vodka, find cranberry juice (or anything sweet, but it was almost always a VC), and then we'd find the room with the loudest music.

Unless the party was really good, with dancing and lunacy, Cyn would start to get this look in her eye that meant she wanted to find some drugs. Parties unearthed the worst of Cyn's drug seekiness because, despite the veneer of good times, they were frustratingly predictable. Getting drunk and horsing around was still pretty tops for me on the entertainment spectrum, but Cyn wasn't all that into alcohol. She also wasn't satisfied, as I would have been, with passing a few hours trying out tipsy come-ons on cute guys. Partly this was because a cute, straight, single fellow was a rare beast at Tiny U, and when one did appear, he was quickly spotted and surrounded by haughty-looking girls with well-presented cleavage. My faded Mr. Bubble tee did not give me much of an edge, so instead of hunting guys, I trailed Cyn.

Cyn wasn't looking for weed. We had that back in the dorms. If the good party drugs weren't immediately apparent, we'd flip into search mode, in which I'd follow Cyn into bedrooms, bathrooms, and backyards. When we busted in on things we shouldn't, like sweaty couplings or the very wasted, we'd hastily retreat with a few words about looking for a missing friend. The subterfuge was hardly necessary. The users, when we found them, were quick to make space for Cyn on the rug, their eyes widening as they took in her bright smile and great length of leg. She was careful to always engage the ladies of the room first, so they knew she came in peace and wasn't after their fellas. Only in these strange moments did I ever see Cyn acknowledge her pull on the opposite sex. She downplayed her feminine charms to the point that she seemed oblivious to them, but other women didn't forget it. They shot me suspicious glances, their eyes warning of problems to come if Cyn created an attention vortex. Competition. Fear. Hate. But even when high, Cyn was too smooth and controlled to inspire any dustups. It was only when she couldn't find what she wanted that I had to look out.

On those nights, she'd become an unguided missile. Nothing could get her mind off the theoretical fun trip she wasn't having, so irritable and jonesey, she'd begin to monologue. She'd get so lost in her rants that I'd have to monitor her like a Seeing Eye dog, lest she step off the curb into the path of an oncoming truck. But by the next morning, she'd snap back to her normal self. If I reminded her of how obsessed and seeky she'd been the night before, she'd laugh it off. She said college was the time to experiment, and despite my reservations, I found it tough to disagree.

It was a typical class day when everything changed. I'd just finished lunch, a real bulge-inducer from the make-your-own-sub-sandwich bar, and I wanted to see if Cyn would join me for a repentance swim. Inside Cyn's room, I discovered Joan shoveling clothing out of her drawers and into a pair of black garbage bags.

"Hey, Joan," I said when she didn't respond to the sound of the door shutting.

Joan glared over her shoulder at me. Her porcelain cheeks were unusually red and blotchy.

"I thought I'd locked that," she snarled.

"Nope." I sat on Cyn's bed. "Open, just like always."

"Exactly!" she shouted. "I've fucking had it!"

"Something wrong?" I offered blandly as I stooped to lift a

book of photography from the floor. The cover featured a nice profile shot of an elephant, its small eye holding unknowable ruminations.

"She hasn't even talked to *you* about it?!"

I made a point never to respond to Joan's agita, a difficult feat at times like this, when she was shrieking in close quarters. I occasionally sympathized with her feeling steamrolled by Cyn, and remembering my own suite mate nightmare, I tried to be kind. Still, hearing Joan's puritanical tirades on everything from the proper maintenance of the dorm fridge to the use of soft drugs on the front steps had eroded my compassion to the point where my dislike for her had crystallized into a manageable gem: sharp, but easy to hide. I took a deep breath.

"Please, stop screeching. I haven't seen her today. What is the problem?"

"Oh, you haven't seen her? Yeah, right! Fuck!" She kicked a garbage bag, creating a hole, and collapsed onto her bed. She emitted a long groan that morphed into choked sobs.

I rolled my eyes but simultaneously felt a small tug of sympathy. I hate to see people cry, even extraordinarily irritating people.

"Joan," I ventured once the choking noise ceased.

"I want to move out. I hate it here with her! Your stupid friend, she lets all these hippies traipse through here and mess with my stuff and sit on my bed. My blanket from home smells like patchouli! And yesterday, that guy, the one who looks like a strung-out Jesus . . ."

"Silence?"

"Yeah, *that* motherfucker! Well, I find him in here, on my side of the room, with this six-foot bong! And when he finally noticed I was there, he was like, 'Yo, can you help me light this?' Cuz obviously it's six feet high and he can't suck on the drugs and light it at the same time, so he asks *me*. So I screamed at him to get out, and I guess he got startled because he knocked the stupid thing over, and disgusting bong water leaked out all over my new rug!"

"Ooh. Bong water. That is bad. Did you try rinsing it out in the shower?"

Joan ignored me. "So I suggested to Cyn, very politely considering *everything*, that she speak with you about switching rooms. I'm in the middle of packing because I want this done now, and since I hadn't heard anything against it, I figured everyone was okay with it."

I did a lightning-speed rundown of the pros and cons. Unless cohabitation led to another round of academic disaster for me (a possibility) or ruined our friendship via overexposure, I didn't see what could go wrong. I did admit to myself that I didn't relish the thought of the unwashed element of Cyn's social sphere lounging on my bed, but that was a sacrifice I was probably willing to make, especially if I could negotiate for some control of the guest list.

Right on cue, Cyn entered. She eyeballed Joan and the garbage bags warily before noticing me on her bed.

"Hey. Heard we're gonna be roommates," I greeted her.

"If that's okay with you. And if you think Annie will go for it," Cyn said, smiling through a flush of embarrassment.

"Annie will go for it," Joan stated flatly. "We've been talking about it for weeks."

This was news. I hadn't known that Annie and Joan were acquainted.

As if answering my unspoken question, Joan rolled her eyes and said, "We're both bio majors. We talk." She picked up the garbage bags of clothes and headed toward the door, stopping on the threshold to glare at me. "So are you gonna get packed, or what?"

I followed Joan back to my own room, my plan to swim

totally forgotten in light of the fact that I was suddenly moving. Joan's ponytail swished its way up the stairs before me. Once inside, Joan dropped her bags by my bed. Annie was nowhere in sight, but her side of the room was suspiciously clean.

"You guys have been wanting this for weeks, huh?" I asked.

"Well, I've been wanting it. Annie was just available. Oh, and in case you were wondering, she doesn't hate you like I hate Cyn."

"That's good. I don't hate her either," I said absently. My stuff was everywhere. Moving was going to be a total bitch.

Joan stood by the door, watching me. "You know, your friend is on a path to total self-destruction. Not that I care about her at all. I don't. She was a horrible roommate. But I hope that maybe you can help her out before she goes truly nuts and takes you down with her. You'll see what I mean."

With that, she and her ponytail of doom were gone.

Living with Cyn required a few adjustments. Back in the old room with Annie, the only person who would regularly pop in was Cyn. Now that Cyn and I were together and Joan wasn't around to glare and hiss, our room was the new gathering spot for everyone we knew. Come sundown, friends slowly trickled in until the room was a veritable salon of slacking. It was fun, but I didn't get shit done, so out of fear of *Academic Meltdown: The Sequel,* I began forcing myself to go to the library for a few hours every evening. Still, it was great to have the party come to us. Even though we were just some chill ladies with a cool room at a tiny school in the middle of nowhere, it felt like we were at the nexus of something big. Cyn's chemistry buddies made the acquaintance of the poli-sci kids. The music hippies made nice with the art geeks. Everyone would trade ideas and swap books and CDs. Random new faces would appear and become regular visitors, and from my lookout point atop my dorm bed, I was pleased to see new friendships bloom. Little did I know that those first few weeks of cohabitation would be the halcyon days of our time together.

The slow, downhill slide began when I returned from class to find Cyn crying. I rushed to her, assuming, wrongly, that someone had died. She gestured to a crumpled letter on the desk. It was from the financial aid office, stating in no uncertain terms that half of her scholarship was revoked. Evidently, she'd misreported her graduation date, because she feared the year and a half she took off would hurt her chances of a scholarship. Midway through the semester, the discrepancy was discovered. Cyn pointed a shaky finger at another paper, an invoice from the school with a sickeningly large number due and owing.

"I'm so totally screwed," she croaked through her tears. "I can't believe this is happening."

"Can't you appeal it? There's gotta be something you can do. I mean, your grades and your scores are all still the same."

"I tried to talk to the lady in Admissions. She's a total bitch. She said that I'm lucky the school hasn't kicked me out for lying on my application."

As Cyn continued to sniffle, I picked up the letter. She would have to come up with almost seven thousand dollars for this term alone. I felt a jolt of selfish terror as I imagined her leaving me at the school alone. I set the invoice down, feeling stunned.

"It's okay. I'll figure something out. I'm not leaving this place, whether they like it or not." She mustered up a broken smile.

"Of course. You can be a student squatter. Or throw a shitload of very expensive bake sales." I was struggling to stay cheery. The amount of money she needed to come up with was staggering.

"Car washes. I will wash cars twenty-four/seven. When I'm not busy studying at this fine, benevolent institution," she snarled.

"You could double your money if you did it topless."

The smile that suddenly manifested on her face had nothing to do with happiness. "I should only do that on prospective student visitation days. Let them and their parents know the whole truth."

"Economics 101."

"Tit-onomics."

Silence poured in around us after the word left her lips. In the fading light, I saw Cyn had a strange look on her face. I should have seen what was coming next, but I didn't.

She dropped the bomb on me the next afternoon when we were out for a sunset jog.

"So, I found a solution to my new economic crisis," she said, the words pulsing out unevenly under the strain of our exertions. I hated to run and had only come along because Cyn didn't often get it into her head to do any real exercise. Her muscles magically required little more than a few hours of weekend party dancing to appear lean and sculpted.

"Awesome," I exhaled. "What?"

"I'm working at Ecstasy II. Dancing."

I stopped running. "Ecstasy II? That dumpy adult store that we make fun of every time we pass it? Are you serious?"

She kept jogging in place as I labored to speak, which annoyed the shit out of me.

"Kelly hooked me up with it. She says when she worked there last summer, she made four hundred dollars on a typical Sunday afternoon."

"Yeah, doing what? Sucking old man cock?"

A small smile of amusement spread across her face. "I knew you'd be upset."

I started jogging, and she easily matched my pace. She was right, I was upset. That also annoyed me. It wasn't any of my business how Cyn made her money, but I hated the thought of her demeaning herself in front of creeps who would only see her as a shimmying tower of T & A. We rounded a corner, and a sharp pain in my side forced me to stop. I leaned on a mailbox for support.

"Side cramp?" Cyn asked.

"Yeah." She waited patiently, not jogging, as I caught my breath. "Okay. Sorry. It creeps me out. But if you can do it and you'll make a lot of money, good for you."

"I hope I will. I made two hundred today, but I had to spend seventy on wardrobe." I caught the perverse twinkle in her eye.

"Oh god, what does that mean?"

She giggled. "G-string and star-shaped pasties, of course. Oh, and platform heels. Ridiculous. I chose this magenta number, on the advice of Gabe, the manager. He says the Barbie look goes over well down here."

"Two hundred is good, I guess. What do you have to do?"

"Nothing too terrible. Nobody gets to touch me, at least. I'm going to be a private booth dancer. The client sits in this little cubicle with me, and I do a strip tease to cheesy pop music. Gabe or some other clerk is always keeping an eye on the situation through a two-way mirror, so I don't think things can go too horribly wrong."

"That's good. And the guys, they just touch themselves?"

She shrugged. "It was half and half today. Two did, two didn't."

"I see." I was feeling light-headed and nauseated. I think it was from running in the heat, but it could have been blood loss from the bruising of my delicate sensibilities. I sat down in the grass in front of someone's house. The cramp in my side refused to loosen.

"What if your professors see you there?"

"I think confetti would fall, and we'd both get an award for being big clichés. Seriously, Glo, I don't care. I know I'm commodifying myself, but that happens at any job. The only difference here is that exactly what I'm commodifying and why is plainly obvious and not accepted in polite society, yet because it's not polite, I get to make more money and work fewer hours. In my thinking, it's the most elegant solution wrapped in a cloak of total seediness."

"Well, if you're okay with it, then I guess it is a good solution. I didn't know you just inherently knew how to perform a strip tease."

"I didn't. The spirit of Grant possessed me and did all the work."

"Grant?" I asked, finally feeling like I might not throw up.

"Dead President on the fifty? Get with it, girl."

"Oh. That Grant." She helped me off the grass, and we began walking back toward campus.

"You wanna jog again, or are you spent?" she asked.

"Spent. Go ahead. I'll see ya back there."

Cyn bounded off, her blond ponytail swinging a wide arc behind her. I knew it was pointless to worry about her, but as she gained distance, she seemed to grow smaller and more delicate.

For some bizarre reason, I thought that Cyn would keep the whole dancing at the adult store thing under the radar. Ha. Our inner circle knew about it by that night, as Cyn went so far as to model her silver platform stilettos for those assembled. No one seemed as shocked as I had been, though Tall Tim blushed tomato red, and I noticed Max shifting around uncomfortably, supporting the rumor that he was as easily excitable as a fifteen-year-old.

"Oh my god, Cyn. Those are so horrible. And awesome. I'm going to make a documentary about you for my Feminist Studies course," Lila said with a gasp.

"Um, thanks, but no thanks. This isn't really a statement job. It's more of a desperation job."

"No, a desperation job would be going all the way," Max interjected.

"Who asked you, Mr. Man," Lila snapped. "I just think it's very bold. Very strong and very bold."

Cyn eased onto her bed and began unstrapping the heels. "Well, if you want to find out for sure, there's plenty of booth time available. I can hook you up."

"Please. This one is not a dancer. Dominatrix, maybe," Max said, wincing in anticipation of the sharp slap that Lila reflexively inflicted on his thigh.

"Ow."

"Don't 'ow' me, you naughty little ass-licker, unless you want another." She raised her thin hand threateningly.

Cyn kicked the heels under her bed. "Well, if anything, I'm sure I'll have some interesting stripper tales to share in my golden years."

Max snorted. "Cyn, I have just one piece of advice for you: don't date anyone you meet at work."

"How could I date anyone, Max?" Cyn demurred. "You know I'm still carrying a giant torch for you."

"And I'm carrying an equally giant torch for you."

Lila smirked. "Giant torch. Yeah, right."

Max pouted.

"Don't worry. I don't think I'll be picking up any guys at the shop," Cyn said.

"The shop," I repeated, laughing.

Tall Tim followed with, "The factory."

Lila rolled her eyes. "The old mill."

"Oldest mill there is. But, right. Of course you wouldn't date anyone from there," Max hectored. "She turns down every guy who asks her out. What's the secret, Cyn? Seriously. I know a lot of dudes who would pay me big cash money to know the right way to ask you out."

I smirked. "The right way? Like at sunset atop a lighthouse? In rhyming verse?"

"If that's what it takes, I'm sure some guys would be willing to try."

"It's not for want of being asked, doofus," Cyn said. "I've always gone after the guys I wanted. I just haven't met anyone here worth pursuing."

"You consider yourself a huntress," Tall Tim diagnosed in his deep basso.

Cyn shot him a look. "The only thing I need to hunt down at the moment is some z's, thanks." She made a show of fluffing her pillow and crawling onto her bed. I yawned loudly in agreement. Max protested that the night was young, but Lila dragged him out the door by his ear. Tall Tim executed a low bow to us before closing the door, his trademark exit move.

After Cyn snapped off her light, we sat in the darkness, staring out at the tops of the palm trees and the sky beyond it, listening to the scattered voices from below in the quad.

"So, do you think you'll find some dude worth hunting?" I asked.

"Dunno," she answered, lying back onto her bed. She was quiet for so long that I had drifted into a half sleep when she began speaking again.

"I sometimes wonder if there's something wrong with me that I don't feel that need. The few guys I've dated . . . they were never serious. They were all relatively smart and interesting people, especially considering where we grew up." She paused. "Sex with Jake was okay, but it wasn't this huge cosmic thing, at least not for me. It was just . . . fun."

I stayed quiet, expecting more. We hadn't talked about sex all that much. I knew she'd had two partners: one briefly, and then Jake, for more than a year. Since I'd known her, she hadn't so much as kissed any of the guys we met at parties, though they always seemed to sniff her out and circle like wolves.

"There's nothing wrong with fun," I said quietly. "Why should there be?"

Cyn rolled over to face me. "Is that what you really think?"

Her voice had an edge that I didn't appreciate. When I didn't respond, she rolled back over.

"You know, you don't have to have a casual attitude toward things just because I do." Her voice sounded strained in the darkness. "I know you still haven't given up the big V, and I suspect that you're one of those girls who believes it should be special. And that's okay. You don't have to pretend."

"Who says I'm pretending?" I snapped, my defenses triggered. So what if I was perhaps harboring soft-focus visions of love and romance? I wasn't a prude, and that was none of her business anyway. I'd been supportive of her becoming a stripper, and now she was belittling me as some sort of blushing virgin?

"There's just a lot of things you don't know about yourself until you go there. Sex isn't all love and romance and explosive orgasms. There's pain and regret, fucked-up power dynamics. It can get dangerous quickly. You can get hurt or hurt other people."

She quieted, and her words hung in the air like the smoky skeletons of spent fireworks. The window of silence that followed seemed like an open invitation to ask the obvious.

"Did you get hurt, Cyn? Is that it?"

She chuckled drily. "Other way around."

"Oh. Jake?" I probed, and got nothing but silence from her side of the room. "Do you want to talk about it?"

"No. Because then I'd have to think about it, and I'm already feeling like shit."

"Okay. Well, if you ever want to, I'm here. Best pal on duty."

I waited for her to answer, and when she didn't, I got up and filled my glass in the bathroom. When I came back in, I saw her silhouetted against the window. She was sitting up, and sniffling.

"Are you crying?"

She didn't respond, but her sniffles increased. I hovered by my bed, glass in hand.

"Hey. What's wrong?"

"My life is just so fucking trashy," she said, her voice tightrope tense and equally quavery. "I wish it wasn't, but it is and that's fine. I never really had lofty ideals for myself and my life, but what the fuck, I'm working as a stripper now? It's just, it's not exactly how I imagined my college experience, and if things are already this low-rent, what the hell is going to happen next?"

I sat on her bed and gave her a hug. After a moment, she shrugged me off. "Tissues," she whispered, reaching for a box on the floor. I sat there as she blew her nose, unsure what to say.

"I really thought you were okay with it."

She sighed and seemed to regain control. "Fuck. I *am* okay with it. During the day, when I was there, I was totally fine with it. But now, when I'm worn down, I start to picture my life from the outside, and it seems so tawdry, like I'm a big, unfunny joke. And now, after today's developments, it's even worse."

She wiped her eyes again, then pressed the tissue to her forehead as another wave of emotion hit and she shook silently. I put my arm around her and waited. She took a few deep breaths and cleared her throat.

"It's not about the stripping. That's obviously a fresh issue.

It's everything. I think I have some major malfunction where I can only get interested in realities that aren't there and people who I'll never meet, and I'm numb to everything else. I'm stuck on the outside and I can't get interested." She looked at me, her eyes shining in the near darkness "You don't know what I mean, do you?"

"I think I do." I was so blindsided by the turn the night had taken that I couldn't think straight. Privately, Cyn was my model of female unflappability, and now I'd seen her completely break down twice in forty-eight hours.

She was crying quietly, a jagged, uneven weeping. She was human, just like the rest of us, so I decided to do what my mother and father had always done for me when I was disappointed after a loss. They told me what they thought I wanted to hear.

"It will happen, Cyn. Someone will enter your life that you'll be crazy about, and things will snap into focus, and all the stuff you're worried about now will seem really small. It just hasn't happened yet. But it will. I know it will."

She groaned and shook her head in disbelief.

"I guess I just thought things would be better. I thought I'd be discovering things and growing and learning to be more empathetic, but instead I'm just pulling away and getting more lost in my head, and the more I meet people, the less I even want to be human. I just thought college would be . . . better," she said. A second later, a tiny smile glimmered across her face.

"But, *honey*, you're in *Flooorida*," I drawled, reviving one of our best inside jokes, an overheard phrase we'd co-opted to deal with any topical disappointment.

"I knew that was coming," she said, rolling her head back in mock agony.

"You bet."

Someone outside howled with laughter.

"Sorry about all this." She gave me a quick squeeze and then brushed her balled-up tissues onto the floor. "It wasn't about you. I love you. I didn't mean to tell you how to be."

"It's okay. You've had a tough couple of days. And anyway, I meant what I said. I think there are good things ahead, for both of us."

"I hope so," she said.

The rest of the spring semester flew by. Since we didn't have the cash to do anything great for spring break, we spent the week at my parents' house and took trips to the beach almost every day. It wasn't full-on beer bong, Jell-O shot, Slip 'N Slide bacchanalia, but it was enough to make us feel young and alive. Cyn even kissed some guy, Danny, at a beach bar one night. Danny was gorgeous, but had eyes only for Cyn, so I spent a long evening discussing war movies with Danny's married serviceman pal. It was an epic shock when I glanced across the bar and discovered Cyn in a deep lip-lock with Danny. I was mesmerized and a little skeeved out, watching his Adam's apple dip up and down as they went at it. It felt like ages since I'd gotten that sort of attention. But, good pal that I was, I swallowed my jealousy and heroically managed to keep smiling at Pvt. Talksalot. We closed the bar down, me waiting impatiently in the car for her to disengage. On the drive home, she thanked me profusely for "falling on the grenade" for her, giggling drunkenly at her own dumb joke while I bit my tongue. When the hangover wore off, she had a happy glow about her, and considering her messed-up month, I couldn't begrudge her some joy. Fittingly, as soon as we got back to campus, she reverted to her prickly ways regarding all things romantic, almost as if Danny from the beach had never happened.

The last two weeks of school were ridiculous. I was drowning in notes for term papers, and Cyn was always at the library, cramming with her science pals for their epic exams. It was nothing but coffee, classes, coffee, a few words of commiseration with equally dead-eyed friends, a small anxiety attack, followed by hours spent stringing words together on a computer screen, hoping they made sense. Lather, rinse, repeat. Just when it seemed like we would all die from sleep deprivation and stress, it was over. Our papers were turned in and tests completed. We were, strangely, free.

The party started on Friday and lasted until Sunday afternoon. Word around campus was that Silence had gotten in a nice supply of pure MDMA. Half of the student body was going to be rolling all weekend. This time, I asked Cyn if she wanted to roll with me. I'd undergone a sea change in the months since my freak-out over the weed. Now I wasn't at all nervous. My papers were in, and I wouldn't need to use my brain for a few solid months. Cyn had told me what to expect: good feelings, happiness, and the uncontrollable urge to dance. It all sounded great, and it was. I remember dancing with my arms around Cyn's and Lila's necks, all of us screaming along with the music. It seemed like there were thousands of people in the quad, every one of them having the best time, every one of them dear friends, even the ones I'd never met.

We danced and got lost trying to find the way back to the dorms, and then got un-lost and decided to walk to the bay. Tall Tim was there, and at some point I was lying with my head resting in his lap, playing with his enormous hands that seemed to block out the gently brightening sky. When it became light enough to see, we all rambled back to our room, crossing through the quad, where a handful of energetic souls were refusing to concede to the sunrise and were still dancing. We closed the blinds and collapsed, passing joints until sleep finally grabbed us.

When I awoke, everyone was gone. Cyn stood looking out

the window, smoking. Her face looked drawn and tired, as I'm sure mine did.

"Is that a cigarette?" I croaked. She had quit a few weeks after we met, with the offhand explanation that smoking wasn't doing anything for her anymore.

"Yeah, I found a pack in my bed. Who they belong to, I have no idea. You want one?"

She walked over with the pack. I shook my head and collapsed back onto the pillow.

"Did you have fun?" she asked.

"Yeah. I did. It was lots more fun than I thought it would be, even. But today is going to suck, right?"

She took a drag and nodded, then disagreed with herself and shook her head. "Depends. Your serotonin levels are fucked, so don't expect to feel happy, or much of anything. Just limit yourself to mindless tasks and try not to get emotional."

She returned her attention to the window.

"Did you have fun?"

She smiled. "I had an amazing time. This sounds weird, but I swear, I really only feel like myself when I'm . . . altered." She sighed and stubbed out the cigarette in an empty soda can. "But I guess last night wasn't really life, though, was it?"

"'Course it was. Just a different part of life."

"I would do it more often, but chemically, it becomes counterproductive," she murmured.

"I'll take your word for it." I yawned. "It's a special-occasion type of thing."

She smiled mirthlessly. "It should be."

She turned away, and her form disappeared into the mid-morning light pouring in through the window. I rolled over and went back to sleep.

Cyn and I opted to stay on campus for the summer, which meant we'd get to keep our coveted room the following year. I picked up two jobs: one part-time gig as a lifeguard at the pool and a waitress job a few nights a week at a seafood place. Max, Lila, and Tim went back to their hometowns, so things were pretty quiet.

Cyn picked up additional shifts at the Treasure Chest, Ecstasy II's sister property across town. Evidently, there was a limit to her marketability at E Two. She still had her regulars, a concept that I didn't quite understand, but apparently many strip club patrons were novelty seekers, so it helped to split her appearances across a geographic expanse.

She quit working at the Chest by the end of the summer. We had made a pact to do nothing but have fun the last week before classes started up, and part of the grand plan was to go clubbing in Miami. Lila booked a room at a posh beachfront hotel, which for us was a serious splurge.

We dropped E and danced until sunrise. Max and Lila ended up making out on the beach, an occurrence both glaringly predictable and unnerving to behold. They'd always shared some psychosexual tension in a queasy brother/sister way, but now, in a cosmic hiccup, Lila was on the outs with her boyfriend. Max was more than solicitous of her tender feelings, and as angels wept with joy, a glorious friends-with-benefits situation was conceived.

"It's like incest, that's all I can say," I growled, watching the palmetto scrub whiz by as we drove home the next day. I was in a rotten mood because of the E's shitty chemical afterbirth, fatigue and jealousy. I wasn't jealous because Max chose Lila; he was a veritable eunuch in my mind. I was jealous because I seemed permanently cast as "girl not being kissed on the beach."

Cyn, well aware of my mood, made vague conciliatory noises

before pointedly turning up the radio. I knew I'd been whining all summer about wanting a love affair, so I took the hint and spared her another onslaught. I closed my eyes and tried to picture the wonderful guy who I'd meet soon enough, when the new students rolled into town. There had to be someone. There just had to be.

CHAPTER FOUR

The first day of classes was accompanied by a late-summer heat wave. By afternoon, the local power plant had suffered a transformer blowout, and the campus was without electricity. No one knew when it was coming back. Classes were canceled because the classrooms were insufferably hot, and students returned to find that their dorm room windows didn't open and their mini fridges were leaking frozen goods all over the all-weather carpeting. I was carrying around a box of quickly liquefying Popsicles, looking to give them away, when I noticed Cyn advancing toward me with a huge smile on her face.

"This is ridiculous!" she shouted, circling her arms to indicate either the heat or the generalized mayhem that had ensnared the campus. She accepted a cherry Popsicle, and I selected grape before handing the box to a threesome of freshmen, who received the gift with hyperbolic delight.

I followed Cyn to a shady courtyard near the cafeteria. There was a slight breeze, but it didn't help much. I could feel individual streams of sweat running down my back, soaking the waistband of my shorts. We raced to finish our Popsicles, the icy sweetness streaking down our palms.

"There's a seriously awesome new guy in my biochem class," Cyn said, licking her stained fingertips.

"Oh yeah? How awesome is seriously awesome?"

Cyn blushed, a rarity. "Hard to say. Physically, he's some sort of ethnic cocktail, like Indian and something else, maybe white, maybe Latino. Tall, shiny Superman hair, fantastic smile. Think James Bond, but with a permanently deep tan."

"Wow."

She nodded in agreement. "Yeah. Wow, indeed. We talked a little, and he seems super smart. And funny."

"Sounds awesome-awesome."

"Could be. I told him about you. Turns out he's a swimmer, too. Hell, maybe we should go to the pool today."

"You told him about me?"

"Yeah. You'll like him, too. I've already decided he should be part of our crew."

"Oh, I see. Does he know he's been recruited to serve with the finest?"

Cyn smiled. "Not yet. A girl doesn't want to come on too strong."

Only three days later, I met Cyn's new favorite person.

I was in the pool, swimming laps. When I was almost in the dead center of the lane, I had this impulse to stop. I wasn't tired or out of breath, I just felt a strong desire to pop my head out and look around. That was when I saw him.

He was walking out of the locker room, dark red swim trunks, toned swimmer's build, sunglasses. He stopped walking and looked at me down in the pool, treading water, staring at him. Then he smiled. His smile literally punctured something in my heart, and I felt this strange sense of relief, like *finally, this is happening*, though what *this* was, I had no idea. All I knew was that I was treading water midlane like a weirdo, glowing inwardly from the smile of a stranger. I pretended like I needed to empty my goggles, then I laboriously kicked back into stroke. I was moving for a few seconds before it hit me that I had forgotten to smile back, or maybe I had without realizing it.

Clearly, he was the awesome guy Cyn had gushed about. She had mentioned the lovely dark bronze cast of his skin, but had not described, or possibly had not yet fully glimpsed, his extraordinary frame. My memory captured him in 3-D Technicolor; wide, graceful shoulders that angled down to a narrow waist, buttressed by chiseled obliques that guided the eye toward his crotch as assuredly as a neon sign. *Did I really just scope out his package?* Yes. I reached the wall and flipped, the aqueous world spinning wildly around me. Before the world righted itself, I imagined tracing the contours of those obliques with my tongue, and conquering the mystery so thinly masked by those red trunks.

My rhythm, which I hadn't fully recovered after the sighting, short-circuited at the thought, and I decided to give up the charade. My mind was clearly no longer focused on my stroke. I swam to the wall and hung on to the floating lane divider, waiting for my breathing to return to normal. I didn't exactly need a periscope to locate the mystery guy, as he had settled on a bench at the end of my lane. I pulled off my goggles and rubbed my face a few times to iron out any pressure lines.

"Hey," he said.

"Hey," I said.

"How is it in there?" He smiled that same smile. Beauty.

I pulled myself up out of the water and sat on the edge of the pool, not quite facing him.

"It's great. You going in?"

"That was my plan." He paused. "I think we have a friend in common."

I smiled. "Oh?"

"I think so. I met a girl who said her roommate was a redheaded mermaid."

I laughed out loud. "You've met Cyn."

"Yes. So you are Gloria. I'm Raj."

I stood up to shake his hand. It felt warm and dry against my cool, wet fingers.

"Just Raj?"

"Oh. Rajveer Nicholas Roy III. Just kidding about the third."

I sat down on the bench next to him, close but out of dripping distance. "Cyn told me about you, too. She said that she wanted to adopt you into our group."

"Did she?" He smiled and looked down bashfully.

In that moment, it occurred to me that he was probably already in love with Cyn. It was an impossibly dismal thought, and sitting next to him in the sunlight, I couldn't make myself believe it. I rapidly steered the conversation in a different direction.

"So how come I haven't seen you on campus before? There's only, like, twelve of us enrolled here. Don't you eat, go to class, things like that?"

"I do. I eat almost every day, if you can believe it. And I take a lot of science classes, which is how I met Cyn. But the crappy thing is, I live in the H Quad."

I shook my head in sympathy. "The Hubble. That explains it."

He furrowed his brow. "The Hubble?"

I giggled. His warm brown eyes were studying me with intense inquisitiveness, like I was the most interesting person on earth. It was making me feel dizzy, so I looked down at the puddle forming around my feet.

"You really haven't heard that yet? H Quad is nicknamed the Hubble because it's so damn far away. Hubble residents are called astronauts."

"Ah, space humor. Excellent." He rubbed his palms against his thighs, producing a faint nylon hum. For an instant, I wondered if I might be making him nervous. Had I been gazing overlong at those surreal abs? Had I lost myself and become a total lech? I forced my gaze elsewhere, locking on to his hands. They were thin and attractive but still masculine, like surgeon hands. "It's way the hell out there. I'm going to have to get a bike or a junker car."

"A horse?" I suggested.

"In this heat, that would be inhumane. I'm thinking more along the lines of a jet pack."

I laughed. "And that's why you appreciate the space humor."

"I do."

We locked eyes, neither of us speaking. Time seemed to blur, and in that moment, I felt myself falling, hard.

He looked away, and I felt a pang of disappointment. I stood up, trying to act casual amid the whirlpool of unexpected emotion that had suddenly seized me.

"You should show up at the dining hall tonight. That's where all the cool kids go to eat grilled cheese."

"I love grilled cheese. I think I will," he said, smiling up at me. I loved his voice. It was warm and smooth, like a radio announcer's.

"Good. I'll see you then. Have a good swim."

I darted away, a blush erupting from my neck upward. I hurried into the ladies' locker room, stripped off my suit, and walked into the empty sauna. More blood rushed to the surface of my skin as I stood there, breathing deeply, unable to even feel the baking heat for the chaotic flurry of desire that was consuming me. I was in love with this guy. In love! I grinned, wrapping my arms tightly around my own humid torso, and felt a strange quiver pass through me like the taut vibration of a plucked bow. Happy as I was, there was also something undeniably frightening about this development; as if in that moment when our eyes met, he had casually reached over and swiped part of my soul, obliging me to chase him forever. It was such a melodramatic thought that I laughed out loud and promptly removed my overheated brain from the sauna. Under the shower, I made a choice. If love required this madness, this exquisite terror of potentially unfulfillable desire, I was ready. For him, I thought, I might try anything.

Back in our room, I found Cyn on all fours, digging around under her bed.

"Hey," she said, not looking up from her search. "I'm missing a sparkle thong. Even if I find it under here, it's gonna be gross."

"You're working tonight," I said, answering the question I was about to ask.

"I'm supposed to be there in half an hour. That seems unlikely." She gave up the hunt and began to toss other stripper paraphernalia into her duffel. The silver platforms were visible inside, as well as some CDs. Cyn had started bringing her own dance mixes. She said it was good for her mental health.

"Guess who I just ran into at the pool."

Cyn's face lit up. "You met him! What do you think?"

I ratcheted my true enthusiasm back by about 95 percent. "He's every bit as awesome as you said."

Cyn nodded. "My god, those eyes."

"Those shoulders."

"That's from swimming, right? I love him already." She stood up and went to her dresser, pulled out something small and rhinestoned, and stuffed it in the bag. Her supply of dazzling lingerie had increased dramatically over the summer. When she did her wash, it caused a sensation.

"Me too," I said quickly, just to get it out there.

Cyn glanced at me. "Do you?" I stiffened, waiting for her to stake her claim. Instead, she smiled. "I'm glad. I think we'll be seeing a lot of him around in the near future."

I should have asked her then and there if she liked him *that way*, too. The sooner I knew, the easier it would be for me to get over it, if I could. But I didn't want to cede him just because she saw him first. What difference could a handful of days make?

"I invited him to eat with us tonight," I said. "I didn't realize you'd be working."

"Oh good." She went to the mirror, applying mascara with quick little jabs. "I want him to meet the rest of the gang, too."

I pictured this reception by "the rest of the gang" and chuckled.

"What's so funny?"

"Max and Tim are going to just love the competition."

Cyn shrugged. "I think Raj might possess the kind of cool that attracts even other guys."

She said *attract*. She was attracted to him. I felt sick.

The moment I asked if she wanted him, it would be all out in the open. Someone would either have to back off, or we might let him choose, or she could just claim firsties. It simultaneously occurred to me that she was being Cyn: falling excessively "in love" with anyone who was new and interesting and rubbed her the right way. Hell, I was case in point. But as I watched her finish her makeup, I felt a troubling tickle of dishonesty. Cyn and I had been utterly straight with one another, and that was why our friendship was so solid. Now I was holding something back. It felt weird and wrong.

"You should meet up with us after work," I hedged, not meaning it and already hating my new talent for duplicity.

"Absolutely."

"Hey, so, does Raj know what you do?" I asked. I might have wanted him, but outing her as a stripper to gain sway was worlds beneath me.

"The dancing? No, not yet. But I'm sure he'll find out sooner or later," she said with a laugh, picking up her keys.

"Okay. Just wondering."

She looked at me in the mirror as she fixed her lipstick. "It's not really a big secret anymore. But I guess, in truth, I'd rather tell him myself." She came back and gave me a kiss on the forehead, leaving a mauve lip print. "Anyway, he'll learn soon enough how debauched we are. It's part of our charm." Before I had time to ask what she meant by that, she was gone.

That night in the cafeteria, I staked out a seat facing the entrance. He appeared in the doorway, gliding in with his panther-like gait, stopping along the way to exchange an elaborate handshake with some guy in an Orlando Magic ball cap. He was laughing, his teeth flashing as he was introduced all around, shaking hands with every student at the table. Someone pulled up a chair and he was about to join them, but then he looked up and our eyes met. Whatever I'd felt at the pool was back with a roiling intensity that made my thoughts slow to a crawl and my mouth go dry. His dark eyes stayed locked to mine as he seemed to rise up in slow motion, murmuring something to the table and again pulling off the handshake, all without breaking our connection. He coasted toward me, wearing an embryonic smile that, as he approached, bloomed lotus-like into a spectacular grin. When he was a table away, he slyly lifted his hands, fashioned them into little guns, and fired them from the hip as he strutted toward me, fully aware, I was realizing, that this was a performance.

When he reached me, he concluded the act with an absurd little spin. It was all so unabashedly ridiculous that I was laughing, hard.

"What the hell was that? You're like . . . a big peacock!"

"Big peacock?" he exclaimed, dropping into the seat next to mine and shaking his head in dismay. "Those are my best moves."

I did not want to be so charmed, but I was powerless. "If that's your best, you've peaked too early, kid."

"Where's your grilled cheese?" he asked, his hands groping about in the space where my dinner should have been.

"I was waiting for you."

He leaned back, the teasing expression fading, replaced by mild astonishment. "You waited for me?"

I nodded.

"For me? This guy?" He patted himself down, uncertainly.

"Yes."

He kissed his fingers and held them up to the sky, like a football player post-touchdown. "I am honored. Truly. It's not every day that a mermaid deigns to eat with a common mortal."

He stood, and formally offered me his elbow. "Shall we?"

I took it, and he escorted me to the hot line while we beamed at each other like Prom King and Queen. I glimpsed Lila paying at the cashier's station, and when she spotted us, her eyebrows flew up to her hairline.

Who is that? she mouthed.

I just grinned.

What happened next was that, predictably, Raj became one of us. This was quickly followed by a sad and uncomfortable weekend in which Tall Tim, who had taken to trailing after me like a lovesick greyhound, asked me out. I think he thought he saw everyone pairing off; Max and Lila were officially a (fully dysfunctional) couple, and I guess he foresaw Raj and Cyn getting together, too. So he asked me out, and I turned him down, as gently as I possibly could, but perhaps without perfect grace.

I was impatient, that was the problem. I was in a hurry to get to the library, because wonder of wonders, that was where Raj and I had engaged in a torrid, aching, make-out session the day before. Our seduction was both mutual and spontaneous. We'd made a date to study at the library after dinner one night when Cyn was working. I led him back to a quiet corner of the library with two big armchairs. Had I previously noted its potential as a possible make-out area? Yes. But frankly, I wasn't that optimistic.

We were still purely friends who flirted, and I would say out of the two of us, he seemed more interested in Cyn. He was always, always talking her ear off, trying to make her laugh. He made up endless variations of these convoluted stories about her, in which she went to India to find a lost ruby, or some other nonsense. She would just sit there and listen, occasionally shaking her head at his silly jokes, smiling this mysterious smile. He never made up stories about me.

But anyway, we were sitting opposite each other, very chastely, when I kicked off my sneakers and put my feet up on the little coffee table that divided us. He did the same, and soon enough, we were playing footsie. I shoved his feet off the table, then he shoved off mine. Soon enough, our battle escalated, and he snatched my book away. Trying not to laugh too loudly, I crawled on top of him to get it back. I was straddling him, and even though I was ostensibly trying to retrieve my book, I knew we were both transfixed by the sensation of our bodies touching. He dropped the book, and with that pretense gone, I was just sitting on his lap. So, I kissed him. And he held me there and we kept kissing. I don't know how long it lasted.

I hadn't told Cyn about it, even though we hung out for a few hours after the fact, and I was worried I might spring an ulcer overnight from the guilt and the stress. At the same time, I felt like I was literally pulsing with lust and joy. He had picked me! I really didn't know what would happen when I told Cyn, and I was too scared to ask Raj what he thought we should do. I was the happiest and most terrified I'd ever been.

We'd made plans to meet again that evening, and I was hoping we would pick up where we left off. I had raced through dinner alone and was rushing around, trying to collect the books that I would hopefully not be opening that night. I couldn't get ready fast enough. Then my door creaked open, and standing there was Tim, holding a bunch of daisies. He said they were for me.

I told him thanks and poured some water into a coffee mug to use as a vase, meanwhile explaining that Cyn loved daisies (an improvised fiction), so we'd both enjoy them, and that also, I was in a hurry to get to the library.

Could he walk me? No thanks, I'd be fine.

At this point, as I was grabbing my keys, he cleared his throat and said, "Gloria, I would very much like to take our friendship to the next level."

Oh no. Had I felt anything for him, that "next level" line would have made me reconsider. It perfectly encapsulated the awkward formality with which Tim always treated me, and which I still hadn't figured out a good way to casually deflect. I looked up to see his face darkening in response to whatever he was reading on mine.

"Tim, that's so sweet. But I think we work better as friends," I responded, the second hand in my head ticking away. I thought of Raj's smell, like pine needles and warm bread. Wonderful warm pine bread, if there were such a thing.

"Oh," he said. Clearly, he had not anticipated that I would say anything but yes.

"Look, I'm sorry, I've got to run." He blinked and then moved out of my way so I could close the door. As I locked it, I felt him looming behind me, quiet as death.

I stepped down the first two steps, then quickly delivered a smile and a cheerful "see ya later" to my erstwhile suitor. The last thing I wanted was this to become a big thing between us, so I figured the more lightly I handled it, the better. This was probably not the best plan. Tim's face just remained frozen, his huge hands twitching uselessly at his sides. Not knowing what else to do, I turned and hurried to the library.

I found Raj waiting for me in our corner. I dropped my bag and sat on the table in front of him.

"What took you so long?" he asked, with a soft smile. Then, he pulled me close.

We eventually wandered back to my room. Our fingers occasionally brushed as we walked, but neither of us took the other's hand. I took that to mean that we were not yet ready to go public. Cyn had just gotten back, and we were going to watch *Hellraiser* together. It was on the tip of my tongue to say something to Cyn, but with Raj having a cigarette right outside the door, I just couldn't. Part of me was hoping that he would say something, but what was there to say, other than that we'd shared two steamy make-out sessions behind the foreign literature racks?

Before we got the movie started, and before I saw the daisies and remembered the other piece of news that I wanted to share with Cyn, Tim was downstairs, bellowing like a wounded grizzly. He was clutching a three-quarters-empty bottle of bourbon, a bad sign, since he was terribly sensitive to liquor and rarely drank. Max had seen him stagger through the quad, six and a half feet of pure inebriation being hard to miss, and followed him, trying to get Tim's attention. Tim ignored him. When Max attempted to slow him down via a brotherly tug on the shoulder, Tim paused long enough to shove him to the ground. The scene was very "drunken Frankenstein's monster on campus rampage," according to Max's description. We got the full picture a few minutes later when he showed up at our steps.

Raj heard Tim coming before anyone saw him.

"Glo-ri-a, I think I've got your num-ber." He was shouting that old pop song that I loathed, over and over, his huge basso

echoing around the quad as he lumbered our way. That I didn't hear him in the room can only be explained by my ace ability to block out songs that I hate. He stopped short when he saw Raj and stood there, swaying slightly, glaring with an intensity that would have melted glass.

"You!" he roared at Raj. "What gives you the right?"

"Tim?" Raj was mystified. "What's the matter, dude? Are you drunk?"

"Fuck you!" Tim hollered.

The shout startled us. I froze like a prairie dog sensing a hawk passing overhead. Cyn went to the door and peeked out just as I registered the stupid mug of daisies by her elbow.

"Stay inside," Raj murmured to us, his eyes never leaving Tim. Through the crack, I glimpsed Tim, rage pulling his features into unfamiliar planes.

"Tim, go home," I called from the doorway. "We can all forget about this."

Tim laughed. He pointed at me unsteadily, as if his finger would help his eyes to focus.

"Tim, please." Cyn had stepped in front of me onto the landing.

"I wanna talk to you, Glo-ria," he demanded.

"We're done talking, Tim. Go home! Go to sleep! You're acting like a jackass." My voice sounded weak and tremulous, and I realized I was legitimately freaked out. Not just for myself, but also for Raj, who was standing there, so calm and collected, like a goddamn sentry. I felt myself flushing furiously, my whole body burning hot, and I started to really hate Tim.

"Tim, buddy, why don't you let me walk you back to your room," Raj suggested.

Tim looked at Raj and unscrewed his bottle, slowly drinking a few slugs before clumsily recapping it. The action seemed to take forever. I hoped it might calm him down.

He looked up at Raj. "Why should you get them both?"

Raj paled, dismayed. Students were stepping out of their rooms to watch.

"Who the fuck are you anyway?" he roared, swinging the bottle recklessly.

Tall Tim waited for an answer, his jaw grinding away furiously. Raj didn't blink. I wanted to drag him into our room and lock the door before Tim weaponized his bottle, but I found myself glued to Cyn, barely breathing.

"She was supposed to be mine," he snarled. "Not yours! You've got the stripper-er," he slurred. In the moment that followed, no one spoke, and Tim's words seemed to echo against every wall. Max appeared from around the corner, followed by a spry cadre of other male students, clearly prepared to intervene. Tim regarded them warily and lifted his elbows in a gesture of harmlessness. He turned and half jogged away, the liquor inside his bottle splashing to and fro with each lurching step.

Wordlessly, the three of us rushed inside to the window and saw him careening through the quad. He suddenly spun and faced us, where we must have all been clearly visible in our brightly lit room. He saluted us with a vigorous "up yours" gesture, then added two well-articulated birds as a coda.

"I think I'm gonna lock the door," Raj said.

"Yeah, let's do that," I murmured.

I ducked into the bathroom, feeling Cyn's eyes on me as the door swung shut. My hands were shaking as I sat on the edge of the tub, trying to collect my thoughts. The spectacle of Tim self-immolating on the dorm steps—and destroying our friendships in the process—was minor compared with what might follow with Cyn when I opened the door. She had to know something was up, and I had no idea how she would react.

Feeling dizzy with fear, I rose, preparing myself for the worst. But instead of facing Cyn's recriminations, I encountered only the back of her head, haloed in the glow of the television we'd picked up from the Salvation Army. She and Raj were sitting quietly, engaged in a game of Tetris. She was kicking his ass.

We spent the rest of the night watching movies. Raj suggested we begin with *Dawn of the Dead*, a fitting selection for the "us against the world" feeling that had settled in the room once we locked the door. We pulled Cyn's mattress to the ground and put it on the floor by my bed, then stacked pillows behind us to make a couch that could fit three. We all cuddled pretty close that night, me on one side of Raj, Cyn on the other. It felt so nice to be next to him that it didn't matter to me that Cyn was there. We all fell asleep on the couch. When I awoke, Cyn and I were on the mattress on the floor, and Raj had made himself comfortable in my bed. I stared at him for a long time, wrapped in my sheets with an arm flung around my pillow. I wanted to keep him there, in my bed, permanently.

We didn't talk about the things that Tim had shouted at us, but the rest of the campus did. Even Max, who was always the first to gleefully venture into uncomfortable topics, didn't say a word. He had spoken with Tim, who was embarrassed but unapologetic about his crazy bender. He told Max he was over our little clique, and he seemed to be. He never showed up to hang out again, and whenever we passed each other on campus, he ignored me.

It wasn't until Lila stopped by the room two days later that I began to understand the nature of the rumors surrounding us.

"Everyone says that you guys are perpetrating some sort of threesome," she said, staring at me coolly between sips of Diet Coke.

When I laughed, she raised her eyebrows. "So it's not true? You're the only one sleeping with Raj?"

"What? No, I'm not sleeping with Raj! He stays over here

sometimes, but that's because he's an astronaut. He sleeps on the floor."

"Oh. Okay. But I heard that you two were making out in the library. Max heard it from Tim."

It all flashed into focus. Tim had seen us. He had probably followed me there and discovered us together. I felt a small pang of sympathy for Tim, the poor bastard. I had inadvertently stomped him when he was down.

I decided against trying to deny it. I wasn't a good enough actress, and Lila was too shrewd.

"So it's true."

"We've kissed a few times, yeah. But we aren't sleeping together."

"What about Cyn?"

"Cyn's not sleeping with him either. We're all just good friends." Lila had this sarcastic look on her face, like I was shoveling lies down her throat. "Jesus, Lila, it's the truth! Just because you ended up hooking up with Max doesn't mean we're all screwing."

She seemed to be coming around. Then she lobbed a grenade at me, hard. "I've got a friend at Hubble who says Cyn's car is outside his place pretty often. Did you know that?"

I felt my gag reflex engage as my whole being recoiled at the idea. "So? They're friends. Friends hang out," I managed.

Lila leaned forward, practically licking her prosecutorial chops. "So it wouldn't bother you if they were sleeping together behind your back?"

I forced a sarcastic smile. "It might, if it were true."

She stood up. "Look, I'm just telling you what I heard. It sounds like you guys all need to have a little chat before shit goes crazier than Tim after a bottle of hooch."

"Thanks for your concern." I wanted her gone so I could freak out in peace. As if hearing my unspoken wish, she gave a cheery little wave and left me to wallow in doubt and misery.

I'm not particularly proud of what went down next.

First I paced around, wondering what to do. Cyn was in class, and I was supposed to be at Spanish Lit in a few hours. If I hurried, I would have time to get to the Hubble and see Raj, and back to the main campus in time for class. I put on my sneakers, and like a stupid cliché movie heroine, ran my ass over to his room.

The Hubble existed as a fleabag motel for drifters until Tiny U bought it, painted it yellow, and rechristened it as a single-occupancy dorm. Raj lived on the second floor. He had a tiny balcony that faced the freeway, and beyond it, the small local airport. I arrived in the parking lot, red-faced and drenched in sweat from my run.

I knocked on the door, and Raj opened it. His eyebrows shot up in surprise, and he swung the door wide.

"Can I use your shower?" I blurted, cursing the lack of forethought that had brought me to his door, stinking like steaming hot roadkill.

He grinned. "Sure. Is yours broken?"

I slipped past him into the bathroom and closed the door. I turned the water on cool, and wondered what the hell I was going to say when I got out. I rinsed my hair with his blue, alpine soap. The clothes that I'd come in were soaked with sweat, so I rinsed them, too, and hung them up to dry. I turned the shower off and wrapped myself in his striped towel.

In the mirror, I saw that the cold rinse had drained the crimson from my face, leaving only a flattering flush across my cheeks. I thought I looked pretty enough to do something terrifying. I opened the door.

Raj was on the balcony, having a cigarette. He turned around, saw me standing in his towel, and came back inside, sliding the glass door shut behind him.

"Better?" he asked, an amused grin spreading across his face.

"Yeah," I said awkwardly.

I hadn't spent much time in Raj's room. Cyn and I had stopped by together once or twice, but I hadn't ever been there alone. It was a typical college-guy man cave. Books everywhere. A futon propped against the wall. The single bed harbored a laptop and a pile of slightly dirty clothing.

"Are you sleeping with Cyn?" The words fell out without ceremony.

He blinked. "No. Who told you that?"

I sensed he was telling the truth. I sat on his bed, my hair dripping down my back. "Ever since Tim-ageddon, we've been at the epicenter of rumor central. According to the rest of campus, we're all three of us sleeping together."

He sat down next to me and rubbed his forehead. "Does that bother you?"

I shrugged. A few seconds ticked by as I continued to drip, just as I had that first day we met. "I haven't slept with anyone. Ever."

He put a hand on my shoulder and pulled my hair away from my neck. Then he kissed me right below my hairline. His lips felt hot against my cool, damp skin.

"Do you want to?" he whispered, his voice husky. "Is that why you came here?"

I wanted to say yes. I wanted to say of course, I want to be yours and I want you to be mine, forever and ever. But I didn't say that. I just used one hand to open the towel.

His mouth dropped open and he quickly tossed the towel to the floor and hastily cleared a spot on the bed to lay me back on. Then he just looked at me, one hand tracing my nipples and belly button, all the way up to the shallow basin at the base of my throat and back down between my thighs.

I was struck dumb. His brown eyes traced my body with what felt like reverence. As he explored me, he glanced back at my face and smiled slightly, his dark eyes dilated with desire. He flipped me over and performed the same tender inspection on my back, stopping to gently kiss the more pronounced of my freckles near my shoulders. When I couldn't stand any more, I righted myself and pulled him close for a long, deep kiss. I took his shirt off. He took off the rest. I didn't have time to investigate his holdings right away, as he was soon on top of me.

It hurt, but I didn't care. It made sense that it should hurt. Seeing the discomfort on my face, he murmured an apology and quickly finished, his face pressed close into my neck, his breath hot and ragged.

He rolled off me, his eyes closed, breathing heavily. I closed my eyes and searched myself to see how I'd changed. I felt happy, because Raj and I were undeniably closer, but that good feeling was almost instantly tempered by a huge wave of doubt.

"Are you okay?" I opened my eyes to find him leaning on one arm, gazing at me languidly.

"I'm great." I couldn't help but smile. "That was unexpected."

He laughed. "So, that's not what you came here for?"

"I came here for you," I admitted.

"I'm glad." We began to kiss.

We stayed there together on his narrow bed all afternoon. The sky became overcast with storm clouds, and Spanish Lit came and went without me there. As I watched the changing light alter the color of Raj's naked back as he slept, I wondered what Cyn would think when I didn't appear for class. I wondered if she would worry about me.

At dusk, I went into the bathroom to check on my clothes. Everything but my nylon shorts were still sopping wet. I pulled on the shorts and picked up a green T-shirt of Raj's. It had an image of a broken lightbulb on it, and I knew that Cyn would instantly recognize it. *It would be a great conversation starter*, I thought grimly as I pulled it over my head.

"Is it cool if I borrow this?" I asked, emerging from the bathroom.

Raj was having another cigarette on the balcony. He nodded. "Looks like there's a storm blowing in." He gestured toward the airport, where heavy purple rain clouds darkened the horizon.

"You're telling me." I picked up my wet socks and underwear and put them in a plastic bag to take back with me. "If I don't tell Cyn about us, she'll just figure it out anyway."

He closed the door and sat on a chair. He ran one hand back through his hair, uneasily. "You think she'll be upset?"

I detected some hopefulness in his tone that I didn't like one bit. "I dunno, does she have any reason to be?"

He sighed. "I don't know, Glo."

He looked ill. I had just slept with him, and here he was, turning gray at the thought of upsetting Cyn.

"Has she said anything to you?" I asked tightly.

"You know how she is. She says all kinds of things. I don't know what to think about it."

I felt my throat tighten. "What do you mean you don't know what to think about it?"

Perceptive enough to notice that I was struggling to contain an emotional explosion, he quickly embraced me. "I'm just saying she's a strange girl, and I would hate to hurt her. Just like I would never want to hurt you."

I gently extricated myself from his grasp. I didn't trust myself not to shove him away. "So has she said she has feelings for you?"

He shrugged, straining to make the case for his indifference. "Does she? Who knows? Did she say anything to you?"

"No."

"Well, if she does, she didn't tell me. But until today, neither did you . . . not with words, at least." He took a deep breath. "Honestly, I've been confused as hell by you two. I can't figure out what the hell either of you wants from me."

"Have you kissed her, too?" It occurred to me that I had only questioned him about sex.

He looked down, and I had my answer. I couldn't believe they had both kept it from me.

"Glo, it was only once. It only happened once." He reached out for me, sensing my fury. I stepped away.

"When?"

"About two weeks ago." He spread his hands wide in front of him and stared at them as if they held the answers. "She stopped over here after work. We got high. Then we kissed. After a while, she said she had to go and she left. The next day when I saw her, we were all together, and she acted like it never happened. Like she forgot."

"And that left you heartbroken, so you came to me," I said with surprising bitterness. "I'm your afterthought."

That really hurt him, I think. I saw him flinch. "That's not what you are to me."

Outside, thunder cracked. I felt confused and ashamed and angry, and I wanted to get out of there so I could pull my thoughts together. "I have to go before it storms."

"Don't go."

His eyes looked so sad and pathetic that I wanted to stay. I wanted to believe, but I couldn't. "I have to go. I have to talk to Cyn. I don't even know what I'm telling her."

He shook his head miserably. Thunder rumbled again, growing louder.

Impulsively, I kissed his cheek, but when he tried to hold me, I wiggled away, close to tears. "Don't worry," I said, "I'm sure you'll find out how it goes."

"Be careful," I heard him say as I flung myself out his door.

It must have been adrenaline, because I somehow had the energy to run all the way back to our dorm, the bag of wet underwear swinging absurdly from my fist. A thunderhead towering above campus gave the twilight an operatically dark edge, but the fiery blitz of lightning bolts were what really got my knees pumping. Getting fried by lightning would have been a fitting way to conclude my short, sorry existence, but I still loved life enough to run in a half crouch. The rain clouds burst open just as I passed the student center, obscuring the dorms behind a veil of water. As I pitched myself blindly through the downpour, I looked up and saw our window glowing brightly. My stomach twisted.

I opened the door, and she was sitting on her bed, a book open in front of her, the stereo tuned to a dance mix. She straightened when I entered, a concerned look on her face. Then, in slow motion, I saw her eyes trace down to Raj's T-shirt, and the blood drained from her cheeks.

I couldn't face her yet. I walked directly into the bathroom, locked the door, and turned on the shower. I stayed in there for a long time, washing redundantly, my skin already prune-like from the drenching. When I couldn't stall any longer, I pulled on my robe and stepped outside.

The dance music was off. Cyn was looking out the window, crying silently.

I sat on my bed and listened to her sniffle. I couldn't think of a thing to say.

"How was he?" Cyn demanded, her voice raspy and bitter. "Aren't you going to share?"

My cheeks began burning, but I still couldn't speak.

"I thought we told each other everything," she snarled.

"Yeah, so did I," I snapped, with unexpected venom.

She looked surprised, but then quickly rolled her eyes knowingly. "Okay, fine. But I didn't sleep with him."

"And why didn't you, if you wanted to?"

"Because I knew what it would do to you, stupid!" she shouted. "I knew that you liked him, but I liked him, too. I just thought if neither one of us did anything, he would choose. And I guess I was right, because now he's chosen you."

She started to shake with sobs. It was terrible to see her so distraught, but her tears didn't extinguish the simmering ball of anger I'd been carrying since I'd left the Hubble. There was no reason for her to be crying. In the shower, I had painfully forced myself to rehash everything that had happened that afternoon. As much as I hated to face it, he clearly cared more about Cyn's thoughts and feelings than mine. I was just the runner-up, and a fool.

"I don't think he has," I said flatly. "I went over there, and it just happened. After the fact, he told me about you, and when I asked him what was going on, he said he was confused. He said we had him totally fucking confused."

Cyn's crying had quieted, and she was studying me intently. She emitted a hard laugh, like a cough.

"Confused. How convenient."

"Yeah," I grunted. We were both silent for a moment. "I didn't mean to hurt you. I'm sorry."

"Well, it's kind of too late for that. If you had suspicions about how I felt, and you actually gave a shit, you wouldn't have slept with him. Now you've trumped me by giving him your cherry, and I'm stuck on the outside because I cared more about your feelings than my own."

"I gave him my *cherry*?" I sneered. "Do you even hear yourself? You make it sound like I snared him in a sex trap just to one-up you, and if you know me at all, you know that's bullshit. It just happened. If you would have told me how you felt, then I could almost understand you saying that, but you didn't, so fuck off. I didn't ask you to stay away from him, and I wouldn't have. I figured things would just work out the way they were supposed to."

"So you think this is how things were supposed to work out? With you being happy and me being miserable?"

"No. I don't want you to be miserable. And just so you know, I'm not fucking happy. I just lost my virginity to a guy who is 'really confused,' and probably in love with my best friend. This situation couldn't suck more."

I snatched some clothes out of my dresser and pulled them on as fast as I could. My mind was lurching about recklessly, and I knew I'd have to get out before I said something I couldn't take back.

She watched me put on my socks. "It does suck," she said, sounding like her normal, equivocal self, "but I don't want to give him up either." She looked up, meeting my eye. "I like him more than I ever expected to like someone, and I know he has feelings for me. You know it, too."

"We both like him," I agreed, standing in the very spot on the carpet where, not so long ago, we had pledged to never let a guy come between us. "Neither one of us told the other one shit because we both knew it, and that's why we're now having this fight."

Cyn's face had grown calm. "We're having this fight because we didn't want to have this fight. We're both fucking cowards."

I got up and opened the door.

"Where are you going?"

"Out. I need air." I was so exhausted, I just wanted to curl up under the stairs and cry myself to sleep.

"It's raining," she protested.

"I don't mind." I closed the door behind me.

The rain was falling at a steady drizzle. I wandered through the quad, the cool drops soothing my simmering skin. A few students passed by carrying umbrellas, but they took no notice of me. I went to the cafeteria and bought a soda, though I would have preferred a few shots of something strong. I sat at a table in the empty room where once, long ago, orientation had taken place, and stared out at the wet parking lot.

I must have fallen asleep. When I opened my eyes, the rain had stopped.

The student convenience store was closed, so it had to be after one in the morning. I dragged myself back toward our room, unable to contain a moan when I saw the light still on inside. I was too exhausted for another confrontation.

I climbed the steps, feeling like a prisoner on her way to the gallows. Inside, Cyn was half asleep on her bed. I was stunned to discover Raj sitting on our floor, staring at the television. When he saw me, he flipped it off. Cyn's eyes fluttered, and she sat up.

"Hey," I muttered to both of them before flopping onto my bed. "Some day, huh?"

Cyn shot me a limp smile and Raj just shook his head. As curious as I was to find out what they'd been discussing in my absence, I was too spent to care. They weren't cuddling in her bed, which was a good sign. If they had been, I would have kicked Joan out of my old room that night and maybe left school the next day. I closed my eyes and collected what little energy I had left, steeling myself for whatever was coming.

"I had an idea," Cyn began, lifting a joint from her nightstand.

I looked at Raj, but he wouldn't meet my eye. Cyn lit the joint and looked to me for my response.

I pushed myself up onto my elbows. "What's your idea?"

Cyn took a long drag and passed the joint down to Raj, who took a small toke and passed it to me. I took a drag and watched as Cyn languidly exhaled. "We share."

I took a Cyn-sized drag. Raj still wouldn't look at me. He seemed to be holding his breath.

"I don't get it," I said flatly.

Cyn smiled and bowed her head knowingly. I passed the joint back to Raj, and when he finally looked at me, his face was awash with worry. I felt a strong desire to crawl into his arms, and that's when I realized what Cyn was suggesting.

"We share *Raj*?" I said, my voice rising precipitously.

She nodded in a way that told me she expected just such a reaction, and that she was prepared to wait it out.

The absurdity of it was astounding. "How? I don't get it. Are we, like, sister wives in this scenario? Do we switch off days of the week?" My head felt foggy, and the many sensible arguments I wanted to make about the insanity of her proposition eluded me. My whole day spun before me; the long runs, the unexpected cherry loss, the drama, and to top it off, the damned joint. I focused my attention on Raj. "You recognize that this is crazy?"

He sighed. He looked as shaken and worn-out as I felt. "We've been talking about it for a couple hours. I'm not trying to push any agenda here. It's really up to you girls."

I looked at Cyn in bewilderment.

"Glo, I can see you're about to freak out, and I understand why. But please, just think about it. The three of us get along so great together, and all these feelings have been there all along; they were just below the surface before. Now they're out. I personally don't see why we can't make the best of it. I mean, maybe it's a gift."

I fell back onto my bed and stared at the ceiling. The room was so quiet, I could have imagined myself alone.

"This is so fucked," I moaned.

"We have to deal with it," Cyn said calmly.

I raised my head to look at Raj, the cause of all this misery. "You honestly can't choose between us?"

He looked positively ill, and I felt sorry I'd said it. I glanced up at Cyn and noted that she registered my regret. Raj groaned and opened his hands wide, as he had done in his room earlier that day. "I won't. Even if I were able to, which I can't, picking either of you over the other would obviously destroy your friendship. We'd all be unhappy. I'd rather we just went back to being in the closet, all three of us."

"It *would* kill our friendship, wouldn't it?" I asked Cyn.

She shrugged casually, as if we were discussing the weather. "Could you stand to be around me if I was with him and you weren't?"

I shook my head.

"I couldn't either." She smiled sadly.

I picked up my pillow and threw it at Raj. "Why can't you just be a eunuch?"

He pulled the pillow onto his lap and shrugged. "Hardly any fun for Raj."

Cyn laughed. I wanted to, but hilarity was lost under a morass of other emotions.

"I'm glad you freaks find this so funny," I growled.

"If you can't laugh, you cry," Cyn said.

"Maybe we should," I countered.

She sighed. "Why? I mean, really. We've been happy for the last couple of months. Now, there's maybe some sex. That's just one element. Otherwise, nothing has really changed between any of us."

"What about jealousy? There's no way—"

"Jealousy is normal. We're not. If we agree to this, we don't have to be jealous. You know I love you. You know it's not in me to want to take things from you. I'm really okay with sharing. Otherwise, I wouldn't suggest it."

"And you're okay with this, too, Raj?"

"I really care about both of you. This has been the most confusing time of my life . . ."

I glanced at Cyn. After "confusing" she raised her eyebrows at me ever so slightly. It almost made me crack up, but Raj continued to pour his heart out, so I held it together.

". . . If I somehow ruined the friendship of the two girls I care about most, I think I'd toss myself off the Sunshine Skyway Bridge. I really do. I don't know what will happen, and that's really terrifying, but yeah, I'm up for it. Life is a grand experiment."

As I listened to his velvety voice, I threw myself into the future, attempting to explore in a millisecond all the possible outcomes of this scenario. They all seemed to lead to heartbreak or social suicide. But the alternative—refusal—appeared a total loss. They could both choose to cut me off right there, and I'd have traded the risk of future failure for immediate, certain devastation.

"This is so insane," I heard myself murmur.

"Glo—" Cyn began.

"I'm not saying no," I interrupted. "I feel like I can't say no. I'm too invested in both of you. You're like love vampires."

Raj smiled and shook his head.

"This isn't a trap, babe," Cyn said seriously. "This is just the best solution for a very unusual problem."

Raj reached out and put his hand on my damp, sock-covered foot. Like a saint in a holy image, his eyes expressed nothing but loving understanding. I wanted him enough to do anything. Even share him.

"And if you fall out of love with one of us? What then?" I asked.

"And if one of you falls out of love with me? Or you two eventually turn on each other?" He shook his head. "Yeah, all these things could happen. We don't get a guarantee that anything will work out in this world."

"I know that. I'm just scared."

"I'm scared, too," Cyn echoed softly. "Raj is right; it's a risk for all of us. But otherwise, we both give him up, which seems impossible, or we have one hell of a knife fight to determine a victor."

"I couldn't stab a sister wife."

I looked up and met the gaze of my rival across the room. I watched her eyes gleam behind unspent tears. Against my wishes, I felt my own vision blur, and I knew I was giving in. She was the best friend I'd ever known, and the last thing I wanted to do was lose her. The tears escaped. I was too beat to do anything about it.

"I wouldn't do this for anyone but you," I managed, my voice thickening against my will.

She inhaled sharply. "Me neither."

Cyn climbed onto my bed and wrapped her arms around me.

"We can't tell other people about this. It's too taboo. Even for this place."

Raj scoffed, his gaze fixed on the carpet. "Everybody thinks it already."

"Glo's right. Let them think it, but we don't confirm anything. We're just what we've always been: very close friends."

Raj shook his head ruefully.

"What's wrong?" Cyn asked.

He looked at us for a moment, serious and unsmiling, but then, as if something shifted in his mind, he laughed.

"I can't believe I can't brag about this to all the dudes." He sighed dramatically, hamming it up for our benefit.

Cyn poked at him with her toe. "What 'dudes'? Do you even know any dudes?"

"I don't, but I should."

"I propose one thing," I said. "As a rule, we keep things as open and honest as possible. Secrets are bad for us."

"No secrets," she agreed. Noticing my silently falling tears, she reached over and wiped them away.

"No secrets," Raj repeated, watching us both. "And if anybody gets scared, or feels left out, we should talk about it."

"Of course," Cyn said.

Raj whistled softly and ran his hands through his hair for about the millionth time that night. "Okay, cool. Multiple catastrophic disasters averted. I just have one question, and please don't think I'm a dick. But just to clarify, we're not all sleeping together. It's just, like, a one-on-one thing?"

Cyn stiffened beside me. I burst out laughing. "I wish you could see your face right now."

Raj turned deep red. Cyn put her head on my shoulder, hiding her face. My body rocked with laughter as an ocean of stress drained out of me. "Your presumption is correct. Cyn and I don't really swing that way," I answered when I could speak again.

"Unless we're rolling, and it's a special occasion," Cyn amended from behind her hair.

"Sorry if that is in any way disappointing," I added.

"No, I knew that," Raj said, getting to his feet. His swagger was all but beaten out of him, but he was still unbearably handsome. "I was just double-checking."

"And we appreciate that," Cyn quipped. I snorted.

Raj stepped back and stared at us sitting together on the bed, as close as Siamese twins. "Jesus, what have I gotten myself into?"

We both shrugged.

"I gotta get back to my space ship. I'm pretty sure I left the door wide open. It's been a strange day." He paused and seemed to shake off a thought. "I'm really hoping this isn't a dream. Is it?"

We shook our heads.

He kissed my forehead, and then Cyn's. "Good night, beauties. I will call for my queens on the 'morrow." He shrugged. "That's roughly adapted from my Brit Lit course."

He closed the door and was gone.

I collapsed against my pillow, and Cyn got up to switch off the lights.

I heard the springs of her bed creak as she crawled on top of it.

"This is one of those nights when the world changes. It seems great, but I have no idea how I'm going to feel about any of this in the morning," I murmured.

"Then the only solution is to go to sleep and find out tomorrow," she answered.

I heard Cyn's alarm go off for her early class. It was a science class, and in my half sleep, I remembered that Raj was in it, too. I felt a stab of jealousy before sleep pulled me away. When I awoke, I was alone. I sat up on my bed and looked out at the palm trees. I had awoken to a unique, new reality; I was in possession, for the first time, of half a boyfriend. Or rights to a boyfriend, half the time. I groaned.

Everything that had made sense the night before was now a huge puzzle. I understood how we could perhaps alternate sleepovers at the Hubble, which would be weird, but doable. Having him sleep over at our place in one of our beds seemed a far less attractive prospect. And how would we handle the whole physical contact thing when it was just the three of us alone together, like on any typical movie night? How would we not slip up in front of our friends?

These were the things we sat down to discuss that night after dinner. We locked the door and set up camp with our coffees in the middle of our room.

"Okay, let's talk guidelines," Cyn said, calling our meeting to order. "Glo has some suggestions she would like to share. Please proceed, Ms. Roebuck."

"Thank you, Ms. Williams," I said with great formality. Raj rolled his eyes. He was also rolling a joint. "I have a few proposals. First off, when the three of us are together, I propose that we keep physical contact limited to our pre-sharing conditions. So flirtation is fine, but groping, kissing, fondling, and so on: not cool. Agreed?"

"Agreed," they chorused.

"Okay, sleeping arrangements. I figure Raj is always free to spend the night here, but if he chooses one bed over the other, it's gonna be weird." I looked at Cyn, who nodded. "So maybe we can chip in and get some sort of air mattress? I dunno."

"That's fine with me. It's no picnic trying to share a twin bed anyway," Raj said.

"Okay, good." I looked at my list and stalled. On it, I had written, *Hubble?* "As far as sleepovers at the Hubble, I guess we can see how that goes. It would make sense to alternate, but I don't know how often we'll be heading out there, unless it's the weekend or something."

"Sounds fair," Cyn agreed.

"I guess that's pretty much all I came up with." I shrugged. They shrugged back at me. "Meeting concluded."

We unlocked the door, but no friends dropped by that night. I don't know if it was the rumors or the fact that there were some freshmen girls performing the role of social hostesses now, but we were getting less and less traffic to our door. Some of the hippies still dropped by, but not as often. We saw Lila and Max, but things with them were suddenly strange. Our get-togethers hadn't changed a bit, but it was as if they knew we were up to something yet couldn't quite place it. It was sad to see them slip away, but honestly, we were pretty happy hanging out just the three of us.

CHAPTER FIVE

Not long after we became a threesome, Cyn and I signed up for a monthlong, full-immersion Spanish course in Costa Rica. We would fly out in January and visit a couple of different towns, volunteering in schools and sightseeing. We'd been kicking the idea around all semester, mostly as a fantastical daydream. Cyn had been busting her ass at the club just to make tuition, but when Professor Pablo said there were scholarships available, Cyn wrote an essay, submitted it, and was selected as one of five winners. Once she was going, I sent in a deposit to reserve my space.

Not that I was exactly rolling in dough, but I had my scholarship, and I'd spent little of the money I'd made that summer. My major purchase was a bicycle, which I used daily to visit the Hubble. Cyn had her car, so she could come and go as she pleased, but I couldn't stomach asking her to drop me off over there, even if she was on her way to work or class. I needed a Raj fix just about every day. It wasn't just about the sex, although I was really beginning to enjoy that; it was having Raj's full attention that I craved.

He made an effort to keep his room cleaner now that he had female guests. I never asked him when Cyn had been by, but I'd find evidence of her visits. Blond hair in his brush. A pair of her flip-flops under the bed. Though there were soon three toothbrushes above his sink, we were both careful not to let our junk accumulate at his place. It reeked too much of marking one's territory.

Despite physical evidence to the contrary, I tried not to think about the two of them together. Raj always seemed delighted to see me, and he made me feel like I was the only one. I pointedly never mentioned her presence in his bed, until one time, about a month after we first slept together, it just slipped out.

We had just made love, and were laughing about our failed attempt at a new position, quickly abandoned after we discovered that key parts didn't meet up properly. In a genius move, I blurted out, "Maybe Cyn can do that, but I sure as hell can't."

The draft I created by kicking open that dangerous door sucked all the afterglow out of the room in a second. Raj loosed a half laugh, cool and bitter.

"Maybe she can," he said, his gaze fixed on the ceiling.

I lay still, trying not to wonder what that meant, hoping the moment would blow past.

He sat up, stiffly, and began to dress. "We're not having sex, Cyn and I. I guess you didn't know that."

That didn't compute. Simultaneously, I realized that the celibacy was clearly not Raj's choice.

"I didn't," I said. "I'm not sure I want to talk about this."

"You two said no secrets, right? Well, now it's not a secret."

My logic had abandoned me, leaving me at a loss as to how to explain why that wasn't what I'd meant by "no secrets." All I knew was that I didn't want any details about their sexual life, or lack thereof.

"I just don't get it," he whined.

At that moment, I learned that hearing your boyfriend complain about your best friend denying him sex is a total buzzkill. Also, it tends to enrage.

"I really don't want to hear about this." I lurched out of bed and began throwing my clothes on.

"She hasn't said anything to you about it?"

"No! We don't talk about what we do and don't do with you. Imagine it this way: Would you ask your brother what he does with his wife? No. Because it's too close. It's weird. And furthermore, it's none of my business."

He emitted a grunt of frustration.

I pulled on my shorts. "You're fucking unbelievable. I just slept with you, and you've got the balls to complain that you're not getting it from Cyn? Guess what? I don't fucking care!"

"You're right, you're right. I'm sorry," he said. "Please don't be angry."

"Too late! I'm angry. Get over yourself!"

He threw up his hands in exasperation, the poor victim of my unreasonableness. That pissed me off even more. I stormed out into the blinding afternoon, letting the door slam behind me.

I got on my bike and started pedaling down a random side street. I whizzed past silent, sunbaked houses, hardly seeing a soul. I rode aimlessly, fuming, until my knees started to ache. Eventually, I found myself back at the mansion by the bay. I tossed my bike down under a shady tree and lay there on the lawn, allowing my thoughts to have their riot.

Why would Cyn reserve the right to date Raj and then not sleep with him? She'd never before mentioned any reluctance to go all the way, or any other weird reservations about sex. I sure as hell heard her tickling out a few solo jollies at night when she thought I was asleep. And I knew she was attracted to him physically. So what the hell was her game?

A really dark thought occurred to me. Though I tried not to frame our agreement as a competition, if it were one, she was scoring a major advantage by *not* putting out. He would desire her all the more because he couldn't have her. By denying him physically, she'd effectively hijacked him emotionally. Or maybe she knew that he would eventually telegraph his dissatisfaction to me, pissing me off so much that I blew up at him like I'd just done. The more I thought about it, the more brilliant a plan it seemed. But the Cyn I knew wasn't a diabolical mastermind. It had to be something else.

I plucked blade after blade of grass and shredded them, deciding one thing for certain: I would not get involved in Raj and Cyn's sexual psychodrama. The thought of it alone made me queasy. But simultaneously, the shadow of worry that I felt for Cyn was thickening. What I'd thought was a small cove of mystery was turning out to be a whole ocean of things that I didn't really know about her. I wondered if it was some failure on my part that she wouldn't open up; if I seemed too naive to get it. Clearly, she must have some sexual hang-ups, but now, with our new arrangement, the subject was unbroachable. I tried reminding myself that Cyn was a smart, capable person who could help herself if necessary, but that didn't silence the worry or squelch my anger. Cyn had said that our agreement wasn't a trap, but from where I sat, it sure looked like one.

I let things cool off with Raj for a few days. I did not pilot my bike to the Hubble. I made an effort to spend time alone and think about what I wanted, which was, lamentably, still Raj. I was perfectly normal with him in front of Cyn, but he knew he was in the shit-house.

After four days, I broke and accepted his dinner offer. I meant to make it hard for him to win me back, but I was so happy to be with him, I couldn't maintain the chilly demeanor that I'd practiced. By the time the check came, I felt no anger or jealousy. I just wanted to be back in his arms.

At the Hubble, we stumbled in the door and began undressing. I was on his bed, enjoying my initiation into the fevered delights of makeup sex, when there was a knock on the door. At first, I thought I'd imagined it, but then it happened again, and I heard a female voice say, "Raj?"

"Babe, stop," I said, squeezing his shoulders. Either because of the music or because he was lost in what we were doing, Raj hadn't heard. The knock sounded again, insistent.

"Glo?" It was unmistakably Cyn, her voice sounding strange and strangled.

Raj rolled off me, and I quickly threw on a T-shirt and some underwear. I wrapped a towel that I found on the floor around my waist and opened the door.

Cyn was standing there with her work duffel, ashen-faced. She looked at me, expressionless, then turned to wave at a police cruiser that was idling in the parking lot below. The cop inside flashed his lights and pulled away.

"Jesus! Was that the cops?" Raj exclaimed, appearing behind me in a pair of basketball shorts. I stepped back, and Cyn walked into the room. She scanned the clothes lying on the floor and the rumpled bed. Raj hastily opened the door to the balcony to let in some fresh air, and I switched on a lamp.

"I'm sorry, guys, I didn't mean to interrupt," she said, a stunned look on her face. "Some guy followed me home from work."

Raj's eyes nearly popped out of his head. "Someone followed you home?"

I sat on the bed and pulled her down next to me.

"Yeah. I saw the guy outside when I was going to my car, and I instantly got this really bad vibe—an instinct, or whatever. So I rushed into the car, and just as I hit the door locks, there was this terrifying redneck face right at the window. I pulled out of there like a crazy person. I swear, I almost ran over his feet. The next thing I know, I'm waiting for the light, and this pickup truck practically pulls up onto my fender. I knew it was the guy. The light changed and I floored it. I was hoping it was just my imagination, but he sped up right after me, and whenever I turned, he kept following me."

"Holy shit," I whispered. Raj sat on her other side, his eyes locked on her face.

"I was too scared to pull off somewhere, because there's nothing open this late other than convenience stores, and I didn't see what the hell good that would do me, running for cover and hoping some high schooler would rescue me. I thought about pulling into the emergency room at the hospital, but I got lost and stumbled on a police station instead. So I pulled in there. Naturally, the truck didn't follow." She waved her hands in a dazed "good riddance" gesture before adding, "I wish he had, because now I have no idea who it was."

"You can't go back to work there," Raj declared. There was an authoritative edge to his voice, as if he had fast-forwarded twenty years and was suddenly addressing a teenage daughter.

Cyn gazed past him, out toward the empty airstrip. "Yeah? Great. So now my income, which is already not nearly enough, will be zero." She dropped her head into her hands. "This fucking night." She looked at me. "You should have seen me in the police station. I was shaking like a little bird fallen from its nest."

I gave her a hug and squeezed her pale wrist. Then I realized I was still wearing the towel, so I scooped my skirt off the floor. "I'll be right back."

"So did the police take a description of the guy?" I heard Raj ask.

Cyn was beginning to answer when I closed the door to the bathroom. I washed up a little bit, mostly to give them some time alone together, and got dressed, wondering what I should do. I didn't doubt that Cyn would want to stay with Raj. If I were in her position, I would want to. But I didn't have my bike, and it was too late to walk back to the dorm by myself.

When I emerged from the bathroom, Raj was cradling Cyn in his arms and whispering something into her ear. He looked up and saw me, and there was something in his eyes that made me feel out of place.

"I think I'm going to head back to the room," I said, remembering I could borrow Cyn's car.

"Okay," Raj said, his focus concentrated on brushing his fingers through Cyn's hair.

I stood there for a moment, feeling the awful sting of being forgotten.

"Cyn, can I borrow your car?" I mumbled, because that was about all I could manage.

"Uh-huh," she murmured. Then she awoke from her fog with a blink. "Shit. It's over there. I parked it, and the cop brought me here. I called the room and there was no answer," she explained hastily, as if worried that I'd be pissed off. "I just didn't want to be alone."

"Oh." I looked out the balcony window toward the airport. The shadows seemed to be crawling with perverts and derelicts. "I guess I can walk," I ventured neutrally, hoping to be shot down.

Cyn scoffed. "Are you fucking kidding me? Glo, c'mon. There's no way in hell you're walking home by yourself now." She looked up at Raj. "Tell her."

"You're staying here, young lady," he admonished, his voice an ironic imitation of the tone he'd employed in earnest just minutes ago.

I put my bag down. "Sorry, guys. I'd like to give you some alone time."

"No, I'm the third wheel in this situation." Cyn sat up and made a gesture to Raj that she wanted to smoke. Wordlessly, Raj produced a glass pipe from his desk and a small bag of weed. I busied myself with putting on some music and settled on the futon, leaving Raj and Cyn across from me on the bed. We silently passed the pipe between us. As the weed hit me, I closed my eyes and listened to Raj and Cyn discuss the chances of running into the pickup truck guy again.

"I wish you would quit," Raj murmured. "It's obviously not safe."

"I would love to quit, but you know I can't."

Raj sighed loudly, and behind my closed lids, I could perfectly imagine the expression on his face. He was protective of Cyn. He babied her. I couldn't figure out why anyone would see a woman like Cyn and think she needed protection, but evidently he did. He wasn't that way with me. But then again, I didn't really do anything dangerous. Cyn had her drug fixations, her perilous job, and, I was realizing, her secrets. I didn't know what they were, but maybe Raj did. Or maybe Raj didn't know, but he sensed they were there. I drifted off.

My eyes opened an unknowable time later, and it was dark in the room. The curtains were pulled over most of the sliding door, letting just a sliver of street light creep in to slice a path across the rug between my futon and Raj's bed. I heard Raj whispering something.

I kept still, barely breathing, and willed my eyes to stay shut. Their sheets rustled, reporting that some sort of caress was taking place. I wished I could be anywhere else. He kept on whispering. Every once in a while, she would respond with a soft utterance. It was a small mercy to me that the air conditioner was on, its low rumble obscuring their words. As the minutes dragged on, I realized that they weren't having sex. But as he kept whispering to her, I felt a jealousy worse than what I would've felt if they had been.

Deep inside, I smoldered. I knew they didn't know I was awake, and even if they had, they weren't doing anything disrespectful. I had no legitimate reason to be angry, but I was steaming. Raj didn't talk to me like that. He didn't make up elaborate stories starring me just to get me to smile. Maybe I had made it too easy for him. Or maybe he just loved us differently, as I'm sure we loved him in different ways. It was a nice thought, but alone on the floor, I couldn't feel the truth of it. I just felt wretched and lost.

True morning.

I woke up first. Cyn and Raj lay entwined in bed. I only glanced. I was not curious. I used the bathroom and found my shoes. Cyn stirred under the sheets. She peered at me through the dim light.

"Hey," she said groggily.

"I'm heading back."

"You sleep okay?"

I shrugged. "Not the best. I'll see you later."

"Glo," she said, stopping my progress out the door. "I'm sorry about last night. I hate that I interrupted you and made you sleep on the shitty futon."

She looked so regretful that I had to smile. "No biggie."

"It is a biggie. You're a great friend. I love you."

"I love you, too. Quit that job today."

She rolled her eyes and fell back on the bed. I closed the door, and in the morning light, made the walk of shame back to my room.

Cyn didn't quit, but she did cut back to just two shifts a week. Raj, or both Raj and I, would drop her off and pick her up in her car so she was never in the parking lot alone. Business was unusually slow; even Cyn's regular clients weren't showing up as often. She would count out her evening's take on her bed and shake her head in disgust.

When she finally sucked it up and shared her money problems with Gabe, E Two's manager, he suggested she try modeling. There was a friend of a friend who needed a girl for some lingerie shoots that were destined for the Internet. Booking the job would require nothing more than his making a phone call. Without hesitation, Cyn agreed.

Raj wanted to be there for the shoot, but Cyn declared it too weird. Instead, I went with her. The shoot was at a photo studio in a strip mall, the kind of cheesy joint families go to for portraits taken in front of a fake fireplace. We were told to show up after business hours. Cyn was wearing huge false eyelashes that made her look even more like a living Barbie. She fluttered them at me while making insect noises at every stoplight, determined to make light of the situation. I think it scared her. But on the surface, she was smiling and happy, so I kept my apprehensions to myself.

We knocked on the door, and for a few minutes, no one answered. We stood there, awkwardly, watching families file out of the frozen yogurt place a few doors down. The door finally opened, revealing a thin guy with glasses who swiveled his head back and forth between us like an oversize praying mantis. He smoothed his wan face and tawny mustache, immediately giving me the creeps in the way that only seemingly normal guys with weird sidelines in pornography can do.

"Lance," he said gruffly, introducing himself.

Cyn shot me a look that clearly said, *Fake name. What a geek.*

He directed his bulgy eyes toward me and extended his hand. "I only need one girl."

"I'm just here for moral support," I said, wiping off the clammy residue his loose handshake left behind.

"She's my pose coach," Cyn enthused, batting those falsies with vigor. I noticed that her voice had risen half an octave. I wondered if this was a defense, part of her burgeoning porn persona.

If Lance was surprised by our tag team act, he didn't show it. He led us back to the larger of two portrait studios. It was dark, except for several bright lights directed at a white backdrop where Cyn would model. There was a cardboard box full of frilly things in clear plastic bags and a checklist. He pointed it out to Cyn.

"Those are the catalog items that we're shooting today. Some of them have props. They're bagged and labeled. Get dressed in the first one. If you work fast, we can bang this out by eleven. Did you bring shoes?"

"Yes," she said, awkwardly dropping her bag and nearly tripping on a strip of wires. Cyn was as nervous as I'd ever seen her. I found a folding chair and set it against the wall, out of the way. She dug out the silver platforms and presented them.

He grimaced. "There are black ones in the box. If they fit, we'll use those."

Cyn pulled out the first plastic bag, a French maid's outfit. She held it up to me and made a face.

"What's the number on that item," Lance demanded, preparing a whiteboard.

"It says 401," Cyn said.

He wrote the number on the whiteboard. Cyn looked around for a dressing room.

"Just go behind the backdrop if you must," Lance snapped, lighting a cigarette. "And make it fast. We've got a lot to do."

Cyn and I exchanged brow raises. She emerged moments later as a naughty French maid, and Lance snapped away for about thirty seconds. Her nervousness had vanished, and she moved through different poses like she'd been doing it all her life.

"Done. Next." He snapped off the principal spotlight and stepped out of the room. The air conditioner was no match for the hot lights, and soon even I was sweating. Cyn took a moment to apply some powder.

"Not so bad, huh?" she whispered. "He's only a little weird. Still, I'm glad you're here."

"You're doing good."

She stuck out her tongue in disgust. "Point curves toward camera and let the lens do all the work. It's just that easy." She grabbed the next bag and hurried behind the backdrop as Lance reentered and pointedly looked at his watch.

She worked through about eight more outfits, which got progressively skimpier as the night went on. The last one didn't have a top to speak of, just a translucent mesh drape. The bag was labeled "The Zenana."

"Tits up and out," Lance grumbled from behind the camera, for the fifteenth time that night. Cyn arched her back. "Better." He snapped off a few more shots. "Good. That's it. We're done. Get dressed."

It was only ten thirty.

When Cyn was dressed, Lance gave her an envelope with four hundred dollars. "I need more next week, if you're available." Then he gestured at me. "This one I can use, too. If you wanna do a girl on girl, I can get a good rate."

Cyn smiled charmingly at Lance as she pulled me toward the exit. "I'm in for next week. My friend is camera shy."

"Well, if you change your mind . . ." He unlocked the door, releasing us into the cool freedom of the night.

And thusly, Cyn broke into the adult photography industry. Her professional name was Cinderella Velvet, and despite what the media said later, her "career" consisted of exactly three shoots. Even to my admittedly conservative eye, the photos she took that first night really weren't that racy; I'd seen worse in swimsuit catalogs at the dentist's office. The lingerie she was modeling was corny and slightly silly, even. It seemed harmless enough.

With the first-time jitters out of the way, Cyn didn't ask me to go to the next shoots. I only know what she told me about them. The second session sounded very much like the first, but at the third shoot, things got sketchy.

When she got there, there was no box of catalog items. Turns out, it was no longer a lingerie shoot but was, instead, a "fantasy" shoot. Cyn balked at first, but she needed the cash.

"What does 'fantasy shoot' mean?" I'd immediately asked.

"I'd rather not talk about it," she groaned, climbing onto her bed. She lay there, face buried in her pillow for a long moment. When she surfaced, she said, "It was a series of pictures aimed at people with particular kinks. Some fetish stuff. Pretty awful. I learned tonight that latex is not one-size-fits-all." She flattened her lips in disgust. "I don't even know if those things were cleaned from the last girl who wore them. I hope to god they were. The only consolation is that it paid six hundred."

"Did you have to show your—"

"No. I was nude at times, but usually with some sort of draping. I had to transition between poses carefully because Lance was working handheld, and I'm sure he was totally gunning for a beaver shot. I kind of kicked him once because he got in too close."

"That sounds very awkward," I commented neutrally. On the TV screen, Lucille Ball's mouth stretched into an O of horror, mirroring the reaction I was having inwardly.

"Yeah." She rolled on her side to face the TV, her hair creating a privacy wall between us. "I tell myself that these pictures will simply disappear into cyberspace and not affect me. I mean, I'm not planning to go into politics or be famous or anything that would make anyone want to dig them up. If people stumble across them, that means they're actively looking for dirty pictures, so if they out me, they'd be implicating themselves, too."

"I think you're right." She needed reassurance, and I was happy to downplay the whole thing. "I wouldn't worry about it. I mean, there are billions of those sorts of pictures out in the world. You've only done a handful, and under a fake name. Odds are, they never see the light of day."

She was quiet for a moment. Then she laughed out loud. "If my parents ever found out about this, it would kill them."

She rolled onto her stomach, a strange smile on her face, and began preparing a joint. Cyn so rarely mentioned her parents that I sometimes forgot she had any.

"I never told you the full horrible tale because it's all too depressing and trashy, but the reason my sister stopped living with us was because my folks disowned her when they discovered she wasn't a virgin."

"What? No."

She nodded. "They made me take her stuff out of our shared room and pile it all by the curb while all the neighbors watched. It was so embarrassing and sad. She was sixteen. I was ten. Part of their rationale, if you can call it that, was that they didn't want her being a bad role model for me." She laughed mirthlessly. "So, Meg went to go live with her boyfriend's family in the next town over. Married him at twenty. My parents didn't even go to the wedding, which blew my mind. They were still angry with her, even though she'd found love and a really good, solid guy. At first, I believed they thought their god would want them to stay angry forever, but now I think it didn't have much to do with faith; they were just stubborn like that. I started to visit her alone, riding across town on my bike, and things changed between us. We got close. She realized that I was almost fourteen, and knew what was ahead for me if I stayed at home. She invited me to move in with them into their tiny cottage for my high school years. It probably saved my life."

She lit the joint and rolled onto her back. Her eyes found the TV and seemed to go far away.

"Saved your life because your parents would have killed you?"

Cyn smirked. "Not literally. Saved my soul, maybe. Saved

my authentic self. For a long time, all I wanted was to please them, but it was getting harder and harder. My parents were furious with both of us. Total cold war. Last I heard, though, they've begun speaking to her again. Small steps."

"What is your sister up to now?"

"She's busy. Three little girls. Her husband, John, is a contractor. Been in and out of work. It's been tough for them financially. She's really smart, though. She does some bookkeeping for a doctor part-time. She could do a lot more, but there just aren't a lot of jobs where they are."

"Would your sister care about the modeling?"

Cyn laughed. "Meg would find it hilarious. She always knew I was going to be a free spirit of sorts. I think that's why she rescued me from my parents. But, no, she's not uptight at all about that sort of thing. She's the one who introduced me to weed." She held up the joint and smiled. "If I have the cash, maybe I'll go visit Meg and John and my nieces during break before Costa Rica. She's like my only family, except for you and Raj. I miss her."

It turned out that Cyn would not have the cash. Lance called Cyn about another shoot. This one would be a longer session and would pay one thousand dollars. Was she interested? She was.

When she arrived at the shoot, it was business as usual. Nothing seemed amiss until she went into the studio and saw a platform dressed like a bed and a male model sitting on a stool, wearing a robe.

"What is this?" Cyn asked.

"The set," Lance snapped.

"Who's the guy?" The model smiled and said hello.

"He's your partner," Lance said, pointedly ignoring Cyn's distress.

"Excuse me," she said to the male model and headed straight for the front door. Having another guy present, especially a big muscular one like the model, was a deal breaker for Cyn. When she started working at E Two, she crafted contingency plans for what to do if she felt endangered. Her approach to modeling was no different. Dealing with two strange men instead of one tipped the scales. It was too easy for things to go awry. She pushed at the front door, but it was locked, and there was no latch to unlock it. She remembered the key ring Lance always carried, the one he would jingle impatiently while she changed costumes. She heard the keys clinking on his belt as he approached.

"Where do you think you're going?"

"Can you unlock this, please?"

"Why? Are you going to run out on me?" Lance said lightly, as if he was joking.

"I left something in my car," she lied.

"You don't need it," he said. Any hint of friendliness was now gone.

"Unlock the door."

He moved in closer. Cyn uselessly scanned the empty parking lot for anyone who might hear her if she screamed.

"And who is going to pay my session fees? I've promised this other model work. Are you going to cover his fees or rent for the studio space this evening?"

"That's bullshit. You didn't say anything about partner work. If you had, I would have told you I don't do it. Your fees are your problem. Now open the door, or I'll call the cops," Cyn said, her voice rising.

"What's going on here?" The male model had emerged from the studio, frowning handsomely.

"Dickface here is creating a hostage situation."

"I'll handle this, Enrique," Lance snapped. "You renege on this job, bitch, and you owe me five hundred dollars."

"No. I don't owe you anything."

Lance nodded his head, then lashed out, explosively slamming his palm against the door, inches from Cyn's face. The glass boomed and wobbled from the impact. Cyn was frozen in shock. She told me that she saw a blur of white cotton, and then Enrique had Lance pinned against the wall, one forearm forcing his head back in a way that looked sublimely painful.

"Why don't you give her the keys?" Enrique suggested.

Lance's hand squirmed into his pocket and fished out the key ring. Enrique nodded at Cyn, and she snatched it from him and unlocked the door. She picked up her bag and fled, leaving Enrique with Lance still squirming and pinioned under his arm.

It was her second close call with danger via the adult entertainment industry, and in my opinion, two times too many. I was surprised when she showed up at the room an hour after she'd left. Unlike the pickup truck incident, the tale of her rescue via male model seemed to delight her. She sat me down and breathlessly recounted the entire scenario.

"I'm only disappointed that I didn't think to thank Enrique. If I had known he was such a *caballero*, I might have stayed for the shoot and taken the one thousand dollars," she said with a laugh. "Anyway, let's not tell Raj about this. He'll probably feel some obligation to go punch the guy out."

"Yeah. I won't say anything. But we're now in violation of the 'no secrets' rule."

She snorted. "Good one, Glo. No secrets rule. As I see it, it's for his own protection. He might look like an action star, but I don't think he's ever been in a fight in his life. Besides, even if he doesn't go all Rambo, it'll still make him angsty."

"You mean, *more* angsty?"

"Definitely."

Raj was in a pissy mood fairly often those days. He was

stressed about fall semester finals, like we all were, but he was also unhappy that Cyn and I would soon be gone for four weeks, leaving him all alone. Confounding us further was that he'd recently started talking about quitting the sciences altogether to become an actor. A professor complimented his performance during an in-class staging of *Titus Andronicus*, and he'd had a revelation: he wanted a life on the stage. He signed up for acting intensives at the local conservatory that same afternoon.

He would come back from these night classes either elated and convinced that he was going to go all the way as an actor or utterly defeated. I never knew which it was going to be before he walked through the door: comedy Raj or tragedy Raj. We were his test audience for whatever new monologue he'd found and de facto scene partners when he needed to run lines. In my eyes, he came to life when performing, and I loved to help him practice. I'd make time to read the plays he was studying, and when we were alone, we'd geek out together about all the different interpretations he could do. Once I got over the shock, and saw how much he cared about acting, I was behind him all the way. Cyn, however, had a different take on it.

"He's a decent enough actor, but this whole thing is just a phase. It's like his college midlife crisis. He's never going to go through with it."

"What makes you so sure?" I asked, my tone rising defensively. I wanted to support Raj's dream. At least he had one.

Cyn rolled her eyes. "For one thing, Mommy and Daddy. And second of all, he doesn't really want it." Seeing that I was about to object, she held up a silencing finger. "He wants it because he thinks it'll be easy since everything in life has been easy for Raj. But acting won't be easy. There's no ladder for him to race to the top of his field, and failure, even perceived failure, would kill him."

She had a point. Raj was used to things going his way and

being the smartest guy in the room. Smarts would only get him so far as a performer.

"So you think it's a rebellion thing?"

"He told me that he likes the 'being someone else' part of it. I think that has a lot to do with it. It's an escape."

"An escape from us?" I joked.

Cyn didn't laugh. "Maybe. Titus Andronicus had it easy compared to Raj and his two harpies."

We sat there in silence.

"I think I'm making him nuts," she said. Her eyes were serious, and I knew with queasy certainty what she was talking about. The non-secret. She still hadn't slept with him.

Give him to me, I thought for the millionth time. *Give him to me.*

My problem was that my initial feeling about Raj—that he was my destined love and the one I'd never let go of—was solidifying into an unshakable truth. My brain advised caution, but my heart would have none of it. His foray into acting seemed like something, in a parallel universe, I might have gone after, and it endeared him to me all the more. I wanted to help him figure his life out. I thought he could do anything and be anything, and I could see myself as the woman standing behind him, giving him strength. We would lie in his bed, wound tightly together, and he'd talk about the future. How we'd move out to Hollywood, how he'd take me to all his movie premieres, how I would be free to lounge about our sunny mansion doing . . . whatever I eventually wanted. I loved this scenario because he never mentioned Cyn.

Hollywood was perhaps just a fantasy for me, but for Raj, it was very real. As he was trying to grow as this actor person, everything was suddenly *Serious*. Every mood needed to be explored and examined. His approach to studying human emotions was, in classic Raj style, systematic to the point of being overly scientific. Sometimes it went off the rails. He started to give in to these dark moods that he would wallow in all day long, taking notes. Then he'd get philosophical and expound on the many ways that nothing we ever did as people mattered, and determine that (ta-da!) life was ultimately pointless. He would gravely inform me of his findings as if they were news, and I'd remind him I'd already walked that primrose path right into the student funny farm. That would shut him up.

Fact was, the future was weighing heavily on all of us. Cyn's only way to stay in school would be to pick up some heavy debt. She began to talk about possibly transferring somewhere less expensive. The first time she brought it up to us together, Raj's eyes went glassy, but then he smiled and said he'd been having similar thoughts. He'd looked into transferring to a school with a theater program, or just ditching school and moving to New York or LA. He didn't look at me when he said it, only at her, making me feel like they were making plans to ditch me, right in front of my face. I abruptly fled our cafeteria table, abandoning my lunch.

Cyn found me in the ladies' room some minutes later, crying.

"Don't worry, it's all just talk." She sighed. "Probably nothing will happen. Everything will probably just stay the same."

Instead of comforting me, that last part made me break down all over again.

Finals and post-finals parties came and went. Cyn and I dropped ecstasy at the big winter bash. Raj, in actor-scientist mode, abstained. He wanted to observe, he said, as if a bunch of trashed kids dancing was something to behold anew with the fresh eyes of Art. As night fell and the music got louder, I lost myself in the pulsing mass of students who had gathered in the plaza. The flashing colored lights and the shimmering strobe gave the night a sense of magnitude, like we were all on the verge of something epic. I felt like I was a flaming top, swirling madly in the dead center of my youth. I would never have as much energy or joy or promise as I had that night, my heart surging along with the dance beat under the graceful palms.

The feeling did not last long. I felt a cool hand on my sweaty arm, and I looked up into the unsmiling face of Raj. Behind him was Mello, the always cheerful RA, a deep bow of concern darkening her brow. I couldn't hear what Raj was saying because of the music, but I had my suspicions. I followed them through the gyrating horde back to Mello's room on the first floor, directly underneath ours.

Cyn was sitting on the floor of Mello's closet, her legs tucked tightly beneath her crossed arms, hugging herself. When I said her name and she saw me kneeling before her, she let out a small howl and clutched on to me. Her cheeks were laced with glittery tear-trails of party makeup.

"Mello found her under the stairs, crying," Raj informed me, a churlish edge to his voice. "I thought you guys were going to stay together."

I gazed into Cyn's eyes, looking for some trace of the girl I knew. She stared out beyond me with the eyes of a spooked fawn. "Hey, babe . . ." I cooed, failing in my efforts to remember how I'd seen her help people out of their bad trips in the past.

Cyn's eyes flipped up to me and back down again.

"I'm worried about her overheating," Mello said. She was a senior, but she had the steady gravitas of someone much older. She lowered her stocky frame to squat next to me, with the calm air of an emergency room nurse who's seen much worse. "Was she mixing?"

"No. I don't think so. I think it's just E, but maybe a lot of it," I said shakily. Cyn's skin was very hot, even through her T-shirt. I was getting scared.

"How much is a lot?"

"She wouldn't have taken a dangerous amount. She's done it plenty of times."

Mello's mouth tightened.

"She's been stressed. Really stressed. That's why she's flipping out."

Mello sighed and seemed to relax. "I'm not seeing signs of overdose here. If it's just a bad trip, it'll pass. Let's get her up to your room and cool her down."

"Hey, Cyn?" I said lightly, helping her to her feet. She looked at me with wide, terrified eyes, and she clung to my wrists so tightly, I immediately began to lose sensation in my fingertips. "It's really hot, don't ya think? I think we should cool off in the shower."

Mello nodded approvingly, and Raj nervously backed up toward the door. He wouldn't meet my eyes, and I wondered if he felt this was somehow my fault. Cyn and I edged slowly up the stairs, Raj following.

"Hey, Raj," Mello called out. "You should go to the store and get some sports drink. Or orange juice. Orange juice always helps."

Raj nodded. I opened our door and shepherded Cyn inside. "I've got her," I told him.

"If you need anything, Gloria, I'm wearing my pager," Mello said.

I sat Cyn on the edge of the tub and turned on the shower. I checked her pockets to make sure they were empty and removed my skirt. I took Cyn by the hand and backed her up until she was underneath the stream. She gasped when the cool water hit, and I held on to her elbows in case she fainted, but she didn't. She just stood there passively, letting the water run down over her face.

"Feels good, doesn't it?" I asked cheerfully, as if showers were a totally cool new thing. She looked up at me, and I was startled by how dilated her eyes were, her irises little more than a thin glaze of sky blue around a center of impenetrable dark.

"Do you love me, Glo?" she asked.

"Of course I do." I gave her a hug, leaning into the drenching flow of water. The water felt good on my skin, too. We stood there like that, in a comfortable embrace, for what must have been a long time. Cyn had dropped her head onto my shoulder, and I could smell the remnants of her fruity hair spray.

"What's going to happen to us?" she murmured.

The water continued to flow over us, mitigating my silence. Eventually, I came up with an answer with no disturbing connotations. "We're going to go to Costa Rica, and climb a volcano, and see lots of monkeys, and put a lime in the coconut every day."

"I can't do this much longer," she said, sounding suddenly 100 percent sober.

I tried to lean back to get a look at her face, but she wouldn't release me. "No," she grunted, and held me tighter. I stopped resisting. I looked down at her head, the blond hair darkened to a muddy gold, and wondered what mayhem was transpiring inside that skull.

"You're gonna be okay. You just gotta relax," I murmured. I caught sight of our reflection in the mirror. Two girls in soaking wet clothes, embracing in a shower. It was almost funny, until I noticed how tightly Cyn was clutching me, and that she had begun to shiver.

There was a light knock at the bathroom door, and Raj appeared bearing sports drink and orange juice. He glimpsed us in the shower and froze.

"How's it going?" he managed. I felt Cyn stiffen at the sound of his voice, but she loosened her grip on me.

"Better. We're feeling a lot cooler. I think this one's even shivering now." I freed myself from Cyn's grasp and turned off the water.

Raj just stood there. The fear that I'd seen before was gone from his face. In its place was relief, and maybe some lust. Cyn stepped out of the shower and stared at her reflection with a diffuse awe, as if viewing an aquarium full of tropical fish. Raj's face betrayed similar fascination, except he was looking at both of us. I shooed him out and closed the bathroom door.

I helped Cyn into a dry robe, and when she was ready, Raj guided her to my bed, which had a better view of the TV. Raj had already switched it to some cartoons as a nonthreatening, come-down distraction, but Cyn just closed her eyes. After a few minutes, her breathing slowed down and she seemed to have fallen asleep.

Raj and I looked at one another. A slow grin of relief spread across his face, and he shook his head. I changed into my own robe and switched off the lights. The flicker of the cartoons flashed across Cyn's sleeping form as I made my way over to Raj on Cyn's bed. The music from the party below was intense, and my body began to respond to the rhythm again, as if reawakening. I lay down beside him, and together we watched the colored lights flash across the palm fronds outside of the window.

"We should stay here tonight, just in case," I whispered. The thumping bass from the party was so loud, I didn't need to fear waking Cyn by speaking, but it was nicer to whisper into Raj's ear anyway.

He responded with a seductive smile, and I felt him slip his hand beneath my robe. I curled toward him, my back to Cyn, and untied the sash. Raj's hands were soon all over me, and we were kissing. With the music and the lights flashing behind my closed lids, I sort of forgot where we were. Before I really realized what was happening, we were having sex. I glanced over at my bed and was relieved to see that Cyn hadn't moved. Raj came shortly afterward, and I rolled out of bed immediately to wash up, hoping to get rid of any evidence of what we'd just done on Cyn's bed, with her right across the room.

The next morning, Cyn was extremely apologetic about the night before. The three of us ate waffles in companionable silence, occasionally pointing out other students stumbling into the cafeteria who looked worse than we felt. I was utterly worn out. Although I didn't share it with my tablemates, I was secretly dying to spend a little time away from school. The previous night's adventure had me worried that we were all spinning out of control.

Cyn promised to visit me at my parents' place for a few days around Christmas, but thankfully, not the entire stretch of winter break. The holidays meant good money at E Two, with generosity and wish-fulfillment perfuming the air, along with the fir boughs and disinfectant spray. While Cyn was quite literally hustling for dough, I was baking cookies with my mom, shaking out the special silver sprinkles, just like I'd always done. Drifting to sleep in my quiet, childhood bedroom, I had the strange sensation of having left my adult self behind on the other coast. I didn't catch myself missing her all that much.

Then, just when the winter holiday pendulum was beginning to swing from pleasantly relaxed to agonizingly boring, Cyn pulled up to my parents' house in her battered red hatchback, with Raj riding shotgun. I'd invited him to stay with us for a night on the way to his own parents' place. Raj introduced himself as my boyfriend and behaved as such, and Cyn, in a wonderful, unspoken gift to me, betrayed no hint of interest in him the entire visit. We drank cocktails and played my old board games into the small hours, laughing. I'd look across my bedroom and see Raj's deep brown eyes on me, and next to him, my best friend, cracking some stupid joke. In those brief flickers, when I could forget everything I knew about the real us, I was truly happy. Then they left, together.

Alone at my parents' place, I found that I weathered the separation well enough during the daylight hours, but as soon as the sun set, I would be hit with a longing for Raj that made me want to keen. It made me nervous and irritable to think about Raj returning to campus in a few days' time. He'd be there with Cyn, and without me, for almost an entire week. I suspected that, in my absence, they'd consummate their relationship. I worried about the potential fallout. I started biting my nails.

I returned to campus for New Year's Eve. Before I had time to blink, we were shoving bathing suits and hiking gear into our thrift-store backpacks. I was out of my head with excitement, barely able to believe that I'd soon be departing for an exotic adventure. The only thing that brought me down was how badly I knew I'd miss Raj.

I slept at the Hubble the night before we left. Raj and I huddled together on the balcony, wrapped in a blanket against the chilly breeze, sharing a bottle of wine. As a plane landed across the freeway, I snuggled in closer, seeking the carnal comfort of Raj's warm body. We didn't talk much. I felt his sadness at our leaving as a palpable force that grew thicker the closer we got to departure.

He'd had a rough time visiting his family. He came out about his acting, and his father, in a knee-jerk reaction, had forbidden it. His mother, he said, had laughed; first at the absurdity of Raj throwing away his scholarship to pursue what she viewed as a hobby, and then at Raj's father's reaction. When the dust settled, she told him to do what he wanted—it was his life—but I think that doubt had taken root. With all of that drama happening, he definitely didn't tell them about his girlfriend. Or his other girlfriend.

The morning Cyn and I left, he was a vortex of gloom, his

jaw grimly set as he chauffeured us to the international airport. Cyn sat in the backseat, her eyes fixed out the window throughout the entire strained and silent ride. Cyn gave Raj a quick kiss good-bye from the backseat and slammed the door, leaving us alone together. Raj looked so miserable that I couldn't walk away without seeing him smile. I kissed him long and slow, and when I pulled away, he pulled me close again. Conscious of Cyn waiting outside on the curb with our bags, I kissed him tenderly one last time and whispered in his ear that I loved him. I'd never said it before, and his stunned smile was worth everything, though he didn't, as I'd hoped, say he loved me back. I locked that smile into my memory and hurried out of the car, and together Cyn and I hustled into the terminal.

All the enthusiasm and glee that we'd been suppressing for the past couple of weeks erupted in the line for security. Other travelers turned to stare as we laughed to the point of tears at nothing in particular, drunk with the knowledge that our adventure was soon beginning.

CHAPTER SIX

We met our group at the gate. There were twelve of us total, as many as could be squeezed into one stretched-out van. Another pair of girls from our Spanish Lit class was also making the trip. Sadie, a wary-eyed, dark-skinned beauty who barely stood five feet tall, and her friend Hannah, who had shaved her head in preparation for the trip.

"Just to clarify, in case there were any doubts, yes, I'm a lesbian," she quipped as we went around the circle introducing ourselves.

Our group organizer, a tall guy named Pete with thinning hair and a wide, toothy grin, urged us to get all the gringo words out of our systems. Once we landed, we were on our honor to speak only Spanish, even among ourselves.

A few hours later, we emerged from the chilly airport into the swampy embrace of the Costa Rican afternoon. As our van zipped through the narrow streets of San Jose, I peered out past Cyn's shoulder at the tropical pink sky, trying to drink in every detail.

We bunked in a hostel dorm all together for most of the first week. We didn't get great sleep because other backpackers who didn't have to work at a school at eight a.m. would stumble in drunkenly in the small hours. They tried to be quiet, but the overhead lights would snap on and off, followed by the interminable rustling of plastic bags, suppressed giggles, and zipping of zippers. Oh, and snoring.

Cyn had nightmares the first couple of nights. The first time, she was moaning, and Sadie reached across from her neighboring bunk and woke her. A night or two later, the same thing happened. Then one morning she woke up crying but couldn't remember the dream that had preceded it.

"Too many *frijoles*," Hannah diagnosed at breakfast, but I was a little concerned. Cyn wasn't eating much, or sleeping much, apparently, but she seemed otherwise okay. I figured it was just the change of environment messing up her biorhythms.

When our week of school volun-tourism was over, we had a few unscheduled leisure days at Playa Tortuga, a beach town not far from one of the best surfing breaks on the Pacific. Our enthusiasm ballooned as our shuttle van drove up to the hostel, all tricked out in Rasta colors. Cyn pointed out a pot-leaf-adorned tapestry of Bob Marley on the wall and smiled broadly. With any luck, we'd be sharing a well-deserved spliff on the shore by sundown.

We spent all day on the beach, but no one was surfing. The ocean was so flat that the guys who rented boards hadn't even opened up shop. Instead, they splayed across their shack's rotting wooden steps, watching the tourists and shooting the breeze. Hannah and Sadie were with us, both of them reading books, ignoring the parade of local guys who lingered by our blanket, many of them openly staring at Cyn's coral-colored bikini and the shell necklace that dangled between her breasts.

"Hello, beautiful ladies," one of them said, in English. I liked his voice, so I looked up from the trashy magazine I had bought at the airport. I liked his face, too, and the rest of him. He was clearly a surfer, the ends of his long, dark hair golden from the salt and sun. He also looked like total trouble. He was our guy if we wanted to find any drugs. Cyn clearly recognized this, too.

"*Hola, guapo*. Why is the water here so flat? We came here to ride the waves," she bantered back, in Spanish.

Clearly delighted to be addressed in Spanish by a gringa, his smile expanded into a wolfish grin. "I'm Marco," he said, and he shook all four of our hands. He even took the time to compliment Hannah on the fuzz that was mushrooming on her scalp. "It's very radical," he said approvingly. She smiled politely, but I could tell that both Sadie and Hannah also saw what we saw, and didn't like it. They pointedly returned their attentions to their books.

"I don't know what is happening with the waves," he said with a theatrical shrug. "I am disappointed myself. Maybe tomorrow. How long are you staying in Playa Tortuga?"

"Three nights," Cyn answered, and laughed when Marco shook his head in exaggerated sadness.

"That is not long enough."

"It's all we have. We're students," I explained.

"From America," he said. "I want to go to America. To Los Angeles."

"It's not as beautiful as this," Cyn demurred.

Cyn and Marco chatted a while longer. Cyn asked him about finding some weed, and he said to stop by the reggae bar that night. It was on the far end of the beach, but there was no sign. "The music is the sign. *Hasta pronto*."

When he walked away, Sadie said, "You're not actually going to go there, are you?"

Cyn laughed. "Why not?"

"Stranger danger?" Hannah suggested sarcastically.

"You used English. You owe us all a beer," I joked.

"It doesn't rhyme as well in Spanish," she said with a sigh.

"I don't think it's a good idea," Sadie warned. "But if you have to go, we should all go together."

Hannah released a loud hoot. "Oh? We should all go together? We see how it is, you little sneak!"

Sadie blushed. "What? It's for safety!"

"No, it's because that guy is a hottie, and you're hoping he has *amigos*."

"Whatever." She snapped her book open, then closed it again in exasperation. "I give up! Am I that transparent?"

"No, honey, but that guy had a body. I may not be straight, but I'm not blind."

Cyn and I bought some cold-enough beers from a guy who wandered past, selling them out of a backpack, and sat in the sand, watching the sunset.

"Man, I can't wait to get some weed," she said for the fourth time, her entire demeanor twitchy with the jones. "Sunset and marijuana are like peanut butter and . . . how do you say 'jelly' in Spanish?"

I shrugged. We sipped our beers, watching the sun sink beneath the horizon.

"It takes a little over eight minutes for light from the sun to reach our eyes here. Eight minutes traveling at the speed of light." Cyn pointed her bottle at the red orb before us, squinting distrustfully.

"Huh."

"If the sun just went out, I wonder how cold it would get, and how fast, after that final burst of light, like, right before minute nine."

"You might not notice right away, if it happened at nighttime."

"The moon would go out," she noted.

"Shit, you're right. Like a night-light gone dead."

"That'd be such a bummer."

"Yeah. Well, it probably won't happen tonight," I opined sagely.

"Not before we get high. I'm not gonna go out like that, Glo!" She jumped to her feet and saluted as the sun disappeared into the water. "*¡Hasta mañana, sol!*"

It was go time.

We got changed and gathered Sadie and Hannah. Together, we hit the reggae bar, or what we thought was the reggae bar. What we found was a dilapidated beach shack with a string of holiday lights above a weathered bar with a few tables set around it in the sand. The bartender was listening to a soccer game when we arrived, causing us to wonder aloud whether we were at the right place. Since our wondering took place in the local tongue, the bartender confirmed that we were in fact in the reggae bar, and accordingly, switched off the game and turned the music way up. We ordered what he suggested, pink rum punch. It was strong and delicious, so we ordered another. More people from our group showed up, and Sadie and Hannah went to greet them.

Soon it was totally dark, the stars supercharged above the black sea. Cyn was almost finished with her third punch when the bartender brought over two more.

"On the house," he said, beaming. His ramshackle beach hut was surrounded by thirsty, Spanish-speaking Americans, and because we'd showed up first, he thought we were responsible for the good fortune. Maybe we were.

Cyn took a sip of the new punch and winced. "This dude keeps putting an extra floater on top of our drinks."

"That's nice of him."

"It seems nice. It might be hell tomorrow."

We clinked plastic rims and looked out at the water. In the distance, we could see the glimmering lights of fishing boats. The breeze was cool, and as I dug my toes into the sand under my chair, I was thinking that the moment was just about perfect. Or it would have been, if only Raj had been there.

Cyn took a long gulp of her drink. "Glo, there's something you should know."

I picked up my cup and sipped, reflexively. With all the weird stuff going on with Cyn, I'd been anticipating a drunken speech from her. I steeled myself for whatever might be coming.

"You see," she began, then sighed. "There are some things I do that I tolerate in myself because I can think, 'That's not really me.' But I've gone to that place so often lately, the place where I'm not me, that it *is* me now. I'm dependent on it. But it's not anything. And when I need to come back to being me again, I'm not sure what it even means anymore."

"Cyn, if this is about your work, then I can only say . . ." I looked for the words, but my sentence stalled out. My head was too foggy to formulate advice.

"I want you to have Raj."

I looked at her and saw her eyes were glowing and wet. She nodded at me with certainty.

"I'm not even a whole person anymore."

At that exact moment, Marco rolled up to our table. I was stunned and speechless, but Cyn was grinning at him warmly. The next thing I knew, I was shaking hands with Hector, a guy who Marco introduced as his brother. They looked so dissimilar that I assumed the "brother" part was slang. Hector was short and stocky, he didn't have a cool hairdo, and he wore glasses. Hector also radiated a much different vibe; while Marco was sex and danger, Hector presented like a shy school teacher.

I excused myself to find the bathroom, which was already occupied by a large green lizard. I went in anyway and watched moths throw themselves against the naked lightbulb above the door. When I was finished, I stood at the sink, feeling dazed. I walked past where Cyn was sitting with Marco and Hector and stood ankle-deep in the surf. The moon was full, or almost full, and encircled by a misty halo. The ocean mirrored its brightness in a gleaming white streak that appeared to end at my toes.

I took a deep breath and tried to chill out. As much as I wanted to hash the Raj thing out immediately, I knew it was no longer the moment. If she really meant what she said, it could wait a few hours. In truth, I wanted to hear it from her when she was sober so there'd be no taking it back.

When I returned to the shack, Cyn and our new friends were leaning in toward one another, absorbed in fervent conversation. Marco was talking quickly about something or other off the beach a few miles down. When I sat, they explained that there was an island nearby that was supposedly haunted on full moons, when the spirits of Mayans would rise up and walk the jungle. When the tide was out, there was a sandbar that you could walk across to get to it. Oh, and that also, we were all going there tomorrow night, which happened to be a full moon.

Cyn nodded happily. "Marco knows a private cove where we can watch the moonrise and have a bonfire, and he thinks he can find magic mushrooms. It should be amazing," she followed up, in English.

"Are you nuts?" I said, also in English.

"What's the problem?" she asked, looking genuinely shocked that I wasn't into it.

"You want to go to a haunted island to do drugs in a foreign country with some local guys we just met. That's the problem."

Cyn laughed, but I was dead serious. Hector was watching me uneasily. "It feels like a lie not to say something. I speak some English. Just so you know," he said, in English. Then he blushed and looked away.

I blushed, too, embarrassed and growing angrier. Cyn laughed even louder.

"I didn't mean to embarrass you," he said, his face strawberry red. Marco asked him what was wrong. "*Nada,*" he replied.

Now I felt like a jackass. Hector seemed like a Boy Scout, and if he was friends or brothers with Marco, Marco was probably okay, too. But I had expressed distrust of both like a typical paranoid American. But this is the thing: I Knew It Was a Bad Idea. I wouldn't have done anything like it in the States with guys I didn't know, but now I felt like a racist, or xenophobe, or just an uptight bitch.

And then Cyn said, "Well, I'm going. If you're uncomfortable, you don't have to come."

I could have throttled her right there. I seethed and finished my drink. There was no way I could let her go alone. If she was determined to do it, that meant, like it or not, I was doing it, too. I vowed that this would be our last trip together. I was furious.

Marco announced that he had some weed. Did we want to smoke? If so, we should take a little walk away from the bar, just to be safe. Cyn nodded, apparently oblivious to how angry I was at her. I followed her out into the darkness, walking side by side with Hector, who wanted to speak a little English. At that moment, I welcomed the distraction. We chatted about college life (he was a student as well) while, in front of me, Marco and Cyn made plans for our haunted island outing.

"Do you believe the island is really haunted?" I asked Hector.

We took a few steps in silence. "I don't think so."

"You don't think what, *hermanito*?" Marco asked. He pulled out a joint and lit it.

"I don't believe that the island is haunted."

Marco laughed loudly, a huge cloud of smoke engulfing him. "Those are just old wives' tales. Or stories to scare children so they don't drown trying to swim there."

"I thought you said it was walkable," I said.

Marco passed me the joint and wiggled his brow. "Only at low tide, you hear me? Otherwise, it really is an island."

"And even at low tide, you have to wade a bit," Hector offered.

"That's true. Leave the long skirts and jeans at home," Marco said with a laugh.

Once we killed the spliff, I announced that I was calling it a night. What I really wanted was a chance to talk to Cyn alone and find a way out of this ridiculous outing. No such luck, since the brothers insisted on walking us back to our hostel, saying the beach wasn't safe at night.

As we passed the bar, Sadie and Hannah emerged, both of them extremely wasted. Hannah ran up and threw her arms around me and began singing some dirty Spanish song the bartender had just taught her. Marco and Hector knew the words and joined in. Our very merry band made a ruckus all the way back to the door of the hostel, and once inside, we became the drunk people stumbling around in the dark.

I found my bunk, which seemed to be swaying on its springs, and the next thing I knew, the room was flooded with painful, eyelid-penetrating daylight. I swear the night was prematurely yanked away like a heavy drop cloth, my sleep stolen in some terrible prank. Across the room, Cyn's bed was empty. Blearily I remembered I had a mission and, ignoring the pounding behind my eyes, found a way to my feet.

I glimpsed Cyn on the hostel's back veranda, nursing a can of pineapple juice, looking hungover.

"Where'd you get that?" I grunted. She pointed toward a small cooler.

"It's part of breakfast. There's coffee and bread, too, if you want to make toast."

I shook my head at the notion of eating anything and snapped open my juice. The hyper-sweetness of the fluid made my stomach quiver dangerously. I sunk into a plastic lounge chair next to Cyn.

"No waves again today," she mumbled, toying with a crust of toast.

I literally didn't have the stomach for chitchat, so I got right to it. "Did you mean what you said last night about Raj, or was that just drunk talk?"

"I meant it." She kept her eyes trained on the ocean, as if she had a ship coming in at any moment.

"Does he know?"

She shook her head.

I looked out at the water, numb to the gorgeousness of the morning. The beauty of the setting, combined with Cyn's abdication of our lover, should have had me trembling with joy. Instead, I felt queasy and suspicious. "Did something happen between you two?"

She looked at me. "I need coffee to have this conversation. Do you want some?"

"Yes."

As she went to the communal kitchen, I forced down the pulpy nectar at the bottom of my can, feeling like I was awaiting grim news at the doctor's office.

Cyn set two mugs on the table and sat down. "There's no milk, so I put in a ton of sugar."

"Thanks."

She took a long sip from her mug. "Well, the quick, sober version of what I was trying to say last night is that I feel trapped. It's not him. He's a wonderful guy, and I do love him, but it just doesn't feel right anymore." She took another sip and glanced at me. "You're surprised."

"Not as surprised as he's going to be."

"Yeah, I know." She sighed. "I've been thinking about ending it for a while, but I haven't been able to pull the trigger. I guess telling you that I'm going to is sort of a dress rehearsal." She raked her fingers through her hair nervously, reminding me, ironically, of Raj. "It's just that he's so serious about everything . . ."

I waited to see if she would continue. She didn't.

"Serious about how he loves you, you mean?"

"Yes, in a way. But I can't fault him for being who he is. I'm the one with the issues."

"Has he told you he loves you?"

"No," she answered quickly. Then she shook her head in resignation and closed her eyes. "Maybe."

Hungover Cyn was not a great actress. "Maybe" obviously meant "yes."

She finally looked at me. "Did he tell you?"

"No." I drank half my coffee in one long pull, not caring that it was steaming hot and scorching the roof of my mouth. Tears filled my eyes and spilled down my cheeks.

"Shit. Are you okay?" she asked.

I angrily wiped the tears away, but they kept coming. I saw with sudden clarity that if it was over between Cyn and Raj, it was over for me, too. He would leave school rather than see her around if he couldn't have her; he was already talking about transferring or dropping out. My love for him wouldn't even be a consolation prize. It would be a painful reminder of what he'd lost.

"He doesn't love me," I whimpered, letting the words tear me to shreds. "It's so obvious. He only really wanted you. I was just the bonus girl."

"That's not true, Glo," she said forcefully. "How can you think that's true?"

"Because it is!" I sobbed. Cyn put her hand on my knee, a warning flashing across her face. I ignored it. "He never told me he loved me, so there's that. And anyway, if he really loved me at all, he never would have complained to me about you not fucking him!"

Cyn squeezed my knee hard, her cheeks coloring. I turned my head to see Hannah and Sadie standing by the cooler, staring at us. Sadie's mouth was hanging open in shock. Cyn dropped her head and let her hair surround her face. When I looked back at the cooler a moment later, they were gone.

"Fuck," I muttered. "Great."

Cyn shook her head angrily. "Who cares what they think? It's not a big deal. None of this is."

"What are you talking about? It is a big fucking deal!" I shouted.

Cyn slammed back the rest of her coffee and shoved the mug across the table. "He really complained to you about me not sleeping with him?"

"Yeah. It was like he couldn't help himself." The memory still carried a fresh sting. "And why didn't you want to sleep with him? Why did you even want him to be your boyfriend if you didn't want him like that? I don't understand any of it!"

"I know."

"Well, you could try to explain it. I think you owe me that."

She bit her lip and nodded vigorously. I looked up and saw Marco on the beach, approaching us with a casual swagger.

"Here comes your man," I scoffed.

We watched him in silence.

"Do you still not want to go today?" she asked after a moment. Her voice sounded indifferent and flat, which was exactly how I felt.

I looked at Marco. He didn't inspire any worry for me anymore. Nor did the thought of a haunted island full of poisonous snakes and hissing tarantulas. It was like my cautious self had packed up and left. I no longer cared about what might happen to me in the next day, or the next year. I could no longer see the point.

"No, let's do it. What the hell," I grunted.

Marco waved lazily at us. "Good morning," he said. He stopped in the sand at the bottom of the steps leading up to us, next to a sign that said the veranda was for guests only.

Cyn got up and met him on the sand. They took a short walk toward the trees, and he paused to pull something out of his pocket to show Cyn. She laughed with what sounded like real delight and touched his shoulder. She pulled a few bills out of her jean shorts and I watched him put on a good show of trying to refuse the cash before finally accepting it. They exchanged a few more words, and he pointed toward the southern edge of the beach. Cyn nodded. Marco extended a hand to me and shouted "*¡Hasta luego!*" I waved and forced a smile.

Cyn came back to the table carrying a red plastic bag. "Take a peek," she said. I glimpsed half a dozen mushrooms with brown-and-yellow-speckled caps.

"Nice," I said neutrally.

Her mood was considerably lifted. "I really think you're wrong about Raj. I think you totally underestimate yourself and your charms. You always do."

I didn't respond to that. It sounded like utter bullshit. "So why didn't you sleep with him?"

She deflated visibly and slunk back against her chair.

"I wanted to. There was never any plan not to. But then . . . God, this is fucking scary to say."

"What?" I demanded, growing annoyed. "How scary can it be? It's just me."

Cyn grasped her empty coffee cup, forgetting she'd finished it, or maybe just stalling. Finally, she looked up. "I had a few clients who I slept with. For money. I was always safe, but I couldn't risk the chance of maybe passing something to you both. So I didn't sleep with Raj, and I didn't tell him why."

Her eyes darted all over my face, fearfully awaiting my reaction. I closed my eyes and took a breath. She kept talking, hurriedly.

"I couldn't tell you about it, either. It was too low. I was in denial about it myself. Dancing didn't pay half of what I told you, and I was scared out of my mind that, despite everything I tried, I'd still have to leave school. So, I did it once, and it wasn't pleasant, but it wasn't so bad. Then I picked up a few more clients; men who I chose carefully. But then, that night when the cops brought me to Raj's, it wasn't because some random person was following me. It was one of my private clients. He was acting sketchy when I showed up for our appointment. He was a doctor, so god knows what he was on. He was flying around the hotel room, all manic, talking some shit about how he was going to 'take me away from it all' which, the way he said it, scared the shit out of me. I got the hell out of the room, saying I was going to get some ice, but he came out and saw me getting into my car and freaked the fuck out and started screaming threats. I really thought he might try to kill me. I was so terrified, I went to the cops with the E Two parking lot story. I couldn't even report the doctor without incriminating myself."

I felt ill. I opened my eyes and focused on the horizon, as if I were seasick.

"So you just slept with random men?"

"Not random. Five men. Including the one who went crazy."

"Jesus."

"When it went right, it was such easy money. A couple hours at most. They were all older guys, most with families. For some of them, it was either get their kicks with me or fuck the babysitter and lose everything."

I tried to imagine what it must have been like for Cyn, selling herself to strangers. The horror of it was so abstract, so beyond my experience, that all I could do was shudder.

"God, Glo, won't you even look at me?" she asked, her voice tearful.

I quickly looked at her, managing a small smile, and she burst into tears. I pulled my chair next to hers and held her while she sobbed. She hardly made any noise, but her shoulders were heaving. A young couple wandered out to the cooler. They saw us, did a double take, and quickly walked past us down onto the beach.

"It's okay," I heard myself repeating, over and over. "It's okay."

She straightened up and wiped her face. "Do you really think so? Because I'm not sure I do."

I wanted to feel pity for Cyn, but pity wasn't what I felt, and it also wasn't what she needed.

"You know what, Cyn?" I murmured. "Who cares?"

She looked at me with horror. "*I* do. *I* care."

"No. I mean, I know you care. And I care. But you did what you had to do. It can be over. You can put it behind you."

She studied the ocean, tears still rolling down her face. Neither of us spoke.

She broke the silence with a harsh, joyless laugh. "I really thought that I could keep that part of me separate, that with my history, I somehow had the personality for it. I didn't foresee what it would cost me. I think my real libido, the Cyn who once liked sex, is gone forever. I've been so stupid."

"You're not stupid. You're a brave person who went a little too far. It was a mistake. We all make mistakes," I intoned. "If things do fall apart with me and Raj, it won't be because of what you did or didn't do."

"That's big of you," she said. "I mean it. You're the best friend I could ever ask for."

"It's the truth." I felt like, as I was speaking, I was channeling some deeper consciousness. Like none of what I was learning could surprise or hurt me, because somehow, deep down, I'd always known it would end up this way. Our relationship was an experiment that was doomed to fail.

"Once we get back, we'll just see how things go," I said. "Obviously, I won't tell Raj."

"You can if you want. It might be healthier for him to hate me."

"He can study his feelings of hatred and use them to grow as an artist."

Cyn chuckled and dropped her head into her hands. "I was hoping I would feel some relief after telling you, but I just feel like an even bigger asshole. You can call me a whore if you want, or any of those things. I deserve it."

"No. I don't want to call you anything. You're my best friend." I felt utterly exhausted. Beside me, Cyn groaned softly, letting her head loll back in the manner of the recently asphyxiated. Above us, the sun shimmered with brilliant indifference.

"Let's go for a swim," I suggested.

CHAPTER SEVEN

We met up with Marco, Hector, and their friend Jorge in the late afternoon. Jorge was going to drive the four of us the few miles or so down to the other beach. We would walk across the sandbar while it lasted, and Jorge would join us by boat later, meeting us at the cove around sunset. Jorge's boat would be our ride back, since by the time we'd be ready to go, the tide would be in and the sandbar gone.

We bought two jugs of water, some peanuts, a couple of oranges, and a liter of cheap rum. Jorge, a hefty guy with an easy smile, helped us into the back of his pickup truck, where we arranged ourselves atop piles of wet, coiled rope. A damp fishing net was piled in the middle of the truck bed, its strong marine vapors attracting seagulls.

The sun was low, and the heat of the day was finally relenting. As we whizzed along the narrow road, we could glimpse the beach through the trees. I looked up, and Cyn was grinning at me, her hair flying wildly in the air. I smiled back. We'd passed the morning wandering in and out of the surf, lost in our own thoughts. My mood had been shifting erratically as I digested the morning's revelations, and I didn't trust myself to say much. After lunch, I passed out for several blissful hours. When I awoke, gazing up at the underside of a palm in a sea of bright blue sky, I finally felt calm. What would happen would happen.

There was no point driving myself crazy speculating which exact way things would self-destruct. Cyn seemed happier, as well. I was now glad she'd cooked up this island adventure for us. It would be a small way of reclaiming life as our own.

Jorge stopped the car along the side of the road. We weren't in a town, exactly, but there were some small shops dotting a short stretch of the road. Hector got out of the cab, and Marco jumped over the side of the hatch. He went over to Jorge's window, and the two began to talk. I grabbed one jug of water and a duffel with a blanket, my camera, and a flashlight. Cyn double-checked that she had the plastic bag with the mushrooms.

"¿Agua?" Marco crowed when he saw what I was carrying. "Didn't you mean to grab the rum?"

I opened my mouth to answer, but he waved my words away. "I'm only joking. Water is always a good idea. Jorge will bring the rest of our things, right, amigo?"

Marco lifted the water jug from my hands as Jorge pulled away. We walked down to the beach and got our first look at the island. It was, as promised, connected to the main land with a ribbon-thin umbilicus of sand barely visible beneath the turquoise water. The island itself didn't look like much: a wide smudge of green that rose to a peak in the middle, surrounded by rocky headlands, with no beach to speak of.

"Our timing is perfect," Hector exclaimed, childlike with glee. He slapped Marco on the shoulder.

"This is as good as it gets," Marco said. "In an hour even . . ." He made a sweeping gesture with his hands. *"Nada."*

At the water's edge, I removed my hiking sandals and put them in my bag. We waded onto the strip, and I took out my camera. I ushered everyone out before me on the sandbar, snapped the shutter, and captured them, arms around one another's shoulders, the island rising in the background.

"Perfect," I said. "I'll take another one when we're halfway out."

We swished along in the ankle-deep water, watching the island before us grow bigger. Cyn chattered happily as we waded along.

"This is so exciting. And dangerous! We're totally unprepared for ghosts."

"That's true. But how do you prepare for ghosts?" Hector teased.

"You don't go on their island on the night they're supposed to be haunting it," I said, or attempted to say. My vocabulary was thin on supernatural terminology.

"Don't worry. We'll keep you safe," Marco assured us, walking backward to face us. "What you need to be worried about are snakes."

"Fantastic!" I shouted.

Cyn kicked water at me. I kicked some back.

Cyn laughed. "Aren't they more afraid of us than we are of them?"

Hector shrugged. "I don't know. I've never asked one. But it's a good idea to make a lot of noise on the trails. It scares things away."

"But it attracts ghosts," Cyn rejoined.

"I prefer ghosts to snakes anytime," he said.

Halfway out, we took some more pictures. The sandbar was already submerged, so it looked like we were walking on water. Cyn and I posed together, back-to-back, with our arms crossed, grinning broadly. The water surrounding us sparkled, the low sun making each ripple appear coated in flecks of gold.

By the time the island drew near, we were wading knee-deep. I paused to look behind us, and the sandbar had disappeared.

"No going back now, *señoritas*," Hector said with a smile.

From the island, I could see upturned fishing boats on the

mainland, but they were too far away to make out any detail. I snapped a few more pictures as Marco searched the tree line for the path across the island to the sunset cove.

"People don't come here as often as they used to," he shouted as he poked around in the trees. "The trail is hiding."

"Over here," Hector called, waving us toward a narrow clearing in the brush.

We followed the brothers into the shade of the trees. The trail was not wide, so we walked single file. Even then, we moved slowly, holding rogue branches aside for one another as we progressed. The muddy sections of the path were marred with footprints, and old cigarette butts dotted the trail like breadcrumbs.

I pointed them out to Marco. "Ghost cigarettes," he said, widening his eyes with goofy horror.

On either side of us, the brush was dense. Long, leafy ferns, thin trees decked out with vicious punk-rock spikes, and swaying palms competed ferociously for light and space. I kept an eye out for snakes or other animals, but other than buzzing mosquitoes and an assortment of butterflies, I saw no trace of nonhuman life.

We hadn't been walking long when the path forked. "We need to go right," Hector advised, "toward the sunset." After another short hike, we began to hear the ocean. The path dropped down steeply and opened up onto a small, rocky cove.

"Here we are," Marco howled, spreading his long arms wide.

"It's gorgeous!" Cyn exclaimed.

I dropped my bag and took my camera to the water's edge. The beach was a narrow crescent of grayish sand, punctuated by large, dark rocks. The beach ended abruptly on both corners of the cove in a rocky abutment, backed by dense jungle. The trees from which we'd just emerged seemed to tower above us in a solid wall. The waves were rolling in strong and fast beneath the sinking sun, teasingly revealing a menagerie of boulders lurking just below the surf.

I snapped a shot of Cyn laying out the beach blanket while Hector and Marco set up the kindling for the fire. When they were done, we sat in a circle on the blanket and divided the mushrooms into four shares. Unless he brought his own, Jorge would not be tripping with us, which was just as well, since he'd eventually be piloting us back to the mainland. I crushed my portion of the mushrooms in my palm. It created a fat handful, probably two disgusting swallows instead of one. I took a deep breath and poured them into my mouth, chewing as quickly as I could. Beside me, Cyn did the same, crinkled up her face in disgust, and reached for the water jug. She gulped hurriedly as I made urgent hand gestures for her to pass it over. She complied, and I passed it to the guys. Marco drank several large swallows, then swished some water around in his mouth and spat over his shoulder.

"*Hijo de puta*, those taste terrible," he yowled, laughing. "Where is Jorge with that rum? I need something to clean the taste out!"

As if responding to Marco's command, Jorge emerged from the trees, sweating profusely, carrying a large canvas bag and, to my surprise, a guitar case. We all cheered in unison when we saw him, and he stopped and smiled, setting down the guitar to wipe his brow.

"I almost couldn't remember which way to go at the break in the trail. But I saw your footprints," he said between gasps. He sat down with a sigh of exhaustion, and we offered him the water. He drank thirstily and then reached into one of the bags and produced a bottle of rum. He cracked it open and passed it around.

I took a large swig, some of the sharp sweetness running down my chin, and passed it to Cyn.

"Har, matey," I said.

"Har, har," she responded, raising the bottle high.

The sun inched closer to the horizon. The guys went into the jungle in search of more wood to add to the few pieces of plywood that Jorge had brought along.

I began to feel weird, a sign that the mushrooms were kicking in.

"You feeling anything?" I asked.

"Oh yes." Cyn was leaning back on her elbows, gazing at the horizon. "You?"

"Just beginning to. I was starting to think these were duds."

"I'm just glad they're not poisonous," she muttered. "They're not, though," she amended hastily. "Don't think about poison mushrooms."

"Don't worry, I'm not."

"This has been a strange day," Cyn said slowly.

My lips and tongue began to tingle, and for the second time that day, I began to feel nauseated. I took a swig of rum and walked into the water, hoping the sensation of the surf might distract my brain from my roiling stomach. The bottom edge of the sun had just begun to kiss the horizon. I watched as it sunk gradually lower, the planet spinning away from it, pulling me along for the ride. I examined the few wispy clouds in the sky. Their edges morphed and twisted in unnatural filigrees; the commencement of hallucination. These mushrooms were strong, and we'd taken a lot. I felt a sudden shock of anxiety, but like the waves wrapping around my shins, it rolled on by as abruptly as it had arrived.

Behind me, I heard Jorge strum a series of arpeggios. They sounded warm and bright, like the setting sun made audible, and I happily returned to the blanket to be with my new friends. I sat beside Cyn, and as the sun disappeared beneath the horizon, she reached over and squeezed me in a tight hug. I looked up and saw that Hector was watching me. When I met his eye, he looked away for a moment, but then looked back, his gaze calm and peaceful. I smiled. Beside him, Marco pulled out a tiny wooden case that looked like a chestnut. He opened it and pulled out a miniature Baggie filled with something white. He inserted the extra-long nail of his pinkie finger and lifted it to his nose. After a quick inhalation, he was grinning wildly, transformed in my eye back into the wolf we'd met the day before. He offered the coke to Cyn, but Cyn smiled and shook her head. He shrugged and returned the case to his pocket.

"We should start the fire," Hector said.

The guys stepped a few feet away to get the fire started, but to me, they might as well have been on the moon. The 'shrooms were hitting me much stronger than I'd expected. I felt dizzy and irrationally anxious that the guys would burn themselves making the fire, so I lay down on the beach blanket and concentrated on the sky. The moment the guys were out of sight, I forgot about them. It seemed like time was passing very quickly, but the sky took forever to darken, slowly blushing from pink to magenta to, finally, a deep plum. Cyn was next to me on the blanket, talking about something. She might have been pointing out the faint traces of emerging stars, because her hands kept darting around before us. Whatever she was saying didn't seem to need a response. My panic disappeared without me noticing, and I was feeling happy again. I relaxed into myself, and soon the guys were cheering. We sat up and the fire was blazing.

Cyn was having a very good time. Every time I looked her way, she was laughing, her white teeth flashing. Hector was all liquidy warm eyes. Marco made me nervous, but I thought maybe he couldn't see me. It was all about Cyn for him. Jorge played song after song. Spanish became so hard to remember that I stopped speaking, but I remembered that *luna* was moon because I was soon shouting at it as it made a shy appearance on the horizon.

The moon emerged slowly out of the water; a glowing, ponderous sea melon. I had never seen it so big, and the shock made me feel like I wanted to cry, but instead I laughed. I tried to take a photo, but I couldn't make my camera work. Cyn scooped it from my hands and snapped the rising moon, then me. I saw my image in the display screen and was startled. My eyes appeared huge and catlike, and I had a wild look about me. We took more pictures of one another, and we remembered the rum. Jorge, who was not tripping, found us all hilarious, and kept inventing funny challenges for the brothers to attempt. Marco tried to stand on his head as instructed, and his little case fell out of his pocket and into the sand.

"My treasure!" he exclaimed, collapsing in a heap. We laughed hysterically. I looked over my shoulder, and the moon was well above the horizon, growing ever smaller. I found myself on a log by the fire. Cyn sat next to me, very close.

I heard a loud pop from the trees. Then one or two more. I thought it was a car backfiring, but then I remembered where we were.

Cyn asked what the noise was. I looked at her to see if she was afraid, because I wasn't sure if I should be, too. She looked calm.

"Ghosts," Marco said, then he laughed too high and too fast. I saw he had the little case out again.

"Firecrackers," Hector murmured, but his eyes darted to the trees and stayed there.

Cyn laughed and made a pair of guns with her hands. "*Narcotraficantes*," she said. Drug runners.

Marco stiffened. He turned and said something to Hector, which I missed because there was another loud pop. Hector rolled his eyes and shrugged, and both brothers got to their feet. They told us they would return soon.

Jorge shrugged and picked up his guitar, singing softly to his own accompaniment. I watched Hector's white T-shirt vanish into the jungle. After a few moments, I noticed that Cyn was rubbing her hand up and down my back. Maybe she could tell I was nervous, or maybe the mushrooms had made her affectionate. We sat that way, staring at the fire, for I don't know how long.

"I love you," Cyn said to me in English. I looked at her over my shoulder. Her eyes were damp and glowing.

"I know," I said in Spanish.

She got up from the log and lowered herself into the sand in front of my feet, gazing up at me. "You look so angelic in the firelight."

I smiled at her and pulled her closer to the log, away from the fire. She seemed far enough gone that she might forget it was behind her. It felt like the guys had been away for ages. Jorge abruptly stopped playing music and was staring at the trees like a spooked watchdog.

"What's going on?" I asked, startling him.

"*Nada*," he said, shaking his head. But he looked nervous. I wondered if it was the ghost thing. He snapped open his guitar case and placed the guitar inside.

"Don't you think they've been gone a long time?" I asked Cyn, dropping the Spanish.

"I don't care," she said, her pupils wide as saucers. "I'm just so glad that we're here together."

Cyn was too blasted for conversation, and now Jorge had clammed up, too. I thought looking at the man in the moon might be a nonthreatening diversion for myself, only I couldn't find the fat-cheeked face that was normally there. I could only see the silhouette of a rabbit that a Peruvian girl in our group had pointed out. The rabbit looked scraggly and feral, and I longed for the fat-faced man, with his expression of startled amazement. My eyes filled with tears. Now that I'd seen the rabbit, the man was probably gone forever.

A sudden cluster of loud pops rattled through the jungle. I locked eyes with Jorge, who now looked very frightened. He stood up and looked into the woods. I reached down and grabbed Cyn's wrist.

"What was that?" I asked.

Jorge shook his head. He picked up his guitar case and began walking toward the trees.

"Where are you going?" I demanded, my voice uncontrollably shrill.

He held up a hand and paused for a moment, listening. He looked over his shoulder at us. "I'm going to go check on something." He walked quickly toward the trail where Marco and Hector had departed and vanished into the darkness.

We were alone.

"I'm worried," I said. "He took his guitar case. Why?"

She smiled up at me. "Don't worry, Glo."

She moved next to me on the log and put her arm around me. I felt her cold lips on my cheek. Then she kissed my chin bone, then the base of my neck. I sat there, frozen and confused. She put her hands on my stomach, and I captured them, holding them tightly in mine.

"Your hands are freezing."

"Are you mad?" she whispered into my ear.

"No," I said, barely breathing, the sensation of her kisses fading more slowly than I would have imagined. *Like magic*, I found myself thinking. I wondered if her kiss was so different than mine, her lips softer, or gentler. I wondered if Raj could tell us apart in the dark . . .

Another loud pop echoed through the trees, pulling me back to the reality of the fire and the sea and the cold, damp sand.

I felt panic waiting in the wings and fought to stave it off. My best friend making a pass at me somehow didn't even faze me. She wasn't in her right mind. My real concern was the darkness behind those trees, and the mysterious noises, and the fact that we were now two women alone and fucked up. The part of me that could still manage logic told me that, best-case scenario, those noises came from other kids, partying and setting off fireworks. The worst-case scenario was that those were gunshots.

I stopped thinking about it because I knew it would freak me out and because it appeared that, between the two of us, I was by far the more sober. I'd have to take care of us somehow. The fire settled, logs collapsing like dominoes, sending a plume of sparks into the air. The fire was so low now. It hadn't been nearly that low when the guys left. Or when Jorge left. How long ago had that really been?

Cyn was rubbing my arm. "You'll have to tell Raj," she said.

"I have to tell Raj what?" I murmured, grateful for the distraction.

"That I don't love him, silly. I love you." She traced a heart shape in the sand with her toe, as if to offer my addled brain physical evidence that this conversation was really happening. "Are you mad?" she asked, again.

"I'm not mad," I repeated.

Wind rushed in from over the water, shaking the jungle and chilling my flesh. I looked up and the sky was clear, the stars frozen in place. The sound of the palms thrashing in the wind rattled my frayed nerves. When I looked at the trees, they appeared as rows of ragged women tossing their hair in despair. My heart began to race, and the air seemed to thicken like gelatin. We were abandoned, and the jungle was full of shadowy dangers. I couldn't even ask Cyn what to do because her spaceship had blasted off for another planet entirely.

A flash of movement came from the trees where Jorge had departed, and I glimpsed Hector, the front of his white T-shirt dirty and his glasses flashing in the reflected firelight. He seemed on the verge of shouting something, but in the next instant, he vanished. In that fleeting glimpse, I read something on his face that made my heart clench in fear. I stared at the place where I'd last seen him, holding my breath. When he didn't reappear, and nothing happened, I began to question whether I'd seen him at all, or if he was just a trick of the mind.

Cyn was facing the opposite direction, and she clamped her hand around my wrist and squeezed like hell. I turned to see what she saw and swallowed a scream. At the far end of the cove, three figures were climbing down the rocks and heading toward us. I didn't recognize their silhouettes. There must have been some signal in their gait or attitude that triggered an alarm in my reptile brain, because I instinctively knew these were predators. We needed to run.

"Let's go," I said, pulling Cyn to her feet. Wordlessly, we ran in the opposite direction, toward the trees at the far side of the cove. They saw us, and I heard someone shout a command to follow.

We made it to the tree line in seconds, but the jungle was impenetrable. We fought our way in against the thorny brush, but got tangled in a waist-deep bog of vegetation only a few steps in. The jungle would rip us to shreds before we were even out of sight.

"Back! Back!" I stammered, breathless with fear. "Let's go in the water. We can hide out there, behind a rock." Cyn nodded, her eyes wide and unblinking.

Over my shoulder, I saw one of the men pause by our campfire and empty our bags. The other two kept running toward us. I grabbed Cyn's arm, and we splashed into the shallow water. Cyn was tripping over the one flip-flop she was wearing. She kicked it off. I noticed as we fled that I had, at some point in the evening, strapped my sandals back on. They protected me from the broken coral and rocks in the shallows, but Cyn had no such luck. She moved tentatively, stumbling, until I began to half drag her with me.

"Glo, wait," she said, but I barely heard her.

We were knee-deep, and already the waves were strong. I saw some rocks not much farther out and made them our goal. If I'd been clearheaded, I would have realized that hiding in the water on the night of a full moon was a really shitty idea, but as things were, that realization came too late. The moon was bright enough to read by, and our retreat was plainly visible from shore.

They shouted for us to stop, but I kept powering forward. Cyn suddenly wasn't beside me. I spun around and saw her ten feet back, standing still, the only movement coming from her fingertips, which gently tickled the incoming waves at her sides.

"What's wrong?" I shouted. "Come on!"

She just stood there. "Go," she said. "I'm not afraid. Go get help."

I slogged back through the hip-deep water to get to her. I saw the two men on the shore untying their boots.

"Cyn, come on! This isn't a fucking joke!" I reached her and tried to pull her in with me, but she backed away. She had this creepy calm about her that made me wonder what she was seeing.

"I knew this would happen," she said.

The men were splashing toward us. The waves were slowing them down and they didn't seem at home in the water, but even so, in thirty seconds, they would reach us. "Cyn, please," I pleaded, "Those are bad guys. We have to swim right now!"

I grabbed her wrist and tried to pull her with me, but she yanked her arm away, and I fell back into the waves.

"Cyn!" I shrieked.

"Go." She looked down at me, half smiling, like a graveyard statue. I sputtered in helpless disbelief, not understanding that she wasn't going to come with me. I glimpsed the men approaching behind her.

"Come on!" I shouted.

"Go," she repeated, and this time, I obeyed. I slipped beneath the waves and swam.

It was all darkness. I pumped my arms and legs as hard as I could, staying submerged. I tried to swim parallel to the shore, navigating by the pull of the tide. I had a hazy idea where the larger rocks were, and that was where I was going. I popped my head above water, gasping for air, trying to keep low. Two more breaths and my knee cracked against a submerged rock. Grimacing at the white-hot explosion of pain, I clutched onto the slick stone, crab-like. Raising my head, I heard Cyn screaming. I clung to the rock and swiveled to see what was happening. A wave rolled over me, bashing my cheek into the rock, but I felt no pain. The terror, or maybe the exertion of the swim, neutralized the effect of the mushrooms, because everything seemed shockingly clear and awful. Cyn shrieked again, a high-pitched siren, and I realized she was saying "No!" I peeked out from behind the rock and saw one of the men wading back toward shore, dragging Cyn with him. Cyn was reaching toward the water, shouting "No, no, no, no."

Her screams were devastating to hear. I wanted to cry out to her, or swim back and join her in her fate, but I kept silent. It wasn't because I had heroic notions that by staying hidden I could get help, as she'd suggested. I was just paralyzed with fear. The other man was still in the water, searching for me. Cyn was dropped onto the sand at the feet of the man who was giving orders. She sprang up, and he grabbed her arms. She struggled to face the water, looking for me.

"She can't swim," I heard her scream in Spanish. She screamed it three times, fighting the man who was trying to restrain her as she thrashed like a wild animal. Then her words were muffled. I didn't see what happened, because the man in the water shone a flashlight in my direction. I clung tightly to the rock, getting slammed repeatedly against its rough, slimy surface by waves I had forgotten were coming. When I dared to look again, he was swinging the beam across the water in the other direction. He turned around and raised his arms in a "beats me" gesture. The man on the beach, the leader, waved him back in. Cyn was sitting on the sand, eerily quiet.

I watched as Cyn was pulled to her feet, the leader speaking to her. I couldn't hear a thing, but I could see she was hanging her head and shaking it back and forth, as if answering questions. They pointed to the fire. She shook her head. One of them pulled out something that produced a light, and they showed it to Cyn. I realized it was my camera. They were looking through the photos. She kept shaking her head. The leader shouted something at Cyn, and I saw her cower. He strode away from the beach toward the trees, and the other two followed, pulling her along with them. She tried to resist, but the leader took her by the arm and dragged her into the darkness.

I waited a long count to ten after the beach was empty before I dared to swim back in. My thoughts were chaotic, but I was feeling hopeful. I hadn't heard any more popping sounds, and the men hadn't been violent with Cyn. I didn't have even a clue who these men were. They might have been park rangers, for all I knew. But even if they were bad guys, she was the smartest girl I knew. If anyone could outwit a horde of potential criminals, it was Cyn.

From where I exited the water, I could see that the bags we had brought were spread out over the ground by the dying fire. It wasn't the smartest move to run out into the open, but I thought there was a chance one of the brothers had brought a phone. A phone meant instant help. I had to try.

I raced across the beach, staying as low as possible. The wind had picked up, and as I rummaged frantically through the items scattered in the sand, I began to shiver. I found my flashlight, half buried, but no phones. I cursed, thinking of my own cell phone tucked into my desk drawer in Florida. I'd thought leaving it behind was the shrewd choice; just one more fuckup to add to the ever-expanding list.

Suddenly I froze. Another cue from my reptile brain told me that someone was watching. I whipped my head around and saw . . . nothing. I stood there dumbfounded, too numb even to cry. I watched a huge jungle ant totter across a wide patch of sand by my toes, my mind a hopeless blank of pure fear.

I had left her. It didn't matter that she'd wanted me to go. I should never have left her.

I sank to my knees in the sand, no longer mindful of being discovered, and wrapped my arms around myself, rocking slowly back and forth. I don't know how long I stayed that way, submerged in misery, but at some point, a better thought burst through my self-recriminations: maybe it wasn't too late.

She'd asked me to get help. Hell, she'd ordered me to. I had to live up to her sacrifice. I had to save her.

I snatched my flashlight out of the sand and hurried to the edge of the beach. I didn't even know what I was searching for, but my adrenaline was racing and I needed to move. Cyn's pink flip-flop was washing in and out with the tide. I saw the footprints of the men who'd taken her. I snapped on the flashlight to see them better, like fucking Nancy Drew. I had no idea what I should be doing. Crabs scurried away from me in all directions, mirroring my disordered wits. Then my flashlight hit something that made my heart climb into my throat. Etched clearly into the sand, among the chaos of footprints, was another heart shape. She had left a message for me. She was counting on me.

I choked back a sob, and then bit my tongue hard, trying to snap out of it.

I had two options: find Cyn myself or get off the island and get help. Either way, I'd have to cross through the jungle.

I followed the footsteps up toward the path. The palm leaves were crashing together in the wind, practically waving me away. I lost my footing in the loose sand that led up to the path, landing on all fours, and as I slid, I was certain I glimpsed a beam of light cutting down the trail.

I scrambled sideways, into the meager cover of the scrub palms. I embraced the spiny fronds like a lover, trying to blend into the darkness. Something stung my wrist, and I inadvertently rose and stumbled sideways, toward the trees. Momentum carried me to the cusp of the jungle, but a crunching sound from close by—footsteps—spurred me deeper.

A few feet into the trees, everything went pitch-black, but I didn't dare use the flashlight and risk giving myself away. Barbed ferns ripped into my flesh, a sharp reminder of why Cyn and I had abandoned the jungle for the water, and the frayed ends of my wet cutoffs quickly became entangled on burred branches. I shredded my fingers trying to free myself, but the tough denim fibers wouldn't give, leaving me anchored where I stood. I heard a crashing sound coming from where I had entered, and I grabbed the branch that held me captive and ripped it off near the trunk. With the bramble still dangling at my side, I took a few frantic steps only to realize that I had gotten turned around during my struggle with the plant. I wasn't sure which direction I had come from, or which way I ought to flee. Fighting panic, I attempted to shuffle in the direction I judged to be uphill, dragging the branch with me as I climbed. A limb snapped behind me, and I impulsively ditched the shorts and the branch in one easy step.

Down to my wet bikini bottom, I moved more carefully. The horror of my situation was threatening to shut me down completely. The dark jungle was more terrifying than any nightmare I'd ever suffered. I knew every step in the darkness risked disturbing deadly, poisonous creatures, and a million other torments. Branches carved deep gashes into me, and I sensed that my skin was crawling with insects. The jungle pulsed with the clamor of wholly unwelcoming species. The noise would periodically quiet, only to rise again in a deafening roar of clattering wings and feverishly twitching membranes. I cowered and covered my ears, waiting for it to pass, trying to think of anything but where I was, trying not to feel my skin where it tickled from god knows what touch, or the burn of the ants that were savaging my feet, or otherwise register any sensory information about my increasing collection of wounds.

In the jungle, I forgot about Cyn and I forgot about the men. If one had suddenly popped out in front of me, I think I would have welcomed the distraction. My fear receptors were saturated beyond capacity. On the brink of losing it, I forced myself to take step after step, graced by the sudden fantasy that I was moving through snow; a photonegative snow world, where black was white and hot was cold. I forced myself to believe in the snow. I told myself that the snow was deep, which was why walking was so difficult, but it was pure and white and there was nothing in it that could harm me. The pain didn't go away, but after a while, pain is just the same message over and over. I could ignore it. My imagination, on the other hand, could undo me. Call it a feat of concentration or a holy hallucination, but for a few crucial moments, there was only me and deep, soft snow.

My polar survival fantasy kept me lifting left after right, and I eventually arrived at the base of a small plateau. I grabbed roots and vines and climbed. As I pulled myself up to the top, the collected jungle chorus was rising into another frenzy of deafening vibration. I fell into a squat and covered my ears, clenching my eyes shut. I reminded myself that I was on a small iceberg, and that if I snowshoed far enough, I would reach the water and I could take an icy plunge, erasing everything. When I eased my hands off my ears, the jungle was quieter. I opened my eyes and saw that I was kneeling on the edge of what might have been a trail. I crawled onto it and brushed myself off frantically, head to toe, in a fitful spasm. I still felt things crawling on me, but not being as closely surrounded by a crush of hostile life was a monumental improvement.

I edged along the trail, moving quickly but still freezing at every sound like a hunted doe. The trail seemed to twist on forever. I startled at shadows and at the ground, which now that I could see it illuminated by patches of moonlight, appeared to be slithering. The path grew sandier, and I prayed that I wouldn't find myself back at the sunset cove. Up ahead, moonlight poured onto the path, I rushed toward it. Nothing can compare to how beautiful the shimmering water looked to my eyes at that moment. I advanced onto the beach and saw a depression in the sand where a boat had recently rested. Jorge had left us. Maybe they all had left us.

I stared across at the twinkling lights on the mainland. The jungle swayed ominously behind me. The island was so small. If the men were looking for me, they would find me on the beach. It was only a matter of time.

I wanted very badly to scream, but there were many reasons not to. Instead, I tried to access my brain—at that point, a very dicey proposition. I was fairly sure that tides changed every twelve hours, and it'd been sunset when we'd crossed. I didn't have the foggiest idea what time it was. The sky was inky black in all directions, no hint of sunrise. I couldn't fathom idly waiting for the tides to change while Cyn needed my help, and I couldn't for a second stomach the idea of hiding in the jungle, waiting to see if the men would hunt me down.

That left only one option.

I ripped open the Velcro on my sandals and kicked them off.

It had taken about twenty minutes to walk across the channel. It couldn't be that far, even if I would be coming from a slightly different point on the island. I'd also have the waves to help carry me in toward the end.

I began to do a few basic stretches, trying not to think about rip currents, or jellyfish, or sharks. At the thought of the latter, I felt my resolve weaken. I had greedily consumed countless shark documentaries in my short life, never thinking that they would come back to haunt me at my darkest hour. I took a deep breath and tied my hair into a fat knot behind my neck as I waded out into the water, the salt igniting my lacerations.

Then I began to swim.

At the start of my crossing, the wind had stilled and the ocean was calm. I employed my basic crawl, a stroke as second nature to me as walking. I would count off fifty strokes and stop to check my orientation. There was a bright orange light on the shore that I made my beacon. Any thoughts that rushed to my head of sharks, or disappearing brothers, or missing friends were quashed. My job was only to count strokes and keep breathing; habit took care of the rest.

After my sixth cycle of fifty, I began to worry. The land wasn't getting any closer and the wind had picked up. Waves began to slap my face when I tried to breathe. Each time, I'd have to stop and tread water for a few moments, giving my imagination the opportunity to conjure up some choice *Jaws* scenarios. Dorsal fins phantomed in and out of my peripheral vision, scaring me back into motion. Eight more sets of fifty and I caught my second wind, but I still didn't seem any closer to shore. The thought that I might be trapped in a current that could whip me around the island and out into the Pacific, never to be seen again, shot me full of fresh terror. Using the extra burst of adrenaline that came when I pictured my skeleton picked bare by barracudas, I kicked into a sprint. I stopped counting after one hundred strokes. Waves were slapping me, my hair was wrapped around my neck, and to my horror, one of my feet began to tingle with an incipient cramp. I rolled onto my back and floated, trying to relax and rest my foot. Floating, I saw the moon and the shadowy eye sockets of the goddamn man in it, very small and very far away. I bobbed on the choppy waves, newly conscious of my exhaustion. I could hardly feel my shoulders, and my upper arms felt like logs. As I flipped over to continue the swim, I noticed that one corner of the sky had begun to blush ever so slightly. No night is ever truly endless.

Either the muscle in my foot relaxed or I got used to the pain. I kept pushing forward, and before long, land was not looking so impossibly distant. My knee hit a sandbar, and I collapsed there, gasping for my breath. The shore directly before me was undeveloped, rocky headland backed by jungle. My orange light was far off to the right, illuminating a stretch of empty beach. Further along, almost beyond the reach of the light, I could make out the faint outline of boat hulls on the sand. Hopefully, that meant people were sleeping not far away. I got to my feet on the sandbar. The water was shallow enough that it was easier to wade along it than swim, and I dragged my exhausted body toward the light. As if in answer to my wishes, I saw a cluster of electric lanterns appear on the beach: fishermen, heading out for the morning catch.

I began shouting for help as I sloshed toward them along the sandbar. The fishermen swiveled in confusion, not understanding where the sound was coming from. When they finally spotted me beyond the surf, they began to call out. I was so wrecked and so full of relief, that I can't be certain what I was shouting. I'm sure it included the words "police," "boat," and "help."

A few fishermen rushed into the water, and I flung myself off the sandbar and began swimming for the shore. Two men helped carry me onto the sand.

In my confused state, what I wanted was for them to take me right back over to the island in their boat, and to help me find Cyn. The fishermen gathered around me on the sand as I raved and pointed. Examining their shadow-lined faces in the darkness, I wasn't sure if they understood anything at all. I kept repeating "*¿Comprenden?*" over and over until one of them lifted me and carried me up to a beach shack where there was an electric light and a phone.

They took a look at me in the light, with my cuts and bruises and undoubtedly wild look. I saw one of them cross himself. Someone forced a bottle of water to my lips and told me to be calm. I emptied the bottle and in an instant, felt a million times stronger. I sat up from the couch where they'd placed me and began re-pleading my case. As they stared at me in wonder, I explained that my friend had been taken by strange men, *dangerous* men, and that it was up to me to save her. I pointed at the phone and told them to call the police.

With all of that out, I closed my mouth and lay back in exhaustion, waiting for my wishes to be put into action. Instead, to my horror, everyone in the room began to argue at once. No one made so much as a move toward the phone. Instead of waiting for a consensus to be reached, I resolved to make the call myself. I stood up and headed for the phone. The room went spinny, and streaks of red and black raced across my vision. Lost in their debate, my rescuers didn't notice I had moved. I saw my finger graze the handset of the wall phone, then everything went dark.

When I came to, it was daybreak and the rain was pouring down. I was in the back of a covered pickup truck. A young woman was sitting on a bench near my head. Two men and another woman with a baby also gradually came into focus. They weren't speaking, and they looked tense. The car hit a bump and I felt a wave of nausea. I closed my eyes.

Cyn was there in the cab with me. I hadn't turned my head, and I hadn't seen her, but I knew she was lying there beside me. I could smell her. If I wiggled my fingers, I was certain to touch her arm, but I was too tired. They must have rescued her, or maybe she swam away, too. I wanted to tell her that I couldn't wait to hear what her story was, that I was so glad she was safe. I could tell her later. I closed my eyes and relaxed into unconsciousness.

The sound of the rotating fan was the ocean, and the pages of my chart fluttering in its wake, palm leaves, swaying in the breeze. When I opened my eyes, or I guess I should say, my eye, since one was so badly scratched they had taped it closed, I was amazed to discover myself not beachside, but in a hospital bed. There was someone in the room, a woman.

"Where am I?" I asked in English. Before I could try again in Spanish, the nurse rushed out of the room. She returned with a handsome doctor in his midthirties. He addressed me in English.

"Hello, I'm Dr. Bayer. You're in a hospital. Do you remember your name?"

"American?" I rasped. My lips, when I explored them with my tongue, were broken and cracked, and the parts that were intact felt like plastic. The nurse offered me a sweet, fruity fluid through a straw.

"I'm American, yes. You're in a hospital in San Jose. Do you remember your name?"

"Gloria Roebuck. My friend, where is she?"

He looked at the nurse, who shot him a "no idea" look.

"We'll check on that," he said.

"We came together." I insisted. "Cynthia Williams. A blond girl. My age."

Dr. Bayer stared at me with concern, but no understanding manifested on his face. The painful thought that I had imagined her in the truck cab with me snaked across my mind. Had she really not been rescued?

"If she's not here, you have to find her. She was with me, on the island. Some men took her. She's out there all alone."

Based on how my luck was going, I expected the doctor to ignore me or sedate me, but instead, he came closer, interested. "Your friend is also an American?"

This small display of understanding almost made me break down, but I was finally getting somewhere.

"Yes. We're students. We went to that island, the haunted one near Playa Tortuga, with some local guys, Hector and Marco." I paused, since the doctor had produced a pad and began taking notes. "There were noises, like gunshots, and they spooked our friends, and it was just the two of us alone, and then these men came, and my friend . . . I tried to make her come with me, but she wouldn't. The men, they took her."

The memory of her expression at the moment when she told me to go appeared from within my memory, as perfect as a Polaroid. Everything that had hurt me that night, and all that I'd suffered was dwarfed by the helpless confusion I suddenly felt. It occurred to me that there was a chance I would never get to ask her why.

The thought broke me.

I lost it.

I was sedated.

When I awoke, I was confronted with a plate of chicken, rice, and beans, and the first of many cops.

You know the rest.

Part II

What Happened After

Seven Years Later

CHAPTER EIGHT

Glo

The coffee mug slipped from my wet hand as I rinsed it, shattering a dish resting beneath it in the sink with a jarring crash. I reached instinctively for the broken plate, as if my quick intervention might somehow undo the damage. My sudsy fingers fumbled across the razor-sharp edge of cornflower-blue porcelain, and I jerked my hand back with a yelp. I looked down and watched a stream of crimson rush across my palm. There was a crescent-shaped gash across my finger just above my wedding band, long but shallow. I thrust the digit under the faucet and cringed as a deeper pain ran up my arm.

"Everything okay?" Raj's voice rolled in sleepily from the living room.

"There's been a casualty. A bread plate. I think we're down to five." *Not too bad*, I thought, wincing as I applied pressure with a paper towel. Only three dishes of that size lost in the three years we'd been married. As long as we didn't plan to throw any dinner parties, we'd be good for another two years at least.

"You're bleeding," he observed, looking up from his phone as I crossed through the room. He rose, preceding me on my way to the bathroom.

"Let Dr. Raj get you a Band-Aid."

The bathroom was still steamy from my shower. He set

aside the tampons that I had forgotten to stash underneath the counter, and in their place, snapped open the first aid kit. In a few days, I would need to go to the pharmacy for another month of birth control, a task I was reluctant to do. The previous night, as my pelvic muscles twisted like taffy, we discussed it again. Or I discussed it, and Raj gazed out the window with a look of studious consideration, humoring me. I knew his position. There was no reason to rush into starting a family. He'd only just gotten his theater company on its feet, and while he brought in a respectable amount of money through his jobs as an actor and voice-over artist, playing a know-it-all beaver on a show aimed toward preliterate children, my salary was by far the more regular. Why not wait until we established ourselves a little more comfortably?

Because the timing was as good as it would ever be. Before we got hitched, we wisely had the whole "kids or no kids" talk and had decisively pointed our compass toward the horizon that read "Kids: at least one, not too many." Now we were three years married, seven years as a couple, and Raj's paternal appetite had apparently dissolved into the ether. I sensed that if I was foolish enough to wait for him to feel really, *really* ready, it would be long after my eggs had become pocked and dusty, tucked away in the dark like a forgotten string of freshwater pearls.

He excised a Band-Aid from its wrapper and pressed it against the cut. I flinched.

"Sorry. Okay?"

I nodded. He carefully wrapped the Band-Aid around my finger, making it snug, but not so tight that it would begin to purple and ache. Then he kissed it. All of this care, this kindness, came so naturally to him. It was as if every moment he was flaunting his ideal qualities as a father, perpetually acing auditions for a job he claimed not to want yet.

"You have blood on your blouse. Maybe that's good for court? Sends a strong message?"

"No court today. Just meetings." I removed my blouse and pulled out the stain remover, dabbing it on the mark. I looked up to see my husband giving me wolf eyes.

"Morning meetings?" he asked.

"Did you perhaps miss the huge box of tampons on the counter?" I watched the mischievous glow fade from his features at the reference to my meddlesome uterus. He balled up the bandage's wrapper and kissed me behind the ear.

"Drats."

"It's not a permanent condition," I reminded him, standing up a little straighter. His eyes lingered on my body as he slipped out the door. I did love the way he looked at me. He was around stunningly beautiful actresses on a daily basis, but not once did I ever see him give any of them what I thought of as *my* look. There was only one other person who had ever made his eyes shine like that, and she was long gone.

My eyes slipped down to the small makeup case where I kept my only souvenir of Cyn, her silver necklace with the star shaped charm. She'd been wearing it the morning we met at orientation, and I'd coveted it even then. Now that it was mine, I never wore it, but sometimes, in late January when my thoughts were inevitably pulled back to that cove, I would take it out and look at it. Sometimes I would shed a tear or two for the girl who had vanished from the planet without a trace.

The Costa Rican police didn't find much to help clear up the mystery. While I had been lying dead to the world in my hospital bed, it had stormed for hours, washing away all the footprints and scattering anything else that might have passed as evidence. The most monumental discovery was a handful of fresh bullet casings and a nearly empty diesel fuel tank. No one knew what exactly to make of it, but an FBI guy let it slip to my dad that the US government had been tracking drug-smuggling submarines in those waters for some time. They hadn't found one yet, and didn't want to alert the public that they were nosing around, lest word get back to their targets. The logical presumption was that the brothers had the misfortune of crossing paths with the smugglers, and died for it. Cyn likely suffered a similar fate. But I knew it had to be worse. It was always worse for women.

My parents, doing what Cyn's parents should have been doing if they hadn't checked out of her life, kept pressing for further investigation but were categorically shut down. The message we received was that discovering the exact details surrounding the death of one American student wasn't worth endangering a massive smuggling sting. Cyn was just gone. Everyone was very sorry. That was it.

Before I made it out the front door, Raj pulled me close, his fingers lingering to caress the tender skin around my collar. "I miss you," he said breathily. I wondered for a moment if our anniversary had passed without my noticing, or my birthday; he wasn't usually so ardent on a random workday morning.

"The weekend's almost here," I said consolingly, even though it didn't mean much of a break for us. Raj had recently landed his first-ever major role in a Broadway show, playing the dashing, if naive, doctor in a British parlor comedy called *The Queen's Keys*. The show was getting great reviews, and it was wonderful for his career. The additional money it brought in was like a steady rain falling on parched land; we'd needed it for so long that it would take a while to make a difference, but we were grateful. The real price we paid was in our time together. My office hours clashed with his night- and weekend-performance schedule, and then there was his theater company gobbling up not only all his available free time, but his mental and emotional energy. I often felt like a single woman, perpetually dining alone in front of the television or playing the third wheel on nights out with our couple friends. I missed him. I missed us. I wondered, often, what *us* would look like in five years' time if nothing changed.

Feeling lonely is an astoundingly dumb reason to have a child, my rational mind chided as I stepped out of our building into the cold, damp air of early spring. My finger began to throb, and I pulled my coat tighter, crossing against the Don't Walk sign to the sunny side of the street. The trees on our block in Astoria, Queens, were still bare of buds. The naked branches reached hopefully past the brick buildings toward the sky, as if imploring the heavens for a warm respite after the long, bitter winter.

If I was honest with myself, I could admit that my desire for a baby was less about a burning hunger for a tiny bundle of joy and more a reaction to the sense that I was fading into the background of Raj's frenetic life. I was lonelier than I had been in a very long time, and I felt his rejection of the very idea of a child as further proof that his notion of our future was possibly less everlasting than my own. The thought made me so sad, and I didn't know whether it was real or just my insecurities rising like the phoenix any time I wasn't the focus of Raj's limelight. The truth was, all I really needed was for him to call my bluff and say "Sure, let's try!" With that sense of permanence in my back pocket, I could wait another year, or five.

I rounded the corner and was smacked with a blast of icy wind that blew right through my wool coat, making me shiver. *You chose this place,* I reminded myself for the thousandth time. And despite the perils of winter, I really loved New York. It had saved us.

The last thing I expected upon touching down on American soil after Costa Rica was for Raj to come to me. The world seemed to me so horrible a place that I all but expected Raj to disappear from my life entirely, just as Cyn had done. But he didn't. He appeared at my parents' front door, ashen and exhausted, speaking words of love, and as firmly as I turned him down and turned him away, he didn't give up.

With Cyn's words about Raj's true feelings echoing in my head, I set him on a task that I thought would put an end to all his nonsense about loving me. He hadn't been at the island, so Cyn's death was to him, still nebulous. Once he was forced to acknowledge that the girl he really loved was gone, I was certain his tune would change.

The task was to go back to our dorm and gather up Cyn's possessions. To me, who was afraid to set foot back on campus, it seemed an impossible ordeal, like something out of a Greek myth. I couldn't imagine climbing those steps and passing under the familiar threshold strung with white Christmas lights. I couldn't bear the thought of seeing all her things; her clothes, her shoes, her seventeen pairs of sunglasses, none of it ever to be touched by her again.

But the school wanted all of our stuff out, so I sent Raj to take care of it with my dad. I expected the task to undo him. As he sorted through her belongings on the all-weather carpet, he would have time to think, and time to let go of her piece by glittery piece. With her passing a reality, he would acknowledge that he had to let me go, too, because how could he ever look at me without thinking of her? I expected a break up call from campus, and stayed within earshot of the phone all day, blackening the eyes of all the models in my mother's *Health & Fitness* magazine as I waited for news of the end.

But that hadn't happened. He'd returned that night with my father, hauling a carful of my things that would be dumped into storage, unbrowsed by me. I wasn't ready.

He looked as drained as I'd ever seen him as he came into my childhood room, collapsing onto a bedspread that was marred with the battle scars of one hundred sloppy manicures.

"It's done," he said, slipping something into my hand. It

was the silver star necklace. "I saw it hanging on her lava lamp. I couldn't give it to the Goodwill. She'd have wanted you to have it."

I squeezed it in my fist until the spires of the star poked deep into the meat of my palms.

"If you don't want it, you can maybe find a way to send it to her sister."

I nodded, unable to speak. We both knew I'd keep it. I was her sister, too.

"How bad was it?"

He sighed, and I saw a sheen appear on his clear, dark eyes. "Your dad kept it light. We listened to a lot of sports radio while we worked."

He smiled at me, and I saw what it was costing him to keep it together. I pulled him into my arms, and held him close. He didn't cry, but I could almost feel the sadness in his body like a layer of varnish on his bones.

"What did you keep for yourself?" I asked after a long time had passed.

He sat up, and looking deeply into my face, took the fist that held the necklace and kissed it lightly. The bandages had come off, and there were scars, light pink like birthday frosting, webbing my flesh. "You, I hope."

We knew that we would leave Florida. Our plans were so amorphous at that point that our decision between New York and California was decided by the flip of a Sacajawea dollar coin. We trusted her intrepid spirit to guide us with care, and heads meant New York City.

Raj grinned and kissed the carved metal face of our talisman. "Awesome. Hot dogs, every day."

Not even Sacajawea could secure us a soft landing in the Empire State, driving up as we had in the dead of winter in a jittery U-Haul, our newly purchased thrift store furniture do-sido-ing noisily behind us all the way up I-95. My parents were understandably chagrined about me putting my education on hold and moving to a neighborhood in Brooklyn with a terrifying reputation, but they were also desperate. I saw in their eyes that the new me, the gloomy, nihilistic zombie that sat at the table masked as their daughter, was even more frightening to them. For a chance at getting the real me back, they would trade anything, including their peace of mind.

We rented our first apartment in Bed-Stuy sight unseen, except for a couple of shady pictures posted on Craigslist. We liked it because it was in Brooklyn, which we heard was cool, and because it had those three-sided bay windows like the house on *The Cosby Show*. It also helped that the landlord didn't care about credit checks or a verifiable rent history. He just wanted a big deposit. We sent a check and prayed that someone would meet us to hand over a key.

The night before we set eyes on our new home, we stopped at a fleabag motel in Jersey called the Swan. The bearded receptionist sat slumped behind a heavy plastic safety window watching television; a shelf of liquor, smokes, and condoms lined the wall behind him. Our room featured a double bed pressed disconcertingly close to a heart-shaped Jacuzzi, ringed with a mossy fur of soap scum. Raj sat up half the night, peering out the window at every sound, worried that someone might commandeer the U-Haul that contained our empire.

Raj's parents weren't as understanding about him leaving school. His father stopped speaking to him, and while his mother was slightly more conciliatory, it was months before she would speak my name. I was "She" or "Your girlfriend," or, when she was being cruel, "The invalid." I think that after what happened, she viewed Cyn and me interchangeably, a pair of equally bad influences on her charming second son, who came so close to doing as she, her husband, and her eldest son had done: gotten that precious medical degree. Raj would never be a doctor, but at least he looked the part enough to play one onstage. For me, it was enough that he could apply a decent Band-Aid.

Once we married, our relationship with his parents improved, though it remained strained. As time trudged onward and Raj failed to tire of me, I could see them making efforts not to be outwardly judgmental, and by the time they visited our current apartment in Queens, they were able to disguise their chagrin with relative success. Our place isn't a palace, but it's a real find for the price, with a dedicated office for Raj and a view of the Triborough Bridge. His father had walked through the space, grimacing with each step, as if he were, at that moment, macerating glass. His mother opened a closet, expecting to find another bedroom, and an errant broom handle tipped out and hit her in the eye. But they didn't actually criticize the place, or Raj's life choices. That was really an improvement, especially because they had just taken the train in from Long Island, where Raj's older brother had recently purchased a vacation house, flush with money after being named "North Carolina's Best Dermatologist," two years running, by *Southern Health* magazine.

As we shivered through that first achingly cold winter in Brooklyn, we were acting on faith, hoping that by drastically changing our location, we might be able to put Costa Rica and all that it symbolized behind us. We naively thought that the world would accommodate our plan for a fresh start, but in New York, my phone never stopped ringing. Every television network had a talking head afflicted with the insatiable desire to rehash the minutiae of our disaster. There was even discussion of a TV movie. The idea of speaking publicly about Cyn made me sick, but the money the networks offered was nigh irresistible. I admit, I would have done it. We were totally broke. Problem was, the networks always wanted both of us: me and Raj together. Raj flatly refused, standing firm even as we stared down the barrel of two sets of tuition bills and astonishingly high rent for that decrepit studio in Bed-Stuy.

I cried all the time those first few months. I cried when rats left droppings across our pillows. I cried when the only job I could find was a minimum-wage retail gig at a children's clothing store called Rag Tag! I cried, secretly, when Raj was accepted into the Actors Studio, thinking that he would soon be leaving my sorry ass behind for some glamorous, bubbly actress. I was a mess. My depression, so impenetrable that it made my Big U episode look like a mild case of the blues, made me miserable to be around. But Raj, my closest, dearest person, somehow caught the brunt of all my agita, and like an enchanted circus juggler, picked it up, tossed it into the air, and handed something wonderful back to me each and every day. I never realized he had such an optimistic streak, but he kept promising me things would get better, and eventually they did.

The darkness faded, replaced by intense moments of discovery and new delights. We watched the sunrise, drinking forties on rooftops with new friends. We strolled hand in hand for hours, strafing the streets of Manhattan, filling our eyes, ears, and noses with a kaleidoscope of stimuli that would later color our dreams. We frequented cheap taquerias, became slaves to Chinatown's dumpling alleys, and haunted the grimiest happy hour bars on the Lower East Side, lavishing our laundry quarters on the jukebox. Hardly anyone knew our story or suspected that we were ever temporarily famous. I grew grateful that Raj had the foresight to turn down the TV money. I liked just being Glo and Raj, without the inglorious past.

As Raj began his conservatory program, I decided it was time to get my own act together. I figured out the minimum credits I needed to complete my BA and signed up for night school. I was done with being a perpetual undergrad, and classwork gave me something to focus on while Raj was away nights, rehearsing. Raj pulled in some cash doing administrative work at his school, and inveterate student that he was, audited directing courses on the side. We didn't buy anything, ever, other than food, booze, and my textbooks, but we were happy. My night school classes were cake compared to Tiny U, and my graduating GPA was sky-high. I didn't take a break to celebrate, though. My sights were fixed on law school. With my wacky transcript, I knew I'd need to ace the LSAT to get accepted anywhere.

Raj took one look at my encyclopedic LSAT study manual and paled. "Honey, you don't have to do this," he'd whispered, as if I'd volunteered to have my arm removed and replaced with a shovel. But I did want to do it. I knew I wasn't the most analytic person by nature, but I was methodical and could process a lot of information. I thought it might even be a way for me to do some good in the world.

"Is this because of her?" he'd asked one night as I struggled, near tears, with the logic games in the practice drills. Before Costa Rica, I'd never mentioned the possibility of a law career, so I understood why Raj might think that it was a reaction to my being, for a short time, a suspected criminal. But my true reasons were less romantic and more practical. Raj's income showed no promise of ever being steady, and our debt was massive and growing. Something my dad said after receiving my lawyer Nocomment's first invoice had also stuck in my head: "*This asshole charges like his goddamn minutes are gilded in platinum.*" I'd seen firsthand what Nocomment could do. I was smarter. I was sure as hell better with people. I could swing this lawyer thing, no problem. I could be the one to save us and make it up to Raj for the many times he'd saved me.

But I didn't become a big-money corporate lawyer. I became a justice-seeking lawyer, prosecuting shifty business owners for the State of New York. It wasn't sexy, nor was it what I'd planned, but for getting a late start on a career, I thought I was doing pretty well. Certainly, I had days that left me questioning whether there were any honest people left in the world, or if my work was making any difference, but even those days were okay, because I'd get to go home to Raj. Those, of course, were the days when I still saw him in the evenings. Now most nights, I struggled to stay awake late enough to spend an hour with him when he returned. I usually didn't make it.

I emerged from the subway near my office and headed toward the deli. As I took a place in line, I told myself that I was there just for coffee but knew full well that I would be walking out with a fresh pack of cigarettes. They helped soothe my cramps, and as it appeared that breeding would not be in the cards for the coming month, I saw nothing wrong with indulging myself. Raj disapproved of my casual habit; vocally, and at length. It had begun in law school for the simple, stupid reason that the smokers in my class seemed to be the cool kids. And it reminded me of Cyn. I missed her, and in a way, I still wanted to be where she'd want to be, going so far as to view potential new friends through the lens of her imagined approval.

Raj wouldn't be home when I returned. Like a bloodhound, he could always sniff out the days I'd had a cigarette or four, and then the sanctimonious lecture would commence. I could shower after the gym post-work, and he'd be none the wiser. I knew that sneaking smokes was a particularly pathetic form of passive aggression, but no one ever gets everything they want in this world, so why should Raj? A few cigarettes was no big deal, and if he wanted me to quit completely, well, he knew what would motivate me.

I ordered my coffee and my smokes. As I opened my purse, I felt a strange tickle at the back of my neck and turned my head to look out the store's front window. There was nothing immediately remarkable. A bus was making a tremendous racket as it rose up on its hydraulics, doors closing as it pulled away from the curb. My eye dragged along its windows, idly, until my attention snagged taut like a fishing line, caught by the uncanny familiarity of one passenger, her profile distinct among the throng.

Nope, I thought, because this happened regularly. Thinking of smokes had made me think of Cyn, so now my subconscious sought to "find" her for me. Any blonde, any female for that matter, could be pegged, scanned, analyzed, and dismissed in this pathological game that my mind so adored. It always ended the same. Not Cyn.

But the woman in profile, she rattled me. The set of her jaw as she looked down, studying something in her lap, the light-colored hair tucked behind a distinctive swirl of ear. The lips, pursed in serious thought. I *knew* that face.

I leaned over the counter, suddenly desperate to catch another glimpse of the now-vanished woman seated at the bus window. The clerk looked at me strangely and repeated the price of my order. A man behind me coughed impatiently.

Mechanically, I grabbed a bill from my wallet and thrust it forward. The clerk repeated the total, and I realized I was offering only a fiver. Not enough. Flush with a sudden sweat, I seized a twenty and slapped it on the counter. The clerk took an eternity to make change, which I shoved in a disordered handful into my purse before rushing out onto the windy street.

The bus was stopped at a light, two blocks away. If I ran, I could catch it, and possibly, probably, confirm to myself that I was again imagining things. I hesitated. *It wasn't her*, I told myself. How could it be?

The light turned green, and the bus progressed slowly down the street, tantalizingly close.

Go see, an inner voice urged.

I stared after the bus, reminding myself that I had been looking through two layers of grimy glass, that I hadn't slept very well the night before, that I was probably overdue a new prescription for my contacts. These were all adequate reasons not to chase the bus, but they did nothing to silence the counterargument, a blaring klaxon of alarm exploding inside my head, making my heart pound like a marathoner's.

I stood motionless in the stream of commuters, hesitating. The bus stopped again, now three blocks away.

I began to run, the searing-hot coffee sloshing out through the loose lid, burning the back of my hand and making my cut finger sting furiously. I dashed through a flashing Don't Walk signal and half leapt over a dachshund that appeared out of nowhere.

Someone shouted, "Watch it, lady!" but I didn't even pause. At each step along the sidewalk, I darted past coat-sheathed bodies shuffling slowly like emperor penguins, newspaper boxes, rickety tables piled high with hats and scarves, coffee carts with lines four-deep. Everything was an obstacle, and the bus kept creeping away, so close, but just out of reach.

Stop this madness, I told myself. I knew I looked crazy. I tossed my coffee into a trash can; I had already spilled most of it down my leg when dodging the dog. A traffic light changed, and I was forced to wait. I craned my neck to see past a garbage truck that was blocking my sight lines to the bus. As each second dragged on, I felt my chances slipping away. The intersection quickly clogged with cars, and I squeezed between a pair of taxis to the next block.

The sidewalk opened up, and I increased my pace to a full sprint, heedless of the poor traction of my wobbly kitten heels. As people and store windows blurred past, I had the sensation of being in a horror movie. I was chasing something that I sensed I didn't want to see. I was the girl venturing down into the dark basement of my past on a stormy night to check the faulty circuit breaker. It could only lead to one thing.

The bus was only a block away. I would make it. I took a step into the street, past a halal cart setting up by the curb, too focused on the bus to realize the light was green for oncoming traffic. A horn blared, and I turned my head to see a cab flying toward me. I saw its front left tire lift into the air as it hit a pothole, meters away. I didn't have time to cross, and my forward momentum was uncontrollable. I was going to get hit by a fucking taxi.

I watched it come at me, holding my breath, waiting for impact like some dumb, cloven creature.

I felt something squeeze my forearm like a vise, and I spun backward toward the curb, pirouetting down to my knees on the gritty asphalt. I felt the whoosh of air and heard the still-blaring horn change in pitch as the taxi shot past where I had been standing one second before. I looked up to see the halal cart owner staring down at me with a mixture of disgust and concern. He hadn't removed his hands from my arm and, breathing heavily, helped me to my feet. The people waiting at the corner stared at me as I blinked back a few startled tears.

"Thank you," I whispered.

"You need to be careful. You could have been killed," he scolded, his accented cadence hitting my ears like a beautiful melody after the harshness of the taxi horn. I nodded, and we both looked down at my badly skinned knees. The light changed, and I averted my face as the gawking commuters surged past. I would be the story told at the water cooler that morning; the stupid lady saved from death by the kebab dealer.

"Wait," he said to me, and I obeyed. I was too stunned to move anyway. My mouth was dry, and my head felt sickeningly light. I leaned an arm against the cart and wiped the sweat from my forehead. Blearily I turned my head toward where the bus had been. It was long gone.

The halal cart man returned with napkins, which he offered to me for my knees. I thanked him again, and he waved me off, a very irritated hero.

I hobbled toward my office, where I spent the rest of the day in a haze, trying to dismiss what my mind insisted I had seen. I could focus on work for short spurts, but a sickening anxiety would shoot through me every time my knees brushed my desk, the sore flesh kindling very raw thoughts. I prided myself on being a rational person, and now I was running after buses like a maniac.

I thought I had let her go. It had been years since I'd chased a woman down the street, driven by the compulsion to *just see*, to make absolutely certain that it wasn't Cyn pushing a stroller freighted with groceries or browsing in a liquor store window. I thought I was better, but perhaps I was wrong.

I slowly crossed my legs, deeply conscious of the fiery burn as flesh grazed flesh. The sharp bite of pain was enough to bring tears to my eyes, and enough to remind me that I was still alive, and she was not. I was not surprised when an instant later, I heard her voice.

Pretty fucked up, Glo.

CHAPTER NINE

Raj

At some point in life, every human being inevitably suffers one horrible incident. The Horrible Thing is ineluctable, buried deep in the contract of existence. Our parents blithely clicked the "Accept" button for us, agreeing to terms and waiving certain rights while bringing us into the world. We can't blame them. No one reads the fine print. The unluckiest among us experience multiple horrors, which is truly a raw deal, an error for which the universe, or God, or whatever crafted this adventure, has some explaining to do. There are other variations, too: one man's Horrible Thing(s) might be tame in comparison to another's, but everyone can point to their own and say, *That was it*, perhaps with a shiver of gratitude that they're still around to do the pointing.

I thought I knew what mine was. Now I'm not so sure.

Recent events have forcefully schooled me that some things can't be sorted out, that some truths remain elusive. When there is no truth to set you free, no clear-eyed vantage point from which to look back on the horrible thing, or forward to the future, the entire world distorts. It's not subtle. Facts take on a wavery, fun-house quality, and history smudges as easily as chalk on a sidewalk. The only thing that is unquestionable is how we feel, and as my feelings have been changing by the hour, even that can't be trusted completely.

The new truth is, everything is different, but nothing much has changed. I hate a paradox even more than ambiguity, and ever since I saw her in the theater, I've found a lot not to like.

The wind is blowing hard outside the dark windows of our apartment. Glo is passed out in our bedroom, but I know I won't rest tonight. I have a near-full bottle of Scotch and a cut-glass tumbler through which to alternately admire and drink the Scotch. I'm in several ounces deep when I pass my glass before the lamp. The color, I realize, perfectly mimics the hair of a strawberry blonde standing below the setting sun on an autumn day. I flash back to fall, to hysterical tumbles in dry leaves, to Glo in her Greek goddess Halloween costume, and rapidly forward again to just this afternoon when Cyn reappeared under her own reddish-gold halo. There was no brash crispness about her then, though, no ruddy-apple cheeks or ruby-red lips. She was pure winter, gazing up at me from the dark, motionless as a wax figure in row D, seat 6.

The expression on her face defied classification. The surface emotion was melancholy. But in our fleeting eye contact, I sensed something else at work underneath, something calculated, like curiosity on a bad day. Glo says that I'm being ridiculous. That, if in fact, our dearest, deadest friend has returned, a possibility she roundly refuses to entertain, we would know. She would come to us. To that I say, maybe she has.

It was the shape of her face that drew my attention. Even in the near dark, my eye sought the heart-shaped gleam of ivory, rising from the unmistakable curve of neck. I was on stage, three-quarters through the production, the end in sight. We were getting laughs. The matinee crowd is great for laughs; everyone a little buzzed from brunch, but not tipsy enough to nod off.

I glanced at her, hazy in the backwash of the footlights.

Cyn, I thought, for the millionth time.

You look for your dead, especially in a place like New York City, where there are thousands upon thousands of doppelgängers to process. For years, I habitually scanned every female of her approximate height and proportion. A familiar gait could make me trail a woman down the block until I inevitably confirmed a false positive. Glo searched, too. Sometimes both of our heads would snap to follow the same golden-haired girl who fit the profile. We never talked about it, but we both knew we did it. So when I thought I'd spotted her, it didn't rattle me. I would deliver my line, and in the buffer of laughter that always followed, steal a second look and confirm my mistake.

Only this time, I didn't think I was mistaken. We had locked eyes. I knew what I'd seen, but for the next twenty minutes, I managed to back-burner all thoughts of her. I didn't steal another look until curtain call, and by then, she was out of her seat, trying to edge past her row mates before they could block the aisle. I watched, grinning helplessly as the audience continued to applaud and her milk-colored coat disappeared out the exit. It took all I had not to leap off the stage and race after her. My thought was, I *have* to touch her. Physically touch her. Don't ask me why. Maybe it was some misplaced idea about ghosts that I ingested along with my Froot Loops while watching *Scooby-Doo.* If I caught this impostor, I could unmask her as a phony, and life would go back to normal.

Before the hem of the curtain hit the floor, I was out the stage door. In the flinty twilight, I spotted the coat, a white speck among a sea of black, and the surprisingly copper-colored hair. She was getting into a cab. I shouted her name. She heard me—the entire block heard me—but she pretended not to, slamming the door closed without even a glance in my direction. Maybe that's why I feel so strange and sick right now. If you can't look a man in the eye, how can he possibly trust that your intentions are good?

In hindsight, I shouldn't have dropped the C-bomb on Glo so cavalierly. There she was, sitting at the bar near my theater, waiting for me with a martini glass lifted to her lips, clairvoyantly prepared for a slapstick spit take. I at least had the good sense to wait for her to swallow before I blurted it out.

"I saw Cyn at my show."

She blinked. "April Fools' is next Sunday."

I pulled my stool close to hers, signaling to the bartender for a dirty martini of my own. My excitement must have read like exhilaration, or worse, elation. It wasn't, but this was colossal news, and who else on the planet would find it as extraordinary as Glo? It had taken all my self-control to not call her and tell her about it immediately, but now that I saw her face, I was glad that I'd resisted.

"I'm not kidding. I really saw her."

Glo didn't say anything for a minute. "She's just on your mind because of my stupid bus 'sighting.' Insanity must be an STD."

"Glo, it was her."

"She's dead," Glo said flatly, all playfulness gone.

We sat in silence as the bartender stood before us, shaking my drink. He set it before me, and I took a hearty swallow, its crisp, salty coolness instantly calming my nerves. I ran my hand up and down Glo's back in a way that I hoped was soothing. Beneath her soft sweater, she was coiled stiff as a carved rattlesnake.

"So, how did this alleged Cyn look?" she asked, forcing a casual tone.

"Smokin' hot," I blurted, trying to lighten the mood. Then I almost bit my tongue, worried that my dumb joke might have stoked Glo's dormant Cyn-related insecurities. She'd been touchy lately, and I really wanted us to have a good night. Glo just rolled her eyes, a good sign.

I took another sip, recalling the moment in the street as I swished the gin between my teeth. Doubt was pouring in, as it always did, drowning my certainty. I didn't get the best look at the woman in the cab; it was dark and there was a reflection from the marquee on the window. I was also notoriously bad with faces, to the point where Glo would have to repeatedly help me identify characters when we watched movies together. "She looked rich. The Cyn I saw looked rich."

"How do you mean?" Glo leaned back in her seat, forcing me to move my arm. But she turned toward me, and the toe of her boot touched my calf. Though I had inadvertently sent our date night careening toward the shoals, she was signaling we weren't wrecked yet.

"Nice coat. White," I emphasized, raising my eyebrows.

"White, in this city? She must have an excellent dry cleaner," Glo said, feigning wonder.

I nodded in solemn agreement. "She was very put-together-looking. Her purse was big and expensive, you know, leather, shiny buckles. She looked like she belonged on the Upper East." I took a sip of my drink and dropped the routine. "This woman's hair was sort of reddish, like yours, but lighter. I ran after her, out into the street just to see, you know, to confirm."

Glo gulped a mouthful of her cocktail, then another, draining it down to the olives. "And when she saw you, she said, '*Raj*? Rajveer *Roy*? I've been totally meaning to get in touch!' "

I laughed. "She literally ran into traffic to avoid me. I mean, if you're going to come back from the goddamn dead, why not hang around for a second and say hello?"

"She was probably in a hurry. Had to get back to the crypt before sundown or something."

"So you're going reverse vampire on this one?"

Glo shrugged. "Sure. Except reverse vampires are bullshit. A body-replicating alien I might have believed."

"You always go with alien. Mix it up a little. You want another drink?"

She nodded and I hailed the bartender. As if by mutual agreement, we didn't talk about our sightings any more that night. Yet when we walked out of the bar to the restaurant, I had the feeling that we were both looking over our shoulders. During dinner, I saw worry dulling the usual brightness in Glo's face. She said she was just exhausted, which was probably true. She hadn't been sleeping much the past few nights.

I had been coming home late, around two or three in the morning. My business partner Tony and I were six months into a five-year lease on a basement black box theater in Hell's Kitchen. Our theater company, the Clockwork Owl, had a new show opening in a week, *The Narcan Journals*. It was by far our strongest production yet, and the one we hoped would get us out of the red. Just as we began tech week, our set decorator abruptly quit, leaving us scrambling to fill a bare stage. Tony had kids, and his wife worked nights as a sommelier, so it fell to me, as artistic director, to labor into the wee hours gluing shitty wallpaper onto plywood and distressing thrift store furniture. The only bright spot was that the play was set in an addict's pad, so my glaring lack of interior design skills didn't hurt the verisimilitude.

Tony and I had made fast friends with the owner and the bartenders of the bar located directly above us, the Copper Dragon. We were there so often, it might as well have been the theater's unofficial office. I sometimes stopped in after working, and the nightcap that Steve, the bartender, offered me magically blossomed into several. This happened more often than was healthy.

The past two nights I had come home expecting to find Glo

in bed, but she was up, staring at the television. She didn't ask me about the show, or work, or why I was swaying like a sailor on dry land. I instantly felt bad, seeing her like that, alone again on a Saturday night, like some hopeless spinster. But she wasn't mad. She let me lead her to bed, and wrap my arms around her, exhaling whiskey vapors into her apple-scented hair. As drunk as I was, I could tell that something was on her mind. It could have been any number of things: our not spending time together, my spending too much time with the company, my drinking a bit too much, my unwillingness to get her pregnant, plunging our already dicey financial status into potential ruin . . .

The thing was, the Clockwork Owl was deeply in debt. Glo didn't know. I wanted to tell her early on, but Tony had me convinced that it wasn't that bad, and by the time it was that bad, I didn't want to worry her. Tony was our finance guy, having already opened a few successful restaurants in Jersey. I hoped beyond logic that he was right; that one successful show could turn everything around, but it wasn't like I'd suddenly lost my ability to do math. We'd spent thousands to renovate the space, and we weren't getting the audiences we needed to keep it afloat. If *The Narcan Journals* was anything less than a runaway success, we'd have to declare bankruptcy and give it all up. Unlike myself, Tony could be sanguine about losing the theater. It was a business to him, but it was everything to me.

In only six months as a theater director, I had already experienced so much more satisfaction than I had in my seven years as an actor. As a director, I wasn't limited by the color of my skin, or my last name, or a million other factors that not-so-subtly tipped the scales in the purportedly "color-blind" casting in New York City. I was relishing my first-ever principal role on Broadway, and the significant paycheck that came with it, but once we closed, there was no guarantee I'd ever win another job like it. Case in point: for the last three years, my ability to pay my rent was largely owed to Bucky Beaver, the cartoon animal I voiced for *The Foresteers!* Sure, Bucky was a lead character who happened to be brown, but he was also a beaver. Having the Owl meant I could put on the shows I cared about, and cast actors who didn't fit the shiny white Broadway mold. When our first two shows, both premieres of new works, came out to positive reviews, I was ecstatic. I thought that I'd found my niche and that the audiences would follow. Of course it wasn't that easy, but I learned from my many mistakes, taught myself Professional Marketing 101 on the fly, and miraculously, our last week of shows played to sold-out houses. Success seemed just a hairbreadth away. If I could keep it up, it seemed like we just might squeak by. With so much at stake, I couldn't not give it my all.

Yet at the same time, my devotion to the Owl was making me a shitty husband. I was so busy trying to hold my dream together that I could hardly spend any time with Glo, and when I did, I was so stressed out that I was only partially present. Of course it put a strain on our relationship. She was suffering patiently, delaying her own dreams of starting a family so that I could get my company started. I was so grateful to her for trusting me to get it right, and the prospect of falling short was looming so large that the only thing I could think to do to solve it was work harder. We were treading water side by side, neither one of us able to push the other toward the shallows.

And then, this apparition. Cyn.

I sipped the Scotch, though I'd already had too much. I shouldn't have poured it, but the next day was my only day off, and the booze was far too good for the sink.

Now that I was alone, I could acknowledge what I hadn't been able to earlier in front of Glo. The run-in with Cyn's doppelgänger had left me shaken.

We had mourned Cyn. Mourned her profoundly. I remember watching the news, Max at my side, when the Costa Rican director of Judicial Investigations appeared to make his report on live television. Even before he said a word, I remember my heart sinking. The man had an honest face, *a fatherly face*, and he looked incredibly sad. When he finally did speak, his words wove together to form a damp, heavy shroud that suffocated the last embers of my hope. *We do not have any confidence in recovering the bodies of Hector or Marco Zamora. Unfortunately, the same is true for Ms. Cynthia Williams.*

"We'll never know," Glo had informed me, curled into the hollow of her parents' rec-room sofa. Her hands and feet were still wrapped in bandages, and there was a large bruise yellowing around her eye socket. "We'll never know who or why or how." Her wounded eyes made a chancy visit to my face. "Maybe it's better we don't know the how."

I didn't know what to say. That whole day, and in the weeks that followed, I didn't have a clue what to say. I just listened during the rare moments when she would break her silence, and held her as carefully as I could. She was hurt in so many places.

She rubbed her temple with a gauzy finger. "The detectives said to me, 'In cases like these, we usually tell the family to bury a portrait. It helps to make it real.' " She sighed, and shrugged. Then an instant later, began to shake with sobs.

It was the saddest fucking thing, but what could we do? We didn't bury a picture of Cyn, but we did our best to leave her in the past. After seven years, it finally felt like her ghost, the one that harbored so much pain and doubt for Glo, and guilt for me, had finally left us. That she was now manifesting on the streets in our imaginations seemed to me an ominous sign. If our lives were out of balance, she was the perfect totem for our unease. Looking out the window onto the dark, still street,

CHAPTER TEN

Glo

My sister-in-law Suneeta is the only woman on the planet who knows everything about my romantic life. I truly hadn't expected to love her like the sister I never had, but perhaps I was due some good luck in the girlfriend department. We bonded immediately. The stiffness of our mother- and father-in-law did much to unite us, but she also came at me like a hurricane of warmth at a time that I desperately needed to be loved. She had always wanted a little sister, and there I was, my heart busted up, hoping for some kind presence to help fill the huge emotional chasm that Cyn had left behind.

We met not long after everything happened in Costa Rica. Phil and Suneeta drove up to visit us in Brooklyn, their baby daughter, Rosie, in tow. They politely masked their horror at the condition of our studio and by the end of a laughter-filled weekend, a rarity for us at the time, were insistent that we come down to North Carolina to spend the holidays in their bright, comfortable house on the lake.

Like everyone else in the United States, Suneeta wanted to hear about what had happened with Cyn. Camped out on her couch with a mug of rich chai tea and a view of the lake, I gave her the exclusive. I told her everything, all the way back to Coach Mike, feeling soothed by the compassion in her brown eyes and encouraged by the mischievous twinkle that would rise up in commiseration. She had been a bit of a wild child herself in college, though you would never know it to look at her.

"You know, Glo, you have never had a man that was your very own. Does that ever bother you? Mike was married, and Raj, you shared with Cyn."

"Do you think that's bad?" I'd asked. She was a trained family therapist, but really, I was asking her as a friend. I trusted her, implicitly.

"I just think you should think about what it means for you." She looked out into the yard where the guys were kicking a ball with Rosie, beers in hand. "It's obvious that Raj loves you. He's yours now, and probably would have been yours alone under different circumstances. But as a woman . . ." She trailed off. "I just hope you know your own power. That's what I mean to say."

I thought of Suneeta's words now, Tuesday morning, two days after Raj had told me about his Cyn hallucination, and four days since I imagined I saw her myself. The sun was barely up, but sleep was off the table.

I had awoken, breathless and choking, from a nightmare of swimming at night across a wide, dark lake. All was peaceful, until something seized me by the foot and jerked me down so suddenly and powerfully that I didn't even have time to scream before my mouth filled with water. I sat up, gasping. *Alligator attack.* As far as nightmares went, that was pretty standard fare. But as I reflected on the vision, rolling the sensory footage back bit by bit, I recalled the pressure on my ankle had been smooth and painless, not jagged like teeth. I realized I'd dreamt of a human hand, dragging me under with a vengeance.

I pulled on my sweat suit and a Windbreaker, tying my running shoes as the sky gradually began to lighten. My footsteps whispered off the pavement as I jogged down the slumbering streets that led to the park. A fog had descended, thick and milky. The graceful elbow of the Triborough Bridge extended up into a mysterious cloud mass, its red aviation warning lights blinking like the eyes of a hidden monster. For all I could see from the top of the park, Manhattan might no longer have existed.

I ran past the empty Olympic-size pool in Astoria Park. It would be months before it was filled. There were a few other joggers out, their forms indistinct in the mist. Dog walkers skirted the periphery, wearing thick coats over thin pajamas against the damp, all of us ghosts to one another.

I puffed along through the foggy, tree-lined trail down to the riverfront promenade, feeling as if I had abandoned one dreamscape for another. I paused by the railing and stretched, watching the swirls and eddies of the currents as the river tumbled in a frantic rush through Hell Gate and out to sea. Another jogger passed me, and I heard the click of solid shoes as a tall man in a trench coat emerged from the haze. He paused by the railing, about fifty yards away, and stared at the water, just as I had been doing. I felt him look toward me, and instinctively turned my back. To be out so early in the park dressed like that signaled he was probably a weirdo or an addict, coming down from the previous night's adventure.

I turned uphill toward the track. If I ran a few sprints, I might not have energy left for nervous ruminations about long lost friends. I'd been doing that far too much lately.

The first few years after Costa Rica, Raj and I would only conjure up Cyn when we were drunk. The alcoholic haze gave me the courage to turn to Raj and ask, "Where is she now?" It was our very dark game; the sad, rather childish way we chose to reckon with her absence.

Answers might be: Foreman of a Chinese Coal Mine, Russian Brothel Mistress, Fortune Teller, Fishwife, Pharmaceutical Company Executive. The more absurd the hypothesis, the better. Our joke scenarios were our attempt to take the sting out of the likely truth: that she was dead. A skeleton, jutting from the sand beneath millions of tons of water.

Raj had asked me maybe thirty times to describe everything that happened that night on the island. The first few times, I thought it was because he was hungry for fresh details that might help him sort it all out. I racked my brain to provide them. Around the tenth time he asked, I began to wonder if maybe some part of him didn't believe me. I worried that he was trying to catch some inconsistency in my story that would blow the whole thing up. It made me paranoid enough that I made a habit of retelling it the same way, using sometimes the exact same words. He told me he knew I'd done everything I could, but I wondered if he doubted.

I had given him reason to. In my most depressed, guiltiest moments, I would confess that I'd killed her. How I should've gone with her to reason with those men, or fight them alongside her. He would listen silently, and then methodically break down my argument against myself.

If I'd gone with her or given myself up, he'd argue, we'd both have vanished. He truly believed this. "By splitting up, you were able to go for help, start a search, and tell her story. It wasn't your responsibility to die with her."

But would she have done it for me?

I hit the track and pushed into a sprint, trying to outrun the thought. I'd asked and answered it a million times, always coming to the conclusion that no, Cyn probably wouldn't have left me, as I'd left her. She was better than me, braver than me. More selfless. A goddamn holy martyr. But I hadn't asked her for that. If I'd had my way, we would have faced whatever it was together. I'd begged her to come with me, I reminded myself. *Begged her*. And she had turned me down.

I rounded the curve of the track, and another jogger overtook me out of the fog. A gleaming blond ponytail swung past my peripheral vision. My eyes swept up and down the woman's body, my breath catching as I identified a possible match.

Let her go, Glo, I told myself, but before I knew it, I had sped up, lurching toward the woman on borrowed breath. As I came close enough to see her face, she shot a startled glance in my direction, the alarm in her eyes decreasing but not vanishing, as she assessed my level of threat.

It wasn't Cyn. Of course it wasn't.

The woman sped up, and embarrassed and ashamed of myself for spooking her, I dropped to a dead halt, panting.

I watched until she disappeared into the fog, noting as I did that the resemblance wasn't really that close after all. I stumbled off the track and dropped into the dewy grass, strangely overcome, not with sadness but with an equally bitter feeling of being cheated by myself, and by fate, one too many times. Wet and cold in the empty park, I was ready to admit why I'd chased the bus, and why I'd always keep searching. In my good dreams, the best dreams I had, Cyn was still alive. I would see her, and she would smile, like, *Gotcha!*, and we would embrace. I'd *see* her, wholly real with her knobby elbows and weird, tiny earlobes and all the irregularities that never manifested in my waking-life memories, and her laugh would ring through my ears and I would feel such incredible joy. I'd be flooded with gratitude and relief that the universe had finally called for an end to the very bad joke of having my best friend, my lost sister, be dead forever. My heart would thrill with the thought of all the catching up we had to do, and the good times that would reign again.

And then I'd wake up and ache like Costa Rica happened yesterday.

I glanced down at my hands, the cut on my ring finger stinging from the sweat. It hadn't yet begun to heal. I twisted my ring so that the diamond faced the sky, struck with a sudden memory of the night that Raj had given it to me.

It was New Year's Eve. We were on our way to a dinner party in Brooklyn, when he asked me to take a quick stroll to the waterfront so we could sneak in one last view of the skyline before the end of the year. It was a warm night for December, and the sidewalks were dotted with couples and groups of friends carrying freshly purchased bottles of champagne, laughing as they made their way to crowded, convivial living rooms.

As I stood gazing at the Empire State Building, watching the sparkle of dozens of camera flashes along the thin rim of the observation deck, Raj had dropped to one knee. I barely remembered what he said, or I said, but of course it was yes, and of course it ended in a rapturous embrace. A couple of people on the street stopped to clap.

Our friends were delighted, and some champagne was popped early. At dinner, the conversation turned to honeymoon spots.

"You should go to Costa Rica," gushed one of Raj's acting-school friends. "I've heard so many great things!"

Raj's eyes met mine across the table, and we shared a private smile. "I'm afraid that's out of the question," Raj demurred, spearing a roasted potato. "My lovely fiancée has a terror of monkeys. Isn't that right, Glo?"

"They're appalling," I agreed, reveling in the way his eyes sparkled at me across the table. My future husband.

That night, after midnight struck, I found myself alone on the balcony. There was a partial view of the skyline, and I was leaning out, marveling at my amazing fortune.

The door slid open, and I was joined by Marcie, the girlfriend of Sarah, the woman who'd suggested Costa Rica. She lit a cigarette and joined me at the railing, smiling at the view.

"I realized something at dinner," she began. "It was you guys, wasn't it? You were the girl who got lost in Costa Rica. Raj was your boyfriend way back then."

She offered me her cigarette, and I accepted a puff, breaking my just-minted resolution to quit in near record time. Considering the moment, I thought I was justified.

"Yeah, it was. No one usually recognizes us."

"You flinched when Sarah said 'Costa Rica.' That's when it dawned on me. Sarah didn't mean anything by it."

"It's cool. She doesn't know. Nobody knows."

Marcie was studying to be a shrink. I was pretty sure she'd be able to read the subtext of my *Nobody knows*, which was, *And we don't want them to.*

She leaned back from the railing. "What a tremendous love story you guys have."

"Yeah," I agreed.

"And they never found your friend, Cynty?"

"No."

"I'm sorry," she said.

"It's okay," I managed, and to my chagrin, burst into tears.

At the thought of Cyn, the tremendous high that I'd been on for hours shattered. Like a kick in the gut, I knew I wouldn't be wearing that diamond on my hand if she'd survived. And just as heart-wrenching was the idea that I'd never get to share my greatest happiness with the girl who understood me best. Far from feeling happy, I suddenly felt uncomfortably fraudulent, and very much alone. I turned my head to look for Raj and saw him inside, helping to set up a karaoke machine that had emerged from a closet.

"Sorry," I said, wiping my face. Marcie gave me a fresh cigarette, and lit it for me.

"Don't be. It's natural."

"What is?"

"Survivor guilt."

"This one's for that gorgeous redhead on the balcony," Raj's voice boomed from the mini-speaker. "The future Mrs. Raj Roy III." All our friends whooped in appreciation.

Marcie stubbed out her cigarette and patted my shoulder consolingly. "You got lucky, Glo. You've got a good one in there."

The familiar opening chords of "My Girl" came thumping out of the speaker like a giant heartbeat.

"*I've got sunshine . . .*" Raj belted, reaching his hand out toward me. I felt the eyes of the party turn to the glass, and with a final brush of my cheeks, I slid open the door. Out of the cold, and away from my thoughts, I felt much better. If only that feeling could have lasted forever.

I rose out of the damp grass and immediately began to shiver.

It was my time to let her go. I had to.

CHAPTER ELEVEN

Raj

Despite the strong, possibly Scotch-induced feelings of impending doom, the days that followed my all-too-rare date with Glo were fine. I was incredibly busy, running dress rehearsals with my company every night after my show. The late nights were tiring, but exhilarating. Our play was rock solid. I had press previews lined up and was hopeful to get the sterling reviews that I was certain the production merited. I envisioned a packed house and mad receipts. In my downtime on the train, I meditated on our bank books transforming from red to black.

Just in case positive visualization alone didn't get the job done, the ever-practical Tony had invited Oona Shaw, a young socialite with a great, old-money fortune and an interest in the arts, to preview our dress rehearsal. She was already familiar with my work as an actor, having seen me in an avant-garde production of *Metamorphoses* in which I was naked, except for a skirt of ostrich feathers, for the entire first act. I remember meeting her afterward at a cocktail gathering in the lobby. Her hot, damp hands had seized mine, holding on for far too long while she smiled at me with sparkling blue eyes, her bobbed hair dyed blond with black streaks, like Daisy Buchanan gone gutter punk. She stood too close to me and touched me too often. I hadn't known who she was then, and was luckily polite, answering her flirtatious banter with my own until a natural lull in the conversation manifested and I could excuse myself. My wife was waiting, I'd said, and noted that the enthusiasm in her gaze had not dimmed in the slightest.

She had shown up for our rehearsal wearing a bright yellow dress more appropriate for a summer barbecue than a late-night underground performance. When she smiled, glitter sparkled from the edges of her eyelids. Her hair was cotton-candy pink, and her lips were coated with a pale glossy lacquer that made them appear to be made of hard candy.

"I know it doesn't look like it, but trust me, she's made of money," Tony had murmured to me before bellowing her name and inviting her to sit with him, front and center. Oona and I shook hands, and I excused myself to the lighting booth. To cut costs, I was running the board for the rehearsals, which at least meant I wouldn't have to sit through the ninety-minute show with Oona's hot hand on my wrist.

The performance went really, really well. My three actors were deep in the moment, so much so that it left me a little frightened when our lead male, a tall, wiry actor playing a heroin addict, tossed the other lead onto the mattress and wrapped his hands around the guy's neck. It wasn't in the blocking, but it was genius. I scribbled a note to keep it. When the lead OD'd at the end and his estranged girlfriend broke down upon finding his body, I saw Oona wipe away a tear.

We celebrated upstairs at the Dragon. I had explained the Oona situation to Glo, and asked her to attend, even though it meant dragging her out after midnight on a work night. I wanted her to be there as a visual aid as to my state of matrimony lest Oona get any ideas. For all I knew, she was Grand Tsaress in her mind, raining money and favors upon the starving artists in her court in exchange for orgiastic delights. Frankly, I would be tempted to indulge her if the price was right, having fielded another call from my manager trying to induce me to audition as lead terrorist in some shitty B movie. I asked him if the role called for someone of Arabic descent, and he told me, "Well, technically, yes, but with a beard, you're pretty close." He's never seen me with a beard, incidentally, but I'm certain that despite my acting prowess, a little facial hair wouldn't magically transform my ethnicity, or make me able to speak Farsi. My Broadway show was scheduled to end in two months. It was possible our run would be extended, but I couldn't count on it. I needed a benefactor, fast.

Glo wasn't there when we arrived upstairs. I took a seat in the booth next to my lead actress, Shari, while Oona sat opposite me. We started with a round of shots, and Oona bought a bottle of champagne. The drinks played powerfully on my empty stomach, and by the time Glo appeared, I was feeling no pain.

Glo showed up looking magnificent. She was wearing a short skirt and tights and a blue scoop-neck sweater that made her eyes shine emerald green. She'd done her hair, and was wearing these boots with sharp heels that I found really sexy. I stood up and gave her a long kiss, and she took Shari's place in the booth next to me.

The next hour or so was blissful. Everyone was in a great mood. Oona could not stop gushing about how much she loved the play and how she would go home that night and contact her theater-critic friends. "I will drag them here by their BlackBerrys if I must," she declared, her champagne glass swaying before her face like a loose pendulum.

"I hope you mean by their phones," Glo quipped.

"I will drag them by whatever region is most sensitive. That is the only treatment those types respond to."

Glo had giggled and raised her glass in a toast.

I looked around, feeling, for once, like everything might just work out. My actors were laughing, lubricated with free alcohol and post-performance adrenaline. Tony was chatting up some friends, and the front of the bar was filled with drinkers. I was happy for the owner of the Dragon and happy for myself and Tony. I squeezed Glo's hand under the table and she squeezed it back. She got up to use the restroom, and Oona scooted in next to me.

We chatted. I was trying to guide the conversation toward our finances, the renovations we'd had to make to get the theater in shape and the outrageous price of advertising, but I kept getting knocked off track. Our group was loud and getting rowdier by the minute, with Tony and his friends playing darts in close proximity.

Just make a good impression, I told myself. *You don't have to seal it tonight.*

I watched as Glo went to join Shari at the pinball machine, each woman working one set of flippers. Oona touched my face. Her fingers were surprisingly cold and clammy, like a corpse's. I couldn't understand what she was saying over the noise, but her eyes made it obvious that I had been asked a question, and an important one.

"I'm sorry, what?" I asked.

One of Tony's friends, a regular at the Dragon, leaned down into the booth, interrupting us.

"Looks like you've got a fan here tonight, Raj," he said, raising his eyebrows.

"What?" I asked, wondering if he meant Oona. This guy was a bit of a boor, but saying that in front of Oona would have been over-the-top, even for him.

"Some chicky. She's staring at you. Right over there."

Oona craned her neck, frowning. "Who? Her?"

I raised my head, and for a split second, my eyes focused on a blond woman half obscured by a pillar. There was a sharp shock of recognition, like the jolt of a joy buzzer. It was the

Cyn doppelgänger. Through the crowd, all I could see was her head, disembodied and ominous. Her eyes were in shadow, but her expressive mouth was set in a line of displeasure. Someone stepped between us, and she disappeared.

"Who is that?" Oona asked.

"Excuse me," I said. Oona was blocking my way out of the booth.

She smiled, being playful, and tapped me on the nose. "Not until you tell me who that is. I've met your wife. That's not her."

"Please, Oona." I attempted to stand up, but the table blocked me. I couldn't catch a glimpse of Cyn.

"No '*please Oona*.' I want names. Dates. Scurrilous Details."

"Sorry," I said. The path cleared, and the woman was no longer there. I pulled my knees up from beneath the table onto the bench and climbed atop the table. I hit my shoulder on a hanging lamp, sending it swinging. My head spun with alcohol-induced vertigo as I looked down toward Tony and his friends. I lifted my foot to take a step as carefully as I could, trying to dodge the swaying lamp, but my back heel slid on some spilled beer. I thought I could recover, but in the next second, I sent a half pint of Guinness crashing into Oona's lap, and fell forward onto the dart players like a deranged stage diver. Even though they were unprepared, they half caught me, and I landed on my knees, feeling shards of broken shot glass (also my doing) dig into my jeans. Oona shrieked from the booth behind me.

I pushed through the crowd, trying to make my way to where I had seen the look-alike. People were turning to stare as I lurched forward, bumping into everyone, unhinged. Perhaps it was because Oona was shouting after me like a scorned lover, but when I tried to move past the pool table, a couple of brawny dudes wouldn't let me pass. I shoved one of them and bobbed and whirled past his buddy. I made a quick surveillance of the front of the bar. Many horrified women stared back at me, but not one of them was Cyn.

I locked eyes with Steve the bartender. His expression was half concern and half "what the fuck?" I rushed out the door and down the stairs.

I looked in both directions. There was no one resembling the woman I'd seen. I took off walking quickly toward Tenth Avenue. She might have slipped into another bar if she thought I would try to find her. I stalked up and down both sides of the block, but saw no trace of activity, just candlelit couples settling up their bills while waiters readied for closing. I doubled back toward the Dragon, peering into basement windows where busboys, disembodied from the waist down by the darkness, collected candles onto trays. A few looked up and saw me peering through the doors and shook their heads. *We're closed.*

I ducked down some stairs to peer into a late-night tapas bar and felt a heavy hand land on my shoulder. I spun around and found Tony looking none too pleased.

"What the hell's gotten into you?" he asked.

"This girl—"

"I know. Oona said you were chasing after some woman. You nearly started a brawl with the Jersey contingent up front."

"Is she upset?"

"Oona?" He chuckled and shoved his hands into his pockets, relaxing. "No. She loves drama. She's even more taken with you now. Your wife, on the other hand—"

Shit. I had totally forgotten about Glo. I turned to head back toward the Dragon. Tony grabbed my arm.

"You can't go back in there. Those guys want to kick your ass through the Lincoln Tunnel and back." He handed me the messenger bag that contained my script notes and books.

"Glo," I said.

"I'll send her out. Wait around the corner."

CHAPTER TWELVE

Glo

It's a special moment in any woman's life when her husband dives off a table to chase another woman out of a bar. As glass shattered in his wake, he dodged and feinted through the crowd with surprising athleticism and singular determination. It was the kind of display that might inspire a warm, beer commercial glow in the solar plexus, a solid *Go get 'em, kid* camaraderie.

That was not what I felt at all.

The instant he disappeared from view, everyone who knew him, which was most of the back bar, turned to stare at me. Their faces offered me a complex sampler of emotions: curiosity, amusement, wonder, pity, and the worst, a sympathetic embarrassment. My husband had chased another woman out of a bar. I took a moment to study the floor.

I guessed immediately what had happened. There was an explanation for Raj's behavior, but not one I was willing to accept. All I could do was pretend that it didn't matter, like I wasn't humiliated beyond belief, like this was just a crazy Raj thing. Problem is, I'm a terrible actress, and an even worse liar.

Shari said, "What the hell was that?"

I took a gulp of my beer and watched Oona climb from the booth, beer dripping from her yellow dress down into her suede boots. It hit me then, what he'd just sacrificed. He'd blown it with this potential money goddess, all because he couldn't keep his shit together for five seconds. My suspicions were confirmed as I heard the word "blond" murmured among his friends. He was so blind drunk that he'd thought he'd seen Cyn.

Oona had locked her sights on me and was headed my way. She absently held a bar towel that she had been handed to dry herself, oblivious to the fact that her boots were getting ruined.

"Did you see that?" Oona asked, her eyes wide and amazed, as if Raj's drunken flailing had been a tremendous feat, appropriate for inclusion in the Cirque du Soleil.

"Everyone saw it," Shari said evenly, leaving the *so what* unspoken but implied.

Oona missed it. "Who was that woman?" She blinked at me brightly, wonder undampened.

"I didn't see anyone."

"She was blondish. She was standing under that Guinness sign, staring at Raj."

I forced a shrug. "Could have been anyone," I said, feeling icy fingers close around my insides as her words ricocheted in my head. *Staring at Raj.*

Oona finally seemed to intuit that this was perhaps not an enjoyable conversation for me. I saw a glimmer of superiority twinkle across her features. She'd solved the mystery. Clearly, Raj and I weren't the happy, secure couple that we'd been making ourselves out to be.

"I just thought you'd know. It was such a strange reaction. Like he'd seen a ghost." She laughed, flashing adorable child's teeth.

"Artist types. They do that," Shari said, waving her wrist dismissively. "Always chasing wild ideas. Raj is on the team, for sure."

"Yeah," I said. I wanted to say something to build a case for this just being a "Raj Thing" but it wasn't. Shari knew it, but she was helping me save face. "I'm really sorry about your dress."

Oona laughed. "This? Don't worry." She turned and looked toward the front of the bar. "Does he normally return after chasing strange women out of bars?"

"Excuse me," I said, before the word *bitch* could escape my lips. Tony caught my eye, and I saw he was putting on his coat.

I went and stood in a stall in the bathroom, my ears ringing and my stomach roiling. I'd drunk too much, but not enough to be sick from it. Not yet. If I let it all settle in my gut, I would have a horrible, angry hangover, and I had to be at the office at eight a.m.

I stuck my finger down my throat, belatedly remembering I hadn't washed my hands since playing pinball. A double wave of disgust hit me and my gorge rose like a tsunami. When it was over, I felt better. My thoughts cleared, and where before there had been groggy confusion, now there was only humiliation and rage.

I picked up my purse from our booth and hugged Shari good-bye. Oona was otherwise occupied, so I was able to slip past without having to face her again. As I passed beneath the Guinness sign, I felt the hairs on my arms rise. I paused and turned to look back. I could see our booth clearly, and the pinball machine. We had been right there, available, in plain sight. The woman, whoever she was, could have pegged us with a Ping-Pong ball.

I pushed out into the cold night, looking for a cab. Raj could find his own fucking way home, or he could spend the night bloodhounding for a ghost. I didn't care.

"Glo!"

I turned and saw Tony and Raj advancing up the street behind me. Tony gave me a curt farewell nod and climbed the steps to the Dragon, leaving Raj and me on the empty street, alone.

"It was her again." His eyes looked wounded, like he wanted

my sympathy, or consolation. I spun on my heel and stalked away from him.

"Hey, wait."

"So the fuck what? So what if it was her? You embarrassed the shit out of me, and yourself!"

"I'm sorry. I wasn't thinking straight. I just saw her, and I reacted."

"And that's okay? That's not okay! You're drinking so much lately that anyone might look like her to you. You need to get control of yourself!"

"I wasn't drunk! I mean, it *really* looked like her." I watched him swallow, and then, lowering his voice, he said, "I think it was her, Glo."

How fucking ridiculous. It was just like drunken Raj to double down on his bullshit instead of just admitting he'd been an idiot. "Of course it was her, Raj. You want it to be her."

"What? What's that supposed to mean?"

"And if by some chance it was her, what would you do? Huh?"

"I don't know."

"I think you do."

"What does that mean?"

"I don't know, Raj, you tell me. Maybe you're not happy with our life. Maybe to you, her appearance seems like some fortuitous way out."

He stared at me, mouth hanging open.

"No."

My laugh sounded so bitter, I hardly recognized it as my own. "No? Just *no*? Because it sure looked that way to me, and to all of your friends."

"I'm sorry I embarrassed you," he said, sounding not very sorry at all. He stepped into the street, looking down the empty block for a cab.

"You want to know what is really pissing me off?" I demanded. The booze that I hadn't managed to evict had me all fired up. I thought of Oona's smug little smile, and I couldn't rein myself in. "You want it to be real. You want her to be here, looking for you, and you don't even have the balls to admit it. Meanwhile, you totally piss off the chick with the money for your damn beloved theater. I don't make enough to support us both and a failing theater company!"

His shoulders tightened. I'd hit a nerve.

"If it's between it being real and me being crazy, yes I would prefer it were real. You can just go ahead and add that to my list of crimes."

"What's that supposed to mean?"

He turned to face me, showing me in that actorly way of his the pains he was taking to not play into my fury. "You can believe whatever you want in that loopy, jealous head of yours, but I don't want Cyn back. If you'd seen this woman, maybe you'd understand it, but both times she's shown up, she's had this look on her face, like, I don't know. I can't even describe it."

"Try."

He sighed and looked up in exasperation toward the darkened brownstones. "She looked like a lot of things, but mostly, she just seemed . . . severe. Like a skin puppet, made to look like her, but filled only with anger. I dunno. Maybe that's just because she was looking at me."

Skin puppet. I stared at him and felt goose bumps rise underneath my coat.

A cab appeared at the far end of the street.

"Can we please just go home, Glo? I'm exhausted. I'm sorry. I don't want to fight with you."

I nodded. I was exhausted, too.

He lifted his arm and walked into the street.

When we got home, he said he wasn't ready to come to bed. He mumbled something about needing to drink some water and sober up. That was as much as we'd said to one another since getting into the cab.

I slid between the icy sheets and listened to the rain that had started pounding down as soon as we crossed the bridge toward home. The radiator in the corner hissed and clanked, but I didn't feel any warmer.

I thought of the woman Raj had described, out there strolling the streets, silent as a wraith, impervious to the freezing rain like some undead thing. I shook the image away, and willed my thoughts elsewhere.

As the radiator fizzed in irritable bursts, my mind drifted to the memory of a cricket that had gotten caught in the wall of my childhood bedroom. It had chirped all day long for days, starting up at unexpected intervals, and continuing for hours. I'd felt sorry for it at first, wondering how it had gotten lost in such a dark place, worrying about whether it had anything to eat deep inside the walls. But as the chirping grew more persistent, I found I couldn't concentrate. The futility of its song at first depressed me, then morphed into irritation and finally rage. I pounded on the wall, trying to scare it out or scare it to death. It would pause, but would resume seconds later, louder and more insistent than before. My dad told me that if it couldn't get out, it would die in another day or so. That wasn't soon enough. I abandoned my room for the guest room a door down, but no matter where I was in the house, I could still hear it. I lit a candle in the bathroom and wished for its imminent demise, like a mini voodoo priestess. What I had once pitied, I now wanted dead, dead, dead. I woke up one morning and the sound was gone, and though I thought myself a kindhearted person, I was gleeful.

I rolled over for the fiftieth time, unable to fall asleep. I shouldn't have come down on Raj so hard about his visions. I knew he was stressed out, and anyway, I had been imagining her, too. I wanted to make up properly so that we could drift to sleep in the comfort of each other's arms, listening to the rain. It had been far too long since that had happened.

I slipped from the bed and wrapped myself in a thick robe, padding silently toward the door. Raj was in his study, the door half-open, and I saw the glow from his computer screen pouring into the hall. I moved to the doorway and paused there. Raj was typing into a distinctive white-and-blue website, unmistakably Craigslist. By some unholy spousal telepathy, I knew that he was on the "Missed Connections" page, throwing out bait, trolling for Cyn.

I recoiled, the breath to speak his name dying in my throat. He said he wasn't hoping to see her. He'd lied, right to my face, and I believed him. The floorboard creaked beneath me, and Raj instantly clicked off the page back to his e-mail, as if away from a particularly vile porn site. I quietly closed the bathroom door, knowing with sick certainty that Raj wasn't done chasing this vision.

I caught my reflection in the mirror and saw the bloodless face of what I'd become; a woman scared to the bone of losing her husband to a ghost.

CHAPTER THIRTEEN

Raj

"What happened out there tonight?" Marshall asked, his small frame perched atop a folding chair in my airless closet of a dressing room.

"I don't know. I just, froze. It's never happened to me before." I cupped my hands onto my knees, fully aware that they were shaking. I had frozen up in act 3, forgotten my lines, screwed up entirely, like an amateur. The rest of the cast scrambled to cover for me while I stared at them blankly, like a zombie, the inside of my mouth coated with what felt like ash. I saw them in slow motion, inventing, on the fly, ways to preserve the jokes that my stunning silence had otherwise killed.

Mercifully, the scene ended. In the wings, the other actors recoiled from me, the wounded animal of the herd. Standing in the darkness by the prop table, I was fairly sure my career on Broadway was over.

"I didn't get much sleep last night . . . ," I began, desperation seeping sourly from my pores.

Marshall looked at his immaculate loafers and sighed. "Your theater company, the Clockwork Bird?"

"Clockwork Owl. Yes?" My heart, which had been thundering, now slowed to a crawl. I'd mentioned my company to a few cast members, but not to Marshall, our director. I thought it best to keep it quiet, so as not to upset the hierarchy of the show by revealing my own directorial leanings. I'd seen it cause tension in other companies, when such actors were perceived as challenging the director's authority, flying too close to the sun on untested wings. I didn't want that to happen on this show. It was too valuable.

"How are things going with that? You've been working hard?"

I did not like where this was headed.

"Things are going well, thanks for asking. Listen, Marshall, I'm really sorry about tonight. In my near decade of performing onstage, it's never once happened before, and it won't again. Ever."

Marshall sighed. "I believe you, Raj, but the producers are a little pissed off. Two of them were in the house tonight. So was the playwright and his mother, visiting from the UK."

"Oh, shit."

"Yes, shit indeed. Had I known, I would have informed everyone, but I just found out myself. The playwright made a big stink. I guess his favorite sequence got dropped. You know how these writers are." He cracked his knuckles and crossed his legs. "I want you to hear it from me. They're putting out a call for potential replacements for the role of Dr. Seager."

"I'm fired?"

"No, no. Not yet. If you're lucky, it will take a few days to get auditions together, and they may not find anyone good. Of course, I will continue to voice my support for you as the best actor for the role. I believe that."

"Thank you." My voice had died away to a pathetic whisper.

"This whole thing might blow over completely, but you must be sure that you are at the absolute top of your game for the next performance, and the next fifty after that. There are no nine lives in show business."

"I understand."

"You might want to back off on your extracurriculars, if you know what I mean. Running a theater company can be exhausting, I know. And considering what's at stake for you here on Broadway, it might be time to reprioritize."

He stood up and folded his chair, tucking it neatly against the wall. He extended his hand like a headmaster finished with administering a caning. I stood and shook his hand. A moment later, he was gone. It was just me, and some doomed failure in the mirror, hunched double, trying not to cry.

After I pulled myself together and washed off my stage makeup, I took a look at my e-mail. There were four responses to the "Missed Connections" notice I'd posted. All appeared to be weirdos. One had included a picture, which I did not open, assuming it would be a penis, or worse. I deleted all of them, and considered removing the post completely. But the thought that it hadn't even been twenty-four hours since I'd posted it stilled my hand.

I understood on some level that what I was doing was delusional. The sad truth was, this was by no means the first time I'd put up an ad reaching out to Cyn. I'd first done it when I was in Florida, searching for a place for Glo and me to live. My search of all the free listings in New York led me to some strange places, and before long I was placing sad little notes on sites with names like LongLost, MissingABroad, and FindHerForMe. I had little faith it would work, but like a sailor tossing out a message in a bottle, I clung to the idea that the gesture itself had meaning. It comforted me, the possibility of hope being not completely dead.

Not completely dead.

A shiver passed through me, just as it had onstage before everything went wrong, and just as had happened onstage, I found myself mired like some tar pit dinosaur in the icy gaze of the woman at the bar. Whoever she was, she knew where to find me. Other people saw her, so I knew she wasn't a pure figment of my imagination. I needed to find out who she was and why she was lurking about, dragging my attention away from where it needed to be, like some terrible siren. I had to get a handle on whatever this was before it wrecked more than just my professional reputation.

I rose and grabbed my coat. It was time to check the bait that I'd left at the Owl earlier that day. When you're fishing for a phantom, you cast many reels.

Earlier that day, I had awoken on my couch in the study to find Glo already gone. Her absence filled me with a sick feeling that was unrelated to my hangover. Glo always woke me from the couch in the middle of the night to bring me back to bed. She claimed she couldn't sleep as well without me there. I had heard her rise once when I was at the computer, but she went directly to the bathroom and then disappeared back into the bedroom without a word. If these were normal days, she would have at least stopped in to kiss me good-bye before going to work. Obviously, she was still pissed about what happened at the Dragon.

The thought of her anger only made me more resolute. I would unravel the mystery and then we could laugh about it all the way to the bedroom. There was the slenderest chance that the Craigslist post would bear fruit, and as my drowsy gaze fell upon my printer, another better idea fought its way to the surface of my consciousness.

One hour later, I'd taken the train to the Dragon armed with a full-color picture from the heady days of Cyn's nationwide fame. She had graced the cover of the *New York Post*, her yearbook picture transposed next to a shot of her kneeling topless on a fur rug, one arm covering just enough breast to be publishable in a "family newspaper." MISSING GIRL MODEL STUDENT? the headline had questioned. I had cropped the image so that it was just her head and shoulders. I found myself staring at the photo from the *Post*, pulled into daydreams as tentacles of lust-tinged nostalgia wormed through me. I hadn't seen a picture of her in years, and it struck me how beautiful, how effortlessly sexy, she had really been. I sat there looking at her photo until I began to feel creepy. A small, under-evolved part of my brain urged me to go all in and plug her name into a search engine. I knew the sort of pictures it would bring up. But I didn't do that. I hadn't done it in the seven years she'd been gone. Whenever I thought of how things ended between us, the desire drained right out of me. I clicked off and powered the computer down, proving, if only to myself, that I was still in control.

I gave the cropped picture of Cyn to Ted, the Dragon's day bartender, and asked him to show it to Steve and the bar-backs when they came in for their shifts.

"If she shows up, call me, okay?"

Ted nodded, and tucked the photo next to the tip bucket, his own wedding band clinking audibly against the metal of the rim. He and Glo were friends. They liked to geek out together about bad horror movies from the eighties.

"I know it's a weird favor, but it's a long story," I said, my palms pressed flat against the bar's still sticky surface.

Ted barely looked up from polishing the draft pulls. "No problem, man. I see her, I'll let you know."

I went outside and paused before the black door of our theater as another bright idea flashed into my mind. I popped into the drugstore on the corner, returning with a box of sidewalk chalk.

As I scrawled out the message, I felt my cheeks burn with embarrassment at the absurdity of what I was doing. I stepped back to check for legibility, and then drew a thin arrow to a dry spot, where I deposited the chalk. I went into the theater and did a few hours of work. When I came out, the door was exactly as I had left it.

Hours had passed since then. Night had fallen. I had committed seppuku onstage and risen to walk again. The clouds were racing high above the peaks of the skyscrapers, shoved out to sea by the force of another incoming storm. The damp air seemed electric, pregnant with possibility.

I picked up my pace as I approached the theater, urged on by the neon flash of the orange-and-green dragon belching red fire. I hopped down the three steps to the theater door, preparing myself for the inevitable disappointment. Then I froze.

There was a response. It was written in chalk in a firm, clear hand.

I'll be at the Chimera Café at midnight. Come.

"What the fuck!" I shouted. A couple strolling by on the sidewalk above startled, and hurried past. "Seriously?"

I leapt back up the steps two at a time, expecting to see someone pop up with a hidden camera and reveal the prank. There were plenty of people on the street, but none of them was at all concerned with me. I hopped back down and shone my phone's light on the wall. I saw the chalk lying on the ground, the chalk that *she* had recently held. I picked it up and held it in my hand, and unaccountably, tears sprung to my eyes. I wasn't crazy. I had been right! Cyn was alive!

"Unbelievable!" I laughed. Then, rereading the message, I checked my watch. It was eleven thirty. I turned and jogged toward the subway.

CHAPTER FOURTEEN

Glo

A gust of strong wind forced its way through my open office window, rattling the blinds. I had thought the bracing, storm-whipped air might help me to focus, but it only served to blow papers around and make noise. Following the trail of an airborne sticky note, my gaze landed on the framed photos behind my desk. Raj and me in Madrid on our honeymoon, arms wrapped tightly around one another's waists in a shot captured just seconds before a heavy downpour left us soaked to the bone. My smiling parents, flush with champagne at their thirtieth-anniversary party. Suneeta and me, sparkling in yellow saris at the wedding of a cousin, little Rosie grinning up at us from elbow height. *All evidence of a full and happy life*, I thought with a derisive snort.

After a near sleepless night, I had the focus and attention span of a hummingbird and was as grumpy as an old crow. A wiser Glo would have packed it in hours ago, but the rain, and the yawning emptiness that was sure to greet me in the apartment, had kept me at my desk. A low rumble of thunder echoed through the urban canyon, and I turned my chin back toward the brief on my computer. Immediately the words began to swim and scatter, and soon my thoughts were back in that plaza in Madrid, and the airy hotel room that overlooked it with the wide bed and narrow balcony. If I closed my eyes, I could still see Raj, naked but for a sheet wrapped around his waist, alluringly smoking a hash cigarette on the balcony as the heavy rain blurred out all life but the one unfolding in our quarters. How painfully I longed to be *that* couple again, so dizzy with love that even four straight days of rain could not dampen our bliss.

My office phone bleeped, startling me.

"Yes?" I looked at my watch. It was almost seven o'clock. I was astonished that our receptionist, Marisol, was still at her desk. No one answered, so I tried again. "Yes?"

"Oh, you are still there." Marisol's voice sounded equal parts weary and annoyed. "You have a late visitor up here. Says he doesn't have an appointment."

"Who is it?"

"A Ryan McMurphy. He's from the State Department. Should I ask him to come back on Monday?"

I rose from my desk and went to my door. The secretarial pool was long gone, their computer monitors blank with sleep. Most of the windows above my colleagues' doors were dark. I'd be seeing this Ryan McMurphy in what appeared to be an entirely empty office.

"Are you staying much longer, Marisol?"

"No, ma'am. Have to catch the express bus at 7:35."

"Okay." I stared blankly at the carpet, indecisive. I was so tired and out of it that I could think of no possible reason why anyone from the State Department would have business with me after hours on a Friday. Wearily, I pressed my finger to the intercom. "Tell Mr. McMurphy that I can give him fifteen minutes. If that's sufficient, please send him back."

I hung up, and suddenly felt leery. Marisol would be leaving in a matter of minutes, and then I would be alone. I picked the phone back up and began a bit of amateur theatrics, speaking louder than necessary to the dial tone in a voice that sounded completely unlike my own. I could hear Marisol's unmistakable carpet-abusing shuffle as she approached.

"Just wanted to let you know I might be a few minutes late, honey. I have one last quick meeting and I'll be done, so it may be more like eight fifteen. Yes. Great. Love you, too. See you soon." I hung up, feeling myself flush in the sudden silence.

"Right in there," I heard Marisol say, her loafers already scrubbing a path back toward reception.

A tall, broad figure filled my doorway. He looked like something out of a vintage comic book, standing with his head bowed in a tan trench coat, an umbrella in one hand and a hat in another. My eyes fixated on the hat. The last time I'd seen a hat like that had been during a screening of *The Godfather*.

The man crossed under the door into my office, ducking slightly as if freshly transported into a new body and unsure if he would clear the frame. He extended a hand, and as I stepped forward to shake it, I was overcome by the lingering ghosts of a thousand spent cigarettes.

"Thank you for seeing me, Ms. Roebuck. I'm Ryan McMurphy."

He set his umbrella down and removed the coat, hanging it over the side of a chair. He ran a hand through his sand-colored hair and made himself comfortable in a chair opposite my desk. For a moment he sat there without speaking, staring past me at my photographs. I swiveled my chair to block his view, and his eyes met mine.

"And you're from the State Department?"

He nodded, and stared at me. I stared back.

He was attractive. Handsome in a rugged, Robert Redford manner, but his eyes were bloodshot and his lips chapped in a way that whispered of despair and joyless excess. Despite my better intentions, I was intrigued. If I was going to be carving time out of my Friday night for some dull government rigmarole, at least they'd sent me someone with character.

"I know you have somewhere to be at eight fifteen, Ms. Roebuck, so I'll get to the point. I've been working on a very sensitive investigation, and I'm hoping you have some information for me."

He narrowed his eyes and rubbed a finger over his upper lip. I waited for him to say more, but evidently, that was the pitch. I almost laughed.

"I think I'm going to need a little more help, Mr. McMurphy. Is this with regard to one of my cases?"

He smiled thinly. "No. It's not."

He caught sight of my scraped knees, and I saw a glint of interest in his eyes as they returned to my face. I smoothed my skirt and scooted my chair closer to the desk, annoyed at myself for running out of tights and annoyed at this McMurphy person for making me self-conscious.

"It's a personal matter, for you."

"Personal?" My annoyance dissolved into fear. Had Raj and I grossly fucked up our taxes? Were my law licenses up to date? Had I made some glaring mistake in my case work that could get me disbarred? None of these possibilities seemed likely, nor, I remembered as the adrenaline ebbed, were they business for the State Department. And then my one major dealing with that particular branch of government burst to the forefront of my mind, like a firework over a dark field.

"Is this about Costa Rica?"

He sat back in his seat. "Yes."

"Oh." I glanced at the clock. It had been five minutes. While moments before my worry had been being left alone with a strange man, I was now concerned about Marisol, notorious water cooler gossip, overhearing our conversation and spreading my story all over the building. She'd be gone soon if she hadn't left already.

"I'm looking for Cyn," he said. "I'm hoping you can help me find her."

I watched the words come out of his mouth, his bared teeth flashing as he spoke her name, but I still could not believe what he was suggesting. "You're kidding, right?"

McMurphy tilted his large head.

"Do you have any identification I can see?" I said, feeling my face flush. I reached for the handset on my phone, suddenly quite afraid that this guy wasn't from the State Department at all, but was instead some weirdo goon with an interest in dead girls and their friends.

He slapped his wallet open on my desk. I stared at his photo. It was the same exact state-issued ID I'd seen countless times. He was legit.

I eased my hand off the phone and sunk into my seat. Nothing made sense at that moment. Not even when he said, in the plainest English, "Cyn's alive."

"No." I said. *She can't be.*

"This has obviously come as a surprise to you. Forgive me."

"Of course it's a surprise! She's been alive all this time?"

His gray eyes were fixed on me, unblinking, and I became incredibly conscious of all the strange things I'm sure my face was doing.

"She's really alive?" I asked, redundantly. My cheeks were aflame. I felt like I might pass out.

"Yes. She's very much alive, and in the city. I take it you haven't seen her?"

"No!" I yelled, and then laughed, loudly. Even to myself, I sounded hysterical. "I mean, I thought I had seen her, but that happens all the time. It's never her."

He nodded. He was studying me intently, absorbed in the spectacle. His presence suddenly felt intrusive. I wanted a moment of privacy to absorb the news, but I also didn't want to leave him alone in my office. He was too curious. His dispassionate observation reminded me of all those cameras surrounding me so many years ago, and I felt my shoulders tighten. But I wasn't that frightened girl anymore. We were on my turf, and it was my turn to ask questions.

"How do you know she's alive, and what makes you think I've seen her?" I asked, doing my best to sound calm and collected, all the while a siren in my head blared, *She's Alive! She's Alive!*

He looked over his shoulder and signaled to the door. "May I?"

"There's no reason for that. We're alone." I regretted the words even as I spoke.

He looked down at his hat. "I know she's alive, and I know that she's here because I brought her here from Colombia."

"Colombia?"

"Yes. You haven't heard from her?"

Asked and answered, I thought, but I noticed there was an edge to the question that it took me a moment to decipher. It was, I realized, hope.

"No."

"What about your husband, Raj?"

He said it casually, but it was obvious he was watching my reaction closely, as I was now watching his. I raised my eyebrows and stated, "No, my husband, Raj, has not been in contact with her either. Is she in some kind of trouble?"

He made a face that would have been a smile had it possessed anything resembling warmth. "She's in every kind of trouble. She is trouble."

I leaned back in my chair as the wind picked up, sending

the blinds bouncing against the window frame. "I can't believe she's alive."

He chuckled drily and raised his wide shoulders in a small shrug.

"How do you know her? Why is she here? What is this trouble you're referring to?" These were the questions I asked, but all I could think was, *Why the hell didn't she let me know she'd survived?*

McMurphy leaned forward over my desk, his head craning to see my computer monitor. From closer up, I saw that he was younger than I'd thought. His gray eyes flicked toward me.

"It appears to be almost seven thirty. Do you have time to hear this?" There was a note of challenge in his tone, as if he knew somehow that my "phone call" was bullshit. It dawned on me that he had probably done his research and knew perfectly well that Raj was not waiting for me anywhere but was instead getting in costume in his tiny dressing room several densely packed miles away.

"I can make time for this, Mr. McMurphy."

"Please, call me Ryan." He shifted in his chair, and his face relaxed into a more pleasant expression. "I've heard a lot about you from Cyn. It's strange for me to be sitting here speaking to you. You're something of a legend to me, like Elvis, or Marilyn Monroe."

Both dead, I mentally noted. The cigarettes caught my eye. The rain was pounding down outside, and the wind kept sucking the blinds outward. I needed a cigarette. "Do you smoke?" I began, on the verge of calling him Mr. McMurphy again. Ryan seemed far too intimate.

"Trying to quit"—he smiled, suddenly boyish—"for about five years now."

I stood, feeling light-headed, and threw the window wide open. The patter of the rain infiltrated the room, softening the silence that had fallen.

"I'm guessing your smoke detectors have also left for the weekend?" McMurphy jested, apparently unperturbed by the thought of the fire department showing up to join our meeting.

The thought didn't faze me either. At that moment, nothing did. Apparently, just the mention of Cyn spurred me toward reckless behavior. It was almost Pavlovian. I offered him my pack and walked behind him to close the office door and keep the fumes contained. We lit up as the wind rattled the horizontal blinds.

"How is she?"

McMurphy ashed into the coffee cup that I offered. "She's troubled. She needs help. It's important, if you see her, that you let me know. I've been working on her case, but last week, she went AWOL on me. Disappeared."

"And you haven't seen her since?"

"No."

"Why are you so certain she'd come to me?"

He puffed and squinted toward the rain. "You were her best friend."

"That was years ago."

"Doesn't matter. Not to Cyn."

"How exactly did you meet her?"

"Five years ago. In Colombia. I was stationed at the embassy, doing visas, going crazy with boredom. Foreign service sounds glamorous, but really, it's a desk job like any other but with shittier air conditioning. Anyway, that's just to say the day she walked into my office was a pretty good day. She came in to talk to me about getting a passport for herself, and a visa for her husband."

I stubbed out my cigarette. "Husband?"

"Some Colombian national. She said he was an engineer. She told me this extraordinary story, I don't know how much of it was true, about being abducted by drug smugglers as a student. She told me the cartel members took her back to Colombia, and for years she had stayed because she was too ashamed to return to the United States.

"I asked her why, and she told me to type her name into a search engine. I had been in the Philippines when she disappeared, so I'd never heard anything about her. But seeing the search results, I understood why she hadn't wanted to hurry back and face all of that. The press really went after her, and she was practically just a kid."

I made a noncommittal noise, which McMurphy interpreted as a signal to catalog the things his search had found. I tuned out. I knew what the press had done, but I didn't believe that shame alone would have kept her from fighting her way home if she wanted to return. She never cared much about what people thought. But being held captive by the cartel made the picture a little clearer. Maybe that was why she hadn't reached out to me.

I tuned back in to McMurphy. Now that his cigarette was extinguished, he was rubbing his large hands together, creating a sandpaper sound. "I asked her to dinner that night. I was honestly very intrigued by her. She seemed so sweet and bright."

My eyes stayed on his hands. He wore a gold wedding band, dull with age.

"You're married."

He looked away, a hint of color enlivening his cheeks. "It wasn't like that. I guess she just reminded me of the California girls I grew up with back home. She was this American girl who had lived out this crazy adventure, and she needed my help. I just wanted to hear more about her life."

With great force of will, I managed to say nothing.

"She turned me down. She was sweet about it, of course. She said she lived out in the jungle, past the jungle, so she had several hours of rough travel ahead of her. She said something like, 'If this was America, and I could hop onto a nice, paved highway, I would happily accept.' " He pressed his lips together and clutched one hand with the other as if it needed to be subdued.

"Who is her husband?"

"I don't know anymore. Let's just say that her story has not stayed consistent."

"How so?"

He sighed, and wiped a palm across his face. I couldn't be certain, but I thought I saw his chin quiver beneath his hand as it passed over. "I really don't know what to believe about her at all, to be perfectly honest with you, Gloria. I've done so much for her. She's cost me, literally, everything, and then just disappeared, as if none of my sacrifices meant anything to her." His voice cracked, and he lowered his head so I couldn't see his face. His shoulders trembled with a weird coiled tension that made me extremely nervous. He exhaled, and with a bashful smile asked, "Do you have anything to drink in here?"

Jesus, I thought. *What a lush.*

But in truth, I could have used a shot myself.

"No. I'm sorry."

He reached a long arm down to the floor. I half expected him to produce a flask, but instead, he lifted a thin laptop case from his bag. "I realize that I may seem a little emotional, but I'm extremely worried. Cyn's more than just another case to me. You've probably already figured that out."

"Yeah," I said, watching as he powered up the laptop. He typed for a second, and turned the screen to face me. I couldn't help but gasp when I saw Cyn, frozen on the brink of speech, seated in a leather chair within a room paneled with wood so dark, it appeared almost black. She was illuminated angelically in the glow of the screen, seeming to ward off the dark shadows that surrounded her by pure force of personality.

He leaned back, watching me as I gaped at the face on the screen.

"She never came back to my office after that first visit. I left Colombia three years ago, thinking I would never see her again. But then, a few months ago, I got an e-mail from her out of the blue saying that she was in trouble and needed to speak to me. We arranged a video conference. I taped it, just in case I needed to protect myself from any liability. Would you like to see some of it? I need your help. This may help convince you that I'm not some nut."

"I don't think that." I'd pegged him as a lot of other things, but staring at Cyn's face on the screen in front of me, I did not think he was a nut.

He stood and leaned over, pointing a nicotine-stained digit at the keyboard.

"Hit that key to play it. Can you direct me to the men's? I'd rather not . . ." He gestured toward the laptop.

"Down the hall on the left," I said, unable to look away from the screen. As he left, I pressed the "Play" button, and Cyn's voice, unnaturally cheerful, chimed thinly through the laptop's tiny speakers.

I felt goose bumps race across my flesh and leaned in close to the screen, willing my eyes to accept it. She'd been around. For seven years. Without a call or an e-mail or a goddamn postcard. *Why?*

I realized I wanted the video. I had to get it, otherwise I might begin to doubt it all the moment McMurphy walked out the door. I reached into my desk and grabbed the first flash drive that I found. I stuck it into McMurphy's computer, opened his drive, and traced the video back to a folder named CynX. There were about twenty other files, similarly named. I held my breath, selected all, and hit "Copy." I was amazed at myself, brazenly stealing McMurphy's private files, but something also told me I was not getting the complete story. McMurphy's laptop began making strange grinding noises, and I fought back a wave of panic, my nail beds pressed white against the surface of my desk as I stared at the screen. My drive showed that it was loading files, albeit at an incredibly slow pace. If McMurphy suddenly returned to find me in the middle of this betrayal, our relationship could take a very, very bad turn. For all I really knew, he was a double agent, sent to reclaim Cyn and drag her back to Colombia, or worse, end her here and toss her body in the Jersey Pine Barrens. With a sense of rising paranoia, I lifted up my office phone and dialed 9 and 1, and rested the handset on my shoulder.

It was killing me to look at the lack of progress on the load bar, so I focused on Cyn, who was nodding encouragingly in response to McMurphy's description of his new life in New York. She was wearing a prim, rose-colored blouse and pearls. A costume, obviously. She'd nailed McMurphy as the type to fall hard for a damsel in distress, and it was clear that she was playing her part for all she was worth. This was the Cyn I knew, with her back against the wall. Something big had to be at stake.

I heard McMurphy's steps coming down the hall, and my heart palpitated, the sweat now rolling down my sides. The download hovered at the brink of completion. I forced myself to breathe and told myself I would count to three, and whether the copy was finished or not, I would eject the drive.

One. His footfalls were three doors away, just past the water cooler. Two. The status bar still read "working . . ." Three. The download completed, and I yanked the flash drive from the laptop, letting it fall soundlessly into my lap. When McMurphy walked in, I was holding his laptop in both hands, awkwardly. I hung up the phone, as casually as possible.

"Trying to find the volume toggle," I lied.

He took the laptop and turned it up, just as Cyn was laughing. He grimaced. "I take it you believe me?"

"Yes, I believe you."

He stopped the video and closed the laptop. "I know she's very brave and very independent, but she needs help. Coming back home to the States was a lot for her to handle." He paused, gently caressing the laptop resting on his thighs. When he began speaking again, his tone was soft and confiding. "We had a disagreement. I overreacted a little. I want her to know that I'm not angry. There's nothing more important to me than her safety."

His eyes had gone dewy, and he hunched in his seat like a defeated giant.

"Can I ask you a personal question, Mr. McMurphy?"

"Go ahead."

"Are you still married?"

His right hand swept across his left, grazing his wedding band. "Separated. Things had been rocky for a while but . . . she didn't want me to have anything to do with Cyn. When she found out I was helping her come to the United States, she left me. Took our two kids." He said it flatly, as if all of the emotions he had were reserved for Cyn. "She served me the divorce papers last week, the same day Cyn vanished from our hotel room. So, you see, considering everything, if anything happened to her, I don't know what I'd do."

"What makes you think something might happen to her?"

"I'm not the only one looking for her." He picked up his laptop, and while attempting to resettle it in its case, dropped it onto my handbag on the desk. My bag fell against the cup with the spoiled coffee and the cigarette butts, tipping it over.

"Excuse me," he said, lifting my bag quickly away from the spill. "That was so clumsy."

I looked up and saw his hands were shaking. I took my bag from his grasp and wiped up the spill. "Don't worry about it," I said. There was a tickling in my head. Something that I wanted to ask, but it eluded me.

McMurphy stood, packing up his laptop. "I should be

going. She might be back at the hotel for all I know." He pulled a business card from his pocket and scrawled a number on the back. "Obviously, I'm not in the office, so when you see her, please call my cell."

"You mean, if I see her."

He pulled on his coat, the movement rousing its acrid funk. "No, I mean when. She's coming for you. Try to keep her in one place, if you can. And take my advice: be careful and don't trust her."

CHAPTER FIFTEEN

Raj

I heard the train coming as I rushed down the slick stairs into the station. I made it into the car just as the doors closed and collapsed into an empty seat. In just a few minutes, less than half an hour, we would meet. The idea simultaneously thrilled me and left me cold with apprehension.

I checked out my reflection in the dark glass of the train window opposite me, beneath which a bone-thin Asian woman sat staring into space, a red plastic bag of groceries balanced on either thigh. I looked passable. Slightly frazzled, certainly damp. I suspected that I still carried the lingering sourness of flop sweat in my sweater, but my scarf, when I tested it, smelled only of the cologne that Glo had bought me for Christmas.

I realized with a sudden pang that I hadn't called Glo after my show like I normally did. In truth, I hadn't been in a big hurry to tell her about my onstage blackout, or the death knell of a conversation I'd had with Marshall. Then I'd seen the theater door. Glo would probably perceive my not calling as neglect, or a cold war continuation of our argument from the night before. Things were already too rocky between us for me to let that idea stand. I vowed to text her just as soon as I got off the train, and tell her an unexpected meeting had arisen. The astonishing details could wait until I got home and could deliver them face-to-face. She'd probably be a little miffed that Cyn had wanted to see me first, but considering the miraculous improbability of it all, she'd get over it fast.

I heard a burst of female laughter and noted a quartet of attractive ladies, all dressed up for a night on the town. They were young, college girls from the look of it. We had been that young not so very long ago. I looked away from their skintight skirts and strappy high-heeled sandals, a truly masochistic choice for such a cold, rainy night. They tittered and teased one another, aloft in a heady world of gritty excitements. So was I, for that matter.

I closed my eyes and inhaled deeply through my nose, like I did whenever I felt the first tickle of stage fright. Seeing Cyn wasn't a performance, but I still felt deeply unprepared, unsure how I should face her or what I would feel when I finally saw her up close. In the bar, she would no longer be a phantom, but instead my living breathing ex-lover, close enough to touch. I had so many questions. Of course I was ecstatic that she was alive and well, but I was also extremely pissed off that she had let us believe that she was dead. That was really, truly fucked. I couldn't think of a reason that would make someone do that, and unless she supplied some really compelling explanation, I couldn't see how we would ever trust her again.

The train stopped and the doors opened, granting release to the college girls and access to new bodies; a great human tidal flow. My car remained mostly empty. In four more stops, and a quick walk, I'd be there.

Printing out Cyn's picture that morning was the first time in years that I'd really allowed myself to revisit her in detail. After her disappearance, it had been too painful. I missed her, viscerally, even when I wasn't trying to think about her. Her smell, the feel of her lips on mine, the way that she would let me hold her in the night, whispering stories into her ear until we both fell asleep. More than that, I'd miss talking with her. For months, a random thought would trigger a memory of some debate we'd had, or some big idea that we'd wondered about together, speculating grandly in that quintessential college-kid way. She always saw things differently. Even years later, I would read something that I knew would light her up and feel a dull ache. Her light was out, forever.

The train stopped again. The doors open and shut.

I found myself flashing back to my college girls, the two of them smiling up at me from Glo's bed on the night that Cyn had the big idea for a binary love affair. I felt like I was floating when I drifted down their stairs that night, but within days, reality set in, and I felt the weight of what I'd agreed to like the heaviest acting role ever. My paired audience, the most exacting critics. The green eyes of one following my every gesture, snapping to crystalline attention whenever I moved within reaching distance of her beloved rival. I touch Cyn, I feel Glo's eyes on my hand, questioning, comparing, calculating, even when she's not in the room. While Cyn, sphinxlike, watched me flirt with Glo with a lazy disinterest, like we were characters in some mildly engaging television show. If jealousy was part of Cyn's emotional roster, I never saw it. I convinced myself it was all a mask. I suspected her as the superior actor.

It had gotten so stressful that I began to avoid them when they were together, sometimes even avoid them alone. I played the part even when they weren't around, struggling to treat them equally in my heart and in my mind, excoriating myself for signs of preference. But inevitably, my heart made its choice. I loved Glo more, and not just because loving her was easier. I slapped the thought down when it arose and vowed to try harder with Cyn. I didn't want to be the one to make the experiment fail.

To cope, I drowned myself in scripts, my socially sanctioned fantasy worlds. The works I loved best were the most clear-cut, their heroes facing death in battle, or loss of liberty or a simple goddamn marriage plot. I envied the characters, even the most miserable, because they at least could take action. I had no idea what actions I could take that wouldn't end up badly hurting one or all of us. I didn't want to lose anything, but I didn't know how much longer I could keep up the act. I was failing, dangerously.

I looked down at my lap and realized my hands had balled into fists. I eased them open and tugged at the neck of my sweater. It was too hot in the train. I couldn't wait to get off and get the meeting over with before my mind dredged up all the bad stuff that I had allowed to sink like toxic waste to the depths of my memory.

As if sensing my rising impatience, the train suddenly screeched to a halt. The jolt sent a teenager, who had been leaning against the door across from me, flying against the side of the seats. He cursed but managed not to drop his phone. There was a pause of a couple of seconds when it seemed like we might resume, but then the train shook with a great shudder and there was a loud hydraulic hiss as the machinery beneath us powered down.

Attention, passengers: Due to an emergency situation, this train is temporarily out of service—

Quite unlike the standard incoherently mumbled announcement, this conductor's voice came through the speakers crystal clear, each syllable vibrating with distress. The intercom remained on, buzzing softly, for a second after the transmission, and I thought I heard her report, "Driver couldn't do anything. Jumper's underneath—" The intercom kicked off, and the train car filled with moans of discontent. Passengers who had been standing shuffled toward empty seats and settled in, arms crossed, radiating dissatisfaction.

It won't be long, I told myself, adamantly denying everything I'd thought I'd just heard.

I focused my thoughts on something practical. When I met up with Cyn, in a matter of minutes, how I should greet her. Handshake? Hug? Kiss on the cheek?

The door leading to the front of the train slid open with a screech, and a Hispanic woman led her tearful preteen daughter to an empty bench. Everyone stared as the mother spoke soothingly to her daughter, stroking the girl's dark braids.

An old woman seated opposite them asked if she could be of help.

The mother shook her head. "We were in the front car. The train hit someone." She nodded down at her daughter. "She saw."

I felt my gorge rise and gripped the seat beneath me. I had an absolute horror of train strikes. I don't know if I watched *Stand by Me* at too tender an age, or fixated on *Anna Karenina* too deeply in high school lit, but I harbored a secret terror of the platform edge. My greatest fear wasn't even that I would get pushed—I kept my back against the wall whenever possible to avoid a psychopath's shove—but that I would accidentally witness a suicide. I had nightmares about it. The blaring horn of the train. The screams of fellow passengers. Bright red arcs of blood splashing up against the white tiles.

I dipped my head and stared at the toes of my shoes, trying to stay calm. Why had this happened *now*, of all times?

I stood, feeling the ground beneath me sway, and noted that the car before ours was filling with refugees from the lead car. The door opened and more people trudged through, every face downcast. A woman who had been holding a handkerchief to her face lowered it as she took a seat next to the Asian woman. As the car began to fill, conversations broke out between the witnesses and their seatmates. I didn't want to listen, but the thing about gory details is, they're enthralling.

"You could feel it when we hit her. Like a *thump-thump*."

"Someone said she ended up under the back wheels."

"They made an announcement not to move, but the smell, it was terrible. I had to get outta there—"

"—even worse when the door opened."

"I didn't look, but someone said you could see her. It was some blond white lady. You'd have to be crazy—"

"You okay, bro?" I heard. I looked up into the face of the teenager who had almost fallen. He was eyeing me warily, as if I might be preparing to puke on his sneakers.

I managed to nod, and caught my reflection in the black mirror of the door. The sight of my sweaty, bloodless face was not encouraging, and I too began to worry about the future of my neighbor's shoes. I leaned my forehead against the disgusting handrail, waiting for the spins to pass.

"This is the second time this has happened to me this year," announced a middle-aged man who wore the muddy boots of a construction worker as he dropped into my abandoned seat. "It's gonna be forty-five minutes, at least, till they fish her out. My advice is, get comfortable."

No, no, no.

I yanked the phone from my bag and pulled up some music, pressing the earbuds deep into my skull. Despite my efforts not to, I'd already imagined the dead woman under the car, her tragically bruised organs drifting to rest across those filthy black tracks.

Some *blond, white woman.*

In my mind, I gazed deep into Cyn's dark eyes in the theater. I recalled the lifeless expression she wore as she threw herself into the cab, and the funereal face she'd directed at me in the bar. She was miserable, that was obvious to me now, but she wouldn't . . . I widened my stance, feeling light-headed as the pieces fell together, forming a truly gruesome picture. She knew I'd be coming from the Owl, knew the train I would be taking.

Was it possible that she'd thrown herself in front of my train as some bizarre statement?

"No. That's crazy," I said, loud enough, and with enough conviction, to make people back away from me. I looked up and saw a collection of wary eyes checking me out, darting away like rabbits the second I looked their direction. I was *that guy* on the train.

I shouldered my bag, and the crowd in the car parted, relieved to be rid of me. I walked through the masses and stepped out onto the small platform bridging the cars, where I paused, inhaling the darkness of the tunnel. If death was present, I didn't smell it in the air.

It was a perverse thought. What the fuck was wrong with me?

I slid open the heavy metal door and moved to the next car. Then the next, trying to focus on my music and outrun my imagination. To get out of my head, I made an effort to notice other people. A bad feeling had settled into the train. I saw it echoed on the faces that surrounded me, all of us hired mourners, destined to get stiffed on the pay. I shrugged off my sweater and scarf as I moved. Finally I reached the last car, the farthest-possible place from the body that I had decided, definitively, was not Cyn's.

She was never, I convinced myself, *that* sick.

I took a seat, feeling my anxiety abate. But then it rose afresh as I checked my phone. It was already 11:50. If Joe Construction was right, I would be an hour late. Would she still be there? I had no idea. I could never predict anything with Cyn, ever, which is probably the biggest reason that things fell apart for us so spectacularly.

It all went down right before the girls left for Costa Rica. Cyn and I were alone together for a week, something that had never happened before. I was feeling a little sorry for myself because I knew as soon as Glo returned, they would both be heading off to Costa Rica. Immature asshole that I was at the time, I held Cyn's excitement against her, mostly because it was happiness that had nothing to do with me. There was also the sex thing, the supercell disturbance over our relationship that only darkened and never broke. Whenever we were alone together in a room with a bed, it thundered, or, at least, it thundered for me.

At first I didn't ask for anything. But as the months wore on, I couldn't hold that good-guy posture, and soon, even to myself, I was the dick boyfriend from every TV movie ever, pressuring my virtuous girlfriend into something she "wasn't ready for." There were very dark moments, like when we'd be making out in my bed at night, and she'd abruptly stop, pull on a shirt, and roll onto her side, cutting off her affection like turning off a tap. Or the times when I would drop her off at Ecstasy II. She would kiss me good-bye, and I would drive off nearly blind with rage. How different, I fumed, was what she gave me from what she gave her paying customers?

I wondered if she didn't want me. If she didn't think I knew what I was doing, or thought I couldn't please her. Maybe despite what she said, she didn't actually find me all that attractive. I needed some answer to wrap my mind around, other than the simplest one: that she was frigid, or cruel. I sometimes thought maybe she was crazy, that her parents had planted some ineradicable virgin complex in her head, which applied only to her behavior with me, while to the rest of the world she flaunted herself as the South's most willing whore. I hated myself for having such thoughts about someone I loved. But I was greedy. I was hungry. I felt entitled. I was, and this is true, desperate to connect with her. Despite all of our big deep talks, I still felt like I didn't really know her. She had this unreachable secret core that seemed impossible to penetrate. Sometimes her face would turn distant and she'd go quiet, and I'd know she was there, in that place that she wouldn't acknowledge and to which I couldn't journey.

My mind insisted that sex was the way forward, since that was the only road we hadn't taken. If she just gave me a chance, maybe we could find each other that way, and even if we failed, even if her secret core remained intact, surely we would be closer without the mutual resentment that perpetually fed the great, horrible storm cloud. If we made love, so many questions and frustrations would be resolved. I would no longer lie awake asking myself *Why, why, why?* Why do this? Why dream up this mad experiment of a three-way relationship, if it could never be balanced?

So I sought that balance, persistently.

"You aren't happy with this anymore, are you?" she murmured a few days after Christmas. She was sitting cross-legged on my floor, silhouetted against the sliding glass door, idly stroking a red felt Santa hat that Glo had given to her. The lights from the airport made the edges of her hair appear gilded as she fluffed the white polyester fur with her fingertips.

I turned off the video game I'd been playing, thinking, *Good, we'll finally have this out.* I turned around to face her. "Now, why wouldn't I be happy with this anymore?"

She stared at me coolly, noting, no doubt, the thinly veiled sarcasm.

"You aren't happy because you aren't getting everything you want."

"That's right. Because you won't let me have it."

"That's right," she echoed. She looked away from me and out at the world beyond the glass door.

We sat there in silence. I'd been expecting more of a reaction. I was at least hoping to learn why she was consciously torturing me, since she'd just admitted she knew what I wanted. But she just sat there, gazing at the airport.

Exasperated to the point of rage, I got to my feet. I suddenly felt like I couldn't even be in the same room with her. I had my hand on the doorknob when Cyn stopped me with a whisper.

"If you really want an answer, my biggest fear is what might happen if I do sleep with you."

"What's that supposed to mean?"

"I'm terrified that it'll mess everything up. But everything is already so messed up. You're going to start hating me, if you don't already. I don't know what to do. I wish I did, but I don't."

She was crying. I stood there stupidly, my anger fading as my confusion rose to a new high water mark. I had no idea what she was talking about. But at the same time, I loved her even more for finally acknowledging what was happening between us.

"You can't wreck this," I told her. "You just can't."

She looked up at me and smiled, tears rolling down her face. "Yes, I can. But I really don't want to."

I pulled her into my arms on the futon, and she pressed her damp face into my neck. My head was spinning questions and theories, uselessly. So uselessly.

"Did something bad happen to you? Something bad, with sex?" It seemed the only explanation.

"No."

"Oh. Okay, good."

"That's not it. It's not." She sighed, her body shuddering against mine. "It's not anything I can explain in a way that makes sense. It's not about you. It's not about Glo. It's me. I'm just kind of fucked."

"I think you're wonderful."

"I know. It terrifies me."

"It terrifies you that I love you?"

I'd never said it; to her, or to Glo. It was a dangerous word, and it had escaped before I could stop it. I meant it, and I regretted it, simultaneously.

Her eyes became softer than I'd ever seen them, and she kissed me. We kissed for a long time, and to my wonder, she began to undress me. Then she lifted my hands and placed them on the buttons of her blouse, smiling coyly. I undid each button, slowly. Then, one by one, removed the rest of her clothes, expecting to be stopped, but hoping not to disturb the spell that was drawing us closer. I swear, that night held a magic that seemed tangible, like some mystic energy was carrying us over the barriers that had risen between us, where we could finally, fully meet.

She didn't stop me. She was quiet throughout, and in the darkness of my room, I couldn't tell whether she was looking at me or her eyes were closed. I kept it simple, standard missionary position, because I was afraid that if I moved, if I did anything unusual, it might upset the balance that had made the moment possible, and everything might abruptly stop. When it was over, we splayed out naked, side by side. I reached for her hand and squeezed it.

"I need a smoke," her voice said in the darkness.

I bounded out of bed to fulfill my queen's wishes. As I flicked on the light and opened my stash box, the world felt full of fresh promise. I caught her looking at me as I rolled the joint.

"You're so happy now," she observed.

"Guilty as charged." I leaned down to kiss her mouth, and she turned her head, offering me her cheek. "Was it okay for you?"

"Uh-huh." She closed her eyes.

We smoked the joint without saying much, and she went right to sleep. It was early, only ten o'clock. I read a book and watched her as she slept. I had no idea that anything was wrong, and by the time I figured it out, it was too late.

The next day she went out before work and didn't come back to my place. When she got home that evening, she came to my room. We had been talking about going out to see a movie, but I think she saw pretty clearly that in light of the previous evening, I had other entertainments in mind.

She tossed her stuff on the floor and lit the joint that I had prepared for her. Since classes had ended she was getting high at noon and staying that way until she passed out.

"You want to fuck, huh? Fine, let's fuck."

Things got really strange from that point. It was thrilling, but also more than a little scary. Cyn became like another person. The girl who wouldn't go all the way was suddenly this sexual mastermind. Nothing about it was normal, but I didn't question it at the time. We did all kinds of things together; things I'd never even thought to do. Some of the things she wanted to do, the games she enacted, weren't even fun, but I did them anyway, because demurring would have felt like cowardice. We got high, and it would begin. We got into some heavy role play where she became this fierce domme, calling me her little bitch, making me do things and doing things to me that I'd never thought I'd enjoy. She terrified me. It was like sex recast as the Olympic ski jump, scary at almost every point in the action, with a safe landing never certain. Sometimes in the midst of it, with the adrenaline surging and all the blood gone from my head, I would crack a joke, or try to catch some hint of the Cyn I knew beneath whatever role she was playing. I never found her. By the end of the week, things were just weird between us. She was high all the time, and if I tried to mention what had passed between us at night, she would look at me blankly, or worse, coldly. The more she shut me out, the more I wanted to talk. That's when she would start taking her clothes off.

As a diversionary tactic, it was brilliant. On the second to last night before Glo was set to return, stoned and drunk, we had sex in Glo's bed. We crossed some lines, a lot of lines. At one point, we pretended she was Glo. I don't remember much of it clearly, but I said something that upset Cyn, and before I knew it, she had stormed out. I followed her, trying to get her to calm down. She was headed to her car, and I was freaking out because she was in no state to be driving. I remember banging on her window, pleading with her not to go. I could barely see straight and was terrified that she would get herself killed or hurt someone else. But she took off anyway, the tires squealing as she tore out of the parking lot. I went back to her room to wait, but she didn't come back that night. In the morning, after zero hours of sleep, I went back to my place and washed up. I cleaned up the mess we'd created over our days of debauchery and called her repeatedly.

I rode Glo's bike back to campus that afternoon and found Cyn's car. I was amazed and relieved to see that it wasn't totaled. I went to her room and found it locked. The lights were on. She was in there. I knocked and waited outside for an hour, trying to cajole her into responding. I delivered apologies in many forms, which eventually turned to un-apologies and then to petulant taunts as her silence continued. I just wanted her to talk to me, but she stone-walled me entirely. Defeated, I left.

She avoided me until Glo returned, and even then, she wasn't the same Cyn. She acted as though everything was normal in front of Glo and stayed glued to her side. I tried to speak to her alone, to clear the air between us, but she wanted nothing to do with me. It was gut-wrenching to have to pretend like nothing was wrong, but seeing as that was what Cyn appeared to want, I played along.

It was obvious that I'd hurt her, but if she wouldn't speak to me, I was powerless to make it better. I also sensed that she was somehow satisfied with how things had turned out, comfortable with seeing me suffer. I rarely ceased wondering exactly what I'd done wrong. I'd lost one of my best friends, even as she sat with me in the same room, smiling through me like a secretly enraged Mona Lisa.

I retreated to my room and listened to a lot of Joy Division. I couldn't stand to be around them as they packed for their trip, twittering happily back and forth like a pair of songbirds. The night before they left, I cornered Cyn by the salad bar.

"Are we not going to talk about this?"

Her icy blue eyes roved over me, unfazed. "There's nothing to talk about."

She lifted the tongs and piled on some romaine, while I stared at her, trying to match her faultless sangfroid.

"Really? Because you seem to hate me, and I'd like to know why."

She dumped the salad back into the bin and tossed her plate aside. "I don't hate you, Raj. Please don't think that."

Before I could respond she had turned and left me alone, holding a plate filled with spaghetti and meatballs that I no longer had any desire to eat.

The lights on the train dimmed, and another announcement buzzed through the intercom. *Please be patient. We hope to be moving shortly*. In other words, we were going nowhere. I felt my blood pressure surge as each passing minute potentially robbed me of the chance to finally get some answers. I balled my hands into a giant fist, lowered my head, and focused solely on the moment that the train doors would release me. Fate wouldn't screw me like this, I tried to assure myself, but even as I thought it, I knew it was a lie. Fate was a real bitch, and I was her plaything.

CHAPTER SIXTEEN

Glo

I sat in my office for twenty minutes after McMurphy left. I needed to gather my thoughts, and I didn't want to risk running into him on the street or on the subway platform. Something was off about him, that was obvious. What I couldn't decide was whether he was that way before Cyn entered his life or she had literally driven him crazy.

Even though our conversation left me unsettled, there was an undeniable flutter of happiness deep in my solar plexus. I suddenly hoped McMurphy was right, that Cyn really was trying to get in touch with me. Imagining that she was out there, still thinking of me with affection, made the torch that I had long carried for her flare up brightly. If it truly was me that she wanted to see, and not Raj, I was more than willing to reconnect. I had so many things to ask her.

I picked up my phone to call Raj, but set it down again, realizing that his curtain call wasn't for another hour. I didn't want to leave him a message about McMurphy; that was a face-to-face revelation, for sure. I now felt a little embarrassed about being pissed off at him all week. I could even forgive him his pathetic Craigslist trolling.

It all made sense now, I thought as I gathered up my bag and my laptop, now locked and loaded with McMurphy's video files.

Cyn was looking for me the whole time, and she kept finding Raj, or finding me with Raj, when she just wanted me alone. I would have to break it to him delicately. I knew all too well how he felt himself to be the one in our threesome who gave far more than he received. This would be salt in the wounds, but I couldn't spare him the sting forever.

I headed up to Woody's, my favorite diner in Hell's Kitchen, to grab a burger and wait for Raj. I called him twice around the time he usually finished up, but he didn't pick up. To kill time and justify keeping the table, I ordered coffee and an enormous black-and-white cookie, which I picked at while gazing at the rain-swept street outside. I called again. No answer. I asked for the check.

I was growing annoyed. I knew he was planning to head to his theater, so I could just find him there, but why hadn't he called me, like usual? I paid, and called again. This time it went directly to his voice mail, which sometimes happened when he was working underground in the theater. The bad weather had probably killed the weak signal altogether.

I decided that sharing my news was worth battling the elements. It couldn't wait until he got home. I shouldered my gear, grabbed my umbrella, and headed west.

I elbowed past a tight cluster of the Dragon's customers who were using the theater's small awning as a shelter from the rain. A woman stepped aside for me, and I saw, on the door, Raj's signature scrawl:

Seeking the Ruby Princess. Please meet me. Anytime. Anyplace.

Below, in a different hand, were the remnants of a response written in red chalk, most of it rubbed away by the smokers' coats and the rain. Still visible was "*midnight. Come.*"

I reeled, feeling like I'd been punched in the gut. The door certainly explained why he hadn't called. He was on his way to meet her and didn't want me to know about his secret rendezvous.

I took a step back, and reread the message. A bitter laugh croaked from my throat as the pain washed over me. One message in chalk, and I was transformed back into the desperate college student, heartsick and trembling, terrified of losing what I loved best.

They were meeting, secretly. *Why?* In an instant, the entire way I'd been thinking about Cyn shifted. She wasn't a friendly force, hoping to find me. She was obviously back for Raj. McMurphy didn't see it because Cyn had him just as snowed as Raj had me fooled. We were a pair of suckers, McMurphy and I.

The hurt and fury that swept through me made my vision go narrow. The next thing I knew, I was pushing my way through the smokers, striding blindly away from the theater. I couldn't focus on anything beyond the radius of my umbrella. I heard people curse angrily as I bumped past them, my trajectory flatly indifferent to the needs of others.

With each soaked step, I wished horrible things upon them both. I wanted them to meet, romantically, in the middle of the rain-polished street, embrace, and get flattened by a speeding dump truck. No. First Cyn dies, while Raj watches in disbelief, a scene that will haunt him for the five seconds he has left to live. He'll see her squashed and mangled corpse and think, briefly, *Well, there's always still Glo*, just as the double bus arrives to pancake him against the asphalt. I laughed out loud through my tears, startled by own my vitriol. A door appeared in my peripheral vision, propped open by a chalkboard. I entered, not caring where it led.

I found myself in the back booth of a dingy bar. Hockey was playing somewhere on a television screen that I couldn't locate. I had a half-empty whiskey on the rocks resting by my wrist. It wasn't my first. My laptop sat open, fifteen of McMurphy's CynX files cued up and ready for view.

I skipped past the initial video that I had previewed at the office. I didn't want to hear the bullshit sob story of the woman who was at that exact moment very likely pity-fucking my extremely grateful husband.

I drank the mental image away and pulled up video number six. I put in my earphones and tilted the screen away from any curious dudes on their way to the bathroom.

She appeared in that same shadowy room, glowing like a ghost. Instead of the prim pink blouse, she wore what looked like a black silk robe. McMurphy, appearing in a small screen at the bottom corner, was wearing a pajama shirt, unbuttoned and wide open.

It was apparent from the look on their faces what was about to happen. I took out the earbuds. I didn't need to hear it. After some conversation, Cyn began to slip off the robe, one sultry shoulder at a time. She revealed a lacy black bra and began to run her hands over her body, pursing her lips like a supermodel.

I paused the video and got up to grab another drink. I clicked "Play," and it continued as expected. McMurphy's face grew sweaty, his arm working furiously. Cyn reached up to adjust the camera, and stepped out of the chair, giving a full view of her body in bra and lace panties. Her white skin appeared luminous in the surrounding darkness. I watched her as she floated in the empty void, mesmerizing, like a seldom-seen deep-sea fish. She pivoted slowly and peeked over her shoulder, offering the rear view. Her hands sought her bra clasp and I sensed someone looming behind me. I clicked off.

I nursed my drink and surfed the weather channel, waiting for the man behind me to be on his way. My eyes drooped toward the little digital clock. It was after midnight. I refused to return home, believing that if I did, I would trash the place like some soap opera diva: ripping our wedding album to shreds, smashing lamps, breaking mirrors, wilding out in a way that was entirely unlike me. At some point, the space behind me emptied. Across the room, the bartender seemed to waver to and fro before my eyes like tall grass in the wind.

I pulled up another video and fast-forwarded to the midway point. It was more of the same. Lingerie, choreographed fondling, McMurphy's embarrassing sex faces. I clicked away, feeling that I had learned all there was to know about McMurphy and Cyn.

As my home page returned, *Moon and Half Dome*, courtesy of Ansel Adams, the rage dissipated. Staring at that mountain, cleaved clean in half, I suddenly felt profoundly sad and completely alone.

As fate would have it, that's when the stranger joined me in my booth. He was on the right side of attractive. Blond. All smiles. Not exactly my type. He was asking me something about the videos. I reached over and closed the laptop, ignoring his questions. He handed me a fresh drink. Even through the murkiness of my drunken haze, I knew that I should not accept it. It could be drugged. If I drank it, the lights would go out for, me and three months later, a vagrant would discover my head in a bowling bag by the river.

His eyes were greenish, and they crinkled when he smiled. He smelled like freshly laundered clothes and Old Spice. When he kissed me, I tasted gin. It must have been a decent kiss, because I didn't shove him off. He pulled me closer, gathering the soft parts of my sides in his large hands. I found myself thinking of Coach Mike, wondering if he'd aged well. Stayed fit. Kept his hair . . .

I squirmed. The sanctity of my drunken reverie was threatened by the rapidly increasing ardor of my bench mate. He was kissing me so fervently that I could barely breathe. I broke away and took a sip of the drink he'd brought. I hadn't forgotten about the potentiality for dismemberment, I just no longer cared very much about my future self. I wanted the kissing to return to how it was at the onset: pleasurably distracting. A moment later his mouth was back on top of mine, but gentler, just as I'd wished. I closed my eyes, and a million thoughts drifted through my head, light as gossamer. Of course, I knew I shouldn't be making out with a random stranger. I had, in fact, only strayed, if you could call it that, once before, with a guy from law school. I couldn't even remember what I liked about him, other than that he passionately professed his absolute love for me. One very late night after too many drinks, I'd made out with him at a bar similar to this one. We didn't go past second base. It had been fun in the moment, and bolstered my ego at a time when I needed it, but I knew it wasn't anything. I loved Raj. When I said I had to go, the guy started to cry. On the way home, I threw up on the train, more sick from the guilt and self-loathing than from the alcohol.

His hands were climbing up my sides. He cupped my breasts and I shifted away. A distant alarm began to sound. His whiskers began to chafe my lips. I felt a hand at the back of my neck, forcing my mouth open wider. I couldn't breathe through my nose, and this strange man was halfway down my throat, as if spelunking for gold. I began to see stars and imagined myself floating on the dark water of the channel, seven years ago. The stars had told me then that it did not matter to them if I lived or died. They would remain whether I sank deep into the salty brine of eternal oblivion or whether I fought my way to shore. It was entirely up to me.

I pushed my paramour away and gasped for breath. He watched me for a moment, blinking. When I did nothing further, he moved back in, his mouth a determined wet suction cup.

"Stop now," I said. I tried to move away from him, but my back hit the wall. His hands found me and latched on tight. I looked at his face and saw that he was blind drunk. He didn't hear me. "Stop it!"

He smiled. He had heard me. I elbowed him and managed to break away for long enough to half stand in the booth. The bar was empty. The bartender was not at his post.

He pulled me back, and I stumbled, cracking my head against the wooden booth.

"You okay?" he murmured, not pausing for an answer before he plastered his mouth to my lips. I elbowed him, hard. His eyes widened with new understanding, and he cast a look around the bar, noticing as I had that we were alone. He resumed, his hands now endeavoring to prevent counterattacks by my elbows. "Be nice," he murmured.

I prepared to bite his lip, my clouded mind suddenly aware enough to inform me that such an act would certainly release blood and reward me with herpes, or AIDS.

I wiggled away, dipping my face toward the table, and knocked over his empty beer bottle with my cheek. His hands squeezed my elbows against my sides as he attempted to reach for my crotch. Suddenly he released me. I looked up and saw the guy being lifted from the booth and flung sideways toward a row of stools. I jolted to my feet and thrashed out of the booth as the jostled bar stools toppled to the floor, along with my assailant. My rescuer turned, and I barely recognized my husband, his face pale and livid.

"You okay?" he asked.

I nodded.

The man righted himself and looked Raj over, and then looked at me, calculating whether it was worth the fight.

"Get up, you piece of shit," Raj said. His hands were balled into fists, and his chest was heaving. The man on the ground scooted away, putting some floor between them before he got to his feet.

Raj took a step forward.

"Whoa, whoa, whoa," the bartender bellowed as he trudged

up the stairs from a hatch behind the bar, carrying a box of bottles. "No fighting in my bar. Take it outside, motherfuckers."

"This shithead was attacking my wife!" Raj was shaking with rage.

"Your wife?" The guy laughed, rising from all fours. "Pretty sure she's a dyke, man. She's one kinky bitch." He turned and limped toward the door.

Raj seemed to be on some sort of broadcast delay. It took him a few seconds to shout, "What the fuck did you just say?"

"Fuck off." The man slipped out the door, just as the bartender appeared in front of Raj.

"You want me to call the police, lady?" he asked. Whether it was an old-school bartender distraction technique or a genuine offer, I couldn't say, but Raj's focus gradually shifted from the door back to me.

I shook my head.

"No. That's okay."

"What the fuck were you doing? Who was that guy?" Raj asked, his cold rage thawing, on its way toward a more personalized boil.

I laughed in his face. "Me? You have the balls to ask me what I've been doing? I know where you've been. Reuniting with your beloved after all these long fucking years with me. How was it? Did she finally let you fuck her?"

With perverse satisfaction, I noticed that he paled.

The bartender said, "You both need to get out of here. Now."

Raj spun on his heel and left. I gathered my laptop, shaking off the beer that had spilled on top of it, and shoved it in my bag. I staggered toward the door under the critical gaze of the bartender, trying and failing to muster some dignity.

Raj was lurking under a streetlight. I pulled out a cigarette and lit it, just to be an asshole.

He stared at me with disgust, and I returned the favor. This was us. This was our great love.

Finally, he said, "I was watching you for a little while. Why were you doing that, Glo? Who was he?"

"I don't fucking know."

"What the hell is going on?"

"You tell me!"

"I didn't see her."

"Yeah, right."

"Glo, I didn't see her."

"Then where have you been? I've been calling you all fucking night. I saw your little messages on the theater. Ruby fucking Princess, Raj? Really? You disgust me."

He stared up the street.

"Can we just go home? You're too drunk and I'm too pissed off to talk right now."

"Why should I go home with you? You're just going to leave me anyway. I don't know why you bothered to come and find me. How did you even find me?"

Without knowing when I began, I discovered I was crying. The cigarette was growing soft in my hand from the rain. I wiped my face and took a determined drag on my failing cigarette, concentrating on my anger.

Raj walked a few steps closer. "I've been calling you for the last hour, but you didn't pick up. We put that missing phone app on both our phones, so I checked to see if you were home. You weren't." He waited for me to say something, but I was silent. "Look, I'm sorry I yelled at you. I just didn't expect to walk in and find you sucking face with some fratty douche bag." I heard him take a breath. "But I'm really glad I showed up when I did. I should have kicked that fucker's ass."

I gulped back a sob. Goddammit, I wasn't prepared for him to be nice.

"I'm glad, too." I whimpered. "That was fucking awful."

He took another step closer, and I saw that his face was calm and deeply sad. I took a step toward him and rested my face on his chest. I felt his arms wrap around me, and I started to sob uncontrollably. We stood there like that for a long time, getting very slowly soaked.

"I'm sorry about the Cyn thing. It's over. I don't know what's wrong with me that I keep thinking she's back. Maybe it's stress—"

I pulled away from him and looked into his face. "She is back."

"How do you know?"

"I met her boyfriend tonight. It's a long story, and I'm probably too drunk to tell it."

He stepped back toward the curb, as if blown there by the power of my revelation. He hailed a cab, ushering me inside. As we sailed across the empty, rain-slicked streets, I leaned my head on Raj's shoulder and began to tell him about Ryan McMurphy and the videos that now resided in my laptop. As I spoke, the hand that had been cradling mine gradually tightened to the point of pain, and his body stiffened beside me. By the time we arrived at our apartment, he was as rigid as a rod of iron.

CHAPTER SEVENTEEN

Raj

I helped Glo into the apartment and fed her a couple of aspirin and a vitamin B. When I went to check on her in the bedroom a few minutes later, she was passed out across the comforter, only half-undressed. I closed the door quietly and went to the kitchen to pour myself a drink.

My night had been a fucking farce.

It had taken an hour and nineteen minutes for my train to shudder back to life. When we pulled forward into the station, it was ghostly empty, except for a few lingering cops. I charged out like a racehorse the second the doors parted, fleeing the overpowering cloud of industrial-strength disinfectant that chased me all the way up the stairs to the street. It was still raining, so I had to dodge umbrella-wielding pedestrians cluttering the sidewalk like so many pinball bumpers. By the time I made it to the Chimera Café, I was breathless and sweaty. I took a moment to collect myself, but not long enough, and pushed through the door.

A bouncer halted me on the threshold, demanding ID. I produced it, all the while craning my neck to search for Cyn. He let me pass, and I spun a quick 360 in the center of the near-empty lounge. A lesbian couple pawed at one another in a dark banquette, and a trio of hipster guys sat rooted to bar stools near the television, but that was it. I walked to the rear of the bar, ignoring the bartender's offer of service, hoping there was some unseen nook or back room that I'd missed. There wasn't.

The defeat I felt was mammoth.

I dragged myself to the bar and ordered a double bourbon. As she poured, I pulled out my phone. I had four missed calls from Glo and a voice mail from an unknown number, received about a half hour ago.

Feeling a surge of hope, I pressed "Play." The message was only a few seconds long and all noise. I listened to it a few times and thought I could make out a female voice in the background. I swallowed half of my drink in one go and called the number.

"Hello?" a female voice answered.

"Cyn? It's Raj."

There was a pause, and the woman's voice broke into laughter, exploding against my eardrums like jagged little crystals. "I'm sorry, Raj. It was a mean joke. Are you at the Chimera?"

"Who is this?"

"It's Oona. I saw your door, and I couldn't resist. Serves you right for giving me a beer baptism and then not bothering to say good-bye. Are you still there? That place was a hovel. I'm at the Delaware, two blocks away. Come. Let me buy you a drink."

I couldn't speak.

"Raj?"

"I can't. I'm sorry. I have to go."

I hung up the phone and finished my drink in one swallow. I couldn't even be angry with Oona. All of my fury and frustration surged inward. I was a tremendous rube. I saw with bitter clarity how deluded I was, how nuts I had been to think that one corny chalked message could magically undo seven years of silence. My own stupid naiveté had rendered me a modern Don Quixote, minus the elevating chivalry. I told myself that this absurd nonsense had to end. I would stop making a fool of myself. It was over.

Except, according to Glo, it wasn't.

I paced in front of the window, completely keyed up, though I should have been exhausted. I spotted Glo's bag, resting where she had dropped it by the front door, and seconds later I was powering up the computer and keying in Glo's password. She hadn't said not to watch them. I went to the Recent file, and found a handful of files with "CynX" in the name. I began with the oldest, turning the volume down low.

When Cyn appeared in full color, live and breathing on the screen, I paused it, refreshed my drink, and took a seat at the table.

Four hours later, I closed the laptop, feeling like a different man.

The few soft-focus feelings that I had harbored for Cyn lay in ribbons, viciously shredded by all that I'd witnessed on-screen. What truly shook me was not the many things she said or the acts performed, but the look on her face throughout. I knew that look. I had seen it many times during our last debauched week together. She had worked me, step-by-step, just as she'd worked this McMurphy.

I saw no conscience in those eyes. No warmth. Only calculation and expectation. Even when playacting the deepest throes of ecstasy, she watched McMurphy closely. You could almost see her tick off each hash mark as she put him through his courses, efficiently moving him toward climax so that she could, afterward, hit him with her next request. If McMurphy had ever once watched the videos with any sort of objectivity, he too would have seen how he was being played. But he was blinded by his love for Cyn. Poor miserable bastard.

I collapsed onto the couch with a lighter heart than I'd had in a very long time. Those videos of McMurphy's were a gift to me. They gave me permission to write Cyn off in a way that I'd never allowed myself before. As the first light of dawn began to trickle through the window, I felt my guilt over our last days together evaporate. Cyn was a creature of a different sort. She operated under different rules than Glo and I. I closed my eyes and drifted into a light sleep filled with strange erotic overtones. Female forms of all colors ghosted in and out of sight, leaving impressionistic glimpses of breast and sumptuous rump. Not one of them was blond. I was, I thought, finally free.

The doorbell rang around eleven thirty. I heard it from inside the shower and finished rinsing off in a hurry. When I came out of the bathroom, I found Glo on the couch, a FedEx envelope ripped open on the coffee table before her. In her hand, she held a single sheet of white paper, covered with large blue script.

"What's that?"

"It's from Cyn. She wants to see me."

I extended my hand for the letter. Glo looked at me, and I saw her hesitate before she handed it over. It was dated yesterday.

Dearest Glo,

I know that this is a surprise, and maybe not a welcome one, but as you know by now, I am alive and in your city. I need to see you. I don't have much time, and in truth I desperately need your help. I've wanted to reach out for so long, and it would mean everything to me to see you again. I have a room in the city. Please call the number below, and let me know if you can meet me today (Saturday). Just you. Once we talk, you'll understand.

Much love sister,

C.

PS—I know you've met RM. This will sound paranoid, but please check your coat and purse for tracking devices.

The one he planted on me was black and about the size of a tube of lip balm. Please understand, I can't let him find me.

I read it once. Twice. Glo picked up her handbag and upended it over the kitchen table. I read it again. I turned it over and looked at the back, to see if perhaps there was something I missed.

Just you. It said. *Just you.*

My mouth was dry. I emptied the mug of cold coffee that I had left on the table earlier and felt a surprisingly strong desire to throw it at the wall, or even better, at the window.

"What do you think?" Glo murmured, as cool as I was steaming. I watched her pale hands comb through the contents on the table.

"It's, uh . . ." Lights seemed to flash on and off in my head as I struggled to settle on a single way to feel. I crushed the paper in my sweaty palm and let it fall to the table between us. "It's pretty clear the only reason she deigned to contact you at all is because she needs something. She can go fuck herself."

I choked up a bit on the last part, infuriatingly showing my hand. Some fantastic actor I was. But still, the absolute gall of it, of showing up and asking for something. But really, that wasn't what had my gorge rising and my heart thundering. It was those scalpel-sharp words that excised me entirely from the picture.

Just you.

They should have been written in blood, they were that malignant. The walls throbbed around me, wobbling like cellophane, my barely contained rage bubbling like magma. I was afraid any word, any gesture from Glo could crack me, and from that fissure, a steaming fury would escape. I didn't want to flip out on Glo. This wasn't for her.

"Son of a bitch," she said, and lifted a small black rectangle from the table. "That fucker planted a bug on me."

She turned to me and showed me the tracker, her eyes flashing with outrage.

"We are not doing this," I stated.

"What do you mean 'We're not doing this?' "

"We're not getting involved in whatever it is she wants."

Glo slapped McMurphy's bug onto the table. "First of all, she didn't ask you for help. She asked me. It's my decision."

"Are you kidding?"

"No. I'm not. What difference does it make to you if I see her?"

"You're joking."

"No."

"Are you too blind to see that she's manipulating you?"

"How is asking for help manipulating me? It's pretty fucking direct."

"Direct? Sure. Maybe you also noticed that her letter makes no mention of me. Does that not seem just a little bit strange to you?"

"I knew it. You're pissed off because, for whatever reason, she just wants to see me. Your ego is hurt, and you want her to suffer for it."

"This is not about my ego. You're getting suckered by your feelings. She's playing you! She's not your friend. She disappears for seven years and only shows up now, needing help? When conveniently, you happen to work for the district attorney's office? Who knows what kind of twisted shit she wants to get you involved in—"

"We don't have any idea what she wants!"

"Exactly! Not to mention this guy McMurphy said she's a danger to you."

"Yeah, and he also put a fucking tracer in my bag in order to find her. She's obviously the one in danger."

"You don't know that! She's not worth this. She's not even

worth a calm, safe cup of coffee in a café. I can't let you do this."

"Oh, Jesus, Raj! Do I take orders from you now?"

We were shouting at one another in our living room. This was not us. I took a breath, trying to get my thoughts in order. I had to get a handle on this before it went too far.

I lowered my voice, speaking as calmly as I could. "Does it make no difference to you what I want?"

"It does make a difference."

"Then don't see her. Don't let her back in."

"She asked me for help. Do you really expect me to tell her no?"

"Yes! I do. But you won't, will you?"

She turned away. I couldn't stop myself.

"You know what your problem is, Glo?"

She turned around, her face steely with challenge. "Can't wait to find out."

"Your biggest problem is you've never been able to tell her no. You've always done everything she's said, and gone along with everything she ever wanted to do, no matter how stupid and dangerous."

"That's not true!"

"It is true! Did you want to go to that island? No! She did, and you went along with it, just like always. Just like you did on that first night after we slept together. You do what she wants at the expense of yourself, and at my expense, too. It was true even when she was 'dead.' She became Saint Cyn, flawless angel, and it got easy to forget what a controlling bitch she was. Well, for me, one thing is certain, and that is I will be damned if I let this all start back up again!"

Glo looked stunned.

"What are you talking about? That night we slept together, I came back to our room and you two had it all sorted out. I wasn't just going along with her, you two were already in agreement! I didn't have any choice at all."

"No, Glo. That's not what happened. I wanted to be with you. I went to your room to find you and found her instead. The whole thing was her idea, and the only reason I didn't speak against it is because I stupidly imagined that you would. You could have told her no, but you caved. You let her win because you valued her more than you valued me. And now, fucking history repeats itself! You're more than willing to walk out that door and put your life in danger for her, without any thought to how it affects us."

Glo seemed to reel, bracing herself against the table with a stiff arm. The letter slipped to the floor without her noticing.

"I thought you liked her more than me. I thought half was the best I could get."

"Of course you did, because *you* liked her more. She was the sun, the moon, and the stars to you."

"That's not how I remember it."

I saw she was trembling, and I pulled her into my arms. She was reluctant to come, but as I held her, she began to soften.

"I know you don't," I said into the warm thicket of her hair. "But, sweetheart, there's a time and a place for certain people in our lives. Her time has passed. Please, for me, don't do this. Don't let her back in."

She pulled back, and I thought we might kiss. But she kept pulling back all the way out of my arms and halfway across the room.

"Manipulation—" she said, the bitter word seeming to catch in her throat.

"What?"

"You just accused Cyn of trying to manipulate me, and now you're doing it. I'm not utterly stupid. I wasn't then, and I'm not now. Do you really expect me to believe that you didn't want to be with her?"

"Glo, I was nineteen—"

"You were nineteen, so your cock had the deciding vote in all matters."

"I'm not saying— Listen. That part of me did want her, yes. I was attracted to her. I liked her. I cared about her a lot. I thought she was a very bright, very mixed-up girl. But I always sensed the crazy underneath—"

"You don't know the half of it," she scoffed.

"Maybe not—"

"She was sleeping with johns. At least one of them tried to rape her. That's one of the reasons she was fucked up."

I watched the words peel off her lips, but somehow I had to run them through my head three times before I understood them.

"You knew that all these years, and you never thought to tell me?"

"I didn't know until that last day in Costa Rica. She—"

"Why the fuck didn't you tell me?"

Glo gave me a look I've never seen before, a nervous scan up and down as if I had transformed into a person of potential violence. I was the bad guy all of a sudden.

"I thought about telling you when I got back, but there was already so much bad stuff on the news, and I thought she was dead. There seemed no point in having you think—"

"You wanted to protect her! Just like always."

"Which is a huge crime in your eyes! What difference does it make? It's all in the past!"

"Is it? How can it be if you go and see her and start it up again?"

Someone pounded on the wall. We had been shouting. We glared at each other with naked hostility.

I lowered my voice.

"You see this, what we're doing right now? *This* is what she does to us. This is what she's always done—"

"You cannot ask me to just turn my back on her and forget it happened." Glo's voice was husky. She wouldn't look at me directly.

"I am asking that. Don't go. Don't see her."

"I'll do as I damn well please! Maybe it hasn't occurred to you that I might have a few questions I'd like to ask her, and quite a few things to say. Stop treating me like some stupid child. I know what I'm doing!"

"Do you?"

"Yes!"

"So your mind is made up?"

She turned her back, folded the letter with excessive care, and tucked it into her purse. Cyn was winning, ripping us apart with a flimsy sheet of copy paper.

"You know what, Glo? Do whatever you want. Fuck danger. Fuck the life we've built together. Do what she wants and hurry over to serve her. Evidently, that's all you've ever wanted."

For a second, the room got very quiet. Glo stared at the table, motionless, except for the quick rise and fall of her chest.

"All I've ever wanted? Since when do you care about what I want? Since when do you bother to lift your attention from your precious theater company for long enough to notice?"

The response I'd been preparing died unformed. The way she was looking at me chilled me to the core.

"Glo—"

"Do you think I've forgotten that you did your best to see her last night? The way you're acting now, all judgmental and self-righteous, it's pathetic. It's a joke. I'm going to go and have one last conversation with her. I need to. If you can't handle it, maybe . . ." She trailed off, gazing past me.

"Maybe what?"

"Maybe we really are fucked. Maybe our relationship is doomed never to move beyond where it was when we were twenty." She looked at me, and her green eyes shone, pitiless and certain. "I don't want to be those same people. I can't live my life wondering if our being together is just a fluke. The past few months, I feel like I've been asking you to double down on our life together, and you have a million reasons why you can't. I don't want your fucking reasons. If you don't see us having a real future together, then you have to let me go."

I watched, stunned, as she repacked her bag, shoving McMurphy's device into her jeans pocket. I felt mildly concussed, unable to respond to how heavy the argument had just become.

"I don't want to let you go," I managed. There was so much more I wanted to say, but I was paralyzed by the fear that I would say something wrong and make things worse. Jesus, was she really talking about splitting up?

"You want all kinds of things, Raj, and so do I."

"Can I come with you? I won't see her. I just want to make sure you're safe."

She gave me a withering look and removed her cell phone from her bag, placing it on the table. It was a wordless commentary on my tracking her down the night before.

"You have your matinee."

I nodded. She picked up her keys and headed for the door. I wanted so badly to touch her, to get some sign that she still believed in our future, but I stood frozen to the spot and watched her walk away.

"Please be careful," I said, but the rusty shriek of the closing door muted my words. I don't know if she heard me.

CHAPTER EIGHTEEN

Glo

Having just thrown down a possible marriage-ending ultimatum, I was surprised that I didn't feel like crying. Instead, my head felt clearer than it had in a very long time. I had said what I needed to say to Raj, deflected most of his bullshit, and now I had one last major task to scratch off my list: meet Cyn.

A shiver of excitement jolted through me at the thought of it, but I shook it off. I was still carrying McMurphy's tracking device, and the idea that he might be lurking somewhere, watching, had me on edge. I mustered up some feigned confidence and walked out into the gray, blustery afternoon. I cast a look up my street, on high alert for a shadowy figure slumped low behind the wheel of an anonymous sedan.

That dumb hat of his will be the tip-off, I thought, and tittered nervously to myself as I hurried across the street. I ducked into a local Internet café and asked to borrow the phone. The woman at the counter looked me over suspiciously and asked if I wanted to purchase an international calling card. I told her it was local and would be brief, but I would pay whatever she wanted. She pushed the boxy desktop telephone toward me with a sigh.

"No charge. Be quick."

I dialed the number on Cyn's letter. It went immediately to a voice mail system. I told her to meet me at the Copper Dragon.

I would be there in less than an hour, and I was coming alone. I hung up and thanked the woman, who didn't look up from her magazine.

On the street, I hailed a cab and asked the driver to take me to the last subway stop in Queens, just before it dove under the river into Manhattan. I had a feeling that Raj would pull some grand melodramatic gesture, like rushing to intercept me on our usual subway platform, begging me to love him forever. His presence would screw up my plan. He would never expect me to ask Cyn to meet at his theater, and that made it the perfect place. I would have the advantage of being on familiar ground, somewhere private where we wouldn't be interrupted. If Cyn really wanted to see me, she would accept my terms. It was as simple as that.

As the driver carried on a mumbled conversation in an indecipherable tongue, I pulled the GPS tracker from my pocket and slid it deep into the darkness beneath his seat. I glanced out the rear to see if any cars were tailing us, but there was a city bus following directly behind, blocking the view. At the subway entrance, I paid the fare and slipped quickly down the steps into the station. As the train pulled in, I found myself smiling, imagining McMurphy trying to follow my electronic trail. He'd no doubt be surprised to discover I spent a Saturday going to and from the city's many delightful airports and halal stands. By the time he figured out he'd been duped, it'd be too late.

As I climbed out of the station into the low gloom of the overcast afternoon, I shook off the first tremor of nerves. My stomach was still reeling from the alcohol, aspirin, and marital drama, and I was running on no more than toast and coffee. I thought a cold soda might help, and looked up to discover the wish-fulfilling doors of a drugstore. The moment I stepped inside, I remembered that I hadn't filled my birth control prescription. Fertility, left unchecked, would resume tomorrow.

Soda in hand, I walked to the Dragon. Before I went inside, I paused by the door of the theater, and with the paper bag from my purchase, erased what little remained of Raj's chalk message. I didn't want Cyn to see it.

I walked into the darkness of the Dragon. It was empty of customers. Ted, the bartender, smiled at me.

"What's this? You've been recruited as set dresser now?" he asked.

"Kind of," I lied.

"That's bollocks," he scoffed, amiably. "Want a drink?"

I was about to shake my head, but my eye fell on a bottle of dark rum, the same brand that Cyn and I had been drinking before everything fell apart. "Yeah, why not?"

"What'll it be?"

"That dark rum, with the silver label. Neat."

"Neat? You got it."

He poured one for me and one for himself. We clinked glasses. "To your good work," he said.

"And to yours."

We slugged back the rum, and Ted screwed up his face. "My god. It's like paint thinner."

I smiled and felt my stomach roar as this latest insult was laid down. "There's a girl coming to meet me. A friend. When she gets here, can you send her down? Phone doesn't work, and I can't always hear a knock."

"Sure. What's she look like?"

"Pretty. Blond."

"Single?" he asked, pretending to fix his hair. "Only joking. Of course I'll send her down."

I descended into the darkness of the theater, groping blindly for the switch to light the dusty iron chandelier that hung in the narrow hallway leading to the auditorium. The space always made me nervous, and this was the first time I'd been there alone. Raj told me that it had been an operating theater in the thirties, and later, the home of a fortune-telling psychic, though he might have been pulling my leg. I made an effort not to think about creepy soothsayers or botched surgeries while I ran my hands up and down the wall, my sweat turning cold as the light switch continued to evade me. I took another step deeper into the hallway, attuned to a dozen creepy creaks and twitches from the utter darkness that surrounded me.

Come on. Be here, I breathed as my hands continued searching. The switch had to be close. I circled my hands like Daniel-san, *Wax On, Wax Off*, but still, nothing. I gulped in air, feeling panic closing in. *Maybe this was all a mistake*, I thought, splaying my fingers wide as my heart began to race. Maybe Raj was right and I had walked into a trap. My fingers ran over something soft and sticky, and I jerked my hands away, panting, unmoored, in the total darkness. In that moment, I imagined the worst: for seven years, Cyn had harbored a furious grudge over what had happened on the island and was now back for revenge, served very, very cold. As the thought took root, I heard a strange hum from the auditorium and my breath quickened. *Was it possible that she was a danger to me?* I asked myself. *Yes.* Now that she was back, anything was possible. *Was it likely?* The hum ceased, and my hand shot out, groping for the wall to guide me back to the front door. Had my fingertips not, at that moment, brushed the light panel, I might have fled, abandoning the enterprise entirely.

I flicked on the light and spun around, searching the dingy velvet walls for haunts and bogeymen. Of course there was nothing. I inhaled slowly and tasted rum in the back of my throat.

As my heart rate decelerated, I returned to my unanswered question. *No, it was not likely*. Cyn wouldn't hurt me. I felt that, deeply. I passed to the end of the hall and switched on a dimmer, raising the house lights to hangover-friendly level of illumination. In the heavy stillness of the deep, empty space, I descended the center aisle between the rows of seats, taking in the set.

Raj had done an admirable job. He wasn't the handiest person with a hammer, but he'd single-handedly constructed a passable apartment setup, with a couple of functioning doors and a window that looked onto a fake brick wall. There was a mattress on the floor, and a battered-looking office chair. A small camping stove rested by a blackened wall, and all kinds of believable junkie detritus littered the floor.

After giving the set mattress a quick sniff to make sure the stains were not authentic, I lay down across it, feeling my anxiety dissolve into pure exhaustion. The pounding in my head was fading. I yawned and let my eyelids fall shut, drifting into a glorious state of mindless twilight.

I was jerked back to reality by the distant click of the theater door closing.

I bolted upright, so quickly that my vision went crimson. She appeared at the top of the stairs wearing a gray raincoat over a white shirtdress, a leather belt accentuating her trim waist. Her legs were bare, and she wore white ballet flats with golden accents on the toes. Raj was right, she did look rich.

"Glo?"

I nodded.

She floated down the stairs toward me. Her hair was shoulder length, like mine, and underneath the house lights, it shone like bronze. Her skin was pale, and she had bluish crescents under her eyes, but her smile, when she released it, had lost none of its commercial brilliance.

"It's really you." She paused at the foot of the stage and stood, beaming up at me. Her eyes were glassy with pre-tears.

"Yeah," I said, getting to my feet. Truth was, seeing her was a little overwhelming, like bumping into a movie star. Even now, on first glance, she seemed to burn at a different brightness than anyone else I knew. I reminded myself to stay grounded, to not allow myself to turn into the starstruck fangirl that Raj accused me of being.

"Thank you so much for meeting me," she said. She clutched a gold-accented leather bag in front of her body, and I saw that she wore a monstrous emerald ring on her left hand and a delicate gold watch on the other.

"You wanna come up here? It looks bad, but it's more comfortable than those ancient seats."

"Sure."

Perhaps confused by the primness of her attire, I was about to offer a hand to help her up, but she made the two-and-a-half-foot climb in one effortless step.

"So this is your theater?" Her eyes swam across the squalor. She stood two feet from me, an arm's length away, but we didn't touch. It felt strange not to hug, but we hadn't, and now it was too late. I shoved my hands in my jeans pockets, and shuffled backward awkwardly.

"It's Raj's, and his partner's. Please, have a seat."

I lowered myself to a cross-legged position on the mattress. She settled herself into the chair, and beamed at me like a Disney Princess about to burst into song. "I've dreamed of this moment so many times. I can't believe it's really you."

"It's really me."

"Thank you for seeing me."

"Please stop thanking me." She colored, and I realized my tone carried an edge. I almost apologized, but an inner voice pointed out that apologizing was exactly the kind of thing a giddy fangirl would do. We were equals. If anything, I was in charge. "Of course I came. I mean, come on. How could I resist?"

"I'm sure you're wondering where I've been all this time, and why I'm here."

"Yeah."

"I want to tell you everything, Glo. I owe you that." She clapped her hands on her knees and sighed happily. "But first, you look so beautiful. How are you? How is your life?"

"It's good, thanks," I said, allowing a frisson of impatience to percolate through my words. My life was not on the table for discussion.

Cyn leaned back and swallowed, recalibrating.

"I've wanted to reach out, Glo. I wrote you so many letters over the years and never sent them. At first because it was too dangerous, and then because I didn't think it would be fair or kind to butt into your life like that."

"You mean, kind of like you are right now?"

She nodded shortly, the color rising in her cheeks.

"What do you want, Cyn? Why come back from the dead after all these years?"

She forced a laugh. "Is it so terrible to see me?"

"It's not the best, no. You seem to be stalking my husband. You've got some demented paramour coming into my office and planting bugs on me, and now you're sitting here, all smiles and sunshine like this is a normal, happy reunion."

"I didn't mean for things to happen this way. I didn't want to drag you into any of it. But I ended up in New York City and looked you up, and with the information in my head, I couldn't resist trying to see you, just once."

"You mean you couldn't resist seeing Raj. You went to his show last weekend, and since then, my life—"

"Actually, I went to see you first," she interrupted coolly. "I watched you shiver your way through lunch in the pavilion in front of the Federal Building. You had a few bites of salad and three cigarettes. You were still so much the Glo that I knew that it surprised me. After seeing you, it was like I couldn't back off. I haven't felt anything good in so long, and seeing you . . . Then last week, upstairs in the bar. It took everything I had not to walk over and sit at your table. Like old friends." Her voice dropped out. "Can I smoke in here?"

I nodded. I had been eating lunch in the pavilion. She could have simply walked up and said hello, and spared me so much worry and angst. Instead, she chose the route of cloak-and-dagger bullshit, and even now, it continued.

She lit up with trembling hands. "Want one?"

I shook my head.

"I know that this has probably been a little unexpect—"

"What do you want Cyn?"

She heard the edge in my voice, and she straightened.

"Your letter said you needed my help. Tell me what you want from me."

She took a long pull on her cigarette, and when she looked at me again, all the vulnerability was gone from her face.

"You loved me once. You tried to save my life back on that island, after you threw me to the wolves. I think we both know you owe me one, so what I need from you now is to save my life. For real this time."

"Threw *you* to the wolves?"

"That's right. You got away, didn't you? Got to spend the rest of your life with your own true love? Well, maybe I don't seem real to you anymore, or human, but I want my goddamn happy ending, too. So please, help me. I promise I will go away and leave you alone forever. Both of you."

"And if I don't?"

She fastened me with a stare of cold disbelief. "Do you particularly enjoy the thought of my blood on your hands?"

I had the sudden urge to hit her, to wipe that haughty look off her face. "I've changed my mind about the cigarette."

She pulled out her pack and tossed it to me. I lit up, all too aware of my own trembling fingers. The first drag steadied me. The second made me bold.

"You want to talk about happy endings? You have no fucking idea what happened to me after all that. The guilt that I went through, and not, as you state, because I threw you to the wolves. I did everything I could to save you."

"But you didn't. I paid the price. You got away."

"You could have come with me."

"You know that's not true. Fucked-up as I was, I could barely tell the air from the water."

"Is that my fault, too? The whole thing was your idea."

"Was it, Glo? Does it matter? You wanted some adventure, too, if I recall correctly. You were dying for it, just like I was. Don't pretend like I dragged you there kicking and screaming. Raj might buy that version of events, but I sure as hell don't. Neither one of us went out to that island as a victim, but one of us sure as hell became one. And here's a news flash, sister: it wasn't you." Her eyes flashed in the dim light and she pulled a tin can off the set, dashing a fiery cylinder of ash into its center.

"What happened to you?"

She laughed drily. "How long have you got?"

I was about to speak, but she interrupted me. "Those men on the beach were drug traffickers. Submariners. The captain thought I would make a fun toy."

She stared at me until I looked away.

"It was terrible in all the ways that you can imagine. They threatened my life, I barely escaped being raped, and because of that small twist in my destiny, of staying so that you could be free, I've seen things that I will never be able to forget. The worst possible things. Beyond nightmares."

I focused my attention on the gold toe of her ballet slipper, unwilling to look at her face.

"The experience inside the sub separated me from myself, from a person who wanted this and that to an animal that just wanted to live. And then, when we got to the United States, I saw the news stories about me. Who would want to be that girl, the one on the screen? Only a madwoman would walk back into that. *Cynty* was dead, and I realized I wanted her that way. Better for me. Better for you and Raj. Better for my poor, sainted parents. It was so natural, that I hardly had to think about it at all.

"I see on your face what you're thinking. If I was so tough and really gave no shits about what anybody said, why didn't I just come back? But ask yourself, would you really have wanted that? Imagine the press at my rescue. I would have become the first slut saint, brought back to grace by a long submersion in the healing waters of the Pacific Ocean." She chuckled, one manicured hand resting on her stomach. "Raj might have taken it as a sign to become a priest, and where would you be then? My staying dead is the best thing that happened to you and Raj both."

"But here you are, Cyn. Why?"

"McMurphy. I chose badly, but I was desperate."

"Desperate for what?"

She leaned back in her chair and sighed.

"There was a man on the sub, Lucas. He was barely a man at the time, only nineteen to my twenty-two. He was an engineering prodigy, the son of a dirt-poor gardener who worked on the estate of a man called El Santo, a man who happened to head a billion-dollar drug cartel. El Santo got wind of how smart Lucas was and paid for his accelerated education. His first job was a redesign of a small submersible. Lucas was there on the island, taking part in the maiden voyage of his creation. He's the only reason that I'm still alive. He looked out for me on the sub and protected me."

"You mean, he kidnapped you?"

"He saved me. The captain, this trigger-happy, coke-addled whack job named Hugo, wanted to shoot me on the spot just for seeing their faces. Lucas wasn't a killer. For him, moving the drugs was just a science project. Then Hugo killed Marco and Hector, and everything went to hell."

I must have flinched, because Cyn paused. "Lucas told me it was very quick. I don't think they suffered."

I nodded, grateful for that added bit of information, even as I doubted whether it was true. A couple of tears fought their way out of me as I remembered the brothers wrestling in the sand, bursting with life. Cyn watched as I wiped them away, and sat silently for a moment before pressing on.

"While Hugo led the raid on our cove, Lucas was wrapping the brothers, kids his own age, in a weighted tarp and dragging them out into the ocean. It messed him up. So when they showed up with me, and Hugo wanted to repeat the process, Lucas told him that if they didn't let me go, he would sink the sub. Hugo argued that it was too dangerous to let me live; I would talk and compromise the two-hundred-million-dollar shipment. Lucas said, fine, we'll take her with us. I wanted to live, so I didn't have much choice in the matter.

"For the rest of the long journey north, Lucas protected me from Hugo, but it was still a nightmare. The inside of the sub was putrid, hot, dark, and claustrophobic. Everyone was stressed to the breaking point. Hugo had cracked through part of the flooring to get at the coke in the hold and was constantly high. The other two crew members were freaked out that Hugo's theft was going to get everyone killed, and of course there was the constant threat of being caught by the Coast Guard. The one bright spot was Lucas. It sounds crazy, but on the sub, we fell in love."

"It doesn't sound crazy. It sounds like Stockholm syndrome."

"I know. But it wasn't. All those hours in the darkness, we lay together on a tiny canvas cot, not knowing if we were going to live or die. He'd taken a huge risk for me, and no one knew how it would play out once we reached the States and El Santo learned what had happened. It may have been an intimacy born of desperation, but the result was real. We told each other everything. By the end, I knew his whole life, I knew his soul, and he knew mine. I told him things that I've never told anyone. No one has ever made me feel so safe, or so loved. Once you find something like that, no matter how it starts, you can't just let it go. I've been with him ever since. I married him, Glo."

"You married the drug trafficker who kidnapped you." I somehow managed to keep the incredulity out of my voice.

"When we arrived in San Diego, I saw the news and weighed my options. He saw it all, too, the photos, everything, and he didn't judge me. When I told him that I couldn't go back to my old life, he asked me to come with him to Colombia. It turned out that El Santo didn't care about what happened on the island. He was just elated that Lucas's sub had gotten there two days faster than the previous incarnation. Lucas told me he didn't know where his life was headed, or if he'd ever be able to offer me a stable home, but he promised that if I went with him, he would upend his life to make me happy."

The cigarette rested between her fingers, forgotten and burned down to the filter.

"I already understood the rational arguments against his proposal: we were basically strangers, he was entangled with dangerous, casually lethal people, and I was probably not yet in my right mind. But on the other hand, I figured if partnering with Lucas was a mistake, then it was just one more for my collection. I'd made so many mistakes, and whether I agonized over the choices or dove in on a whim, the outcomes seemed equally random. So I made the decision to stop always worrying about the worst possible result and just live my life."

"And have you avoided the worst possible outcome?"

She shrugged and tossed the butt into the can. "Everything is relative. I had four good years, two bad, and one truly terrible. If I can't change my circumstances quickly, I won't have the luxury of any more years to evaluate."

"Why not? McMurphy?" A heavy truck passed by on the street outside, rattling the metal theater door in its frame. I felt a shock of adrenaline, and began to rise, wondering if Cyn had thought to lock the door behind her on her way in.

"I locked it," she said with a wry smile. I knew better than to be surprised at her ability to read my mind. "What did you do with the bug?"

"I left it in a taxi."

She laughed drily. "Good thinking." She pulled out another cigarette. "McMurphy is more a disappointment than a real threat. He reminds me a little of your Tim. Remember Tall Tim, with the alcohol intolerance?"

I allowed myself a small smile. "I can see some similarities. Height, for one. What's his deal?"

She lifted an ankle and slowly rolled her foot, studying the golden tip of her shoe. "I would have given him so many things, but not the one thing he wants. Turns out his marriage has been in the shitter, and now she's gone and he's all in when it comes to me. That wasn't the plan, and now it's gotten . . ." She sighed, her clear blue eyes meeting mine. "Difficult. Very fucking difficult."

"I see. Do the police need to get involved?"

She looked at me and laughed, loudly. "Police. Good one, Glo."

I blushed, against my own wishes. It was a stupid thing to suggest.

"I met McMurphy early on, when Lucas and I still thought we had a chance of getting out of the business. I was still an American citizen, and I wanted to find out if I could bring

Lucas back with me once he had completed his contract. After that first run, Lucas told El Santo that he didn't want to be part of the cartel. El Santo agreed, feeding him some line that drug running was a terrible business, not fit for dogs. But each time Lucas would ask to leave, we were always told, after the next project. It's been seven years now. I'm here to do whatever it takes to get free from that life. Our time is running out."

"You said Lucas was designing subs?"

She looked away. I sensed the wheels turn a couple of clicks as she decided how much to share.

"Yes, at first. Then he moved on to more complex projects. Making improvements on existing systems."

"Systems?" I waited, but she didn't elaborate. I guess she didn't need to. I got the picture. Lucas was too valuable to just be allowed to wander off into the American sunset. In gumshoe terms, he knew too much.

"I haven't asked about Raj," she said, in a blatant change of subject. "Thank you for not bringing him, by the way. I didn't think he'd appreciate hearing me wax on about me falling in love with some other guy. How is he?"

"He's great. He's an actor now, as you know. Also a director."

She nodded, sphinxlike. At that moment, I realized what about her had changed, or maybe what about me: other than the revealing way she talked about Lucas, I no longer had the slightest clue what she was thinking. Her outward expression was simultaneously completely amiable and totally guarded. If I hadn't known her at a more sensitive time, I may not have noticed it. It was a finely honed mask. I felt a sluice of adrenaline flow into my blood, wondering if I was somehow being played.

"You went to see his play. Why?"

"I just wanted to see him, Glo. One last time. I fell in love with someone else, but I did love Raj, in my own way."

"How did you think that would make me feel? Or Raj feel?"

"I'm sure it freaked you out. Both of you. I'm sorry, Glo. I really am. I bungled that one, big-time. I bought the ticket on impulse, not really checking where the seat was. It was idiotic, but I didn't think about the fact that, duh, it's not television. Stage actors can sometimes see you, too."

She looked genuinely contrite, and I felt my pulse begin to slow. Until she added, "One of the delights of my strange life has been that you and Raj made it. I followed you, on the Internet, as much as I could. It makes me think that on some weird level, all of this was supposed to happen."

"You seem to think it was easy for us. It wasn't."

"But you guys pulled through. It was fated."

A dark, dry laugh escaped me. "Fated? That's a fun way of putting it."

"How do you figure, Glo?" She leaned toward me, exhibiting signs of authentic interest.

"You do realize that your actions were the catalyst for what happened, right? Not all of it was bad, and not all of it was your fault, but it's hard for me to hear you describe it as some random chain of events that just happened to have a happy ending. We went through some terrible shit."

"I didn't mean it to come across—"

"You decided when to leave," I continued over her, swept up in my own prosecutorial spiel. She blinked at me through a plume of smoke, and I corrected my misstatement. "You at least decided not to return, and now you've changed your mind. That's not fate. That's the cause and effect of your choices, many of which continue to affect my life. That's not fate. Let's get it straight."

She waited for me to finish before pinning me with those cool blue eyes. "Question: Would you rather not have known what you know now?"

"Well, I already know it, so that's not really an option."

"Okay, then, thought experiment. Remember we used to say that about random hypotheticals? If you hadn't heard from me, and some man on the street came up and handed you an envelope that told you what happened to me, would you not have opened it?"

"I'd have opened it, yes. Because I'm a human being and a very curious one at that. That's largely the reason why I'm here. I had to see for my own eyes if it was true. And just so you know, I'm happy that you found love and your life has been mostly great. I'm really glad to hear it."

She released a tight, joyless laugh. "It's not mostly great, Glo," she managed, her neck tightening as if garroted by an invisible scarf. "In fact, it's not great at all. I'm really sorry for showing up like this, but after things fell apart with McMurphy and the money I brought in ran out, I didn't know what else to do." She smoothed away fresh tears, inhaling deeply. "I'm fucking scared and I'm desperate and if I don't figure something out, everything that makes my life worth living is going to be destroyed. I thought I was smart enough to do this on my own, but my plans keep falling to pieces and I'm running out of time. I know you probably think I'm a piece of shit because I'm both fucking up your life and asking for help, but you are honestly the last good person I know who I can trust."

She looked up at me, her face damp with tears. If we were your standard set of old friends, this was when I would have risen and moved close to give comfort. But as it was, McMurphy's warning not to trust her repeated in my head like a particularly ominous broken record. Instead of following my instinct, I folded my hands in my lap and gazed at the floor, reminding myself uncomfortably of my Big U shrink.

"Why don't you tell me how you think I can help?"

She looked toward me, but not at me, her mouth loose. "Glo, babe, I want to come home."

I stiffened.

"Home? As in, the United States?"

"Yes."

"What's stopping you?"

"We're trapped. We can't get out. But we have information. My hope is that the United States would be very grateful for this information. Grateful enough to offer a way out, and . . . protection."

"Protection from whom? El Santo?"

She lowered her eyes. "El Santo is dead." Her tone made me think she might suddenly genuflect, Catholic-style. "His son, Ernesto, is in charge now. He's the exact opposite of his father; reckless, coldhearted, cruel. He's a true, clinical psychopath, only goal in life is to make more money and get more power than Daddy. He always resented Lucas's relationship with El Santo. Thought Lucas was some little guttersnipe, looking for handouts. Now that he has all the power, Ernesto has made a point of making Lucas suffer. Making us suffer.

"I really thought that when El Santo died, we'd maybe have our chance. But two days after the funeral, Ernesto summoned Lucas to his home around midnight. When Lucas got there, he was herded onto a helicopter. In the copter with Lucas was the pilot; Ernesto; Ernesto's bodyguard; and a bound, blindfolded man. When they were in the air, Ernesto removed the blindfold, and Lucas recognized Gabriel Arroyo, an older friend who also worked for the cartel. He was crying and begging for his life. Lucas pleaded with Ernesto to reconsider whatever it was they were doing, but it didn't help. The helicopter flew to the center of town, where there was a church with a plaza, and at its center, an old fountain. Ernesto ordered the pilot to ascend. When he decided they were high enough, he opened the door and without a word, kicked Gabriel out into space. Lucas couldn't hear him scream over the roar of the blades, but the entire town heard the impact of his body. It completely shattered one side of the fountain.

"Ernesto turned to Lucas, and just stared at him. Didn't say a word. Once he decided that Lucas got the message, he signaled the pilot to return home. You see, Lucas knew Gabriel wanted out, too. Gabriel had told Lucas of his plan to rent a boat and take his family to Lima. Lucas didn't tell another soul, but somehow, Ernesto found out anyway."

Her hands were trembling as she stubbed out her cigarette. "Funny South America thing—El Santo used to pay for the maintenance of that plaza, out of pocket, because he thought every respectable town needed a nice place for people to gather and socialize. Now Ernesto refuses to allow the fountain to be fixed, so it just sits there in ruin. No one goes there anymore except for the old men, because they've seen it all, and the homeless. I feel like it's a message just for us."

"Jesus." I watched as she started to crumble into herself like a sand sculpture.

"I can't live like this anymore, terrified that any day Lucas is going to leave and not come home or that someone will come for us."

"How did you get away? How are you here?"

"Vacation." She smiled wanly, through her tears. "Actually, the official story is that my mother is dying. If they sent anyone to track me, my cover is already blown. But I can't think about that."

"And Lucas remains there, wherever there is."

A cracked smile bent her lips and she nodded.

There was one thing about Cyn's story that didn't quite make sense to me. Cyn may have changed, but I couldn't imagine her sitting idly while her husband went off to do mysterious things at the cartel every day.

"What exactly have you been doing the past seven years?"

She chewed her lip and muttered, "Housewifing."

"Bullshit."

She grinned. Her eyes exhibited a reckless twinkle that I knew well. "You don't believe that ol' Cyn would be content to sit around doing laundry and watching telenovelas all day?"

"No, I don't."

"Well, you're right. You've put your finger on the button. I got involved. I am so fucking involved. If I would have kept my head down and just been a normal wife, and watched the damn TV, things might have been okay, or maybe less terrible. But I had to get interested. Had to offer suggestions. Ideas. It seemed like a harmless way to help my husband, at the time."

"Fuck, Cyn. This complicates things, you realize."

She closed her eyes and leaned her head back, exposing her throat. "I know, Glo. But after what happened with Gabriel, I thought to myself, *His wife wasn't involved*, but that doesn't make him any less dead."

My head was beginning to throb. I uncapped my flat soda and took a sip. When I looked back up, Cyn was studying me, her fingers knotted together in a tight bunch.

"Can you forgive me, Glo, for vanishing? Or worse, for coming back like this, asking for favors?"

"Yeah, sure." My thoughts were spiraling around the logistics of who I could call to help with something like this. It was absolutely out of my field of knowledge, more like something for the FBI or the State Department. And how exactly did McMurphy, bona fide employee of the State Department, play into this, and why was she no longer relying on his help? I glanced up, and she was fixing me with big questioning doll eyes.

"You do? Really?"

It took me a moment to remember what she'd just asked.

"Jesus, Cyn. With your problems, does it even matter what I think?"

"Yes!"

"Why?"

She dropped from her chair onto her knees before me and put a hot hand on mine, her face softening in a way I'd never seen.

"My daughter, Glorianna, is three. She is my most treasured thing. I named her after you. And I know it may seem strange because we've not known each other much longer than we were friends, but it was a very happy thing for me, knowing you. A bright spot. It really was. That's why it matters. My life has been such a bizarre mix of things, good and bad, that I've stopped trying to make sense of it. I'm just doing all I can right now to not fall apart, so if you don't like me or don't trust me, I'll just drop the pretense of dignity and start begging—"

"Cyn . . ."

She pulled her hands away and wrapped them around herself, a hysterical smile distorting her face. "Who knows? Maybe I can get used to it. I mean, seven years and I rarely see any of the murders. I mostly just hear about them from Lucas and if I'm very lucky, see the photos in the newspaper—"

"Cyn." I took her wrist and shook her. When her eyes snapped to my face, I heard myself say, "I will help you. I'll do whatever I can."

She stared at me, wide-eyed, and emitted a single moan of relief. She opened her arms to me, and sensing eminent breakdown, I caught her as she collapsed into tears, sobbing like it was rinsing something out of her. I was crying a little, too, as a rough picture of the horrors she faced formed in my mind.

"Where is she? Your daughter?"

She sniffled violently, her breath coming in uneven heaves. "With Lucas. Back there. That's why they didn't even have to follow me here. They knew I'd come back. They have everything that's important to me. They have all the cards."

I smoothed the hair from her face as her tears crested and then slowed to a painful shiver. We sat huddled together on the mattress, neither of us speaking for a long moment. A dark look had settled across her brow, and beneath it, a scowl that looked well-worn-in. I imagined her wearing that face, pacing a balcony at night, cigarette in hand, waiting for headlights to appear on the road. Waiting for her husband to come home, only to let the worry begin anew the next day. I tried to put myself in her position, and my mind recoiled in horror. If that was her life, she was right to call it a nightmare.

"Tell me about her. Glorianna."

The hard lines strafing Cyn's brow softened. "She's a wonder. She's very cheerful and she loves birds and animals and is a complete daddy's girl. Wants to follow him everywhere. We're teaching her to swim."

"Just like her namesake," I remarked.

Cyn smiled and, after a moment's hesitation, opened her purse. She fished out a cheap clamshell cell phone and pulled up a photo. "She was born with this curly, reddish hair. No idea where it came from. That's when I knew for sure what to name her." She stared at the image on the screen as if reluctant to look away, and then handed it to me. "I only brought this one, and even carrying it makes me nervous. I've kept our lives off the Internet as much as possible. The less identifiable we are, the better our chances of getting away. Lucas wanted me to bring her with me, but it wasn't allowed. I think they smelled a rat."

I looked at the grainy image on the phone. A small girl with dark copper hair squatted on a lawn, one pudgy arm extended toward a kitten. Glorianna's face was in profile, and her mouth was open, frozen in a squeal of delight. I felt the corners of my mouth rise in response, and handed the phone back, feeling my cheeks burn under Cyn's gaze.

"Are you and Raj planning—"

I cut her off. “We need to approach this delicately.”

“I know.”

“The fact that you were personally working for the cartel makes it difficult.”

“We know everything about their organization. That has to be worth something.”

“I would think so, but I don’t know. This really isn’t what I do.”

“I know you’ll do your best.”

I felt a shiver of recognition. She had said the same words, in the exact same way, to McMurphy in one of the videos.

“They’ll probably put you into hiding. You’ll go dark.”

“Yes, I know.”

She put her phone away and sighed. Stretching her legs out toward the empty seats, she reached for the pack of smokes, offering me one.

As she lit up, she sighed. “So Raj hates me, doesn’t he?”

There was no reason to lie. Whatever veil she had drawn between us was lifting, and the look on her face said she already knew exactly how Raj felt. It reminded me at once of how eerie their connection had been. Long-suppressed memories of watching them argue some metaphysical abstraction, the heat rising as they parried like fencers, making points that I struggled to follow, crawled out from the past to wound me. The intimacy of that connection was why I’d so feared their becoming lovers. She was already sharing with him so many things I couldn’t, even if I tried my best. I hated to even remember it because it so stirred my jealousies, but Raj and Cyn had had something special.

“He doesn’t exactly trust you.”

“In light of everything that happened, I was glad that you and I had that talk at the hostel, about everything. I hope it made it easier for you guys.” She paused. “I would have liked the chance to apologize to him. But there on the street, I just couldn't. Tell him I'm sorry."

"Tell him you're sorry for what?"

"For how it ended. He didn't deserve it. I warned him I was sick."

"What are you talking about?"

Her eyes searched me, and she allowed the slightest flicker of surprise to wash across her features. She flicked her wrist in the air as if shooing a fly or, perhaps, dismissing a servant.

"It's nothing, really. I was cruel to him before we left on our little adventure. I've felt guilty about it all this time. How did he take it when you told him I planned to break up with him?"

I tapped my cigarette on the tin can, though there was nothing yet to ash. "I never told him."

"You what?" she leaned forward, her blue eyes aghast.

"You were dead. Why would I tell? It would only hurt him."

"But what about you? Telling him might have helped you."

"How? I don't hurt people I love for no reason."

"It wouldn't have been for no reason for Raj. I thought I'd done all I could to kill our relationship before we left, but even that didn't work. The poor bastard's probably been carrying a torch for me all this time."

I looked at the floor, feeling the heat rise into my face.

"Sometimes you have to hurt people to help them see the truth. It's not the same as being cruel for no reason." Her tone grated on me, as if she were this wise woman and I, a naive child.

"Was that your technique with Ryan McMurphy? Is he drinking himself to death due to one of your acts of kindness?" I felt her eyes on me but couldn't look at her. "Since we're being all brave and honest and kind, I should tell you: I know about the videos."

She stiffened. "What videos?"

"He recorded all your video . . ." I struggled to find the appropriate word, "sessions. He showed me one."

She looked away. "I told you, I was desperate."

"Yeah, well. You're always desperate, aren't you?"

She flinched like I had slapped her.

"I don't expect you to understand the choices I've made, and I'm not asking you to. You haven't lived my life. You have no idea what it's cost me just to stay alive. And you're right, I may be desperate, but I'm not ashamed. Everything I've done, I've done for my family."

"Does your husband—"

She cut me off. "My husband is a fiercely proud man, but I have no doubt that he would have slept with McMurphy himself if it meant Glorianna could be free. She is innocent, and she deserves better. Maybe someday you'll understand that when your back is against the wall, there is little you won't do to save the ones you love."

"I already know that."

"No, Glo, you don't."

Her eyes were burning. She was talking about the island.

"I was scared," I said.

"I was scared, too."

When I mustered the courage to look up again, she smiled at me through her anger, a quick, sad smile. She had been my best friend, my sister by choice, and I had let her down in the biggest way possible. I had come in to the theater wanting an apology, but now I realized that wasn't what needed to happen at all.

"I'm sorry I left you that night."

She inhaled. "Thank you, Glo. That means a lot to me."

"It's haunted me . . ." I heard my voice thicken and break.

"Glo. It's okay. I know you're sorry, but don't be. Not anymore. There really was no right decision."

My vision went blurry under a gush of stealth tears. The relief I felt was beyond anything I expected. "I just wish—"

There was a subtle pressure change in the room, paired with a quick intrusion of street noise as the theater door quickly opened and shut. My tongue collapsed in my mouth like a popped tire.

Cyn clamped her hand onto my wrist and squeezed. "I thought I'd locked it," she whispered, her eyes wide with fright. She pulled me to my feet and opened one of the set doors, which I knew did not lead anywhere at all. It was too late. Out of my peripheral vision, I saw a man enter the auditorium.

CHAPTER NINETEEN

Raj

"Convincing as it looks, that door doesn't go anywhere, ladies," I said.

Glo spun around to face me while Cyn remained halfway hidden behind the false wall.

"What are you doing here?" Glo demanded.

"Sorry, I thought this was my theater company."

"It's past three. Shouldn't you be onstage?"

I sauntered down the steps, playing it cool. Cyn had emerged from behind the set and was watching me, her head lowered like a lioness tracking prey.

"I thought that maybe this was more important. They're going to fire me anyway."

"What!" Glo exclaimed. "Are you kidding?"

"No. I'm not. Call me crazy, but I thought it was worth losing one acting job to make sure you were safe. Hello, Cyn."

I took a seat in the first row of chairs, where I usually sat if I was directing, and crossed my legs. I was trying very hard to appear at ease, but sweat was already dotting my forehead.

"Hello," she responded, her tone battling mine for the low end of the thermometer.

"How the hell did you know I was here?" Glo was half shouting. "Did you follow me?"

"Ted called me. I asked him last week to give me a heads-up if your ghostly best friend manifested at the bar." Both women were glaring at me, and honestly, it felt great. I was burning my whole world down in a single day. It was the only way forward. "So, what did I miss? Are you besties again? Is she moving in with us?"

"Raj—" Glo began.

"You look right onstage, Cyn. You always were my favorite actress. You look really good on film, too." I winked at her. I had never had the occasion to mine the true depths of my dickishness, and I found the waters were deep.

I saw her face go white. She took a step toward me. She knew exactly what I was talking about, just as I knew she would.

"Did you really think so, Raj?"

"Yes. I enjoyed many of your performances. Your costar, not so much. I would have recast him. Too desperate."

I saw Glo step backward, toward the wall. Her face was blank with shock. She was still too stunned to be disgusted with me.

Cyn cast a look over her shoulder at Glo, and turned back to me. I saw something working behind her eyes, and my heart began to accelerate.

"And what exactly did you like about the videos, Raj?"

"Seeing you. Seeing you for what you really are. It was . . . a relief."

She nodded, and paused, coyly slipping one foot out of her shoe and using it to casually scratch her calf, like some exotic bird. "And what am I?"

I let the question hang in the air as she lowered herself to a seated position at the edge of the stage. There was four feet of dead space between us. Her eyes glimmered challengingly in the low light, each blink an unspoken dare.

"A whore."

Glo exhaled. A second later, Cyn's throaty laughter filled the silence.

"Oh, Raj, is that really the best you can do? Don't forget, I've been called that in five languages all across the national press."

"It's the right term, though, isn't it? You use people. You're using Glo because you know she's got a soft spot for you. You use your body to get men to do what you want. You did it with McMurphy, and you did it with me."

"And what did I want from you, Raj?"

She was mocking me. I felt a rush of anger and confusion.

"I don't know."

"Love. I wanted your love."

"Bullshit."

"It's true. But I gave up on that dream when it became clear that all you wanted from me was sex. And when I finally gave it to you after your months of pathetic, ceaseless begging, the light went out of your eyes. You were disappointed."

"No."

"Yes. But I know it wasn't my failing. I was a practiced, professional-grade whore by then. Did you know that?"

I could see a fucking twinkle in her eye. She knew that Glo hadn't told me. She knew, and she thought it was funny. I stood and moved toward her, like she was an electromagnet, sucking me out of my seat.

"You think it's funny?"

"I do. I think it's a very funny joke. I think your feelings for me were always a joke. Always more about you and what you needed and what you could get out of me. And for what? Your silly little ego. Do you remember those last nights we spent together?"

I stared at her, unable to speak.

"All those things you let me do to you? Well, here's a secret: I didn't enjoy it. I thought maybe if we fucked enough I might feel something real, but you just couldn't turn it on for me. I was faking all of it, every moan, every orgasm, just like you were any other sad, pathetic john."

She smiled at me with vicious sweetness, and then next thing I knew, my hands were around her throat. I wasn't squeezing, I know that. Through a great force of will, I kept them relaxed, but I felt the hot flesh of her neck against my palms and the delicate contours of her windpipe, so vulnerable in my grasp. What a glory it would be to squeeze. I felt a rumble beneath my hands and realized she was speaking.

Glo was shouting so loudly that I could barely hear what Cyn was saying. She looked at me evenly, and there was no fear in her face. I leaned in closer so I could look her directly in the eye.

"Do it!" she urged as the tears began pooling in the corner of her eyes. "Do it. I'd rather die by the hands of someone I once loved than by some hired thug."

The fierce certainty of her words shocked me out of my rage tunnel, and I pulled my hands from her as if scorched. Glo's arms were around my neck, yanking me backward. I stumbled and fell against the seats, landing hard on the floor.

"What the fuck is wrong with you?" Glo was shouting. I cowered as she came dangerously close to kicking me, opting instead for the seat beside my head. "You put your hands on her goddamn neck? Who the fuck are you? What kind of person does that?"

"It's okay," Cyn said. "He wasn't going to hurt me."

"Yeah? It sure didn't look that way to me! And what the fuck is wrong with you? *Do it? Do it, Raj?* So he can go to jail for the rest of his life? You're both fucking crazy people!"

"Glo—"

"Shut up!" she shouted at me. She was as unhinged as I'd ever seen her. "You gave me such shit because I didn't tell you she was a prostitute, and you never thought to tell me that you'd slept with her?" She stared up at the ceiling, and a fountain of delirious laughter bubbled from her throat. "It's funny, because

I don't even care. It doesn't matter. She hates you. He hates you. I think you're both absolute lunatics, and maybe I am too. It's finally the neat and tidy ending I always hoped for."

"Glo—"

"No!" She pointed at Cyn. "You, solve your own fucking problems! You're dangerous. That's what you've always been, whether you mean to be or not. It follows you, and I don't want it following me any longer."

She spun around to face me. "And you—"

I braced myself, waiting for the hammer to drop. Glo's voice broke off abruptly, and I looked up and saw her head swing toward the rear of the theater, as Cyn stood, her face ashen and mouth slack.

"Ryan," she said.

I clambered to my feet and faced Ryan McMurphy in the flesh. He stood at the top of the stairs, a glowering tower of discontent. I couldn't see his eyes underneath the shadow of his brow, but it was pretty clear that he was looking at Cyn.

"Surprise," he deadpanned.

"Mr. McMurphy, you need to leave. You're trespassing on private property." I marveled at how quickly Glo had regained her composure. She stood straight as a rail, the flush in her cheeks spreading down across her chest. "Did you hear me?"

"I hear you, Gloria, I just don't care what you have to say." He shuffled toward the center aisle and glanced at me, distaste quivering across his features. He turned his large head back toward Cyn, and his mouth bent into an odd grimace. "You had to see them. Just had to. I knew it. If you had just resisted, I might never have found you. Do you know that?"

Cyn shifted nervously. Before she could answer, I said, "Listen, pal. This is my theater. Get the hell out of here before I throw you out."

He chuckled, thick and low.

I glanced at Glo, frozen wide-eyed like a mannequin, and remembering my regrets from the previous night at the bar, found my courage. I wasn't going to allow some beat-looking asshole to stride into my theater and menace us without taking some action. I began advancing up the stairs toward him, slowly, watching his hands, wondering what the hell I was going to do when I reached the top. The closer I came, the taller he loomed. Of course Cyn had managed to snare some deranged giant for the role of scorned paramour. I just hoped he wasn't armed.

I was six steps away when, in perfect movie slo-mo, I saw his right hand ease out of his pocket, and in his palm, a dull gleam of metal. *Gun!* my neurons screamed in unison. The full muzzle slid into view and slowly swung my way, the yawning blackness of the barrel blotting out all other thought.

"Stop, right there."

I halted midstep. "Is that a gun?" I exclaimed, in case the girls hadn't noted this very important shift in our circumstances. My body was largely blocking McMurphy's sight lines, and I was hoping they would take the hint and get themselves to some semblance of safety. Unfortunately, there wasn't anywhere particularly safe for them to go. A small dressing room backstage was a dead end, and the sole emergency exit was also at the top of the stairs, on the opposite wall. McMurphy had the high ground, and we were all trapped.

"Raj!" Glo yelped.

"Ryan, don't."

"Back off, *pal*," McMurphy sneered.

I lifted my hands and took a step backward.

I heard footsteps, and suddenly Cyn was beside me. "Go to Glo," she murmured to me, never taking her eyes off McMurphy. "Go." She glanced at me, and in her face, I saw something of the old Cyn; a reckless confidence that made me think that maybe she knew how to handle this.

I stepped down to the ground floor and put Glo behind me. She reached for my hand and squeezed, hard.

"Ryan, please, put that gun away," Cyn said. I couldn't see her face, but her voice sounded warm and mildly cajoling, as if the gun were just a camera and she didn't feel especially pretty.

"I just need one thing from you, Cyn, one honest answer. Will you leave him?" McMurphy swayed dangerously.

"What should we do?" Glo whispered into my ear.

"I don't want to talk about it here, in front of my friends. You want to talk, get rid of the gun, and we'll talk somewhere private."

"I want an answer. I think I'm entitled to one honest answer from you." His voice stayed terrifyingly flat.

"Ryan, sweetie. You're scaring my friends."

Cyn began to speak again, but McMurphy interrupted her.

"What's his name?" he demanded.

"Who?"

"Your future ex-husband. I want to know his name."

"You know it. Lucas."

"No. His full name. I want you to tell me his full fucking name."

"Why?"

"Because otherwise, you'll lie. I've been thinking about it, since you left, and I think that's been your plan all along. Use me, dump me. Run back to your true love. I want to know his name so I can call my people and put a trace on him. So I can end him if you screw me on this." He was breathing heavily. I saw his enormous shoulders rise and fall.

"End him? Drop the posturing, Ryan, please. We both know you were fired. You can't *end* anyone." Cyn's exasperation was audible, and I watched McMurphy's face darken dangerously. I took a step forward, but Glo's iron grip anchored me in place.

"You're right. I was fired. Because of you. And will soon be divorced, because of you. And will lose my children, because of you. And what do I get? Lies and empty promises. How do you think that makes me feel? I love you and you lie to me! Just do what you said you would. Haven't I earned that much?"

He was shouting. I saw tiny specks of saliva fly from his mouth, sparkling briefly under the house lights. The air in the room felt absolutely spare, as if we had been transported to the highest Himalayas. Every molecule of oxygen was elusive.

"Yes," Cyn said.

McMurphy stiffened, and she stepped forward, her voice honey sweet, her gestures, though she didn't touch him, soft and nurturing. "Look at me. It's okay. You're right, darling. I shouldn't have left like I did, but I was frightened and I wasn't sure I could trust you. Surely you can understand that? It's not personal, it's just . . . me." She shrugged, and her voice grew a touch playful. I watched McMurphy watching her, mesmerized. "I want to make it up to you. I will do anything you want. I know I owe you, Ry, and I know what you've given up for me. Will you say something? Please?"

McMurphy hesitated. Glo and I were both holding our breath. She was squeezing my wrist so hard, I'd lost feeling in my hand.

McMurphy exhaled with an audible moan, and the glower dropped from his face like a Halloween mask. "Cyn, angel. I know I've fucked up so bad. This . . ." McMurphy used the gun hand to gesture to his torso. "This really isn't me. You know that."

"I know that."

"Look at me. I'm a goddamn mess." He smiled, and his face lit up, a demented jack-o'-lantern. He took a step down toward her, arms spreading wide.

"So you'll give me another chance? You'll come back?"

"I will. We can go right now."

"Don't—" Glo exclaimed.

Cyn turned to face us. She looked calm and, if anything, mildly irritated. "It's okay, Glo. Ryan and I understand each other, don't we?"

She took another step toward him, gradually closing the gap between them. It seemed like they might embrace, but she stopped short. "Can I have that please? You know how I feel about guns."

I noticed McMurphy was now staring at us. After a moment, he looked back at Cyn, stone-faced.

"No."

"Why not?"

"I did it again. I gave in too fast. I told myself I wouldn't cave to you and your pretty pink mouth without some proof, some real proof that your old life is done. What's his name?"

"Ryan. Think for a minute. I could tell you any name. How would you know?"

I cringed. Not the time for real talk, Cyn. I felt my heart pumping as McMurphy stared down at her dumbly, like a puzzled golden retriever.

"I don't have any reason to lie to you, Ryan. I wanted to see my friends, one last time. I'm sorry. But I've done it, and I'm yours now, for as long as you want."

He shook his head and chuckled softly. "Very convincing. I don't even . . . know how you do it." He looked up toward the ceiling as if blinking back tears, his pitch rising alarmingly. "You're so, so good at it. You hate me, despite everything. You despise me. I can see it. I'm not an idiot."

"Ryan," Cyn lifted her hands, palms open, desperation creeping into her voice. "Please—"

"No! I should turn you in myself. No, I should hold you for ransom. Get some big money for you from the motherfucking cartel. That would solve my problems, and it would serve you right."

"No!" Glo shouted, releasing my hand.

Cyn raised her arm, gesturing for Glo to stay back, all the while keeping her eyes on McMurphy. Glo slipped past me, fast as the shadow of a passing jet, and I saw the dark holes that hid McMurphy's eyes turn toward her.

"Glo!" I yelled, my fingertips just brushing the hem of her blouse as she lurched forward into space.

I saw Cyn's face, white as a ghost, as she glanced over her shoulder and saw Glo rushing the stairs.

My life is over, I thought as McMurphy's gun hand began to pivot toward Glo. My own body had finally settled on a response, which was to jump in the air, throwing my arms wide, in an attempt to wrest McMurphy's attention away from Glo. But it was too late.

I was staring right at them, fifteen feet away, and I'm still not sure exactly what happened those next few milliseconds. I know that Cyn jolted toward McMurphy, her elbows lifting like a bird about to take flight. I almost expected her to rise into the air, when in a stunning reversal, her body collapsed like a doll's, pounded earthward by a giant, unseen fist. Only then did I hear the bang, chased instantly by Glo's piercing shrieks. Glo dropped into a tight crouch on the steps, her panicked eyes meeting mine in the instant before she rolled for cover behind a row of seats. I watched, frozen, as McMurphy stared open-mouthed at Cyn's body, crumpled at his feet.

"Oh. No," he murmured. He looked at the gun in his hand, and then up at me.

Before I could even open my mouth to shout, he pressed the gun beneath his chin and pumped the trigger, hard. I saw it all in terrible detail. His crown exploded into a cloud of dark matter, and he dropped backward, collapsing at a sickening angle against the wall.

There was a second of utter stillness before Glo clambered,

sobbing, up the stairs to Cyn. Together, we turned Cyn over. I held her head. Her eyes were closed, dark blood was soaking her white dress. There was an open wound over her left breast, just where her heart must have been.

"Oh god, no," Glo wailed. "Cyn!"

"Go upstairs. Call an ambulance," I urged.

"Cyn!" she screamed, shaking her as if she could be readily awakened.

"Glo! Please get help. Hurry!"

She heard me. I watched her lurch over McMurphy's body and I heard the theater door slam behind her.

I held Cyn's body in my arms, and pressed my hands over her wound. I could feel her heart still pumping, faint and weak. Hot blood sluiced through my fingers at a pitiless rate, and I watched the skin around her eyes go paper white. I willed those eyes to open, and when they didn't, I found myself speaking to her, urging her to hang on, to keep it together, to not give up. My voice grew hoarse and my clothes became soaked with her blood, and with McMurphy's, which was dripping down the stairs in gruesome rivulets.

It's hard to say what I was thinking in those agonizingly long minutes before the firefighters arrived, followed in quick succession by the paramedics and then the police. Toward the end, as the color drained from Cyn's lips, I leaned close, and whispered all the true, sweet things that were the flip side of the vitriol I'd disgorged only moments before, in what already felt like a different lifetime. I wept as I asked her forgiveness and told her that she was loved, always. Forever. I wanted her to take that with her, to enter whatever was next fully wrapped in a shroud of love, as if that could mitigate the violence that had sent her there. I was so, so far from the perfect person to send her off, but I could offer her that much. *She was loved, Next World, she was. Please be kind.*

CHAPTER TWENTY

Glo

She didn't die. Not that day at least.

As the doctor explained it to me, the nose of the gun had bucked upward when McMurphy fired, sending the bullet on an upward slant through the space just above her heart, ripping a hole just millimeters away from her pulmonary artery. She was very lucky, he said, as if this were news to me.

She coded a few times in the ambulance. Raj told me as much. He rode with her to the hospital, bloody and stunned like the lone survivor from a horror movie, while I stayed behind to run interference with the cops. When the paramedics arrived and said she was still alive, I somehow had the wherewithal to get right on the phone with both the FBI and the State Department. It gave me something to focus on, and I also knew if her name were released, if she became a story again, her life would be over even if she survived. This time I would not fail.

The local police weren't exhibiting any willingness to listen to me until the FBI showed up, at which point things got a little easier. I convinced them it was worth it from an intelligence standpoint to pressure the NYPD into declaring a "Jane and John Doe situation" until Cyn's prognosis became clearer. The State Department was also happy to oblige, considering they were facing what looked like a scandalous and shameful crime involving one of their own. I spent the next several days on the phone, stammering vague responses to questions for which I had no answers. "She'll tell you everything when she regains consciousness," I uttered, over and over, the knot tightening in my stomach as I wondered if it were true. I was putting my reputation on the line on the basis of Cyn's promises of future information, and in truth, I had no idea if she really knew anything at all.

Meanwhile, the press had descended upon the story of the mysterious attempted murder-suicide in the dramatic environs of an underground theater like horseflies to spilled blood. Raj declined all interviews and postponed the opening of his play, which, due to all the press and the new allure surrounding the "haunted" theater, had sold out well into the foreseeable future. He had been rapidly rehired as Dr. Seager in *The Queen's Keys*. The producers weren't stupid, recognizing that his newfound mystique was box office manna. His agent, too, made a robust reappearance, calling him up with auditions for principal roles in major feature films. There was a new happiness in his eyes that I hadn't seen in years. If I hadn't been so stressed out about maybe going to jail if Cyn's tale turned out to be fantasy, I would have been happy, too.

It took about a week for Cyn to stabilize. They had a pair of armed guards stationed outside her door twenty-four/seven. I stopped by a few times to check up on her, but the blinds on her window were always closed, and she wasn't conscious. No one was allowed in anyway.

It was Sunday when I got the call that Cyn was awake. Raj was onstage, so I texted him the news.

A new stoicism had settled over him since that afternoon at the theater. "Cyn and I weren't good for one another," he told me. "We never really were."

That he had been painfully and deliberately guided toward

that conclusion was not obvious to him, but I saw otherwise. When Cyn goaded him into the rage that culminated with his hands around her throat, she and I alone knew that it was an exorcism she was performing. By all accounts it had worked. When Raj and I talked about her now, there was no frisson of tension underlying our words. By shattering her spell over Raj, Cyn had given us both one last gift.

I went to the hospital and was stopped, as always, at her door. There were new guards stationed outside, not the crew I had grown used to seeing.

"Someone called and told me to come," I explained when they summarily dismissed me. "She wants to see me."

"She's not seeing anyone, ma'am," the older guard informed me.

"I'm the closest she has to next of kin," I said. When that did nothing, I persisted, "Someone here called me, and I'm her de facto attorney. I'm not leaving until I speak to whoever that was. Can you please check it out?"

With a heaving, soap opera sigh, the older guard disappeared into her room, closing the door quickly, but not before I glimpsed two suited figures seated at her bedside. Square shouldered, gray haired; they had to be the feds. My palms began to sweat as I wondered how far they had gotten in taking her statement. I prayed it would be sufficient. I waited in silence with the other guard, my nerves making me so twitchy that I forced myself to take a quick walk to the water fountain to chill out. As I returned, I noticed the horizontal blinds in the room were slowly opening. The first guard reappeared, firmly shutting the door.

"They said you can't go in, but you can visit through the window."

"Okay, thanks." I slowly turned to the window and raised my hand to block the glare. Cyn was propped up in bed, looking pale and small in her sea-foam green hospital gown. Her arms were laced with tubes, and her bed was bookended by twin towers of monitoring equipment.

With obvious care, she turned her head toward me and smiled. It wasn't her typical megawatt beamer, but it was enough that I could see her spirit remained intact. She raised one arm a few inches and wiggled the fingers in greeting, then winced and rolled her eyes.

I laughed, and raised my own hand in salute, pressing it against the window.

One of the feds turned around to look at me. I searched his face for some indication of how things were going, but his expression was impossible to read. One of the men must have spoken, because Cyn looked at him and frowned. She turned her face back toward me and smiled again, only this time the smile was underscored with sadness. I knew it was good-bye.

Good-bye, Glo, she mouthed.

"Bye, Cyn," I said aloud, even though I knew she couldn't hear me. "Good luck."

She lifted her hand as high as she could and presented me two fingers, a peace sign, just as one of the suits rose and moved toward the window. I blew her a kiss, trying not to tear up as the blinds slowly closed. I knew, somehow, that it was the last time I would ever see her.

Raj was waiting for me on a bench outside.

"You saw her?" he asked, rising as I approached.

"Through the glass. They were interviewing her, so I didn't get to visit."

"Oh."

We began walking north, slowly, like an old-timey couple out for a promenade.

"That was it. I'm not going back."

"Really?"

"Really. I've done what she asked. She knows it. I meant what I said in the theater. She's dangerous. I want her to have a good life, but I don't want her in mine."

"You'll probably never see her again," he said, reaching for my hand.

"It's okay." We walked for a while, in peaceful silence. "You know what I got from this, and you did, too?"

He looked at me quizzically. "I dunno. Night terrors?"

"No. We got a better ending. She's not dead or missing or lost. Presumably, she'll go on to be a normal person out there, living her life with her family. Just like us."

He nodded, thoughtfully, but I knew there was a rebuttal coming.

"And that makes these past couple weeks worthwhile to you? You could have been shot." He pressed his hand against his chest dramatically. "This man right here could have been shot."

"Worthwhile, no. Worth something, yes."

He shook his head and pulled me toward him as a spring rain, thin and vaporous, began to fall. He wrapped his arms around me, holding me tight. "Well then, best of luck to her."

"Yes, best of luck."

I thought of our magnanimity that evening outside the hospital eight months later, when we were on an airplane, flying down to Florida to surprise Raj's parents with the news of my pregnancy. I was flipping through the cheesy in-flight catalog, amusing myself with pictures of Victorian canopied dog beds, when one image caused me to choke on my ginger ale.

Available for the price of $24.99 was a rainbow-colored polyurethane pinwheel, featured in a tidy suburban lawn. Sharing the scene was a tiny girl with curly reddish hair, one arm reaching out toward a kitten.

Glorianna.

I sucked in air and placed my hands on the photo to frame the image as Cyn had showed it to me on her phone. It was unmistakable. I imagined her taking the photo on her flight in from wherever it was she had come from, tucking it away just in case she needed added leverage to get me on her side. It had worked, flawlessly. She knew me so damned well.

I flashed back to her face the last time I saw her in the hospital, shooting me that peace sign. Only now did I realize, perhaps it wasn't a peace sign after all. Her eyes had been saying something else, and at thirty-five thousand feet, her true message hit me like a shock wave. *Twice, Glo.* Twice she had thrown herself on the grenade for me. Two times I would walk away intact, with my true love at my side. Those slender fingers were a reminder to me of a much larger truth: I may have been a sucker, but I was undoubtedly the lucky one.

Something flipped in my head, and I started to laugh. Tears rolled down my cheeks, and I began to hiccup uncontrollably. It was several minutes before I could even catch my breath to explain to Raj what was so hilarious. At first, his face went flush and his jaw tightened in that old familiar way. But he watched, side-eyed, as I ripped the picture out and folded it carefully so that it fit into the picture window of my wallet. When I was done, I heard him snort.

I looked up and met his laughing eyes.

"Do you want to see my daughter?" I asked, holding it up.

"She's beautiful," he said, his composure breaking in tandem with mine.

"I named her after you," I managed, before losing it completely. I pressed the photo facedown against my tray table, and together we shook with laughter, delirious and attracting stares.

"Wait, wait. Let me see her again," he said breathlessly.

I presented it anew, my face glowing with motherly pride. "Here she is!"

"So precious," he said. "Congratulations."

At that moment in the air, we truly understood that we would never, ever get any answers. We would never find the real truth about who Cyn became, or who she ever was. And we realized there was only one real response.

If you can't laugh, you cry.